A House *on* Liberty Street

PRAISE FOR THE TONY VALENTI THRILLERS

* *A House on Liberty Street* *

Turner hits the mark in a spellbinding, page-turning thriller featuring a worthy underdog hero and prose that tugs at the heartstrings. The author has a great sense of plot and timing. **IndieReader 4.5 Star Review**

Neil Turner unravels an ever-deepening drama that exposes the lengths one man will go to protect his family in *A House on Liberty Street,* a suspenseful and heartfelt thriller. Tapping into evocative themes of family, fatherhood, and second chances, this is a fast-paced read with a clever protagonist ducking and dodging in a classic pursuit of justice. The storytelling is casual but compelling, with memorable characters, intriguing dynamics, and an unpredictable case for readers to piece together. …there are also touching moments of paternal wisdom and honesty that shine… *A House on Liberty Street* is a neatly penned thriller that will keep readers guessing to the very end. **Self-Publishing Review**

** Plane in the Lake **

Neil Turner's latest Tony Valenti thriller, *Plane in the Lake,* pits the no-nonsense lawyer and his fiery partner against entrenched power in this classic Chicago crime story. Lawyers and liars go hand in hand in the pearly offices of the city's underworld, as a well-to-do family's desperate attempt to cover up the truth behind their daughter's death spirals into something much more. As Valenti is faced with saving not only his firm but his family too, Turner skillfully wields an incisive pen that takes on the seemingly untouchable upper classes and shady crime families. With his trademark breezy style reminiscent of Dennis Lehane, Turner has produced another devourable thriller. **Self-Publishing Review ★★★★½**

Plane in the Lake is a satisfying blend of tense thriller and whodunit that calls into question and ultimately strengthens Tony Valenti's bonds with friends, family, and peers. The novel works on many different levels to involve readers in a puzzle that remains murky up to its surprise conclusion. It's a fine story that will keep readers (whether newcomers or prior fans of Tony's gritty streetwise style) thoroughly engrossed to the end. **D. Donovan, Senior Reviewer, Midwest Book Review**

** A Case of Betrayal **

In his third powerful Tony Valenti Thriller, *A Case of Betrayal,* author Neil Turner puts his charming and brilliant defense attorney back into the fray, where his loyalties to old friends will be tested against his passion for justice. Diving into tough subjects - from the deeply rooted racism in America to the struggles of single fatherhood - this installment stands out from other thrillers; there is real heart in this prose, as well as nuanced character development that keeps the read continually engaging. Packed with suspense, and a page turner from the start. **Self-Publishing Review ★★★★½**

** A Time for Reckoning **

"A character-driven thriller that fearlessly reveals the dark corners of human nature – misogyny, greed, violence, power, and control. Driven by strong dialogue, unpredictable twists, and more than a dash of colloquial country charm, this savagely honest novel is a stellar addition to the *Toni Valenti Thriller* series." Self-Publishing Review, ★★★★½

** Scared Silent **

"A brutal and gritty novel of survival on the merciless streets of Chicago, *Scared Silent* is a gut-wrenching ride. Given the national spotlight being recently turned towards the desperate plight of the poor, this gripping story is not only expertly penned, but also timely and fearless." **Self-Publishing Review, ★★★★★**

A House *on* Liberty Street

Neil Turner

First Edition

Published by Neil Turner Books, Canada 2021

Published by Neil Turner Books 2021

Cover and interior design by David Prendergast
Library and Archives Canada ISBN 978-1-7775179-0-8 Trade paperback
Library and Archives Canada ISBN 978-1-7775179-1-5 Kindle edition
Library and Archives Canada ISBN 978-1-7775179-2-2 ePub edition

CHAPTER ONE

The first sign of trouble is a Cedar Heights police cruiser blocking the intersection. A tangle of other emergency vehicles clogs the street halfway down the block. Red, blue, and yellow emergency lights explode like multi-colored flash-bulbs, their reflections skittering across the windows of the stout brick bungalows that line Liberty Street. If the cops aren't at our house, they're damned close.

A uniformed cop looks over his shoulder and waves us away when I coast to a stop a few feet short of the cruiser. *Like hell.* I creep closer. The cop glances back and waves me away again. When I stay put, he whirls and advances on us with the blinding beam of his flashlight aimed at our windshield. Crisp autumn air floods in when I open the driver's side window of my Porsche Panamera and turn on the interior lights.

"Street's closed, sir," the cop announces impatiently. "Move along."

"What's going on, Officer?"

"Street's closed."

There's a newsflash. I point beyond him and make an announcement of my own. "I live down there."

Interest flickers in his eyes before a hand shoots to my window. "Driver's license."

He gives the car a longer, appreciative look while I wrestle a lambskin wallet out of my back pocket, flip it open, and push it outside.

"Just the license," he snaps without touching the wallet.

I jerk the license out of its plastic holder and hand it back.

He glances at it. "Georgia?"

"We moved back a few weeks ago."

"You staying?"

"I plan to."

"You gotta go to the DMV and get an Illinois license," he says. "Plates, too."

"Sure."

"You got ninety days."

Who the hell cares? *Take it easy, Valenti,* I caution myself. Bulletheads like this guy think bullshit rules are all that stand between law and order and chaos. I lock my eyes on the flashing lights dead ahead while he studies the official plastic in his hand.

His eyes narrow. "Your name's Valenti?"

"That's right. Tony Valenti."

He aims the flashlight past me, blinding my fourteen-year-old daughter, Brittany. She shrinks lower into her seat.

"My daughter," I tell him while easing forward to shield her. "She's a freshman at Saint Aloysius. We're on our way home from orientation."

"What number do you live at?"

"Forty-seven."

"Wait here," he says tersely, then turns on his heel to march back to his car with my license in hand.

"What's going on, Officer?" I shout at his retreating back. He doesn't break stride until he leans into his cruiser and pulls out a radio microphone. He stares back at us while he talks. I look beyond him to the cluster of emergency vehicles.

Jesus. The cops are definitely in our driveway and buzzing around the front porch.

I roll my shoulders to release tension, then give Brittany's hand a reassuring squeeze. Her scarlet scrunchie is wound so tightly through her fingers that they're turning white. My eyes drift to the stately old elm trees towering above the damp pavement. Each is rooted precisely five feet from the curb; one per narrow, Chicago-style lot. Their branches wave high overhead to link limbs with their neighbors—much as the mostly Italian immigrants here have done since the trees were saplings. The glow of streetlights shrouded in an early autumn haze struggles to reach the street below. But Liberty Street isn't especially dark this evening. Porch lights are on as the neighbors drink in whatever drama is unfolding at our house. They're mostly older now, retired, people of my parents' generation—grizzled men who wear sleeveless white undershirts and fleshy women in voluminous floral dresses. The residents of Liberty Street are gathered on wooden porches, perched on lawn chairs in their tidy yards, or huddled together along the edges of the pavement.

"What's going on, Dad?" Brittany asks. "Is Papa okay?"

How do I answer that? Cops. An ambulance. Hardly the makings of a Disney moment, especially knowing that my father—Papa in the vernacular of our fairly traditional Italian family—should be home. The cop tosses the radio into his cruiser and marches back toward us. "I think we're about to find out," I tell Brittany.

Bullethead jerks a thumb toward the curb. "Pull it around the corner and park."

"What's up?" I ask.

He waves us toward an open spot without answering. I jam the gearshift into reverse to back away from the cruiser, then slam the car into drive and zoom into the open spot, leaving the back end of the Porsche jutting into the intersection. I throw my door open and step into a puddle left behind by an early evening thunderstorm. Cursing under my breath as my shoe squishes every step of the way, I stride straight toward the cop waiting beside his car and say, "I want some answers."

The cop yanks the rear door open without a word and motions us in. He's in front of me in a heartbeat when I try to brush past him. "Where do you think you're going?"

"Our house."

"You can't."

"Why can't I go to my own damned house?"

"It's a crime scene. The detective will be here as soon as he can."

Crime scene? Detective? I stand my ground with my nose within a foot of his. I've got maybe an inch on him. "Tell me what's going on."

Malice stirs in the wintry blue eyes glaring back into mine. "Get in the car."

"My father was there when we left," I retort while looking past him.

"Your old man's okay."

I cross my arms and meet his gaze. "Good to know, but I still want to see him."

"Not yet."

Pin a badge on these clowns.... I inch close enough to smell mint on the cop's breath. "Why not?"

His nightstick materializes under my chin. "Because I said not yet."

My manufactured machismo melts away when the weapon brushes the underside of my jaw. I take Brittany's arm and steer her back to the police cruiser, where we slide onto the cold, brittle vinyl of the rear seat. The door slams shut. My anger gives way to a moment of frank curiosity; it's my first time inside a police car. Beyond a battleship-gray grated metal partition that separates us from the front seat, a shotgun stands menacingly at attention against the dashboard. The sour stench of the drunks and whores and other deadwood of Cedar Heights clings to the battered upholstery. This is no place for a corporate attorney and his teenage daughter.

Brittany inches closer. "Can't you do something?"

Nothing that won't get me arrested. "Patience, Britts. We'll know what's going on soon enough."

"I'm scared."

Join the club. A morsel of my recently deceased mother's matter-of-fact wisdom bubbles forth. "Mama used to say that people take years off their lives worrying about bad things that might happen. Know what?"

"What?"

"Most of it never does."

"Yeah," Brittany mutters sullenly. "But sometimes bad shit just happens, right?"

We've learned the truth of that over the past few months, haven't we? I'm debating whether or not to let her profanity slide when I notice a smallish man hustling toward us in a beige suit straight off the rack at Sears or J.C. Penney. With the aid of a sharply receding hairline and a frost-tinged mustache, I peg him for around fifty.

He pauses to speak with the uniformed cop, steps over to open the back door of the cruiser, and waves us out. "Jake Plummer," he says while extending his hand for a crisp handshake. "I'm the lead detective assigned to the case."

What case? I wonder.

Plummer turns to Brittany and shakes her hand. She's as tall as he is, though considerably more slender and graceful—not to mention infinitely better coiffed with her head of thick, shoulder-length auburn hair. "I hear you're on your way home from school," the detective says.

She leans a hip on the cruiser's rear fender and nods.

"Pretty late for school, isn't it?"

"We had orientation for the freshman class. You know, parents getting to know who the teachers are. Like that."

Plummer smiles. "That's ninth grade, right?"

"Yeah."

"New school for you?"

Her eyes drop to study the pavement. "Yeah." The move hasn't been easy on her.

"Starting the year in a strange school is tough," Plummer says sympathetically. "I'm an Air Force brat, so I know what you're going through. Sometimes it seemed like I went to a different school every year. Somehow or other, things always worked out."

Brittany shrugs but says nothing, so he turns back to me. "I need to ask a few questions. Is it just the two of you, or is there a missus or significant other we should be speaking with, as well?"

"She's in Europe," I reply stiffly.

The detective cocks an eyebrow. "Whereabouts?"

"She lives in Brussels. Divorce." That's new, too.

We both glance at Brittany, who now looks thoroughly miserable. When Plummer's eyes meet mine again, they carry a silent apology.

"Let's get on with it," I suggest.

The uniformed cop, who's been hovering nearby, takes a step closer. "Want me to take the girl somewhere?"

"That's up to Mr. Valenti," Plummer replies.

I wrap an arm around Brittany's shoulders, draw her close, and wave Bullethead away. "She stays."

The detective nods. "Just as well. She'll hear about this soon enough anyway."

"First off," I begin, "I understand my father's okay. Is that true?"

"It is."

I look past him toward our house. "I'd like to see him."

"He's not here."

My patience with this cat-and-mouse bullshit is wearing thin. "Where is he?"

Plummer studies me for a long moment. "Mr. Valenti, your father shot a police officer."

"He did *what?*"

"A Cook County Sheriff's Deputy was sent to serve papers. Your father shot him."

"Legal papers?" I ask. Inanely, I realize immediately.

He nods again.

"There's got to be some confusion, Detective. Papa's never had a legal issue worth mentioning. I doubt he's even had a parking ticket."

Plummer calmly stares back at me. "Yet here we are."

We continue our stare-down while I grapple with what he just told me. If it's true, only one person can explain it. "I'm a lawyer. When can I see my father?"

The lawyer comment gets the detective's attention. He glances at his watch. "I'll be wrapping up here in twenty or thirty minutes but the crime scene folks will be here awhile yet. Go have a coffee or something and come by the station in an hour. No promises about seeing your father, but maybe we can clear up a few things."

"How's the deputy?" I finally think to ask.

"Dead."

CHAPTER TWO

We loiter over a couple of apple fritters and Cokes at a Dunkin' for the next hour, then waste forty-five minutes at the police station waiting for Detective Plummer. When he finally arrives, he escorts us to a squad room ripe with the caustic stench of burnt coffee. A row of four battered beige metal desks occupies one wall; offices line another. The detective leads us to the last desk and waves us into a couple of folding chairs placed in front of it.

My ass is barely on the battered seat before I repeat my demand. "I want to see my father."

"Patience, Mr. Valenti."

I ease forward and level my eyes on his. "Why can't I see him now?"

"I said *patience,* Mr. Valenti," he replies tersely. Then he stares me down for several seconds.

I eventually get around to nodding. The cops may tell me Papa's okay, but I'm anxious to see him with my own eyes. I'll wait to see what this guy has to say before I go to the mat with him about seeing Papa.

"Okay then," Plummer says. "Coffee?"

Not the burnt swill I smell. "Got a fresh pot somewhere?"

"I put one on a few minutes ago." His eyes shift to Brittany. "Soda?"

"Can I have coffee?" she asks weakly. She's been alternating between bouts of catatonic silence and uncontrolled sobbing since Plummer cut us loose on Liberty Street.

"Sure can," he says. "Two coffees coming up. Cream and sugar?"

"Yes," we say in unison. I look around the room after he ambles away. Beefy men in shirtsleeves occupy two of the other desks and a few uniformed cops wander in and out. The stares we attract range from curiosity to outright rancor.

When Plummer returns, he sets three white Styrofoam cups of steaming coffee on his desk. A red stir stick bobs in each. "Someone is on the way over from the Public Defender's office," he tells us while he dumps a mound of creamers, sugar packets, and sweeteners in the middle of the desk.

My eyes cut from the condiments to the detective. "A public defender? Why?"

"Your father had enough sense to ask for a lawyer when we brought him in. When my partner told him that his defense will probably run into six figures, your dad said he doesn't have that kind of money. So we called the Public Defender's office."

After my brain catches up to my mouth, I realize that was probably the right call. My knowledge of the criminal justice system can be written on the back of a post-it note. Still, Plummer is mistaken if he thinks his "trust me" schtick is going to wash with me. I don't see his angle yet, but I'll sniff it out.

The detective leans back in his seat and crosses his arms. "So, you're a lawyer?"

I nod while stirring two creamers and two sweeteners into my cup.

"Illinois Bar?" he asks.

I can practice law in Wisconsin or Georgia and even joined

the bar in New York for business purposes, but I've never worked in Illinois. "No."

A flash of annoyance flickers in his eyes—probably because he realizes I played him with the lawyer revelation to weasel my way in to see my father—but he says nothing before Brittany interrupts.

"Deano?" she asks.

In a dazzling display of having my head up my ass, I hadn't thought of the other family member at Forty-seven Liberty Street this evening until Brittany brought it up at Dunkin'.

"Before we go any further, Detective," I say, "where's the dog?"

"He was in the backyard when I left."

"Poor Deano!" Brittany exclaims. "He must be terrified."

"He's okay," Plummer assures her. "The poor old guy was a little agitated, obviously, but he was taking things in stride."

"Good to know," I reply, briefly wondering what we're going to do with the apple of Mama's eye.

"Yuck!" Brittany blurts with a pucker after she takes a sip of Plummer's high-test coffee.

The detective drums his fingers on the desk while we watch her dump four more sugars and five creamers into her cup. He turns his attention back to me. "Your father says you're unemployed. No interest in applying to the Illinois bar so you can take on his case yourself?"

"I'm a corporate guy. I wouldn't know where to start."

"Are you thinking of hiring an attorney?"

"Maybe," I reply with a frown. "I hear public defenders aren't exactly the cream of the defense attorney crop."

"I don't want to waste their time, Mr. Valenti," Plummer says with a hint of annoyance. "If you plan to hire someone else, do it soon."

Can I afford to get Papa a real lawyer? Can he afford not

to have one? He's got the house and his pension and there must be some savings. Will that be enough?

As if reading my thoughts, the detective asks, "Do you have any brothers or sisters who can help?"

I shake my head. "My sister died a long time ago. There's a brother I haven't spoken to in years."

"Can you reach him?"

I haven't spoken to Frankie since the final beating he administered to me in our teen years. That one left me hospitalized for a couple of weeks. Hell, he didn't even bother to come to Mama's funeral. Estranged understates the distance between us. "I'm not even going to try," I tell Plummer.

He nods and moves on. "You know your father's being evicted from the house?"

A gasp escapes Brittany as we absorb another sucker punch.

"What?" I ask in disbelief.

"The deputy was serving him with an eviction notice."

"But he owns the house outright!" I argue. "How can he be evicted from his own home?"

"We're a little fuzzy on what's going on there. I'll have someone look into it tomorrow morning. Maybe it has something to do with that eminent domain circus a year or two back?"

He's referring to an attempt to expropriate the neighborhood to build a shopping center and condos. "All water under the bridge," I answer confidently. "The developer pulled the plug on the deal."

Something in Plummer's gaze suggests skepticism. "Titan Development was behind that proposal, wasn't it?"

"Yeah. Why?" I ask. "Do you know something I don't?"

He shakes his head. "Not really, just a passing thought. Given this eviction business, your father might not have the house to help pay for his defense. Something to think about."

Great.

Brittany hasn't let go of the doggy bone. "Can we go get Deano?"

"You can swing by when we're done here," Plummer replies. "You won't be able to go inside the perimeter but I'll give them a heads-up to expect you. Someone will bring the dog out."

"Thank you!" she says.

I resume my push to see Papa. "When can I see him?"

Plummer's eyes drift beyond me while he thinks. "Not tonight," he finally replies. "We'll see what the public defender has to say."

My initial instinct is to argue—what with me being a lawyer and all—but I'm way out of my depth here. Turning help away might not be the wisest move.

"And here he is," Plummer announces.

A tall black man whose lengthy gait suggests athleticism is striding toward us. The hem of his colorful knit sweater ends below the waistband of a well-pressed pair of pleated slacks; a navy-blue windbreaker is slung casually over his shoulder. He's a sharp looking guy. The slender folio tucked under his left arm is the only indication that he's here on business.

Detective Plummer extends his hand, which quickly disappears into one the size of an oven mitt. "Mike," he says to the newcomer. "This is Tony Valenti and his daughter Brittany."

I look into Williams's inquisitive, deep-brown eyes. He's a shade taller than me, probably 6′ 6″ or so.

"Michael Williams," he says in a deep, silky voice as he grasps my hand and pumps once. "Pleased to meet you."

"Mr. Valenti is the suspect's son," Plummer says. "He's also an attorney."

The public defender's alert eyes turn to mine. "What kind of law?"

"Corporate. Not a member of the Illinois bar."

Williams stares at me. I stare back. His next query isn't

verbalized but I see it in his eyes: *Are you gonna be a problem?* I'm wondering the same about him.

He rests his ass on the edge of Plummer's desk. "What have we got, Detective?"

"A dead sheriff's deputy, a sixty-nine-year-old suspect named Francesco Valenti, male, apprehended with what appears to be the murder weapon. The suspect confessed to the first uniforms on the scene. Pretty cut and dry."

"Aren't they all," Williams mutters wearily.

"There's no question who pulled the trigger," Plummer continues. "I don't know why, though, and that's bothering me. It doesn't add up."

No shit. I'm not buying this Papa shot a cop bullshit. The supposed confession to a couple of uniformed cops is a little too convenient for my liking. To purloin and build upon Plummer's trite phrase, that story adds up like one plus one equals pi.

Williams frowns as he asks Plummer, "Witnesses?"

"We're canvassing the neighborhood to see if anyone saw the shooting."

"Local cop?" Williams probes with a cocked eyebrow.

Plummer shakes his head. "Cook County Sheriff's Deputy named Andy O'Reilly. He was one of ours for a couple of years before he went to the Sheriff's office ten, eleven years ago."

Something in Williams's demeanor shifts, suggesting this isn't the first time he's heard the name. "Did you know him?" he asks Plummer.

The detective drums his fingers on the armrest of his chair for a few seconds before answering warily, "To see him, but I never knew the guy well. He lived in town. I'd see him around now and then but we didn't talk."

"Why is that?" Williams asks.

"Different circles," Plummer replies with a shrug. He seems less than grief-stricken over the passing of his former colleague—an odd reaction from a brother officer. Williams doesn't look heartbroken, either. Who in hell was this O'Reilly character?

Williams studies the detective for a moment before moving on. "Is the suspect going to qualify for a public defender?"

"Looks that way."

Williams's curious eyes turn to me. If I were him, I'd also wonder why the father of a corporate attorney needs a public defender. I try to look less ashamed than I feel. Williams breaks eye contact with me, steps away from the desk, and looks down at Plummer. "Where can I talk to Mr. Valenti?"

"I've got a room set up," the detective replies. Then he turns to me. "This may not be suitable for a fourteen-year-old. Have you got a relative who can pick up Brittany?"

"Papa's all we've got here."

"Friends?" he asks.

"We've only been back a few weeks. I haven't had a chance to reconnect with anyone."

The corners of Williams's mouth turn down. "Neighbors?" He doesn't seem too keen on the idea of having Brittany around, either. Why don't these guys want her here? Too many witnesses to what they're up to?

"Nobody she knows," I reply. "I don't want to leave her with strangers tonight."

Brittany finally pipes up to ask me, "Can I stay? I'd rather be with you." She underscores the plea with the distraught, doe-eyed entreaty she perfected long ago—a gambit straight out of her mother's playbook. I've succumbed to both of them many a time.

Plummer's gaze shifts to her. "How about I give you something to read and you can wait in one of the offices?"

Brittany's eyes remain locked on mine while she squeezes the blood out of my fingers. "Please, Dad?"

"She stays with me," I tell Plummer, hoping to hell I'm making the right choice.

"Fair enough," he says with a frown. Then he sits up straight, places his hands on the desk, and gets down to business. "Any history of mental instability with your father?"

"None," I reply.

"You're sure?"

"Absolutely. Why do you ask?"

"I've got him on suicide watch."

Brittany stiffens at my side. *Suicide? Papa? How ridiculous.* Are the cops setting up one of their "suspect died in custody" incidents?

"He's not in the lockup with the herd?" Williams asks.

"I didn't want to lock him up with the regulars," Plummer replies. "He's in an interview room. I cuffed him so he can't do anything dumb."

Williams leans his hands on the desk and stares hard at Plummer. His voice is pure ice when he asks, "Cuffed?"

"For his own safety."

"Jesus! You've had a sixty-nine-year-old man cuffed to a chair for"—Williams glances at his watch—"what? Three, four hours?" Maybe Williams smells the same "died in custody" scenario I'm worrying about.

"For his own safety," Plummer repeats through clenched teeth.

Williams snorts. "How did you come by that confession, Detective?"

Plummer is on his feet in a heartbeat. His hand shoots toward the bigger man's chest and his index finger punctuates each word of his response without quite making contact. "Don't you ever insinuate that crap with me again, Williams. Ever! You got me?"

Cook County has a long history of cops obtaining questionable confessions from suspects before they see a lawyer. It seems to be a sore point for Plummer; there's quite a temper under that seemingly calm façade. At heart he's probably just another asshole cop.

Williams backs down immediately. "Sorry, Detective. I know better."

The fire in Plummer's eyes subsides as quickly as it flared. "You know that's not my style," he mutters as he settles back into his seat.

"I know," Williams replies contritely. "I was out of line. Sorry."

"Fair enough," Plummer replies with a curt nod. Then he turns to me. "I'm concerned about your father's emotional state. I want you to observe through the mirror and tell us what you think."

"I should be in the room with him," I reply. Plummer and Williams both shake their heads. I slide to the edge of my seat. "That's my father you have penned up in there, Detective."

"I know," he replies. "He's not 'penned up,' he's in custody."

"Semantics," I retort. "I want to make sure he's okay and that you guys haven't been screwing around with him."

The detective slaps a palm against his fingertips in a "time out" gesture. "I'm not going to debate this. Either accept what's on offer or go home."

"You told me to come here to see him!"

Plummer's eyes turn to ice. "No I didn't! I said you *might* get a chance to see him, Mr. Valenti—*after* you informed me that you're a lawyer and conveniently forgot to mention that you can't practice in Illinois. I could hardly say no. Besides, I realize this can't be an easy situation for you."

Horseshit! Whatever this guy's game is tonight, empathy has nothing to do with it.

Perhaps intuiting my thoughts, the detective rests his elbows on the desk and leans over them while he fixes a stare on me. "Let me make things clear to you, Mr. Valenti. Your father is the prime suspect in a capital murder investigation. The *only* people who get access to the prisoner at this stage of the game are cops, prosecutors, and defense attorneys licensed to practice in the State of Illinois. As you are none of the above, you're *not* speaking with your father tonight. Understood?"

"This is bullshit!" I retort in a mixture of frustration and helpless anger.

Plummer points at the door. "I've had enough of this. Get out."

We glare at each other, but I don't budge.

Williams steps in. "Let's not lose sight of why you wanted Mr. Valenti here, Jake. I'd like to hear what he has to say about his father's demeanor."

Plummer sighs and meets my gaze. "Are you going to accept my conditions?"

Not trusting myself to utter a civil reply, I clamp my lips shut and nod. What the hell else can I do?

"For what it's worth, I think this will be easier for your father if you're not in the room," Williams says.

I don't answer him, either.

Plummer stands. "I'm gonna go make sure the room's ready."

Williams steps in front of me after the detective leaves. "I'm not thrilled to have you along tonight, Mr. Valenti."

"Why?"

"Your father didn't do himself any favors talking to the police earlier. I need him focused on me when I'm with him. If he sees you, he's likely to blurt out more that the police don't need to hear."

I square my shoulders in a corporate power move to signal that I'm about to impose my will. "I'm going to do whatever I can to help my father."

"I understand and respect that," he responds with a nod. "I'm glad you want to do what's best for your father. So do I."

I let the comment go, maintain eye contact, and wait for him to fold.

Williams shakes his head with a bemused expression. "You trying that 'first person to blink loses' bullshit with me?"

I feel the color rising in my cheeks after he calls my bluff. Now what?

"Do you have *any* experience in criminal law?" he asks.

"Just what I remember from law school… but two heads are generally better than one."

"Sometimes that's so, sometimes not."

"I intend to be involved."

He looks resigned. "I think the best thing you can do for your father right now is to let me handle things. We can't afford any missteps in a potential death penalty case."

I'm shocked into momentary silence. Illinois did away with the death penalty years ago. "A death penalty case?"

Williams nods grimly. "Looks like he killed a first responder."

"But Illinois abolished the death penalty."

"The Republicans brought it back this year," he informs me with a look that telegraphs his awe with my legal expertise. "You missed that?"

"I've been out of state," I murmur sheepishly.

"Folks can get the needle for killing a kid, a first responder, or for multiple killings."

The death penalty revelation fuels my determination to have a say in things. "All the more reason for you not to be cozying up to the cops. You're supposed to be here to help Papa, not grease the skids for Plummer."

Williams's eyes smolder while he bites back whatever angry retort is on his lips. Then he shakes his head and sighs. "Look man, you're confused. You're angry. You're scared. I get it."

"But?" I snap back.

"Plummer's right. You can't be in the same room as your father right now. It isn't done."

I nod tersely. Bitching and arguing hasn't gotten me anywhere to this point. I'm done wasting my breath.

"I'm surprised he has you here at all," Williams continues.

I shrug.

"What happened at your house seems cut and dry, yet something is niggling at Plummer. If he's nothing else, Jake is a fair-minded man, a cop who is interested in getting things right. He must sense that he doesn't have the whole story. That could be a rich vein for us to mine. Park your anger and keep your eyes and ears open for clues as to what's on his mind."

Is this guy for real? "Like there's a cop on the planet who's interested in a damned thing besides getting a conviction."

"Don't confuse good street cops and detectives with prosecutors, Mr. Valenti," he shoots back. "Those of us who practice criminal law don't make that mistake."

My finely tuned lawyerly instincts warn me that I may be talking out of my ass again.

Plummer's return spares me further humiliation.

"You folks ready?" he asks.

We all nod. He leads us out of the squad room and into the hall. We follow in silence until he stops outside the first of two adjacent doors. Both are labeled Interview Two. Brittany and I are ushered inside a cubbyhole with a wooden bench along one wall and the viewing side of a two-way mirror on the other. When we sit down, our noses are within two feet of the glass. Brittany's trembling hand slips into mine when Williams and Plummer walk into the next room.

Francesco Valenti, my father and alleged cop killer, is shepherded into the interview room. It's as if someone let the air out of him. The collar of Papa's prison-issue shirt seems at least two sizes too large. He looks wilted—inches shorter than his true 5'10" height; even his olive Mediterranean complexion seems bleached. His eerily vacant eyes look first to Plummer and then to Mike Williams, who is a stranger to him. The detective settles into a straight-back chair and gestures for my father to sit. Papa sinks into a chair across the table, appearing to leak a little more air as he does.

Williams steps forward. "I'm Michael Williams from the Public Defender's office, Mr. Valenti. I'm here to assist you."

"You asked for a lawyer earlier," Plummer explains. "Mr. Williams is a criminal defense attorney."

"I wanted my Anthony," Papa answers, his voice barely audible through the cheap speaker hanging in the corner of the viewing room. I'm stung by the disappointment in his eyes when he asks, "Why he no come?"

"Your son isn't licensed to practice in Illinois," Plummer informs him. "Mr. Williams is here to protect your interests."

Williams steps in. "Mr. Valenti, my job is to advise you and make sure you're afforded all of your rights. Did the first police officers to arrive at your house read you your rights before they questioned you?"

Papa shakes his head no. "They not do that until we come here."

Excellent! That invalidates his so-called confession.

Williams, who appeared momentarily taken aback by Papa's fractured English—even after almost fifty years in America—leans in closer, "You understand what your Miranda rights are?"

"I know about this," Papa replies.

True enough. Papa loves his cop shows.

"I need to be sure, Mr. Valenti," Williams presses. "This is a serious matter. They should have told you that you have the right to remain silent, that anything you say can and will be used against you, and that you have the right to an attorney."

"I understand," Papa retorts with a flash of irritation. "I did what they say. I shoot the policeman."

Brittany goes rigid at my side while my stomach twists

like a towel being wrung out. Papa *did* shoot the cop? Why? Where in hell did the gun come from?

Williams settles back and sighs in exasperation. "I was about to say that you don't have to answer questions about that."

"It no matter," Papa announces. "Now they will kill me—an eye for an eye. This is the way of things."

"Well, I guess we're done," Williams mutters to Plummer.

No shit. The horse isn't just out of the barn, it's already somewhere in the next county.

After the detective nods in agreement, Williams kneels in front of Papa. "I or someone else from my office will see you at bond call tomorrow. Do you have any questions, Mr. Valenti?"

Papa's reply is a disinterested shake of his head.

Plummer summons a uniformed cop into the room. "Take Mr. Valenti back to his cell and keep him in a paper suit tonight. Understood?"

"Yeah," the officer replies as he jerks Papa to his feet.

Plummer's eyes flare. "Gently!" he admonishes the cop.

I watch in disbelief as Papa shuffles out of the interview room.

Brittany's fingers tighten their grasp on mine and her voice quivers when she asks, "What's wrong with Papa? He looks awful!"

He looks awful? That's the least of our worries—he just said he shot a cop. No, I can't accept that. There has to be some other explanation. Getting back to Brittany's question, I'm not sure how to reply. Do I tell her that maybe her grandfather has grown weary of the world? His home of almost fifty years is being taken away from him, he just watched cancer devour his wife, his daughter Amy has been dead over fifteen years, and he's estranged from his eldest son. As for me, I've just returned from Atlanta, but maybe that isn't much of an incentive for Papa to carry on. No surprise, I suppose—I've been absent for most of the past two decades, physically and emotionally. Maybe Papa's playing out the string, anxious to join Amy and Mama.

Plummer opens the door and summons us out of our cubicle. "Well?"

"He's whipped," I announce.

His eyes search mine intently. "Enough to do something crazy to himself?"

I finally understand what he meant about the paper suit. Aside from a possible self-inflicted paper cut or two, Papa won't be able hurt himself. "No," I reply with a little less certainty than I had a few minutes ago.

The detective picks up on my hesitancy. "You're sure?"

I nod. "The Catholic Church forbids it."

Plummer raises his eyebrows and calls bullshit on my logic. "I'm not sure they encourage parishioners to shoot police officers, either."

Good point. Maybe the paper suit isn't such a ridiculous idea, after all.

Plummer hands me two business cards—his own and another with the address of the Cook County Criminal Courthouse. "We'll take him down for bond call around one tomorrow afternoon."

Williams, who has been watching silently, turns a questioning gaze on me when Plummer walks away. "You coming to bond call?"

"I'll be around. I'm not giving the cops a free ride to railroad Papa."

"You've really got it in for the police, don't you?" he notes with what seems to be genuine curiosity. "Do you have some history with the law that I should know about?"

"No record, if that's what you're suggesting. Don't forget that I'm also an officer of the court."

Williams nods and wordlessly walks toward Plummer,

who is waiting for us. I take Brittany's hand and trail Williams.

A cop appears in the doorway at the end of the hallway. "Peter Zaluski's on the phone for you again, Detective."

Plummer sighs heavily. "What the hell does he want now?"

"Says he needs to speak to you." The cop glances at me before adding, "about this."

"Christ!" Plummer curses. "Get a number and I'll call back when I'm done."

I briefly wonder who Peter Zaluski is. Then my thoughts turn to the more pressing matter of where we'll sleep tonight. "Can we go back to the house now?" I ask Plummer.

"Not tonight. They'll be bagging and tagging evidence for a few hours yet."

So, a hotel for tonight. Just tonight? "What about tomorrow?" I ask.

"I imagine we'll be done by morning."

"What about the eviction notice?" That scares the hell out of me. We've got nowhere else to go and we sure as hell can't afford to live in a hotel.

Plummer rubs his chin. "Hadn't thought about that."

"Have you got any objection to us going home tomorrow? You're in control of the house, aren't you?"

"Yeah, I guess I am. If our people are done, you can go home in the morning."

"Good," I say in relief before pivoting to the other concern that just cropped up. "Who's Zaluski and what does he have to do with Papa?"

Plummer rolls his eyes. "Don't ask."

Oh, I'm asking. "Is he the Chief of Police or something?"

"Nope. He's the village manager."

The cops are after Papa. It sounds like the village is after his house and no less than the village manager has his finger in the mix. It's not enough that I already feel like a drugged mouse trying to navigate a maze; now they have to blindfold and spin me twenty times to make sure I can't tell up from down or right from left? "What's he got to do with this?"

"It's nothing," Plummer replies. "Forget it."

Like hell I'll forget it. I add Village Manager Peter Zaluski to my mental checklist of people and things to investigate. If nothing else, a checklist might organize the puzzle pieces of fear and suspicion that are ricocheting around my skull.

I take Brittany's hand. "Let's go pick up Deano and get a room."

CHAPTER THREE

After a restless few hours and too little sleep at a Best Western Inn—rated two stars by AAA, at least one of which must have been a pity point—Brittany and I are on our way home at seven o'clock the next morning. The temperature is already in the low sixties, there's not a cloud in the sky, and a hint of breeze blows off the lake. The sun filters through the trees to speckle the Porsche's windshield with winking bursts of light when we turn onto Liberty Street. It's a beautiful morning that heralds a gorgeous autumn day in Chicago.

The neighborhood seems as peaceful as ever when we cruise past the tract housing that was slapped together by a long-forgotten postwar builder. The cookie-cutter houses gradually took on something of the personality of their owners as the two long blocks of Liberty Street matured into a vibrant neighborhood. There were many happy hours for those of us who grew up on this street: baseball, swimming, cloud-gazing, and lemonade stands in summer; backyard skating rinks and snow forts in winter. We kids fought a lot, as well, the squabbles generally forgotten by the next morning, if not sooner. Our folks also did battle, often loudly over a beer or two on someone's front porch—usually with an abundance of boisterous laughter tempering the verbal salvoes. Show me a neighborhood without petty jealousies, catty cliques, and silly squabbles, and I'll show you a street of strangers. Not us. We ate at one another's houses, had sleep-overs, pitched tents in backyards, and went to plenty of weddings and the occasional funeral. The more ambitious of us earned our first few dollars cutting lawns and shoveling snow. Like most of us who grew up here, my first fumbling efforts at necking and beyond took place in the nighttime shadows of Independence Park at the end of the street.

My trip down memory lane ends abruptly when I touch the brakes and steer into our freshly resurfaced driveway. The Porsche's fat twenty-inch tires crunch over bits of sooty asphalt as we glide to a stop. A silent foreboding settles over me when I kill the engine. Turning my attention to the house, my eyes quickly traverse the weathered sidewalk leading to the front porch, where a diagonal slash of fluorescent yellow crime scene tape stretches across... nothing? What the hell? Where yesterday a storm door had fronted an elaborately carved mahogany entry door—one of the few extravagances of Mama's sixty-four years on earth—this morning only a gaping rectangle of emptiness remains.

The unlatching of Brittany's car door stirs me to action.

"Deano?" she calls uncertainly.

Deano, indeed. When we'd come by last night to collect him, Bullethead was still manning the perimeter. He wouldn't let us by, claiming they hadn't heard from Plummer. Then he blew us off with the explanation that "the dog's been taken care of."

"What the hell does that mean?" I'd asked the snot-nosed bastard.

He didn't seem to like my tone. "It means you've got no business here. You best be on your way."

I'd stalked away and called Plummer. No answer. Three times. When I returned to the perimeter to again demand our dog, Bullethead warned me that I was on the verge of being arrested for interfering in a police investigation. When Brittany burst into tears, the asshole had softened a bit and said, "Come back in the morning. It'll be quieter and you can get the dog."

Brittany had seemed mollified. Given that I didn't even know if the motel would let Deano in, I decided to let it go.

We stand side-by-side in the driveway and gawk at the vacant doorframe. Our noses wrinkle in disgust at an odor that reminds me of the gag-inducing reek of the Milwaukee Cargill slaughterhouse from my Marquette University days. I turn around to look up and down the street while Brittany takes a step toward the house. No police presence at all—not a single cop! How many hours has our home stood open to the public? What's been taken? More alarming, who or what might be inside?

Brittany starts retching behind me. She's frozen at the bottom of the steps with her face twisted in horror. I hurry over and find myself staring down into a lake of congealed blood that covers a good portion of the green indoor-outdoor carpet. Well, that explains the slaughterhouse stench. Do all murder scenes smell like this?

I wave my hands wildly in a futile attempt to disperse the horde of feasting flies. *Bastards!* I rail at the cops for not cleaning this up. No fourteen-year-old should have this sprung on her—granddaughter of a cop-killer or not. I take Brittany's trembling arm, lead her back to the car, and ease her into the passenger seat. "Wait here while I get Deano and check things out."

Satisfied that she'll be okay for a few minutes, I jog down the driveway to the rear of the house, unlatch the gate, and cross the empty yard to the back step. At least the bastards locked this door before they left last night. After unlocking it, I nudge the door open and step into the kitchen. Papa's nightly bottle of *Birra Moretti* Italian beer sits in its usual spot on the maple table, the sports page of the *Chicago Tribune*—predictably opened to a Chicago Cubs article—is folded neatly alongside… all as if he just stepped away for a moment. He must have been here when the doorbell rang. The dog's water bowl and his food dish with a few stray bits of kibble sit in the corner. Where the hell is Deano? Had the cops locked him in a bedroom? The basement?

My next stop is my dead sister's bedroom. It now temporarily houses Brittany. Until our arrival four weeks ago, the room had remained much as Amy left it the final time she was home. It's now overflowing with stuffed animals and other refugees from Brittany's Atlanta bedroom, which had been at least twice the size of this—only one in a litany of injustices done to her by our move north. No Deano. Nor is he in either of the other two bedrooms, the bathroom, or the L-shaped living/dining room. After bypassing the front entry, I trudge down the stairs to the basement. Again, nothing seems out of the ordinary except the flies, a handful of which have found their way into the bowels of our home.

Still no dog. Surely, the cops didn't leave him loose in a house without a front door? They better not have impounded the poor old guy. Assured that I'm alone in the house and that the only vandalism perpetrated last night was done by the police, I stomp back up the stairs and head for the front door. After a quick peek to make sure Brittany is still in the passenger seat of the Porsche, I turn my back on the bloody porch, then pull out my iPhone and Detective Plummer's business card.

"Your pals ripped out the front door and left the house wide open for who knows how many hours!" I shout when he answers.

"Who is this?"

"Tony Valenti. How could you do this to someone's home? Anybody could have waltzed in here!"

"The doors were evidence."

"Fine, so take them. You couldn't call me? We'd have been back in ten minutes!"

"Anything else?" he snaps.

"Where the hell is our dog?"

"You didn't pick him up last night?"

I relate how that circus played out.

Plummer sounds concerned for the first time. "He's really not there?"

"Would I be asking if he was?"

"I'll look into it."

My anger over the dog, the door, and this entire nightmare explodes. "This is bullshit, Plummer! It's your investigation, so I hold you responsible. You haven't heard the last of this."

The bastard hangs up on me.

I'm furiously stuffing the phone in my pants pocket when someone behind me asks, "Giving Plummer an earful?"

I spin around and find Public Defender Mike Williams standing at the bottom of the steps. "Damned right I am!"

"The cops left the place open all night?"

"Yes."

His eyes track from me to Brittany in the front seat of the Porsche. "Hey, I'd be pissed, too, but you might want to dial things down for her sake."

"Easy for you to say," I mutter, but the empathy in his words tempers my anger.

Brittany climbs out of the car and exchanges greetings with Williams.

"Where's *Due*?" she asks, pronouncing it Doo-ey. Mama had named our first dog "Deano," in honor of Dean Martin, who she always spoke of wistfully with a pat over her heart. Taciturn Maria Valenti was a Dean Martin groupie, something that amused the hell out of us. When Deano the dog passed at fifteen, a replacement black lab puppy had waltzed into our home and straight into Mama's heart. She had christened him Deano *Due—due* being two in Italian. I just call him Deano.

"He's not here," I reply lamely. "Plummer's looking into it."

Brittany's face falls. "Can I go to my room?"

I nod. "Go in the back door."

"This is just beginning, my friend," Williams says after Brittany disappears around the corner of the house. "You'll make yourself crazy if you let the anger consume you."

He's right. The storm of emotions unleashed last night is already wearing me down. Taking care not to step into the atrocious mess on the porch, I hop down to the sidewalk. "What are you doing here?"

"I wanted to set the scene in my mind so I can visualize how things played out. Helps to see the sightlines so we know where to look for potential witnesses and whatnot."

We both turn to survey the scene from the base of the porch, then walk to the end of the driveway and look back. Our front yard landscaping continues to flourish even as winter gathers on the meteorological horizon. Papa retains the upper hand in the holding action against our side of the Vaccaros' exploding lilac hedge next door. The freshly mown lawn gives way to tidy flowerbeds that border the sidewalk and foundation. Bits and pieces of the concrete steps leading up to the porch have flaked off after being pounded by years of countless footfalls, but a comfortable sag is all that betrays the age of the freshly painted wooden porch itself. A pair of glossy green ceramic planters flanking the base of the steps overflow with the last batch of scarlet and white geraniums Mama ever planted.

The brick facade of the house features an oversized picture window to the right of the porch and a couple of high bedroom windows on the left. Decorative forest green shutters bracket each window. A steeply pitched roof sits atop it all, crowned by a fresh umbrella of black shingles. Our home looks much as it did at this time yesterday—indeed, much as it has year after year after year. The only difference is the gaping wound in the front entrance and the moat of blood guarding the door. Will I ever stand here again without picturing that?

Once Williams is done looking at "sightlines and whatnot," he turns to look me in the eye. "There's nothing to be gained by antagonizing Detective Plummer—or the rest of the cops, for that matter."

Like I need a lecture from this guy. "What they did here was bullshit."

"Sure was," he agrees. "Some petty asshole delivering a little payback."

"Asshole indeed."

"This is just the tip of the iceberg, Mr. Valenti. Nothing infuriates law and order types more than a dead police officer. As luck would have it, we've got a whole nest of law and order zealots in local and state politics these days—from the governor and attorney general right on down to the state's attorney. This is all politics to them."

"Great," I mutter as we begin a slow walk back up the sidewalk toward the house.

"Did I hear that a dog is missing?"

I explain the Deano mystery. "Plummer is checking into it. I don't even know where to begin looking."

"He probably hasn't wandered far if they left him here," Williams says reassuringly while his eyes track up and down the block. "Why don't you take a little walk around the neighborhood?"

I shrug noncommittally. Leaving Brittany on her own doesn't seem like a good idea. Deano will probably wander back looking for a meal if he's in the neighborhood. I'll give him and Plummer an hour before I go looking.

"I gather you're planning to hire a real lawyer to replace me?" Williams asks.

Even if I wanted to, there's no money—not at the moment, anyway. I'll see how things play out. "Probably not."

He looks surprised. "So, we're good?"

"For now."

He holds out his hand and we shake. "Gotta run along. See you in court later?"

"I'll be there."

He nods and turns to go.

"Just a minute," I say. "Did you learn anything here?"

He tilts his head toward the row of houses across the street. "Lots of folks might have seen what happened. I don't imagine the police are around here often?"

"No."

"Someone might have been curious enough to watch the action. We just need to figure out who. The cops should have canvassed the neighborhood last night looking for witnesses. I'll look for that in discovery."

The thought hadn't occurred to me. He's probably right. Maybe this guy knows what he's doing, after all. He showed up last night and he's here again this morning, so he gets an E for effort. "Why don't you send an investigator yourself?"

Williams gives a little snort. "Who's gonna pay?" he asks before he walks away and climbs into a battered old Toyota Corolla. I look between the Porsche and the Corolla. Both are the vehicles of lawyers, one of whom pursues justice in life and death struggles. The other chases a buck. Judging by our wheels, guess who society values more? The realization unsettles me. The ringing of my phone rescues me from deeper contemplation.

"Tony!" a hearty Midwest voice booms when I answer. "Gavin Townsend from Executive Solutions."

My greeting lacks my headhunter's over the top enthusiasm. "Hello, Gavin. How are you?"

"Great! I, uh, saw the news this morning and couldn't help wondering...."

"Was that Tony Valenti's father?" I ask.

"Yeah."

"It was." My admission is met with silence. "Do you have something for me?"

"I sent your CV to a bank holding company that's looking for corporate counsel," he replies. "They expressed interest yesterday and asked when you might be available to meet with them."

I don't know what the next hour has in store for me, let alone the coming few days, but I desperately need a job. "Early next week?"

"We'll see, bud. Like I say, I saw the news this morning and couldn't help but wonder."

"And?"

"My client called ten minutes ago with the same question."

I deflate like a punctured balloon. Overcoming the stigma of being associated with my most recent employer poses a potential wrinkle in my job search, but I'm confident of overcoming that. The collapse of Sphinx Financial had been spectacular—yet another signpost along the road of corporate degradation—but it's not as if I did anything wrong. But Papa has. That might touch me in ways I've yet to imagine.

"Tony?"

"I'm still here," I mutter.

"I'm sorry, buddy, but I'll have to get back with my client on this. I'll call you."

"When?" I ask before realizing the line has gone dead. Just great. Out of work. Zero prospects. Trouble with the law. Maybe homeless sometime soon. All that and no money to be a successful father to my daughter. What kid wants anything to do with a destitute failure of a father?

Speaking of Brittany, it's time to see how she is. I find her flung across the bed in her room, racked by sobs and drenched in tears. I step across a pile of clothing strewn over the floor and settle beside her. "What's up?"

"Just all of this… this shit! I can't deal with it, Dad! Why the hell did your father do it?"

Not Papa or even Grandfather—just "your father." "It'll be okay, honey."

"No, it won't ever be okay again!" she wails.

I cradle her head in my lap as I've done for years when she's upset. While she sobs, I ache at the cruel contrast between my early teenage years and what Brittany has endured over the past few months. First came the death of one of her grandmothers. A month later, the stock option wealth that helped make her sheltered upbringing possible vaporized in the scandal-ridden implosion of my employer. Then Brittany's mother walked out on us. This morning her grandfather sits in jail, accused of murdering a police officer on the front step of her new home.

I absently watch her goldfish Puckerface putter around his bowl until the crying peters out. She looks up at me through bloodshot eyes. "I'm not going to school."

I'll be glad for the company. I nod and brush my hand across her brow, pausing to run my thumb around her puffy eyes, which are the same somewhat startling shade of Caribbean blue as her mother's. Her gaze cuts away to the iPhone in her hand.

"I guess I'll leave you to it," I say, hoping she'll ask me to stay for a few more minutes.

She nods and starts tapping on the keyboard. "See you later."

I reluctantly walk out of her room and down to the basement. After venting my frustrations on a couple of flies that cross my path, I gather up a handful of towels and rags that are set aside for cleaning and yard work, then head back upstairs and change into an old pair of jeans and a t-shirt. I check for rubber gloves and find none, so I pluck a couple of freezer bags out of a kitchen drawer to cover my hands. I steel myself to what awaits outside and slip under the police tape onto the front porch, then hesitate at the top of the steps. Dare I clean this up? Will the cops be back, pissed with me for destroying evidence? Screw it, they had their chance. While battling waves of nausea and clouds of godforsaken flies, I bend to my task, spreading towel after towel after towel to sop up the grotesque lake of blood before working the towels and rags into a pile. By the time I stuff the sopping mess into a green trash bag and fling it into the yard, I've worked myself into a towering rage against the cops, a God I don't even believe in, and the arbitrary inequity of fate in general. What the hell have I done to deserve any of this?

My next stop is the garage to collect a battered two-gallon tin bucket and a stiff brush. On the way back, I unspool the garden hose, drag it to the porch, and sweep jets of water back and forth across the porch until the run-off cascading into the flowerbed and across the sidewalk loses most of its reddish-brown tinge. Then I make a couple of passes across the carpet with the brush. I'm wasting my time; the carpet needs to be replaced. Who the hell do I call to take care of something like this? I retrieve the garbage bag and drag it to the curb, then rehang the hose and carry the bucket back to the garage.

When I come around front again, our next-door neighbor is waiting by the end of the hedge, dressed in the same style of Dickie work pants Papa favors. The neighborhood uniform is completed with an untucked open denim work shirt over a white t-shirt. Mr. Vaccaro's craggy face is awash in sadness. His eyes search mine. "What happened here last night, Anthony?"

I'm as bewildered as he is, so I just shrug. "Have you seen Deano?"

Mr. Vaccaro's eyes widen in surprise. "The police didn't tell you?"

"No," I reply while my mind races. Did something happen to Deano last night? Did some asshole cop shoot him?

"We have him," Mr. Vaccaro says. "The police were going to leave him in the yard, so we brought him here. They were supposed to tell you."

Assholes. I keep that thought to myself and say, "Thank you."

"How is Francesco?"

"I don't really know. I'll see him in court soon."

"Today?"

I look at my watch. "In a couple of hours."

"We're thinking of him. Tell him. Wish him our best."

"Thanks. He'll appreciate it."

"The door," Mr. Vaccaro says, looking up at the hole in our home. "Have you bought a new one?"

"Not yet," I reply with another glance at my watch. *Damn it!* No time now.

He eyes the door, then puts a hand on my shoulder and looks me in the eye. "You go to court, Anthony. We'll keep Deano until you have a new door."

"Thank you."

"Actually," he says, "I'll go to Home Depot. What kind of door do you want?"

Given the litany of oversights and failures I've been piling up lately, it's probably best not to trust any decisions to me. "Don't bother with anything fancy," I reply. "Whatever you think."

Brittany appears at the door as Mr. Vaccaro departs. "Deano?" she asks. Her face lights up when I tell her what happened. "Can I go see him?"

I'm about to reply when I see a cyclist dressed all in black racing toward the house. A hoodie pulled low keeps his face in shadow, but as soon as he turns towards us, he brakes hard and skids to a stop at the end of the driveway. Brittany's eyes track mine so we're both watching when the rider points at us and then draws a finger across his throat in a violent slashing motion. My eyes cut to Brittany, whose mouth is open in a little O. I angrily turn my attention back to the street as the cyclist rockets away and disappears into Independence Park.

Brittany's voice is a hoarse, bewildered whisper when she asks, "Dad?"

"Could you see who it was? He looked like a teenager."

She shakes her head and wraps her hands tightly around my arm.

I decide that I don't want her alone in the house. "Tell you what. Mr. Vaccaro's going to pick up a new front door while I'm at court. Why don't you hang out at their place with Deano until I get home?"

Her spooked eyes stray to the park and then back to mine. She looks relieved when she nods and says, "Yeah. Good idea."

There's no doubt in my mind that the lowlife in the hoodie will be back.

CHAPTER FOUR

It's warm but not sweltering and I've got the Porsche's A/C cranked, yet I'm mopping my brow with my sleeve as I cross the Chicago Sanitary and Ship Canal on my way to Papa's bond hearing. Fear. Nerves. Heat isn't the only thing that makes you sweat.

Cook County Jail looms ahead. A massive four-story prison block glides by on my right and several older blocks stretch a half-mile to the north on my left. I recall seeing some strutting peacock from the Sheriff's office proclaim that the Cook County Jail is the largest facility of its kind in the United States—as if the incarceration of ten thousand citizens in a single county is something to be proud of. The thought of Papa penned up somewhere within this mix of run-down brick and concrete cellblocks is repellent. If he doesn't make bail, tonight will be the first of many nights he'll spend as an involuntary guest of Cook County.

I walk into a bustling courtroom inside the Leighton Criminal Courts Building ten minutes later, spot Mike Williams tucked away in a back corner, and slide onto the bench seat next to him.

"Hey," he mutters. Williams spends the next couple of

minutes extracting the highlights of Papa's life from me before he delivers a one-minute tutorial about the bond call process. Then his eyes fall to the paperwork in his lap. "Sorry, but I've gotta get this stuff done."

"Have at it," I say. My attention turns to the exhibition of hardened cops, scruffy criminals, and hardscrabble lawyers who ply their trade in bond court. I watch them cut corners and deals as a steady stream of Chicago's underbelly parades before Judge Myron Mitton.

The judge looks like he'd rather be somewhere else. I imagine we all do. His long, pallid face is set in a perpetual frown. Misshapen strands of graying hair sweeping back from a high forehead testify to encroaching baldness. The judge shows little outward interest in his decisions; he's either weary of or flat out bored with the monotony of the dreary dramas that play out before him. Sheriff's deputies escort an accused before Judge Mitton, who limits himself to a perfunctory question or two unless the charges threaten a significant jail term. In those cases, Mitton stirs himself to ask if the accused can afford a lawyer. If not, he appoints counsel. Bail is set and the prisoner is marched out of the courtroom. The lucky ones who can swing bail go home. The rest will languish in Cook County Jail awaiting trial. Hit replay.

The door swings open yet again and Papa shuffles in between a brace of sheriff's deputies. Swimming inside his orange prison coveralls with his hands cuffed before him and his feet shackled together, Papa could hardly appear less threatening. The law enforcement types in the courtroom nonetheless snap alert while the deputies maneuver Papa into position before the bench. Then the jailers step away, leaving their shrunken charge alone to face Judge Mitton. There's no sign of the strapping, energetic father I'd once had to run to keep up with.

I nudge Williams, who looks up from his paperwork.

"State of Illinois versus Francesco Pascal Valenti," the court clerk announces while I watch in disbelief.

The judge, more animated than he has been since my arrival, sits straighter while he peers over his glasses at Papa. "Francesco Pascal Valenti, you have been charged by the People of Illinois with the crime of murder in the death of Cook County Sherriff's Deputy Andrew Sean O'Reilly, a violation of Illinois Criminal Statute 720 ILCS 5/9-1 (b)(3), felony murder in the first degree with aggravating factors, filed as case number 03639."

Williams pops to his feet and starts making his way to the center aisle.

"Do you understand the charges against you, Mr. Valenti?" Mitton asks.

Papa nods in reply.

The judge sighs. "Please answer the question aloud so the court reporter can record your response."

It takes Papa a moment to catch on. "Yes," he mumbles.

"Do you have an attorney, Mr. Valenti?"

Papa looks around in confusion.

"You are entitled to representation. If you are unable to afford an attorney, I will appoint one to represent you."

"No lawyer?" Papa mutters.

Mitton's manner inches towards impatience. "Would you like the court to appoint counsel for you?"

"May I be heard, Your Honor?" Williams asks when he finally reaches the bar.

The judge's eyes lift to him. "What is your interest in this case, Mr. Williams?"

"If it pleases the Court, my office will represent the accused."

"I assume the Public Defender's office is aware that appointment of counsel remains the prerogative of this court?"

Williams nods. "Of course, Your Honor."

Mitton appears placated by Williams's deference. "Has an investigation been made into the financial resources of the accused?"

"A preliminary assessment suggests Mr. Valenti will require a court-appointed attorney."

Mitton turns to his clerk. "Give Mr. Williams a copy of the complaint."

"May I have a moment with Mr. Valenti, Your Honor?" the public defender asks while the clerk collects the paperwork.

"A moment, Mr. Williams."

The judge gives them a minute before he turns to the prosecutor, a trim and serious-looking brunette I guess to be in her early thirties. "Are you ready to argue bond, Miss Dutton?"

"We are, Your Honor."

"Mr. Williams?"

Williams leans close and whispers to Papa, then replies, "Ready, Your Honor."

The judge asks his clerk for the bail review, which is a report completed by the probation department. He instructs the clerk to give Williams a copy and then drops his eyes to read. A couple of grunts punctuate his progress before he sets the report aside. He gives the public defender a "come on" gesture and says, "Go ahead, Mr. Williams."

"We believe the defendant should be released on his own recognizance pending trial, Your Honor." Everyone in the courtroom, with the possible exception of the accused, knows this pro forma motion is a waste of breath.

"Does the State wish to be heard, Miss Dutton?"

She gets to her feet. "The State does, Your Honor."

"Go ahead," the judge says. "Be brief."

"Thank you, Your Honor," Dutton says before cutting a withering look at Papa. "Given the seriousness of these charges, the wanton and unprovoked killing of a peace officer engaged in the performance of his duties, the People ask that the defendant be held without bail."

The judge's eyes swing back to Papa's attorney. "Mr. Williams?"

"Mr. Valenti has lived an exemplary life in this community for some fifty years. He has no criminal record. He owns clear title to a home in Cedar Heights, and what family he has left resides with him there. I see no reason to deny bond, Your Honor."

Like that's going to happen, I think. Now comes the obligatory give and take before the judge proclaims a decision he's probably already made. Dutton is on her feet before Williams's words reach the back of the courtroom.

Mitton's eyes swing to her. "Miss Dutton?"

She makes a point of looking indignant. "The People ask that the Court bear in mind the harm done to society by this defendant's crime, Your Honor. Irreparable damage is done to the fabric of our community when police officers are gunned down in the street. I don't need to remind the Court that the killing of a peace officer is among the most serious of crimes."

"You're quite right, Miss Dutton," Mitton says tartly. "You *don't* need to explain the law to me. Have you anything substantive to add?"

Dutton flushes momentarily before resuming her attack. "The People draw the Court's attention to the blatant misrepresentation of the facts by the defense. Further—"

"What misrepresentations are those, Miss Dutton?" the judge asks sharply.

"The defendant is in the process of losing his house in a foreclosure action. He is not employed and, in fact, lives alone. The relatives staying at his house appear to be transients."

Where in hell did that come from?

The judge's questioning eyes turn to the public defender. "Mr. Williams?"

It's Williams's turn to look indignant. Unlike Dutton, he has cause to. "Your Honor, I take exception to the People's assertion that I've attempted to mislead the Court. I ask that you admonish the People against making reckless accusations in your courtroom."

"Perhaps you can explain how Miss Dutton's allegations are reckless, Counselor?"

Williams crosses his arms on his chest. "Your Honor, Mr. Valenti isn't unemployed, he's retired from a job he held for three decades. To state that he lives alone only months after the death of his wife of forty-seven years is not only disingenuous, it's callous and mean-spirited."

Judge Mitton nods and cuts his eyes to the prosecution table. "The People are cautioned against personal attacks on defense counsel, Miss Dutton. Kindly make your arguments without further editorial content."

Dutton bows her head ever so slightly. "I meant no disrespect to the Court, Your Honor."

Mitton's voice drips with sarcasm when he grumbles, "Nor, I'm sure, to opposing counsel."

Following the briefest glance in the direction of Mike Williams, Dutton shakes her head. "Of course not, Your Honor."

"Do the People have anything to add?" Mitton asks.

"Without boring the Court with the details of the foreclosure action, Your Honor, suffice to say that it's the result of the defendant's refusal to pay property taxes. Sheriff's Deputy O'Reilly attended the Valenti property on Wednesday evening to serve legal papers in that case. In the course of an attempt to cheat the village out of a few thousand dollars, the accused took the life of a law enforcement officer."

Williams bounces to his feet. "Your Honor!"

The judge holds up a hand. "Are you going to argue that Miss Dutton's version of the foreclosure proceedings is prejudicial, Counselor?"

"I am."

"You're quite right, and I'll give her commentary the

weight it deserves." Mitton is a cantankerous old bastard, but at least he seems to be an equal opportunity son of a bitch; much better than a toady for the prosecution. He turns back to the prosecutor. "Do we need to schedule a preliminary hearing?"

"Not at this time, Your Honor."

Meaning they intend to have a grand jury rubber stamp the charges. Williams expected that. The attorneys fall silent, as does the rest of the courtroom. The judge reviews the papers before him for several seconds and then looks up. "The Court denies the request for the defendant's release on his own recognizance. Bail is set in the amount of ten million dollars."

Ten million?

Williams explodes, "The defense objects, Your Honor! The amount is excessive and clearly beyond the resources of an accused requiring the services of the Public Defender's office. We ask that bail be reduced to a reasonable sum."

The judge turns a poker face on Williams. "Bearing in mind that your client stands accused of a capital offense, Counselor, what would you consider reasonable?"

I'm tempted to blurt, "Something smaller than the credit limit of my American Bar Association credit card," but wisely keep my mouth shut.

"Scale suggests something in the neighborhood of one-hundred thousand dollars, Your Honor. Certainly nothing in excess of a million."

"A sheriff's deputy is dead, Counselor," Mitton replies tersely. "Bail remains as set. The defendant is remanded into custody pending further proceedings."

"Your Honor?"

The judge looks up at Williams in annoyance. "What is it?"

"Given the circumstances of the accused, the defense submits that setting bail at ten million dollars amounts to *de facto* denial of bail. We therefore respectfully request that the Court go ahead and deny bail outright so we may request a denial of bond hearing."

Williams is right, of course— not that it's going to do us any good. Still, I suppose it's never too soon to start making and preserving a record for the court of appeals in case things don't go well.

"Request denied." Mitton punctuates his refusal with a vigorous crack of his gavel.

With the game barely afoot, the scales of justice already tilt heavily against Papa.

CHAPTER FIVE

Mr. Vaccaro and his son-in-law Phil Russo meet me at the top of the driveway when I arrive home from bond call. "You know Sandy's husband Phil?" Mr. Vaccaro asks as we shake hands. Sandy is the Vaccaros' daughter.

"Hey, Phil," I say before inspecting their handiwork. The new front door is a bland substitute for the masterpiece the cops ripped out, but it will keep the weather outside where it belongs and Deano inside where he belongs. My gaze settles on a roll of indoor/outdoor carpet that sits at the head of the driveway. I cock a questioning eyebrow at them.

Phil waves a hand toward the porch, where the old carpeting has been ripped up and tossed aside. "We figured you'd wanna get that outta here."

I nod and pull out my wallet. "Thanks, guys. What do I owe you?"

"Nothing," Mr. Vaccaro replies. "Your parents helped us many times and asked for nothing."

"Let me pay," I insist while extracting a thin sheaf of bills. The set of our neighbor's jaw warns me that I'm offending him. "At least let me give you a hand."

Mr. Vaccaro summarily waves my offer aside. "This won't take long, Anthony. Go. Your daughter needs you."

"The move's been hard on her, even before... this," I say with a catch in my voice.

Mr. Vaccaro frowns. "Francesco told me that your wife is in Belgium."

I nod.

"Is she coming back to help?"

I'll have to let Michelle know what's going on. The odds of her helping me are a shade worse than the odds of a viper snuggling up to a mongoose. "I doubt it."

Mr. Vaccaro purses his lips. "A mother belongs with her child at a time like this."

I won't argue with that sentiment, but this isn't a topic I want to dwell on. I turn to Phil. "What kind of work are you doing now?"

"Still with the Toll Authority."

"Doing?"

"Assessing maintenance needs and scheduling the work. I'm a supervisor now," he adds with a wan smile. "A little more money but plenty more headaches."

"I'll bet," I reply. Have I ever known what he did for a living? In all likelihood, I never bothered to ask.

Mrs. Vaccaro marches around the hedge. Her daughter Sandy is in tow, carrying a flowered casserole dish. Sandy, a bookish and withdrawn girl, was a couple of years behind me at school. Even as toddlers, we only played together when our regular playmates weren't available. I don't think I've spoken ten words to her since I graduated high school.

"We brought you something to eat," Mrs. Vaccaro announces. She reminds me of Mama: stolid, uncompromising Italian matriarchs who were the glue of the neighborhood and its families.

I nod gratefully. Dinner. Another domestic necessity that

slipped my mind. I'd probably be assless if it wasn't attached. "Thank you."

Her eyes drift away to the porch. "How is Francesco?"

"Not well. Did you see anything last night?"

"No," she replies gravely. "The storm."

I know there was a brief but intense thunderstorm. "Is that when it happened?"

She nods. "You know who is behind this, don't you?"

"I have no idea."

"Peter Zaluski and the mayor," she replies with disdain. "Find out what they're up to and we'll know why this happened."

Zaluski again? He moves to the top of my list of people and things to research.

Sandy holds out the casserole dish. "One of Mama's herb casseroles."

I take the dish from Sandy and set it on the railing, uncomfortably aware of how badly she's shaking. *What's that about?* I wonder while my eyes track between her and her mother. "Thanks for dinner."

Mrs. Vaccaro nods. "I will send Brittany and the dog home." Then she leads the procession of two back to her house.

I give Phil's arm a squeeze before placing my hand on Mr. Vaccaro's shoulder. "Thanks again."

"We are neighbors," Mr. Vaccaro replies, as if no more needs to be said.

I collect the casserole and head inside. I'm pulling plates out of a kitchen cabinet when Brittany and Deano arrive. He races through the house with his toenails scratching for purchase on the tile and hardwood as he checks every room and the basement for Mama or Papa. Unsuccessful, he shuffles back into the kitchen and flops forlornly onto his bed.

"I know how you feel, old fella," I commiserate while

giving him a quick ear massage. He edges onto his back and folds his forelegs to demand a tummy rub. I oblige him.

"Smells delish!" Brittany exclaims while turning an accusing look my way. "All I've had to eat today is Fruit Loops for breakfast."

"I had a banana," I reply while getting up to rummage in the silverware drawer for a serving spoon. We'd feasted on the meager offerings of the Best Western's free breakfast this morning. After shoveling towering portions of casserole onto our plates, I snag a couple of sodas from the fridge and sit down.

Brittany forks up a couple of mouthfuls before she starts talking. "What happened in court? Papa was supposed to get bail or something?"

"They set bail at ten million dollars."

"Isn't that a lot?" she asks in surprise.

"The prosecutors want to send a message that cop killers don't belong on the street," I explain while pushing noodles around my plate. "They can do that by denying bond outright, which would mean a court hearing to explain why Papa's a flight risk and / or a danger to society."

"He isn't, is he?"

"No, he's not," I reply firmly. Which is why Mitton wouldn't risk a denial of bond hearing.

"So, why ten million?"

"Maybe someone was worried I keep a few extra million in the sock drawer."

Brittany's eyes widen. "Can you get that much money?"

"Not a chance. I kicked the problem around with Mike Williams. I'll see what I can cobble together and then we'll file a motion asking the court to reduce bail."

She looks surprised. "That's the lawyer guy from last night and this morning?"

I nod.

"But you're gonna find someone else, right? You said guys

like Williams are pretty much scraping the bottom of the barrel."

Hearing my ill-advised words is a bit jarring. "That might have been a bit harsh."

She cocks an eyebrow. "Yeah?"

"Yeah," I say contritely.

She forks up more noodles and gives me a long look while she chews. "Now what?"

"Williams thinks they'll arraign Papa next week," I reply, doing my best to sound like someone who knows what the hell he's talking about.

"What's that mean?"

"It's the first step in the trial process. The judge will read the charges and ask Papa if he pleads guilty or not guilty. Then they'll set a date for the first hearing."

We eat on in silence until she lays her fork aside and levels her eyes on mine. "I miss Atlanta, Dad. This is so different."

That it is. Our house in Atlanta had been at least six times the size of the bungalow we're sitting in. The neighborhood was, of course, *nouveau riche* exclusive. "Wildercliff: One of Atlanta's most sought after gated communities," in realtor-speak. At least that was our realtor's spiel when we put the place up for sale. It's still listed.

"I'm not exactly fitting in at school," Brittany moans.

Which I don't understand. She's smart. Personable. Pretty. Talented. I could go on. I reach across the table and take her hand. "Sometimes, these things just take time, Britts. You're a great kid. They'll figure that out soon enough."

"I dunno." She squeezes my hand back and then gets up to collect the plates and deposit them in the dishwasher. "I don't have any friends here."

"You will."

"When?" she groans theatrically. "I need friends now!"

"Patience." The platitude sounds lame, even to me.

"You know what I think?"

"What?"

"I'm gonna be some sort of freak kid now," she says in horror before continuing sotto voice, "Hey! That's the chick whose grandfather wasted a cop!"

The hell of it is, she's probably right. I get to my feet and wrap her in my arms. We cling to one another for a long minute before the doorbell rings. Leaving Brittany to clear off the dishes, I march to the front door expecting to find Phil and/or Mr. Vaccaro on the step. Instead, a pair of Cook County Sheriff Deputies confronts me.

"Good afternoon, sir," the taller one says while his partner hangs back. "This is the regular address of Francesco Pascal Valenti?"

"It is."

He thrusts a sheaf of papers into my hand. "Your name, sir?"

"What's this about?" I ask while studying the papers. I'm holding an eviction notice.

The deputy stares back coldly. "We need your name to confirm service."

"Why don't you serve my father?" I ask. "You know where to find him."

His expression plunges from cold to frigid. I give him my name. "Is that Tony or Anthony?" he asks sharply.

"Anthony," I reply with a touch of contrition. I've just realized why they're here. The deputy who tried to serve the papers last night can hardly file an affidavit to prove service.

"You regularly reside at this address?" the cop asks.

"I do."

"For now," the smaller deputy mutters under his breath from the bottom of the steps.

Asshole, I think as I stare back.

"That's all, Mr. Valenti," the taller man says. Without another word, he spins on his heel and marches off the porch.

The second deputy pauses to give me the stink eye before following.

"Who was it?" Brittany asks when I return to the kitchen.

"The cops."

My daughter's eyes widen in fear yet again as the assault on her formerly well-ordered, sheltered world continues. Her voice is barely more than a frightened whisper when she asks, "What did they want?"

"They were serving another eviction notice."

"We have to leave?"

"Not necessarily," I reply. I hope to hell we don't. Where would we go?

Brittany looks horrified. "But we might have to?"

I nod reluctantly.

"That's just great," she snaps with her lips twisting in anger before she stomps off to her room. "Just frigging great!" she shouts as the door slams shut.

Briefly considering and immediately discarding the impulse to follow—experience tells me it's best to leave Brittany alone for a while—I browse through my phone's contact list to find her mother's number in Brussels. All I've got is her new office number. I get voice mail.

"Hello. You've reached the office of Michelle Rice, Executive Vice-President of Human Resources for Coca-Cola Europe," she says in her crisp Ivy League business voice. Then she pretends to care about my call. *Blah, blah, blah.*

I wait for the beep. "Michelle, it's Tony. It's Wednesday evening. Papa... uh, Papa shot a sheriff's deputy last night. Dead. Call me." I pause and look at the phone in my hand. What else is there to say? My thumb is hovering over the End Call icon before I hastily recite my number and hang up. Who knows if she's erased my number in an effort to wipe me from her life? It had been quite a ride, but the end was about as pleasant as wrestling a wolverine barehanded.

Michelle had captivated me from the moment I first laid

eyes on her at Marquette. I've often wondered how I landed her. She had enjoyed being seen around campus with a star collegiate athlete, so I'd always known that was part of the attraction. We dated through our undergraduate years, then she set off for an MBA at Georgetown and I stayed behind for law school. I assumed that was the end of it—people from families like hers didn't marry down to my level. We hooked up again five years later at a Marquette undergrad class reunion. Michelle was by then an HR up-and-comer at Coca-Cola and I was running errands at a prestigious Milwaukee law firm. The rest, as the cliché goes, was history. She'd had to teach me how to rise above the limits of my less-than-*GQ* looks, beginning by clothing me as if I were one of the hereditary hoity toity. Then she'd taught me how to carry and comport myself with the proper attitude. To my amazement, it worked. I suddenly found female eyes following me around rooms and had reveled in my inclusion within the circle of other men dressed and prepped for success.

I live in perpetual fear that the thin veneer papering over the real me will blow away to reveal my mediocrity… especially now that I don't have Michelle to cover for me. I've often wondered if marrying me had been nothing more than an act of defiance against her overbearing father. What other explanation could there be?

I stuff the phone in my pants pocket and turn to Deano, who deigns to wag his tail before rolling over for another belly massage. I oblige him again.

"What next?" I ask myself after he nods off. A quick read through the eviction notice confirms that it has to do with property tax arrears. How can that be? Mama was always fastidious about paying bills. Can I check the Cook County court records online? I plug the modem line from my MacBook Pro into a wall jack and dial my ISP. My homepage begins loading, seemingly one pixel at a time. I lean over and open the drawer where Papa keeps his papers. Recent utility bill stubs are on top. All marked paid. Below that is a collection of crap: shopping coupons, a newsletter from the village, another from the library district, and bank statements. At the bottom of the drawer is a staggering invoice from Smolinski's Funeral Home. The bastards had really soaked Papa for Mama's funeral. *How do they sleep at night?* I wonder while I slam the drawer shut. There must be more papers somewhere. A cancelled property tax check or a property tax bill stamped "PAID" would be a welcome sight. I make a mental note to ask Papa about that.

My homepage is still loading. How the hell did the internet ever take off in the age of dial-up modems? I abandon the dial-up effort and connect to my iPhone personal hot spot while adding a high-speed internet connection to my to-do list. Then I open the refrigerator and stare at an Eli's cheesecake. I could probably entice my daughter out of her room with this; Brittany shares my weak spot for Eli's. Sphinx Financial had obligingly had an ongoing supply delivered to me in Atlanta. They'd also shipped in the Rowntree's Fruit Pastilles I developed a taste for during an English vacation. With such a sense of entitlement in the corporate suite at Sphinx—excesses initiated and blessed by President and CEO Hank Fraser—it's no wonder things ended badly.

Deciding that it's best to leave Brittany to herself for a bit longer, I reluctantly defer the cheesecake feast and gobble down a handful of chocolate chip cookies. Then I return to the computer and Google "Peter Zaluski, Cedar Heights, Illinois." Who is the guy that Mrs. Vaccaro claims is behind the eviction notice? Twenty-three entries scroll onto the screen. Some are official village links, others connect to news stories, and a few lead to dead ends. I open the link for the Village of Cedar Heights and click through to the Village Manager page. Peter Zaluski smiles back at me. He's a good-looking guy with startling blue eyes, a neatly trimmed mustache, and vaguely Slavic features under a thick mane of black hair. The smile betrays a hint of arrogance, or so I imagine.

"So, you tried to kick my parents out of their home," I say to his image. Just the sight of this guy rubs me the wrong way. The website includes a brief bio. Business Admin grad from Northern Illinois University. Married, five kids, active in his parish—the Catholicism explaining the litter of children. Membership in the Polish American Association. A quick peek at their website suggests he's very active indeed. To give the devil his due, he seems to have a history of doing some good things there. Polishing his career apple? Back to the village website bio. Played football at NIU. That's all it says about his athletic career, so he couldn't have been anything special. The bio tells me that Zaluski put in years of service at the civic and county level before he landed the Cedar Heights job. So, he's achieved nothing of consequence. Typical bureaucrat.

The news stories amount to a handful of references to village business, plus a couple of press releases from Cedar Heights applauding Zaluski's accomplishments on its behalf. I'm not going to uncover any of his misdeeds on the village website. I backtrack to Zaluski's picture and stare with an unreasoning antipathy at this stranger who made life difficult for my parents.

"If you really screwed them over, I'm coming after you," I promise the image.

Deano lumbers to his feet and strolls over to rest his head in my lap. He's a hefty old guy now with a salt and pepper face betraying his age—"dignified" in Mama's telling. I scratch behind his ears while his soulful brown eyes stare up into mine as if to say, "Where's Papa? What the hell's going on?"

I gaze down into his eyes. "I wish to hell you could talk. I'll bet you know exactly what happened here last night."

CHAPTER SIX

My nerves are wound as tightly as they were in the lead-up to a big match during my collegiate volleyball career: sweaty palms, rubbery knees, and a stomach in turmoil. It's the day after bond call and I'm at the Cook County Jail to visit Papa in lockup for the first time. The door swings open. A beefy, acne-scarred Latino guard marches Papa to our designated cubicle and backs away, leaving us to stare at each other through a scratched-up Plexiglas partition. Papa's haunted hazel eyes convey unfathomable sadness. Mama had loved those eyes, claiming more than once that she'd been drawn into their twinkling light like a moth to a flame, albeit with happier results. Today that incandescence is utterly extinguished—yet another victim of Tuesday night's shooting.

Papa slumps into a battered blue plastic chair. "I am sorry, Anthony."

I pull my seat forward to get my nose right up to the glass. "What's done is done, Papa. We need to look ahead."

His eyes flicker to mine. "They leave me here now?"

"We'll ask the court to review the bail decision."

"I think they no want me out of jail," he says with weary resignation. "Why we fight them?"

Because my life is in shambles and I came back to be with you in our home—not to visit you in this hellhole. Brittany might be a great kid, but I need adult support. I need someone else's strength to draw upon. I think all this but say nothing.

"You no borrow money for bail, Anthony."

As if I could. A call to our realtor in Atlanta suggested that it's time to lower the asking price on our house there. I'd been hoping to squeeze a few bucks out of the place. Not that there's much equity to begin with—especially after broker fees and closing costs. Our Atlanta banker says Michelle will have to co-sign any loans while I'm out of work. That's the type of proposition the term "non-starter" was coined to describe. The bail bondsmen aren't interested in our sliver of equity, nor would they touch Papa's house—not with an eviction notice and tax foreclosure in the works. I suppose some loan shark might offer a few bucks on the house at thirty percent interest, with the added attraction of having me kneecapped if I default. I'm not that desperate. Well, not yet anyway.

I inject an unfelt note of optimism into my reply about the bail money. "We'll think of something."

"Brittany is ashamed?" he asks morosely while running a hand across his head in a gesture that used to smooth a full head of largely vanished coal-black hair.

True, but Papa doesn't need to hear it. "No, she's just worried about you."

His expression calls bullshit on me but he doesn't pursue it. "I wish I not buy this gun," he mutters in a voice heavy with regret.

"Since when have you had a gun, anyway?" I ask in bewilderment. Papa never allowed so much as a cap gun or BB gun into our home and made us promise to leave any house if a weapon turned up.

"We buy it after the home invasions happen," he explains with a sad shake of his head. "Mama, she get scared. She not trust the new renters."

I recall Mama telling me that she was afraid of what was happening to the neighborhood in the wake of the eminent domain episode, especially after a couple of violent home invasions—the first serious crime I recall taking place on Liberty Street. I'm shocked to hear my parents had been frightened enough to purchase a gun.

I decide to change the subject. "I found an attorney through the Marquette Law Alumni Association who can advise us on the foreclosure. His firm also has a criminal defense guy. I'll talk to him, too."

"This defense lawyer, he does something the Williams man does not?"

"They're both criminal defense attorneys."

"We not pay Williams?"

"That's right," I reply. "He's a public defender."

"Who pays?"

"The state funds the public defender's office."

"This other lawyer, who pays him?"

"We would."

"He does this all the time?" Papa asks.

"Well, maybe not a steady diet of murders, but he defends people, yes."

"Williams works on murder cases all the time?"

"I think so," I reply uncertainly. "Mostly violent crime, anyway."

The look on Papa's face when he responds recalls the moments of my childhood when I'd uttered yet another idiocy. "Then I think we want Williams. Experience is best teacher, no?"

Put that way, running with Williams seems like a no-brainer. Unfortunately, it assumes Williams isn't a public defender because he can't cut it in private practice.

"You not spend your money for lawyer," Papa says. "*Capisci?*"

Yes, I understand—Mike Williams is our man by default. I hope Mama's dictum that "you *always* get what you pay for" doesn't turn out to be prophetic. The next issue to tackle is the alarming possibility that Brittany and I may be on the verge of homelessness. I prop my elbows on the ledge in front of me. "Papa, I don't understand this eviction thing. The court papers say the house is in foreclosure because you didn't pay your property tax. It also mentions repairs and maintenance not being done. What's going on?"

"Your mama, she look after these things. She talk about the sunroom and more tax. Always more tax," he mutters with anger creeping into his voice. His hands are beginning to move in time with his words, a sure signal that he's growing agitated. Do Italians *really* talk with their hands? Damned right they do. This one does, anyway.

"They reassessed you because of the sunroom?" I ask.

"Yes, she say something like that."

"And you didn't pay the taxes?"

"Your mother talk to lawyer so we not have to pay."

"She filed an appeal?"

"She talk with Mr. Rosetti. They do this to him, too. His lawyer, he send some papers to court for us."

"You won the appeal?"

Papa shrugs. "I no know what happen. When Mama get sick, I tell her no worry about this no more."

Great. Clear as mud. Why the hell didn't they just talk to me? I lean in. "There's got to be more, Papa, something we don't know. The village didn't go to court and get an eviction notice without demonstrating a pressing need to get you out of the house."

"I no understand these things, Anthony. After your mama pass, I no listen to them no more. I tell them leave me alone, you no have my home to make stores!"

"What about papers?" I ask. "I looked in the kitchen drawer but didn't see anything about this."

"Mama keep in box in bedroom closet. When more papers come, I put there."

Well, that's a starting point. I'll review them over the weekend and drop in on Mr. Rosetti to find out what he knows about the reassessment and appeal. "Mrs. Vaccaro mentioned a Peter Zaluski from the village. She seems to think he's got something to do with this."

An ember flares in Papa's eyes. "It no matter no more," he says with an air of finality. "We no speak of him again."

"For God's sake, you're going to go on trial for murder! I need to know about this guy."

Sullen silence greets my outburst.

"Papa, please talk to me."

"It no matter now."

Jesus! I slap a hand on the table. "Damn it, Papa, you wouldn't be here if you'd come to me with this in the first place! The least you can do now is give me a hand when I'm trying to help!"

Papa's eyes narrow dangerously in a look that had presaged the occasional backhand in the years of my youth. "I ask your mama what you say to do. She tell me you always busy but you listen to what she say. She say no worry. If big problem, you will fix for us. 'No one can take our home, Francesco,' she always tell me, 'Not in America!'"

"I never heard about anyone bothering you after the shopping center plan fell through," I mutter lamely. "I didn't know about the tax lien, either."

He scrutinizes me from beneath those menacing bushy eyebrows. "Maybe you no listen so good to your mama."

Did I always pay as much attention as I should have? Probably not, preoccupied as I was with scaling the corporate ladder and living the good life in Atlanta. "Maybe I could have paid more attention."

Papa waves the comment aside and stands up. "I am tired, Anthony. I go to sleep now. You come back tomorrow?"

"Uh, sure," I stammer, scrambling to my feet, as well. "Are you okay?"

He nods and gives me a half-hearted wave before the jailer leads him away.

The potential implications of my neglect finally register. I recall my bemusement while listening to Mama prattle on and on about the little events of their life. I usually made the dutiful calls to Cedar Heights from the office, pecking away at my computer keyboard or doodling on a notepad while Mama talked. At least half of what she told me went in one ear and out the other. I'm staggered by the realization that I may be partially at fault for what has befallen Papa—perhaps even wholly culpable. I'm incensed with and sickened by myself as I leave the jail.

The message indicator chirps when I power up my iPhone in the parking lot, so I call voicemail.

"Tony, it's Michelle." I can picture my ex-wife gathering her thoughts in the ensuing silence. Her response to my call last night had been a terse email saying she was sorry about what happened. I'd left another message to call me, this time mentioning that I have to raise bail and need to know what assets we have that I can use. The mention of money was sure to get her attention. Thanks to the Rice family fortune, Michelle had walked away from our marriage as wealthy as she'd entered it. Probably at Daddy Rice's insistence, she hadn't invested a dime of her own wealth into our marriage. I'm now effectively broke, despite the hefty annual incomes we'd burned through and the mountain of now worthless stock options I'd been so enamored with. She declared the outcome "equitable."

"This underscores why I needed to leave and come here," her voice mail continues. "I can't afford to be involved in any way—not in this court thing of your father's and not with you. I'm sorry, but that's the way things have to be."

There was a time when I admired Michelle's ability to relentlessly pursue her own agenda to the exclusion of all other considerations. What I didn't anticipate was *me* becoming a potential liability when Sphinx failed. Within a month, I was cast aside on the scrapheap of people who had outlived their usefulness. So much for the pledge in our wedding vows to stand by one another "for better, for worse, for richer, for poorer" and so on. Maybe there was an asterisk I missed, a clause buried in the fine print of the paperwork we signed. I've landed on the "for worse" and "for poorer" side of the ledger all by my lonesome.

Michelle's voice takes on a reproving note. "I'm concerned about the effect this is having on Brittany. I think you should be, too. Maybe she should be here."

Really? After bailing on us to protect her precious career? My anger, bubbling hotter and hotter as I've listened, finally boils over. I savagely rip the car door open. My phone goes flying when the door rebounds into me. I scramble after it and put it back to my ear.

Michelle is still talking. "On the advice of my attorney, I've closed the joint credit card and bank account we've been maintaining until the house sells. I've asked the bank to wire an extra couple of thousand dollars with the child support this month. That covers your share of the account balances and should help out with whatever you need there. You have my personal email address if there's anything else. Don't contact me at work again. Have Brittany call me."

"Fuck you!" I bellow, channeling an incomprehensible degree of rage into the scream. Rage is new to me. Disconcerting. Maybe even a little frightening.

I ignore the startled looks of the people in the parking lot and slam the door behind me after I climb into the Porsche. I put every one of its three-hundred-and-thirty-three supercharged horsepower to work peeling out of the jail's parking lot. Even they aren't enough to escape my anger… or to outrun my burgeoning guilt.

CHAPTER SEVEN

Mike Williams slams a hand against a wall in the hallway outside the courtroom we've just exited a few days later. "This reeks of politics!"

The depth of his anger surprises me, coming only moments after he'd remained calm throughout Papa's latest court appearance. A grand jury handed down a true bill of indictment over the weekend, which cleared the way for the state's attorney to officially charge my father with first-degree murder only a week after the shooting. Papa has just been arraigned and has pleaded not guilty. The next step on the way to his trial will be hearings and arguments ad nauseam while the prosecution and defense jockey for pre-trial advantage. The case has been designated a priority prosecution, a tag Cook County courts can apply to five trials at any given time. It's a tactical maneuver by the state's attorney to limit Papa's time to prepare for trial.

"What's political about it?" I ask.

"There's always friction between the courts and the cops, the city and the cops—seemingly everyone and the cops," he says bitterly. "Cops never think they get enough respect or support from the court system. They never think the city throws enough cash their way."

"What's that have to do with Papa?"

"Things have been worse than usual lately with police corruption trials. The state's attorney probably hopes prioritizing a cop-killer's trial will salve some wounds."

"You think Papa's a bone being tossed to the police union?"

"And the rest of the law and order crowd," he mutters in disgust.

As if the deck isn't already stacked high enough against us. "When will we go to trial?"

"In a couple of months. Longer if I have anything to say about it."

I notice her while Williams is speaking—a woman standing just inside the courthouse doors twenty feet ahead of us. When certain we've made eye contact, she smiles and offers a little wave. I don't recognize her but lamely lift a hand in reply as we approach. She betrays a trace of amusement at my predicament.

Williams slows our pace. "Met with anyone yet to replace me?"

"That's not happening," I reply while struggling to place the woman's increasingly familiar face. She's enjoying my confusion.

"No?" Williams asks with a smile. The smile throws me until I realize he's noticed my interplay with the woman and finds it entertaining.

"No, and quit looking so smug," I reply, turning a smile on him for probably the first time since we've met. "It's not like you're going to get a bunch of billable hours out of this."

"We public defenders work for a mite more than minimum wage," he retorts with a chuckle. The smile fades when he asks, "Any luck with the house? You were looking for help with that, too, weren't you?"

"I'm seeing someone this afternoon."

"Which firm?"

"Butterworth Cole." The woman, by now a major distraction, has drifted a few feet closer. She's keeping just out of earshot.

"Butterworth Cole, huh?" Williams says with a whistle. "Watch your wallet, my friend."

My eyes return to the woman I finally recognize as Pat O'Toole. Once upon a time, Pat was my colleague on the St. Aloysius High School newspaper. She went on to become a real-life reporter with the *Chicago Tribune.* I haven't seen her since our high school graduation.

"You still wanna be involved in your father's case?" Williams asks.

My eyes snap back to him. "Of course."

"If you don't mind doing some legwork for me, I can ask my boss to let me list you as a member of the defense team once you pass the Illinois bar. That will get you into the attorney-client rooms at the jail to visit your father. Beats the hell out of the civilian visitor pens."

The ice between us thaws a little more. "Make sure you mention that I work pro bono."

"Damn straight you will," he retorts with a laugh as he turns to go. "I ain't gonna be the only guy working on this case for peanuts. Talk to you in a day or two."

"Right. Thanks again."

"Say hi to Brittany for me," he calls over his shoulder as Pat O'Toole moves closer.

She stops a couple of feet in front of me, smiles, and holds out her hand. "It's been a long, long time, Tony Valenti."

I take the proffered hand. Her grip is firm, the hand slender and cool in mine. She smells of soap and shampoo, much as she did twenty-five or so years ago. "A very long time, Pat."

"So, you *do* remember me," she says with a soft chuckle. "I could tell you were struggling."

"Guilty. In my defense, it *has* been a long time."

Her eyes dance with humor. "You could always say it's because I look so much better than I did as a gangly schoolgirl."

"Okay, let's go with that." I'm enjoying the developing banter.

Her eyes settle on mine. "I'm sorry about everything you're going through."

"Thanks." *She's a reporter. Be careful,* I caution myself as I start walking toward the doors.

Pat falls in beside me. "I was so sorry when I heard about your mother and sister passing."

"Thanks again," I say with a sideways glance at her. "How's your family?"

"Everyone's doing well, thank you."

"I'm happy to hear it." Not that I remember her family.

Papa's prosecutor, Alexander Dempsey, marches past us. His salt and pepper hair, heavy on the pepper, has only just begun to recede. He's trim, of average height, and is clean-shaven. He struts the same way he talks—as if he's got a stick up his ass. This morning had been my first look at the humorless man whom Williams warns me is a barracuda in the courtroom. Nothing he's done over the past thirty minutes disabused me of that notion.

"He scares me," I tell Pat.

"He *should* scare you. I wouldn't want Alex Dempsey gunning for me."

That's reassuring. I push through the courthouse doors into the dazzling sunshine of a crisp autumn afternoon. Pat follows. The pleasantly acrid tang of leaves being burned in a barrel floats on the breeze. Isn't leaf burning illegal now? Stupid damned law if it is. We slide away from the doors to stake out a position on the sidewalk.

"Who's Brittany?" Pat asks.

"My daughter."

"Really?" She cocks her head and tucks a stray strand of collar-length auburn hair behind an ear. "I'm trying to picture you in the doting father role."

"That's not so hard to believe, is it?"

Her soft, lilting laugh sets her eyes alight. I'd forgotten that laugh and the magical way her eyes—an arresting sea green—can change in a heartbeat from instruments of cool appraisal to glittering jewels of amused delight. "Relax, Tony. I'm here as an old friend. I *may* consider you a friend, right?"

The apparent sincerity of the question disarms me. "Sure. Why not?"

"I don't want you to think I'm here in the dastardly guise of Pat O'Toole, inquisitive and heartless newspaper scribe."

"Okay."

"Glad we got that out of the way," she says with a smile.

"Not that we were all *that* close in high school."

"Not my fault," she replies drolly.

True enough. Bespectacled Pat had been a little too tall and angular to fit the pom-pom queen mold. She'd also been a little too smart. A "joke" amongst my crowd was to refer to Pat as Stick. This was a mean-spirited reference to her slender build. I was painfully aware of how deeply the cruel taunt cut her and battled back as best I could without causing too deep a rift with my friends. To my mind, Pat was more attractive than most of the cheerleader types I hung out with. Still, while our interaction on the school newspaper had been an acceptable breach of the battlements between cool kids and geeks, it wouldn't have done for me to be seen hanging with her socially. I smile inwardly when I recall that my sister Amy surmised, correctly as it turns out, that the years would be kinder to Pat.

"Sorry about that," I mumble.

"It never mattered to the rest of us as much as it did to

you hot shots," she says with a bemused shrug. "Pissed us off some, but we got over it soon enough."

"I wish we'd spent more time together," I admit after an uneasy laugh. She was always easy to be around. Bright. Funny. Interesting. Seems that hasn't changed.

She studies me with an appraising eye before a smile lifts the corners of her mouth. "We reporters develop a bit of an ear for the blarney, you know."

"You do, do you?"

"Sure. I'm happy to report that my bullshit meter didn't just go off, so I'll admit I would've liked to spend more time with you, too."

I try to echo her drollness of a moment ago. "Really?"

She laughs. "While your crowd were pretty much an insufferable collection of jerks in high school, you were maybe a little more sufferable than most."

"I believe they call that 'damning with faint praise.'"

"Before we start squabbling about how wrong you were and how right I was, let's get back to the safe topic of your daughter. Forgive me, but I can't say I ever pictured you as the fatherly type."

"For fourteen years now."

"You any good at it?" she asks skeptically.

Not lately, if ever, I think before replying, "I try."

Pat glances around. "Where is she this morning?"

"Back in school. I figure she's seen enough of the real world over the past few days."

Pat's expression softens. "This must be hard on her."

"It is."

"And you."

I nod.

She stretches her hands high in the air and arches her back. "I strained my back training this summer. Standing around tightens it up. Can we walk a bit?"

"Sure," I reply as she begins pacing north. I follow along. "Training for what?"

"Just training," she says with a shrug, then shoots me a sideways glance after we reach the north end of the building and reverse course. "Is there a Mrs. Valenti to help out?"

"Not anymore."

"What happened?"

I really don't want to get into this. "You reporters ask a lot of questions."

Pat stops and takes a step back from me. "Sorry. Curiosity's an occupational hazard. I didn't mean to pry."

"Apology accepted," I say lightly to temper my ill-advised comment.

She considers that for a moment, then takes a step closer. "Coffee?"

I steal a peek at my watch and realize I'm cutting it close to make it to Butterworth Cole on time. "I've got an appointment."

She cocks an eyebrow. "He says, terminating the interrogation?"

"No. He *says* he's got an appointment when he realizes he's due in an attorney's office in thirty minutes. Why *are* you here this morning, Pat? Surely the *Trib* doesn't make a practice of sending people to cover arraignments."

"I can't help noticing when something interesting happens in the neighborhood," she says as she resumes walking. "I recognized your father's name. I was, to say the least, surprised."

"You know they're trying to evict him?"

She nods in reply and says, "Yet another odd thing about this story. I guess I came hoping for some answers."

"Odd barely scrapes the surface. The detective on this, Plummer—you know him?"

"I know who he is. Seems to be a good cop."

I pause and look her in the eye. "Yeah? As in 'a good guy for a cop' or just a competent cop?"

"Both."

"Good to know. Anyway, he asked if I thought this was related to the shopping center bullshit a couple of years ago and I said no. He didn't seem to be convinced. Think there might be something to that?"

She looks at me for a long moment while she processes the thought. "I wouldn't put it past Brown and Zaluski."

"Peter Zaluski, the village manager?"

"One and the same."

"His name keeps popping up. Who's Brown?"

"Cedar Heights Mayor," she replies with evident distaste as we reverse course again at the south end of the courthouse. "Quite a pair, those two."

"How so?"

"Too tight with developers. Rumors of kickbacks."

"Anything to it?"

She nods slowly. "Yeah, I suspect there is. The whole Liberty Street/Independence Park redevelopment deal reeks to high heaven, Tony."

I steal another glance at my watch. *Damn, just when this is getting interesting.*

"I know," Pat says with an easy smile. "An honest-to-goodness two o'clock appointment."

"Sorry," I say, and mean it.

"No need to be. I'd like to talk more, though."

"About the case?"

"Not necessarily. I'd like to catch up. Maybe I can help you with the other stuff, too."

"The house?"

She nods. "Yeah, and also your father. Something's not right with that."

No kidding.

"The paper has resources you don't, Tony. Besides, you look like a guy who desperately needs a friend."

I can't help but smile. "Were you this perceptive in school?"

"Maybe if you hadn't been such a self-absorbed shit you wouldn't have to ask," she says with a laugh as we come to a stop in front of the courthouse doors.

"Touché."

"Call me," she says, handing me a business card before she turns and strolls away down California Avenue.

CHAPTER EIGHT

An elevator whisks me to the forty-ninth floor of a Wacker Street skyscraper twenty minutes later and deposits me in the hushed reception area of the Butterworth Cole law offices. The building and lavish lobby echo the corporate headquarters of Sphinx Financial on Peachtree Street in Atlanta. One of two receptionists behind a curving façade of highly polished mahogany pastes an efficient smile on her face. "May I help you, sir?"

"Tony Valenti to see Mr. Cumming."

At the mention of a full partner of the firm, she dials the wattage up to a dazzling smile and reaches for the phone. "I'll let Mr. Cumming's office know you're here."

I gaze around. The decorating is a combination of rich woodwork and exotic fabrics, accented with a few select pieces of minimalist artwork and understated furnishings. All *very* top drawer. All obscenely expensive and, of course, all made possible by squeezing every possible billable dollar out of their clients. I gulp. Suckers like me.

"If you'll come with me, Mr. Valenti, I'll walk you back to Mr. Cumming's office," the receptionist coos as she sweeps around the desk.

We pass through a labyrinth of offices and cubicles before we arrive outside an enormous office. A brass plaque affixed to a mahogany door announces *Herbert C. Cumming, Jr., Partner*. Expansive views of Millennium Park and Lake Michigan make for an impressive backdrop. The man inside is shrugging into a suit jacket.

"Mr. Valenti! I'm Herbert Cumming," he booms while giving me an overenthusiastic handshake after I'm shown in. "Always a pleasure to meet a fellow Warrior," he says while closing the door behind us.

"Golden Eagle," I correct him with a smile. Marquette University had retired the Warrior name and mascot around 1993 or 1994 in deference to American Indian sensibilities. Marquette teams now compete under the moniker Golden Eagles.

"A shame," he grumbles before leading me to a sitting area larger than the entirety of Papa's living/dining room. We settle in a matched pair of brocade French Provincial wing-back chairs that flank a gargantuan coffee table. The table is a foot-deep cross-section cut from a tree of enormous girth. It's all a bit pretentious, not unlike my office at Sphinx.

"It's an honor to meet the shining star of our national championship volleyball team," Cumming says with a shit-eating athletic supporter grin.

"Long time ago," I reply. However pleasant it may be to be remembered as a campus athletic hero, I'm impatient to depart memory lane. "Let's move on to my problem."

He shifts gears smoothly, albeit with a hint of disappointment in his eyes. "You mentioned that you're in the process of relocating back to Chicago."

Cultivating Herbert C. Cumming wouldn't be a bad career move. He's well connected in the world of Chicago law in addition to the Marquette network. "That's right."

"Have you found a position?"

"I've got a headhunter working on that."

"Have they forwarded your CV to us?"

"Good question," I reply.

"What type of practice did you leave in… Atlanta, wasn't it?"

I nod. "I was in the corporate law department at Sphinx Financial."

A cloud crosses Cumming's face. "Corporate counsel, perhaps?"

"I left when it became clear how deeply the rot had set in," I reply with a hint of defensiveness.

His face registers disappointment. "At the end then?"

"Almost."

His hail-fellow, well-met deportment dissolves and I understand that no further mention will be made of my job search. He leans forward to open a drawer cut into the table and removes a yellow legal pad. Then he slips a gold pen from his monogrammed shirt pocket. "Why don't you tell me exactly what you're hoping we can do for you?"

I relay what I know about the house situation.

"My goodness, I wonder what prompted an eviction action?" Cumming asks, then glances up at me with a half-smile. "Of course, that's why you've come to us."

That, and to put myself the rest of the way into bankruptcy.

He purses his lips. "So, the first order of business is to quash this eviction notice."

"Right. An injunction while it's litigated."

"You also mentioned an eminent domain action?"

I recount the episode, stressing that the matter is in the past.

"That's a dangerous assumption," he says. "Municipalities have grown quite aggressive in pursuit of their eminent domain objectives."

Cumming's disparaging tone stings. Yet another thing I didn't know.

He edges forward. "This promises to be a rather complex matter. Perhaps we should discuss billing arrangements?"

My heart falters when I hear "complex matter" used in conjunction with "billing arrangements." I manage to talk him down to half the retainer he originally suggests. Then I hand him photocopies of a sheaf of papers from Papa's bedroom closet and make my escape before he can turn me upside down and shake out my pockets. I shudder to think what their criminal defense attorney would charge to take on Papa's case.

I put that thought firmly out of my mind and call my headhunter as soon as I'm on the road.

"Executive Solutions. Recruitment Solutions for a New Century," a chirpy woman's voice announces.

"Gavin Townsend, please. Tony Valenti calling."

"Tony!" Townsend booms when we're connected. "Great to hear from you."

"You never told me what happened with that bank holding company."

"Sorry, bud," he replies. "They decided to go in another direction."

He couldn't call to tell me?

"We knew the Sphinx situation might scare some people off," he continues. "I've had a couple of clients get a little testy with me for shopping you to them."

"That's ridiculous!"

"You stayed until the bitter end, Tony. That bothers some folks."

"Are these people familiar with the concept of loyalty?"

"Loyalty is a tired concept in today's workplace, especially at this level," he says patiently. "The situation with your father isn't helping."

"Surely everyone in Chicago doesn't connect me to that?"

"Some have. Look, we're going to have to live with this stuff, bud. Sphinx *and* your father."

A creeping sense of dread steals over me. "Suggestions?"

"I can keep banging my head against the wall or we can modify our search parameters."

"Lower our sights?"

"Yup."

"You have some positions in mind?" I ask while coasting to a stop for a red light.

"I've got three or four firms that should jump at the chance to interview you."

I respond with a touch of dark humor. "I'm not going to be clerking again, am I?"

He laughs a little too quickly. "Of course not. A manufacturing concern with a few hundred employees spread across six plants might be a good fit. They want someone to handle their HR legal."

"Strictly HR work?" I ask, hoping my horror at the prospect isn't evident in my voice.

"Not entirely, but HR is the primary focus. The workforce is unionized."

Great. Probably open warfare between management and the union. Grunt work. But it will put food on the table and keep us living indoors, at least until the legal bills start rolling in. "See if you can set up an interview."

Ironically, the traffic light turns green in time with the realization that my career as a high flying corporate hot shot has come to a screeching halt.

CHAPTER NINE

The sharp crack of the screen door slamming against the house heralds Brittany's announcement of Pat O'Toole's arrival late Sunday afternoon. "She's here!"

Pat's suggestion to give her a call led to lunch at Howells and Hood in the Tribune Tower. We caught up on our lives since high school over fish and chips and a beer, then spent a half-hour talking about Papa and the house. I enjoyed the visit so much that I invited her for Sunday dinner on the Columbus Day weekend.

It's one of those days when the atmosphere sucks all the moisture out of the Gulf of Mexico and dumps it like a lead weight on Chicago. Unusual for October, but not unheard of. Great day for a barbeque, shitty day to be on my hands and knees picking through backyard dirt. It hasn't been a good few hours for Tony the Home Handyman. A sprinkler system replacement head that was supposed to take "fifteen minutes, tops" to install lays temporarily discarded in the garage. *Fifteen minutes, my ass.* Then again, how was the Home Depot irrigation guy to know I can't tell one end of a hammer from the other? Hell, even weeding is proving to be a challenge.

I poke my head above the roses and see Brittany planted

on the back step with her hands on her hips. Pat stands beside her, dressed in an almost identical outfit of cut-off denim shorts and abbreviated tee shirt.

"Give O'Toole a beer," I tell Brittany as I sweep past them and into the house. "I'll wash up and be with you in a few minutes."

I emerge from the house fifteen minutes later, showered and decked out in a canary yellow golf shirt over a tan pair of Docker shorts and my habitual loafers. Brittany and Pat are stretched out side-by-side on a pair of patio loungers. Deano has already latched onto the newcomer and is settled in the shade under her lounger, busy licking Pat's calf through the webbing. I plunge my hand into a galvanized metal tub filled with ice, snag a Sam Adams, and plop my aching ass in a zero gravity chair.

Pat lifts a hand to shield her eyes from the sun, then shoots a glance Brittany's way. "Wanna hear about this guy's high school follies?"

Brittany nods enthusiastically. "Yes!"

I'm pleasantly surprised by the easy camaraderie I re-established with Pat over a couple of hours together. She seems to be replicating the trick with Brittany. I tip my bottle in their direction. "You two are going to be trouble together, aren't you?"

"You've got a lotta beer for two of us," Pat says while hoisting herself into a sitting position. "Expecting a crowd?"

"Nope. Tales of you hard-charging, beer-guzzling reporters are legion."

"Yeah, right," she replies with a wry chuckle. "It wasn't *my* crowd who spent their high school years chasing around from beer bash to beer bash."

"Daaad!" Brittany exclaims with a delighted clap of her hands. She turns to Pat. "Really?"

Yup, these two are definitely going to be trouble. "O'Toole exaggerates," I protest with mock indignancy. "We did not *chase* from beer bash to beer bash, and that's all *you* need to know about my school years, young lady."

"Pshaw," Pat sneers before she winks at Brittany. "Stick with me, kid. I'll give you the straight goods on this character."

Brittany beams. "I will!"

Pat's eyes roam over our surroundings. "This is a great yard. I feel like I've fallen down a rabbit hole and come up outside a Mediterranean villa."

"Exactly the effect Mama and Papa were after," I reply.

"*Love* the swing!" Pat gushes.

My eyes settle on a handcrafted Western Red Cedar swing for two. It's nestled beneath a Hawthorne tree whose branches are beginning to sag under the weight of clusters of red autumn fruit. This is where Mama and Papa retired after dinner on summer evenings. I can almost see them sitting there when a gust of wind sets the swing in motion.

"Who did the fence?" Pat asks.

"Papa," I reply, looking along the length of the four-foot tall side fence of creamy stucco that separates our yard from those of our neighbors. Folks on Liberty Street didn't hide from their neighbors, hence the modest fence height. The Valentis and Vaccaros spent hours chatting over that fence. I'd always suspected Papa decided on stucco while feeling a touch homesick for Italy. The Mediterranean flourishes became more frequent with the passing years. "Mama and Papa loved it back here."

"Let me guess," Pat says. "Your mother babied the roses and your dad fussed over his tomatoes?"

I smile and nod. "You, too?"

She returns the smile. "Pretty much." Such is Cedar Heights.

Phil appears in the Vaccaro backyard. I hold up my beer for him to see. "Hey, Phil, can I buy you a beer?"

He nods and walks over to the fence. I snag a bottle of

Sam Adams and the bottle opener, then pop off the cap on my way to meet him. After shaking his hand, I nod toward Pat. "Phil, meet Pat O'Toole."

"Hi, Pat," he says.

She waves back. "Hey, Phil."

"Phil is Sandy Vaccaro's husband," I tell her.

Pat's smile widens. "I remember Sandy. Sweet gal."

"Sure is," he replies before tilting the bottle back and draining half of it. "Speak of the devil," he says while wiping the overflow off his chin with the back of his hand. Sandy has just walked into the Vaccaro backyard, looking none too pleased with her husband.

"Hi, Sandy," I call out. "We've got Sam Adams."

Her eyes meet mine for a millisecond before she turns to Phil. "I need you to start the grill, honey. Mama and Papa and the kids are waiting and we need to leave for mass in an hour and a half."

Phil's eyes meet mine as his wife stalks back into the house. "Sorry, pal. She's really wigged out about what happened over there. I guess she knew the cop from school."

"They were friends?"

"I don't think so. Maybe an acquaintance. She didn't sleep after she gave the cops her statement."

"She saw it?" I ask.

"Naw, she just heard them arguing."

I didn't know. "Arguing about what?"

"She won't discuss it. Coupla cops came by to talk to her the day after." Phil holds his beer up before he turns to leave. "Thanks."

"Anytime," I reply as he departs.

The awkward encounter puts a damper on things. Pat looks pensive. Brittany looks frightened. Maybe food will help.

"I'll get dinner started," I announce before starting the gas grill. Then I head inside for the meat and a skillet of vegetables. Once dinner is sizzling over the flames, I wander over to rejoin Pat and Brittany.

Pat cocks her head to study my daughter. "You remind me of your aunt."

"Auntie Amy?"

"Yup. Don't know what happened to Chubby here," Pat says while hooking a thumb in my direction, "but his sister was a looker."

"Chubby?" I ask indignantly while Brittany howls. Maybe I've gained a pound or two and some gray hairs since high school, but *Chubby*?

"Sorry," Pat says without a trace of remorse.

"Did you know Auntie Amy?" Brittany asks Pat when they stop laughing.

Pat's expression sobers. "Not well. Amy was a couple years ahead of us at school and helped coach my softball team one year. Great gal. I was crushed when I heard she died."

Brittany points across the yard at a mural painted on the fence. "She made that."

"Really?" Pat sits forward to stare at the painting.

Amy had done it after graduating high school. A vision of her with paintbrush in hand fills my mind—the image as fresh as if it had been yesterday. It was the summer she'd briefly imagined life as a Bohemian *artiste* toiling along the left bank in Paris. If only she'd gone.

"As I recall, she painted it from a snapshot of Papa's hometown," I reply. "She claimed the style was inspired by the Italian fresco school, or some such." I'm about as conversant with the business end of a paintbrush as I am with the part of a hammer that hits the nail.

"It's brilliant," Pat says with her eyes riveted on the depiction of lush rolling hills dotted with picturesque pastel houses and trees. A wagon sits at rest alongside an earthen road; the horse hitched to it has buried its snout in the tall grass edging the path. Gentle mounds of purple and gray mountains rise in the distance.

I nod in agreement. "Papa loves that mural."

We quietly gaze at Amy's masterpiece, each alone with our thoughts. I still miss my sister fifteen years after her death and remain outraged about how she died. Amy was an Army helicopter pilot who told us she was bouncing around the country in puddle jumpers when she was actually flying Special Forces missions in Colombia. One night her chopper never returned. The Army told us she crashed on a joint training exercise with Colombian troops and that her body hadn't been recovered from the swampy jungle. There was mention of crocodile-infested waters. Not having a body to bury was tough, but the nightmare got worse when a guy named Joe McIntyre showed up on Liberty Street a few years later. He'd been a helicopter pilot in Amy's unit in Colombia and had a different story to tell. McIntyre told us they'd been in Colombia helping the Colombian Army put down some sort of rebel faction—effectively taking sides in a civil war. He and Amy were inserting ground troops into a mountain clearing the night she died. Unfortunately, the wrong people expected them. It was all over by the time the cavalry arrived. The Pentagon could hardly send the bullet-riddled corpses of Amy and company home and still pretend they'd been killed in an accident, so the bodies were quietly buried in a Panamanian military cemetery. After they were outed by McIntyre, the Pentagon bastards still managed to convince Mama and Papa to keep the whole sordid business quiet. Mama's price had been that they bring Amy's body home to be reinterred in Cedar Heights.

I'm pulled back to the present when Brittany pops to her feet and scurries to the back door. "Gotta go potty!"

Pat scooches to the end of her lounger and leans close once Brittany is inside. "I didn't want to mention this in front of Brittany. I've heard rumors that what happened to Amy in Colombia wasn't a training accident."

"What did you hear?" I ask cautiously. So far as I know, Joe McIntyre's story has stayed within the family.

"That she was killed in one of our glorious covert operations."

I'd never agreed to keep quiet. Screw the Pentagon. I meet Pat's gaze. "You heard right." Her eyes widen while I recap Joe McIntyre's revelations.

"How is it that the truth never came out?" she asks while Deano stretches to nose her foot. She absently rubs behind his ears, which produces a contented doggy sigh and what I swear to God is a toothy canine smile. Or maybe he's just panting in the damned heat like the rest of us.

"I wanted to scream it from the rooftops," I reply. "Mama and Papa agreed to keep it quiet after the Pentagon bastards insisted that they do so for national security reasons."

"How do you feel about that?"

"Like we betrayed Amy."

Pat's eyes bore into mine. "And your father? How does he feel about it?"

"Mama dealt with it a little better than he did. Not that she didn't grieve, but she seemed more willing to accept the Army's reasons for bullshitting us. Papa held his tongue about it for Mama's sake, but he was incensed that the government lied. He couldn't forgive them for wasting the life of his daughter."

"That's how he sees it?"

"We discussed it once after we brought Amy home. He never mentioned it again."

"A helluva thing for parents to endure," Pat murmurs. She touches my arm. "Her brothers, too. Speaking of which, how's Frankie?"

"No idea. Haven't seen him in years. Haven't even talked to him."

Pat's brow furrows. "I didn't see him at your mother's funeral."

"He fell out with them years ago." The night Mama stumbled on him beating me near to death. Papa argued that it was just boys being boys. Mama was having none of that.

"That's a shame," Pat mutters. "Kids should honor their parents—good parents, anyway. They should be there for their folks when times get tough."

"Yeah," I reply bitterly. Not that I'd been much better than my brother. My response to Amy's death had been to plunge deeper into volleyball and my studies to fill every waking moment so there wasn't time to think. I eventually realized that I had shut out my parents, as well. Like some sort of precursor to the foreclosure business, I hadn't been there for them then, either. Her mention of Mama's funeral registers. "You were there? I didn't see you."

"Didn't want to bother the family," she says with a shrug.

So kind. So considerate, I think.

"That's a potentially interesting twist," she says thoughtfully.

She's lost me. "Twist to what?"

"Your father's case."

I lean closer. "How so?"

"Just wondering about his state of mind."

"What are you two babbling about, looking all serious and stuff?" Brittany asks when she bursts back through the screen door.

Pat glances up at her and replies, "Your grandfather's trial. I've been wondering what could make a man like him snap the way he did. Maybe he's been dealing with more than we know."

"Maybe," I allow. I don't want to have this conversation in front of my daughter. I get to my feet. "The meat should be done. Should we eat out here or in the house?"

"I *hate* flies on my food," Pat says.

"She's always been quite a nature lover," I tell Brittany, who rewards my lame humor with a half-hearted smile.

"He's got a point," Pat admits. "My idea of roughing it is leaving the window open overnight."

Once we're inside and settled around the table—Pat and I passing our knives through a pair of sumptuous T-Bone steaks as if they were pats of butter while Brittany munches on a burger—I steer the conversation back to mundane matters like school, work, and the weather. We keep the conversation light for the rest of the meal.

Pat smiles across the table when she finally pushes her plate aside and dabs her lips with one of our gourmet paper napkins. "Great meal! Thanks."

"Our pleasure," I reply. "Dessert?"

She groans. "Maybe after coffee?"

Brittany bounces up. "I'll make the coffee."

Pat and I follow her into the kitchen and are rinsing silverware and glasses when the phone rings. The Caller ID reads: *Butterworth Cole.* They called earlier in the week asking for permission to bill my credit card for additional costs. I was afraid everything might come to a screeching halt if I said no, so I gave them the okay to whack my ABA Visa. I didn't have the stomach to ask what the damage was—my next statement will tally the carnage soon enough.

"May I speak with Anthony Valenti?" a crisp female voice asks when I answer.

"Speaking."

"Good afternoon, Mr. Valenti. My name is Penelope Brooks, Associate Counsel with Butterworth Cole."

"Yes?" I ask as I wander into the living room for some privacy.

"Mr. Cumming assigned me the eviction matter you discussed with him. I've completed our research and am filing paperwork to request a hearing. Mr. Cumming asked that you be kept apprised of our progress."

"On a holiday weekend?" I'll bet Herbert C. Cumming isn't in the office today. Looking on the bright side, associate counsels bill less than full partners. "Sorry I'm costing you your Sunday."

"You're an attorney, Mr. Valenti?" she asks.

"Afraid so."

I can hear the smile in her voice when she says, "Then you understand what it means to be a lowly associate. This is what we do."

I chuckle and slide a memo pad in front of me. I'm tempted to ask if the research effort went much beyond obtaining copies of the village filings and reading the paperwork I left with Cumming. Part of the village's pleading for eviction is based on damage done to the garage last spring when a truck smashed into it. The repair work still isn't done, but it's not because Papa's been dragging his feet. I sent Butterworth Cole a copy of a building permit request filed in May by Papa's insurance company's contractor, along with a letter from the contractor to Papa listing monthly follow-up calls made to the village licensing office. We're still waiting for the permit. "I'm glad you called, Miss Brooks. Any idea when we'll get a hearing?"

"Hopefully no more than a week to ten days."

"We haven't filed an appearance form or answer to the complaint, have we?" It's been eleven days since the eviction notice was served. We have thirty days to respond.

"Let's wait to see if we get our injunction," she suggests. "No point wasting your money if we don't have to."

Thinking like that won't get her into a corner office anytime soon, but *I* appreciate it. "Thanks. Speaking of my money, I'm hoping to keep costs down on this."

My comment is met with a lengthy silence she finally breaks by asking, "Why don't you join me as co-counsel?"

"Pro-bono?"

"Doesn't get any cheaper than that," she replies with a chuckle.

"How will your office feel?"

"I don't think anyone's paying much attention."

It's her ass, I think before I reply, "Deal." Now I've got two jobs and no income—not exactly a sustainable career path. I let her know that I'm sitting for the Illinois Bar exam next week.

"Well then, we'll talk afterward."

"Think we'll get the injunction?"

"Have the tax arrears been paid?" she asks.

"I thought I'd wait to see if we're getting kicked out of the house first."

A soft chuckle comes down the phone line. "Given that the village is the party holding up the repairs, I'd say our chances are pretty good."

"I tend to agree, but courts do surprise us now and again."

"True, but I like our chances. We'll argue that your father's murder charge leaves him unable to defend himself in the foreclosure matter. If the court bites on that, which I think they will, it follows that an injunction is required to stay proceedings until he's in position to respond to the complaint."

I find myself nodding as she speaks. "I like it. Anything else?"

"Not at the moment. I assume you'll want a copy of our filing?"

"Right again."

"Is there a fax number?"

Beside the answering machine sits a spanking new $129.99 all-in-one printer, copier, and fax, complete with scanning capability… courtesy of my overburdened ABA Visa. "Same phone number," I reply.

"I'll send it as soon as we're off the phone."

"And then you should go home, Miss Brooks. I appreciate

the call and how quickly you've gotten this done. Thank you."

"You're welcome, Mr. Valenti. I'll be in touch with the hearing date."

Pat and Brittany look at me expectantly after I hang up and walk back into the kitchen, so I fill them in on the details of the call.

Pat's eyes roam around the kitchen. "This is Peter Zaluski's idea of urban blight, huh? With that mindset, he's gonna have to pave over most of the village. I mean, what's the deal here? Any idiot can see this house is in great shape."

"I guess Zaluski is a special kind of idiot."

"Speaking of Zaluski, I got the names of a couple of people at Village Hall who might have a story or two to tell about him. According to a pair of writers on the *Trib*'s Metro staff and a gal I know who writes for the *Cedar Heights Voice,* he's a real piece of work."

"Do you know him?" Brittany asks.

"Not really, but he doesn't exactly give me the warm fuzzies," Pat says with a frown. "Mayor Brown is an even bigger jerk."

Brittany cuts to the chase. "So, Dad, when are we gonna know if they're kicking us out of the house?"

CHAPTER TEN

Pat calls at the end of the week to ask if she can stop by after dinner with a little Zaluski news.

"Let's take a walk," I suggest when she arrives. "Britts has an assignment due tomorrow and she won't get it done if she knows you're in the house."

"Can I at least say hi?"

I hold the door open and step aside.

Pat walks to the kitchen door. "Hey. How's it going?"

Brittany rushes over to hug Pat, then glares at the schoolbooks scattered across the table. "Just having a little homework fun."

"What kind of monster makes a big assignment due on a Friday?"

"Mrs. Griffin."

Pat shakes her head. "Termites. Hemorrhoids. Mrs. Griffin. Some things we just don't need."

"Pat and I are taking a little walk," I tell Brittany.

"Do you guys hafta go right away?"

"You've got homework to finish."

She scowls and slumps into her chair, managing to make the act of sitting insolent.

I shake my head and frown when we're outside. "She's developing quite an attitude."

Pat shoots me a sideways look. "She's a good kid dealing with a lot of crap. She told me last week that she's been struggling—especially since the shooting."

"Have kids been picking on her about that?" I ask in surprise.

"Shunning her is more like it." There's an edge in Pat's voice when she adds, "She ran into O'Reilly's son at school. He said she'd be smart to keep her stay in Cedar Heights short. It freaked her out."

She hasn't mentioned the run-in with the dead deputy's son. Why doesn't my daughter open up to me?

"I asked around and it sounds like he's one of those kids who's in and out of trouble as a matter of course," Pat continues. "Fights, a little vandalism, underage drinking."

"Typical high school bad boy. Pretty much harmless."

Pat's eyes flash. "Don't blow it off, Tony. Maybe she's right to be scared."

"Okay," I mutter as Papa's disregard of Frankie's "boy stuff" pops into my mind in flashing neon letters. Could that have been O'Reilly's kid threatening us from the bicycle the morning after the shooting? If so, the little bastard better not touch my daughter.

"What's the deal with your wife anyway?" Pat asks icily. "What kind of woman leaves her kid to fend for herself at a time like this?"

"Michelle can be a little self-absorbed."

"A *little?*"

"Well, maybe more than a little."

She slows and turns to me. "What happened between you two?"

"The Sphinx thing was pretty big news in Atlanta. In short, when it fell apart, Michelle was afraid she'd get splattered."

"Professionally? Personally?"

"Both."

"Not every woman ups and leaves her husband and daughter on the off chance her precious career and social standing might hit a little speed bump if she sticks around," Pat fumes.

"Sphinx was a bone of contention between us long before it collapsed. Michelle wanted me to get out but I stayed until the company imploded. After that, things between us fell apart and she stormed out."

In fact, when signs of trouble began to swirl around Sphinx, Daddy Rice had informed me that my continuing employment there was something of an embarrassment. He offered me a job at one of his companies that was "more appropriate" to his daughter's standing in society. Michelle had urged me to take the position. I refused. There was no way I was going to be in Prescott Rice's debt. *Or* under his thumb.

"Maybe there wasn't much there in the first place," Pat suggests while we resume walking.

Was there? We'd had years of history together. Careers. Most everything money could buy. Brittany, of course. The sex was spectacular right to the end, yet we never became the best of friends. Michelle always had other people for that.

"Getting back to Britts," I say. "Once I'm working and get a few dollars together, we'll be looking for a new place and school. She'll get another fresh start."

"I figured you'd stay here."

After Wildercliff? "Not really our type of neighborhood." Not Brittany's, anyway. Me? I kind of like the familiarity of being back in Cedar Heights, especially the good memories. Brittany has neither.

"Since when?" Pat asks. I get the sense I've offended her.

"Britts is used to things being a little more upscale. I suppose I am, too. We're going to poke around the suburbs this weekend. Maybe the prospect of a bigger house will lift her spirits."

Pat looks mortified by the idea. "The burbs? Really?"

"She's not happy here," I reply with a shrug.

"She doesn't even know the neighborhood. Give it a chance."

"It's not what she's used to."

"By suburbs, do you mean way the hell and gone on the edge of Iowa or Wisconsin?"

I shrug. Surely, we won't have to go *that* far to afford a good-sized house?

She gives me a searching look. "What about you? What do *you* want? This is your home."

How *do* I feel about waking up to rows of corn baking under the prairie sun? Not that my feelings matter a whole helluva lot. Brittany wants out of St. Aloysius. Me? I'm fourth in the household pecking order after her, Deano, and a goldfish. "I don't want to lose Britts."

"Lose her?" Pat asks sharply. "She'll go live with her mother if you can't keep her in the style she's accustomed to?"

"That's exactly what I'm saying."

"Maybe you're selling her a little short."

"What the hell do you know about parenting?" I shoot back.

Her eyes flash. "I've seen a lot of good parenting and what you're describing isn't how it's done. Kids can't be in charge."

We're rescued from further argument when we find Mr. Rosetti in his front yard. He's changed little over the years. His black hair has thinned and grayed only a little. His shoulders have rounded a bit, but his posture otherwise remains erect. He continues to dress well. Tonight it's a pair of black dress slacks topped by a burgundy cardigan over a white button-down shirt.

"Mr. Rosetti, this is Pat O'Toole," I announce.

"From the *Tribune?*" he asks.

"That's right. Pat's an old friend from St. Aloysius."

After they exchange pleasantries, I tell Pat that Mr. Rosetti returned home from Florida last night.

"Different time of year to go," she says. "My folks and I wait to go until winter sets in."

Mr. Rosetti studies her with interest. "You vacation with your parents?"

"Every year."

He nods in approval. "Your family is nearby?"

"I grew up over on Newberry Street. My folks still live there."

"And you?" he asks.

"I bought a little house up by Humboldt Park."

Mr. Rosetti smiles. "It's good to see at least one of our young people living nearby." The smile falters when he turns to me. "And you, Anthony? Are you home to stay?"

"For the time being, at least. Things are a little confusing."

His face clouds over. "I heard about Francesco this morning. How terrible."

"It is," I agree before turning to the topic I've come to discuss. "Papa told me they reassessed your property taxes as well as theirs."

Mr. Rosetti nods grimly. "Yes, they did."

"Papa says you gave Mama a hand with that."

"I brought Maria to my attorney. We filed appeals. We lost."

"You paid up?" I ask.

"Of course."

I shake my head in a demonstration of my continuing bewilderment about how the hell this happened. "The village is foreclosing on a tax lien and somehow managed to convince a judge to issue an eviction notice, so I guess Mama and Papa didn't pay. Is there anything else you can tell me? Maybe Mama told you what she planned to do?"

Rosetti winces and shakes his head. "Maria's illness was such a shame. The Lord takes the best of us, no?"

My thoughts turn to Mama. With her couple of years of college, she and Mr. Rosetti had been among the better-educated and well-spoken people on Liberty Street. They had always gotten along well but I've never completely warmed up to him. I've long suspected him of harboring a vague distaste for Papa's fractured English as well as the rural mannerisms and idiosyncrasies of his native land. In comparison, Mr. Rosetti is urbane and educated, his career as the manager of a community bank further differentiating him from most of his neighbors.

"It's not the same street with these renters," he grumbles. "I should have sold out along with the DeLucas and Palumbos and Priolos."

"When was that?" Pat asks.

"Just after we made the village and its vultures back down on their shopping center plan two years ago," he replies. "An investment group offered several of us more than our properties were worth. Some took the money—maybe they were the smart ones. The DeLucas now live in Maine, the others are in Florida." He waves a hand down the street, where a chained Rottweiler rails at the world from what had been the Palumbo's front yard. "The rest of us are left with this trash."

We stand at the end of his sidewalk in silence. How ironic that it had been those three couples who, along with the Valentis and Rosettis, had formed the principal resistance to the shopping center development. Maybe the prolonged battle had simply exhausted them and sapped their passion for the neighborhood.

"Come," Mr. Rosetti says. He leads us to the alley and thrusts an accusing finger at the broken-down fence at the back of the Rottweiler property and hisses, "Look at this!"

The wooden fence has been ripped out and the splintered remains litter the yard. Trash is scattered between clumps of unkempt grass and sinewy weeds. The rusting hulk of an old Chevy pickup on blocks towers above the litter.

His rant continues as he walks back to his door. "The curbs are a disgrace, the potholes aren't repaired on time and when they do fix them, they just toss a shovel of asphalt in and bang it down—not like they used to do."

"That's odd," Pat says. "They still do things the old way on Newberry."

"I know," Rosetti mutters before he bids us good-bye and stomps back into his house.

"I'll show you what's left of the pool and park," I say as we near the end of Mr. Rosetti's sidewalk. With his complaint fresh in my mind, I notice curbs crumbling in a couple of spots and take a look at the former homes of the Priolos and DeLucas. They haven't fared any better than the Palumbo property.

"You had a job interview yesterday?" Pat asks as we resume our walk.

"Yup. Forty-five minutes on the expressway and another fifteen lost in a suburban office park. Good times."

"Ah, suburban living," she says with a smirk. "How did the interview go?"

"There were some issues. The HR guy was a bit of an asshole."

"How so?"

"He was concerned about Papa's trial being a distraction. He was also fixated on what he called my 'demotion' at Sphinx."

Pat's eyes cut to me in surprise. "What demotion?"

I explain that I wasn't the Chief Legal Officer for my entire tenure with Sphinx. "Once we became a Wall Street darling, I was doing as much PR spinning as legal work. We really needed someone with more Wall Street savvy to handle the press. Hank Fraser and I talked it over and decided it would be best to let someone else stroke The Street. He brought in outside counsel for that and a few other matters. We dropped my CLO title but I was still the senior in-house corporate counsel. Things might have ended better if Hank hadn't taken so much of the legal oversight out of my hands."

"How close were you to Fraser?"

"He's a dynamic personality—a very magnetic and inspiring leader. It was easy to fall under his spell."

"Are you still close?"

I shake my head. "We haven't spoken since the day I quit."

"Any regrets?" she asks while her eyes search mine.

This is a topic I've avoided. The suspicion that I'd been a witless dupe that enabled my former boss to loot the company is too painful to contemplate. "I probably should have left when the first serious allegations of trouble surfaced."

"Why didn't you?"

"Loyalty. I'd been there a long time and wasn't about to bail at the first sign of trouble. Plus, I trusted Hank." And I stubbornly refused to accept how rotten Sphinx had become until it was impossible to hide from the truth any longer. After all, we were all lining our pockets—or so we thought before our stock options turned to ash.

Pat nods but looks troubled.

"Anyway, enough about Sphinx," I say. Nor do I want to dwell on my dimming employment prospects.

"Wow, they've really let this place go to hell," Pat murmurs when we arrive at Independence Park. "I remember coming here almost every day in the summer."

It's appalling—especially the pool, which has been closed for a few years. The weathered wooden beach house is rotting. The once baby-blue concrete sides of the pool itself are blackened with mold and have several large chunks hacked out of them. Old sheets of newspaper, sales flyers, and other flotsam and jetsam are piled in corners or pasted against the rusting chain-link fence. Beyond the pool enclosure, the goal posts at either end of the playing field totter at odd angles, their yellowed paint peeling in long, ragged gashes.

"I pretty much lived in that pool when I was a kid," I say while thrusting my hands deep into my pockets. "How could they let this happen?"

"There aren't so many kids in the neighborhood now. Children today have better things to do than flop in the water to cool off."

I think of Brittany's lifestyle. "Malls are air-conditioned."

"Don't get me started on malls," Pat gripes as we pass through the park.

Rotting fabric on rusting swings and the bent and twisted rails of a derelict merry-go-round greet us at the playground. Hard to believe this place was once filled with peals of laughter and the simple joy of kids at play. We pick up the pace.

"You've got something to tell me about Zaluski?" I ask, belatedly remembering the reason Pat had stopped by.

"There's no smoking gun," she replies. "But I talked to a gal in the tax department who told me Zaluski had 'suggested' the village assessor might want to poke around the neighborhood a couple of years ago—right after the developer scrubbed the shopping center project."

The bastard! I think while I absorb the news.

"She thinks the village is getting ready to take another run at the shopping center plan."

Great. "Anything else?"

"Not really. I just thought you should know." Pat stops dead when we reach the crumpled rear corner of our garage. A tattered sheet of black plastic flaps in the wind. "What happened here?"

"Some idiot ran into the garage last spring. Papa put up a

couple of tarps, but they were stolen. Eventually he just slapped the plastic up and hoped for the best."

Pat's brow furrows. "Doesn't he have insurance?"

"He does." I tell her about the building permit delay and conclude, "They're still waiting on the permit."

"How long has he been waiting?"

"Believe it or not, almost five months."

"That's ridiculous!"

"Tell me something I don't know."

Pat's eyes narrow. "This wouldn't happen to be the deferred repairs cited on the eviction notice, would it?"

I nod, immediately seeing where she's going. When Cumming's office had gotten the paperwork that was filed with the eviction request, it had come with pictures of the garage and copies of three *Notice to Perform* demands to make the repairs.

She turns on me as if she's face-to-face with the village idiot. "I doubt this is a simple case of bureaucratic tardiness, Tony. Someone's targeting your family."

After she leaves, I plunk an imaginary dunce cap on my head, climb into a bottle of bourbon, and ponder the depths of my stupidity and utter worthlessness. Perhaps it would be best for Papa and all concerned if I skipped the bar exam and kept the hell out of the way.

CHAPTER ELEVEN

A week later, Penelope Brooks and I stand outside a Daley Center courtroom where we'll seek an injunction to postpone the foreclosure action. I'm terrified at the prospect of the village winning in its pursuit of the "the public good," *aka* the theft of our home. Penelope is trying to calm me down when I spot Pat O'Toole beckoning me from the far end of the corridor. "I'll be right back," I tell Penelope before I make a beeline for Pat.

"I've only got a minute," I tell her when I arrive.

"Did you pass?" she asks.

Against my better judgement, I sat for the bar exam. "Yup."

"Congratulations!"

"Thanks," I murmur, still uncertain whether or not I've done the right thing. When she gives me a curious look and appears ready to probe, I remind her that I'm in a hurry.

"How would you feel if the truth about Amy's death came out now?" she asks.

"In the *Trib?*"

She nods.

Sonofabitch! I should have seen through her "old friend"

gambit to get close to us. "You've been looking for a story angle the last few weeks?"

"What?"

"You heard me."

"I didn't have to ask, you know," she snaps after my accusation registers. "You told me enough last week for me to get the rest of this story on my own—*if* that was what I wanted."

"I'd like to believe that."

Pat plants her hands on her hips and stares at me with an expression of disbelief, tinged with a sprinkling of pain. "You don't trust anyone, do you?"

"Maybe not." Hank Fraser at Sphinx. My ex-wife Michelle. My brother Frankie. A host of others before them. *Why would I?*

"You're planning to take on the world alone?"

"If I have to."

"Now, there's a losing proposition if ever there was one," she says with a mixture of anger and regret.

Don't I know it. If I've learned anything from team sports, business, and marriage, it's that partners and teammates make any challenge easier to face—at least until they decide to desert you or bury a knife in your back. "You think I *want* to face this alone?"

"You'd be nuts to try, Tony."

"Almost as nuts as trusting a damn reporter!"

Pat recoils as if she's been slapped. Then she's gone. I'm standing stock still in shock when I notice Penelope urgently summoning me from the doorway to our courtroom.

"Everything okay?" she asks after I hurry back.

I shrug and follow her inside, where we settle in to await the judge. Cedar Heights has dispatched a platoon of four lawyers to argue its case.

"Still nervous?" she asks.

I nod, forcing my mind away from Pat's betrayal to the matter at hand.

"Don't be. I think the court's going to see this our way."

Penelope submitted a masterful brief arguing for the injunction. We've chatted on the phone a few times and met briefly earlier in the week to plan for the hearing. Logic and the law suggest things should go our way. Fear says otherwise.

My gaze drifts across the aisle and lands on a village attorney who immediately tries to stare me down; the preppy punk must think this is a boxing ring or something. I deliver my best look of disdain before turning back to Penelope, who's been watching.

"Were you that obnoxious right out of law school?" she asks with a smile playing on her lips. She's in her late twenties and wholesome in a Midwestern country girl way; shoulder length brown hair, a shade over five-feet tall, athletic build but not overly muscular. What sets her off is a pair of enormous chocolate brown eyes and a smile that makes you feel good every time she dials it up.

"I hope not," I mutter as my thoughts drift back to the confrontation with Pat.

Penelope chuckles. "He'll lose some of that swagger soon enough."

A sheriff's deputy strides into the courtroom. "All rise. Circuit Court of Cook County, County Division, is now in session, the Honorable Judge Marsha Jackson presiding." A heavyset African American woman about my age sweeps into the courtroom and quickly settles behind the bench. She shoots the sheriff's deputy a quick smile and winks at her clerk.

"Not your average fire-breathing judge?" I ask quietly as we retake our seats.

"Good judge," Penelope whispers back.

Our case is announced. Penelope advises the court that she and I will represent Papa.

To our surprise, the punk I've mentally dubbed Junior

rises across the aisle. "Luke Simpson on behalf of the Village of Cedar Heights, Your Honor. My associates this morning are Tammy Wright, Andrew Goldstein, and Lester Henderson."

"I guess young Luke needs to start drying out behind the ears sooner or later," Penelope says softly. "This could be our lucky day."

Junior leads off. "We wonder if the Court is aware that Mr. Valenti is incarcerated."

"The Court is aware of that," Jackson replies curtly. "Tell me, Mr. Simpson, do you offer that information to enlighten the Court or is the disclosure made purely for its prejudicial value?" Without waiting for an answer, the judge turns her attention to Penelope. "Miss Brooks, I've read your motion and supporting brief. For the record, you're seeking an injunction to stay proceedings in an eviction and foreclosure action."

"Yes, Your Honor."

"Do you have any oral argument to make at this time?"

Penelope shoots a sideways glance across the aisle. "Perhaps after the Court hears from the village?"

"Fair enough." Jackson turns back to Junior. "You have more for me this morning?"

Thoughts of my blowup with Pat recede as I watch the developing drama.

Junior rises, straightens his lapels, and marches to an easel I hadn't noticed. He dramatically throws back the cover sheet to reveal a photo enlargement of our damaged garage. "We have been forced to take action to prevent further waste to the property, Your Honor. As you can see, the premises are sadly in need of repairs—repairs that Mr. Valenti has not seen fit to effect despite village demands that he do so. The value of the subject property declines every day this situation is left to fester."

Penelope stands. "Objection!"

"Grounds?"

"Assumes facts not in evidence, Your Honor."

Jackson looks to Junior. "Mr. Simpson?"

"The pictures and the defendant's neglect are evidence enough, Your Honor."

"Might I remind counsel that *I'm* the finder of fact in this courtroom?" Judge Jackson replies sharply. She glares at Junior for a moment longer before she turns back to us. "Has the garage been repaired?"

"Not yet," Penelope replies.

Jackson's eyes narrow. "Am I missing something, Miss Brooks?"

"There's a story behind that," Penelope begins.

Jackson glares down at her. "This is not story time, Miss Brooks."

Penelope freezes like a deer in oncoming headlights.

As the seconds tick by and the judge begins to grow impatient, I get to my feet. "If I may, Your Honor?"

"Yes, Mr. Valenti?" she says while Penelope settles back into her seat.

I pick up a copy of the building permit application and pass it across to Junior. Then I identify the document for the judge. "The estimated cost of the garage repairs is $3,748.76."

The judge pulls out her copy of the papers supporting Penelope's motion. "I've got a copy here. Are you familiar with this document?" she asks Junior.

"I am not, Your Honor."

"You *do* represent the Village of Cedar Heights?" I ask him.

"I do," he mutters.

Jackson's eyes swing back to me. "Mr. Valenti?

"May I ask opposing counsel a few questions, Your Honor?"

"By all means."

"Is that a village document?" I ask Junior with a nod toward the permit application dangling from his fingers.

"It appears to be," he replies before all but flinging the document back at me.

I accept the paper graciously and am the very voice of reason when I ask, "Did you happen to notice the date on it?"

"No."

"It's dated May seventeenth, Counselor," I say in my best Mr. Reasonable Lawyer voice. Then I figuratively place my foot on his throat. "Did you know that the plaintiff's contractor has called several times and is *still* waiting for the village to authorize that building permit?"

"I'm sure there's an explanation," Junior mutters through clenched teeth.

"Oh, I'm sure there is, Counselor, but I doubt we're going to hear it here this morning. I can't imagine why it should take several months to approve a building permit for something as simple as fixing a hole in a wall. Has it occurred to anyone at the village that if this permit had been issued in a timely manner, there would be no grounds for the eviction notice?"

"Taking that thought a step further," Jackson interjects with an edge in her voice, "if the eviction notice hadn't been issued, Francesco Valenti wouldn't be in jail this morning and Deputy O'Reilly would be alive." She lets Junior and his cohorts stew for several seconds before she turns back to me. "Do you have anything further, Counselor?"

Damned right I do. "Is the village aware of any encumbrance on the subject property beyond its own tax lien?" I ask Junior.

"No."

"I'm not a real estate appraiser, but can we agree that this property is worth more than, say, $20,000?"

"I suppose that's a reasonable assumption," Junior replies with a weary nod.

"So, we've got less than $4,000 worth of repairs to be made and a total tax bill of approximately $10,000, including penalties and interest due," I say. "A tax sale of $20,000 or so should comfortably cover the entire risk to the village."

"I can't say," he retorts with a poisonous scowl, going from weary to surly in a heartbeat.

"You know the answer as well as I do, Counselor," I shoot back. "The Village of Cedar Heights is in no danger of losing money in this matter. Is there some other reason you're so anxious to get your hands on this property?"

Junior glares back at me but doesn't reply. I wonder if he's growing as incensed with Peter Zaluski's bullshit as I am.

"Does the village have any further argument?" Judge Jackson asks.

Junior shakes his head.

Jackson scribbles some notes before again fixing the Cedar Heights attorneys in her sights. "I'm vacating the eviction notice and suspending foreclosure action for a period of one-hundred and eighty days."

Judge Jackson next turns her attention to us. "I'm aware of your client's circumstances, but property taxes must be paid. This ruling is conditional on payment of all tax arrears and penalties. Deliver proof of same to this court within ten days."

Penelope stands. "Thank you, Your Honor."

Jackson nods at Penelope and then locks her gaze on me. "See that those taxes are paid, Counselor. I will not be pleased to find this matter being litigated in my courtroom again."

The six-month stay is at least double what I dared to dream. I have no wish to antagonize the judge at this point. Reasoning that a verbal reply is neither required nor expected, I merely nod.

Village Attorney Andrew Goldstein gets to his feet. "Might not a hundred and eighty days be overly generous, Your Honor?"

Jackson gently bounces a pencil on her blotter. "If Mr. Valenti's home was in another village, perhaps so, but he lives in Cedar Heights, Counselor. Who knows how much longer it will take for that building permit to work its way through Village Hall?"

"I think we can assure the Court that the permit will be expedited," Goldstein responds with an oily smile that reminds me of Zaluski's.

"Pity it should take a court hearing to get your people off the dime, Counselor," Jackson replies.

Goldstein plows ahead. "I suggest the injunction be amended to thirty days, conditional on the village issuing the building permit within seventy-two hours."

"I've already ruled, Counselor," the judge replies. "But I'm sure Miss Brooks and Mr. Valenti appreciate your efforts to correct a past wrong. I'll include your seventy-two-hour commitment in my ruling." With a rap of her gavel, Judge Jackson dismisses us. If I had to hazard a guess, I'd say she's pleased with the outcome.

Penelope falls into step beside me as we leave the courtroom. "Thanks for bailing me out, Tony. You were great in there."

"You were doing fine," I lie. Some lawyers are great in a courtroom, others do their best work behind the scenes writing masterful briefs and motions that give the rest of us the material to stand up and argue our cases. Without Penelope's brief and research, I would have been lost in there—an actor with no lines.

I spot Pat as soon as we reach the hallway. She's talking to a man who is scurrying to reach the same elevators we're heading toward.

"Need to talk to your friend again?" Penelope asks with a knowing smile when she notices me watching.

"I do," I reply as I hurry ahead. Pat's in reporter mode with notebook and pen in hand, unsuccessfully maneuvering to block her target's path to the elevator. I break into a jog when the man turns his head and I recognize Peter Zaluski.

He sees me coming and warily watches my approach as he reaches the elevator. Pat stands aside.

I park myself three feet away. "I want a word with you."

"Who are you?" he asks.

"Tony Valenti, of the Liberty Street Valentis. You remember my parents, hot shot?" All the helplessness and rage that has been building within me over the past month wells up and threatens to explode. I step a little closer. "Do you realize what you've done to my family, Zaluski? My mother died recently, in no small part due to the stress you put on her by pushing your shopping center boondoggle. Now your bullshit has gotten a police officer shot."

Zaluski is backed up against the elevator doors. His expression has progressed from annoyance to alarm. I inch closer until I'm towering over him. I can barely suppress the urge to wring the bastard's neck.

"No, Tony!" Pat cries. She grabs my arm and pulls me away as a *ding* announces the arrival of the elevator. Zaluski backs in without breaking eye contact. His eyes reflect a myriad of emotions as the doors close: fear, bewilderment, pique—all tinged with a hint of anger.

Pat looks aghast at me. "What were you doing?"

I wanted to intimidate the bastard. I want Zaluski to understand that he's not facing off with Mama and Papa this time. I want him nervous and afraid and looking over his shoulder at night—not that I want to articulate any of that with the way Pat is studying me. "I guess I just lost it a little when I saw him," I reply. "What the hell was Zaluski doing here?"

Pat stares at me for a long moment, then steps into a second elevator without a word. With her goes the afterglow of our court victory—as if it were nothing more than a puff of smoke in a stiff wind.

CHAPTER TWELVE

I'm home an hour later after a stop at the Cedar Heights Village Hall to charge the tax arrears and penalties to my credit card. We're on track to be pretty much broke in another month—maybe two if we're lucky. Thankfully, there's the possibility of a job on the horizon. Gavin Townsend is optimistic, so I've allowed myself to get my hopes up a bit. Even that little pinch of optimism vanishes when I recall the painful image of Pat's perplexed face disappearing behind the Daley Center elevator doors. My angry outburst about Amy's story was out of proportion; I was hurt as much as I was angry. The thought of having a friend had been comforting.

A late lunch of leftover stir-fry is in the microwave; an empty afternoon and evening yawn in front of me. A lazy afternoon puttering around the house and yard in the undemanding company of Deano promises some welcome downtime. I'll hang out with Brittany after school. Given her fondness for animals, maybe a jaunt to the Lincoln Park Zoo? With any luck, the world will look brighter by bedtime.

Then the telephone rings.

"This is Mrs. O'Connor from St. Aloysius School. Is this Anthony Valenti?"

I think back to registering Brittany and recall Mrs. O'Connor as a pleasant middle-aged woman in a frumpy dress. "It is."

"Is Brittany at home?"

"No, she's at school. Isn't she?"

"There was an incident between Brittany and her English teacher at the start of fourth period," O'Connor says. "Brittany was asked to report to the office. She seems to have left the school instead. We're looking for her now."

I snatch my keys off the counter. "How long ago was this?"

"No more than twenty minutes."

The front door crashes open and footsteps thunder through the living room, solving the mystery of the missing Brittany. Her bedroom door slams shut.

"She just walked in."

"Thank the Lord!" Mrs. O'Connor exclaims before she speaks to someone in the background.

"Can you tell me what happened?" I ask.

"Just a moment," she replies. I rock impatiently from foot to foot while I wait, anxious to get off the phone and see what's up with my daughter. Mrs. O'Connor finally comes back on the line seconds before I hang up. "Father Ramone would like to see both of you."

"When?"

A brief consultation at the other end of the line ends with, "This afternoon?"

"Let me talk to Brittany first. We'll be down afterward."

"I don't want to talk!" Brittany howls in response to my rap on her door. I push it open anyway. She's sitting cross-legged in the middle of her unmade bed. The haunted face looking back at me suggests the hounds of hell have come for her.

"The school called. What's going on?"

"I hate that place!"

"What happened?" My question is met with stony silence. "We're going back to speak with Father Ramone. Do you"

"I'm *not* going back!" she explodes.

I pluck her sneakers off the floor and toss them to her. "This isn't debatable. We *are* going back. Are you going to tell me what happened or let Father Ramone explain?"

She yanks on her shoes in a fit of temper and drags herself off the bed. "Who cares? He'll just take *her* side anyway."

"I'd like to hear your version."

She shrugs and pushes past me with a look that could melt a glacier. Car keys in hand, I follow her out of the house. She doesn't say a word until we pull into the school parking lot, then turns on me. "I called her a miserable old bitch and told her to get out of my face."

I twist the key in the ignition to kill the engine. "You *what?"*

"You heard me," she snaps while hopping out of the vehicle.

"I did but I don't believe it," I mutter as I scramble out after her.

"Believe it." She spins away and slams the car door before stomping inside.

Father Ramone, swathed in the robes of his vocation, is waiting for us. A puff of Old Spice aftershave tickles my nose when he glides forward to fold his soft hands around mine. "Thank you for coming." The priest's cocoa-colored eyes, buried deep within the fleshy folds of a clean-shaven face, shift to study Brittany, who stands rigidly with her eyes fixed on the floor. "Your disappearance upset everyone. Thankfully, by the grace of God, our prayers for your safe return were answered."

Given that Brittany came straight home, the melodrama seems overdone.

The priest steps aside and waves us into his office. "Come, let us talk."

We settle on a chrome-framed vinyl couch that would be right at home in a Goodwill store. The only items breaking the monotony of the off-white walls are a graphic crucifix flanked by a full color portrait of the Pope. The priest rolls a ratty office chair from behind his desk and parks it in front of the couch, then leans forward to cover Brittany's hand with his. She stiffens at the touch but doesn't move her hand or look at him.

"Brittany told me what happened," I say when Ramone looks at me. "I'd like to know why."

Father Ramone settles back in his seat with a heavy sigh and turns his gaze on Brittany. "Did you tell your father *exactly* what you said to Mrs. Griffin?"

Brittany's eyes remain glued to the floor. "Yeah, I called the old cow a bitch."

"You know better than to swear at teachers!" I snap.

The initial shock that registers in her eyes when she looks up quickly mutates to fury and a wordless accusation of betrayal. "Are we done now?"

"No, we're not," I retort. "Tell us what Mrs. Griffin did to you."

Brittany replies with barely suppressed rage, "One of the kids told me that Griffin's brother is a cop. She glares at me through every class. She talks to me like I'm garbage. It's bad enough I have to deal with crap from kids—do I have to put up with it from my teachers, too?"

"I know this is a difficult time for you but none of our St. Aloysius family would mistreat you," Ramone says solicitously.

"I'm no part of your precious family," Brittany fumes. "Your *family* hasn't wanted me here since the day I showed up."

The degree of hostility and pain in my daughter stuns me.

Pat's caution that things at school were bad rings in my ears, a warning I failed to heed. Who knows how different things might be today—on a number of fronts—if her father talked less and listened more?

"Ever since Papa shot that cop," Brittany continues, "I've had kids taunting me—cop-killer this, cop-killer that. I'm sick of it!"

Father Ramone turns to me. "St. Aloysius draws students from the working class, many of whom are the families of police officers and firefighters. What happened is their worst fear. When kids are scared, they act out to express their fears and anger."

"O'Reilly's son goes to school here, doesn't he?" I ask.

Ramone nods.

"You know he's threatened my daughter?"

"He's angry and confused about the death of his father," he replies with an almost imperceptible shrug. "He may act out on occasion."

"*Act out?* A delinquent threatening someone isn't the same as a toddler throwing a tantrum, Father. What have you done to punish him and to protect Brittany?"

"I believe it is best to allow children to express their anger," Ramone replies calmly. "We do not believe it is being directed at Brittany."

"Who *do* you think it's directed at?"

He doesn't reply. Mindful of my admonition to Brittany about profanity, I bite back my suggestion that the good Father pull his head out of his ass. "It didn't occur to anyone to monitor the situation?"

"We must consider the welfare of the child."

"I wish you'd said *each and every child*, Father," I reply icily.

"I will ask the staff to watch more closely upon Brittany's return."

"So, she's being suspended," I say. No surprise there, I suppose. "For how long?"

Brittany looks from Ramone to me. "Nobody cares what Mrs. Griffin did to me?"

"She did nothing to you," Ramone says with finality.

Realizing that prolonging this is pointless, I get to my feet. "We've all spoken our piece now, Father. We'll be on our way."

The priest rises and extends his hand. "That might be best."

"When can Brittany return to school?"

He ponders the question for a moment. "One week from Monday."

The Porsche is silent all the way home. Brittany simmers in the passenger seat while I'm lost in thoughts of where I've gone wrong as a parent.

"I'm *not* going back to that dump," she announces as soon as we walk into the house.

"We'll see."

"*No,* we won't 'see,' Dad. St. Aloysius is history."

"We can't afford private school right now."

"So? Send me to a public school!"

"Not in Chicago, honey. You've seen them. No way."

"Another Catholic school then."

"St. Aloysius is the high school for this parish. It's that or nothing."

"Then it's private school or no school. I'm *not* going back to that shithole."

"Maybe we can swing something once I'm working."

Brittany goes ballistic. "Then get a damned job already!"

I bite my tongue as shame overwhelms my initial burst of anger.

"Maybe I need to talk to Pat," she says. "Someone who understands me."

"Pat's out of the picture."

"*What?*"

"We had an argument."

"About what?"

"She wants to write about how Amy died."

"So?"

"What if that's the only reason she looked me up?"

Brittany's voice edges toward hysteria. "Jesus, Dad. She's the only friend I have in this shitty city!"

I shrug helplessly. Her words and the realization of how true they are cut deep, but not as deep as her follow-up explosion.

"Sometimes I hate you!" she screams with her face contorted in fury.

She marches straight to her room and I head for mine, snagging the cordless phone as I go. Whether she wishes to acknowledge it or not, Michelle is still Brittany's mother and she can damn well pitch in. While the line rings in Brussels, I decide that I'll beg for money if I have to—whatever it takes to get our girl into a private school.

Michelle picks up after three rings. "Hello."

"It's me."

A pause. "Do you know what time it is here?"

"No." Four thousand miles, several time zones, and an ocean of acrimony separate us.

"I'm trying to have dinner," she announces, as if I'm a telemarketer calling at an inopportune moment. "Did I give you this number?"

"Brittany has it." I'd asked her for it after being told not to call Michelle at work.

"What do you want?" she asks impatiently.

I fill her in on the afternoon's events.

"What's going on there? She told me there was an altercation with another student a week or two ago."

"That was just kid shit." Does Brittany talk to everyone *but* me?

"I'm glad *you're* taking it all in stride," Michelle snaps. "This whole idea of running home to Chicago isn't working out very well for Brittany though, is it?"

I'm in no mood for Michelle's scolding or cheap shots. "She won't go back to St. Aloysius. We need to get her into a private school."

"*We?* You've found a job then?"

"Not yet," I admit while holding my phone in a death grip.

"Then how do you plan to pay for private schooling?"

"Her mother works."

Michelle's tone turns frigid. "I will not support you, Tony."

"I'm not asking you to support me. I'm asking you to help with your daughter's goddamned education. Is that unreasonable?"

"How much will you be contributing?"

"Once I'm back on my feet I'll pay for it all myself. Right now, we need some help."

"Hopefully you'll find a job soon. Until then, we'd best consider Brittany's options. Let me talk to her."

"Now?"

"Yes. I'd like to speak with my daughter," she replies in her "I will brook no argument" voice.

"What about school? We haven't made a decision."

A long-suffering sigh crosses the Atlantic. "Let me speak with Brittany first."

"Damn it, Michelle—"

"*Now*, Tony."

"Hang on." After tossing the phone onto the middle of the bed, I set out for Brittany's room. I have to pound on her door to be heard over the music blaring inside. The volume dips but she says nothing.

"Your mother's on the phone."

The door swings open immediately. The smile on her face, coupled with the light shining in her eyes, are like a knife to the heart when she excitedly asks, "Mom's on the phone?"

"That's what I said," I reply dejectedly.

She stares at my empty hands. "Where's the phone?"

"On my bed," I reply with a wave down the hall.

She's gone before I take my next breath. I follow Brittany back to my room and lean on the doorframe to listen to her end of the conversation.

"I'm sorry about swearing, Mom, but these people are *sooo* nasty… all of them—the kids, the teachers, even the priest. They act like *I* shot the stupid cop."

The anguish in Brittany's voice almost brings me to tears.

Her face lights up as she listens to her mother's response. "Really? Can I do that? When?"

I start to worry.

"Too cool!" she exclaims before asking, "What about school?"

They can't be discussing what I think they are. I step across the room and hold my hand out. "Give me the phone for a minute, honey."

She ignores me. "You've got room?"

"I said give me the phone, Britts."

After she turns away, I snatch the phone out of her hand. "What the hell are you up to, Michelle?"

"She'll be better off here with me."

I bite off my angry reply and take a deep breath. Brittany hasn't exactly been putting up an argument. If I'm honest with myself, the school troubles and the O'Reilly kid lurking have left me a little on edge. Maybe a break from Cedar Heights isn't such a bad idea. "What are you thinking?" I ask. "How long?"

"As long as it takes her to get over this."

"A week or two away probably wouldn't hurt. Give me a few days to think about this and kick it around with her."

"Two days, Tony. Call me back in two days."

Brittany is staring at me, her expression suspended between residual anger and excitement about escaping Cedar Heights. My heart sinks at the prospect of losing my daughter.

CHAPTER THIRTEEN

I arrive at the Cook County Jail almost two weeks later to visit Papa in an attorney-client conference room. After a drawn-out battle, Mike has persuaded his office to list me on the defense team roster at the jail. He assures me this will be a huge improvement from seeing Papa in the public visiting pens. Despite this welcome development, I've been bitchy all morning. Taking the dog out for his morning walk and finding all four of your $600 tires slashed wide open can set you on the road to bitchy in a hurry. This kind of crap didn't used to happen on Liberty Street.

A bored jail guard sitting behind a glass partition glances up and asks how he can help me, managing to do so without conveying the slightest interest in being of assistance.

"Tony Valenti. I have an eleven o'clock appointment with Francesco Valenti."

He taps on a computer keyboard before issuing a little grunt, then points at a clipboard sitting on the counter on my side of the glass. "Sign in."

I record my name and the time.

He reads it and frowns. "Got some ID?"

I hold out my brand-new Illinois driver's license.

He studies it and grunts again, then picks up a phone and punches in a couple of numbers.

"Taylor at security. I've got a Tony Valenti here to see the cop-killer in an attorney room at eleven." He shoots a pointed glance at his watch and cuts his eyes to me after he hangs up. "Cuttin' it close, pal. Don't make a habit of it."

Screw you, pal. See how punctual you are when someone slashes your *tires.*

The guard fishes a visitor card out of a drawer and records the number beside my name in the visitor log before he drops it into a slot that he spins around to face me. "Wear that around your neck at all times."

I slip the lanyard over my head while a buzzer signals that he's unlocked the door.

"You hear me?" he asks as I enter. "Wear it at all times."

I nod. *May a thousand piranha devour your testicles in the bathtub, big guy.*

I head inside. Seeing Papa wasting away through a sheet of Plexiglas hasn't prepared me for the physical shock of embracing his emaciated body. The birdlike grasp of his fingers clinging to my shoulders startles me. His once-powerful hands had unwittingly left me squirming in discomfort many a time when we horsed around during my childhood.

He finds his voice first. "Is good to visit here. This room is much better."

"It certainly is." I make a mental note to thank Mike Williams once again.

Papa nods toward the door. "Williams, he say I should no talk out there."

"He's right." The guards are trained to hover and eavesdrop on the detainees in the public visiting areas. Anything damaging they "happen" to hear is admissible at trial—yet another thing about criminal law I've either forgotten or never knew. The list of such revelations is uncomfortably long.

Papa sinks into a chair and props his elbows on the table. Anguish seeps from every pore. I slide onto a chair and cover his hand with mine. "We'll have plenty of time to talk now, Papa."

His eyes flicker to mine before dropping back to the table. He's a million miles away. The two topics most likely to capture his interest are his daughter and Brittany, not that there's any good news to impart in either case. Though Amy has been dead for years, Papa still mourns and clings to any mention of her. I wonder how he'll react to the idea of the *Trib* going public with the truth about her death. As for his granddaughter, Brittany flatly refused to return to school at the end of her suspension last week. The conundrum about her school plans was resolved by an email from Michelle this morning announcing that she's purchased our daughter a plane ticket to Brussels for this weekend. After managing to fend off Michelle for over a week, I was allowing myself to imagine that she may have had a change of heart about letting Brittany stay in Cedar Heights. I should know better than to get my hopes up about anything these days.

After a deep breath, I decide to lead with my sister. "Pat O'Toole from the *Tribune* knows what really happened to Amy. She pitched the idea of running the story in the paper. Would you object?"

Papa looks up. "This Pat, she is the woman you go to school with?"

I nod.

"Your Mama, she would not like this."

"I'm not asking Mama. Would *you* like to see it happen?"

His eyes search mine. "Why do this now?"

So someone can finally hold those Pentagon bastards accountable—whatever accountable means for an institution that seems to operate beyond the reach of the law. Instead of venting, I simply reply, "Why not?"

After a lengthy pause, he nods. "Maybe now is time for truth."

Goddamned right it is. I squeeze his hand. "It was time for the truth many years ago."

He shrugs and nods. "Yes."

When tears well up in his eyes, I decide to switch gears. "Brittany's going to Europe."

"To Michelle?"

"Yes."

"When she come back?"

"I'm not sure."

The imperious father of my youth surfaces. "You no tell me everything, Anthony. Why does Brittany leave?"

I freeze. There's either the truth or something close to an outright lie. I've never been a guy who lied to his parents. Well, not much anyway, and that was many, many years ago.

He isn't put off by my prevaricating. "You tell me what is wrong! Brittany has trouble at school?"

If the topic can't be avoided, I can at least downplay things. "Kids, you know," I say airily. "They squabble and do stupid things."

Papa's eyes bore into mine. "What stupid things?"

"She had an argument with a teacher."

"This happens because of me?"

"She's a kid, Papa. It wasn't a big deal."

My father leans closer with fire in his eyes. "Anthony, you no lie to your Papa!"

Well, if nothing else, I've put a little fight back into the old coot. "It was about the shooting," I admit.

His lips tremble and a moan escapes him while tears begin to stream from his eyes. "Now she run away. She leaves from shame!"

Well, there's some truth in that, isn't there? I wrap him in my arms. "There's more to it than that. She misses the life we had in Atlanta. She misses private school."

He sobs for a moment longer before he eases out of my arms and straightens up. "This divorce is wrong. Brittany, she need her Mama and her Papa. This is not right for her."

"Marriages don't always last," I reply weakly.

He stares at me for a long moment while another tear dribbles down his cheek. "Because people now not do what is right, only what is easy."

I can't argue the point, nor can I explain modern sensibilities to Papa—I don't always understand them much better myself. Maybe, instead of putting the work into our marriage that I've always heard is necessary, Michelle and I simply masked the shortcomings of our union with relentless material acquisition and the pursuit of career advancement. I'm rescued from this unaccustomed self-reflection when the door opens and Mike Williams walks in. His eyes quiz me after he looks at Papa, who has turned away to stare at the ceiling while he wipes the tears from his eyes.

"Brittany got into some trouble at school and is going to stay with her mother for a bit," I explain.

"Sorry to hear that," Mike says. "What happened?"

"I'll fill you in another time," I reply with a shake of my head to wave him off the topic. Perhaps upset to have Mike find him in tears, Papa has broken into a fresh outbreak.

Mike glances at Papa and nods his understanding.

I decide to steer the conversation somewhere less painful. "You got any kids?" I ask Mike.

"Nope, and I'm not married—much to my mother's dismay."

"Does she scout prospects for you?"

He rolls his eyes. "Only every unmarried young lady at her church."

Papa wipes his eyes a final time and tunes in. Family talk —anyone's family talk—always catches his interest.

"The hours I work are a problem," Mike continues with a resigned shrug. "At least that's what my last couple of girlfriends told me. That, and an inability to leave work at the office."

"You want the wife and kids?" Papa asks him.

"Yeah, I guess I do."

"An obsession with work isn't all it's cracked up to be," I say. Mike should listen; I know what I'm talking about.

"My work and what you do are worlds apart," he replies.

He's right. Not for the first time, I'm reminded that the weight of responsibility he carries is crushing—especially given his passionate devotion to the work. Still. "All work and no play isn't good for you."

"Yeah, I know."

I reluctantly get back to trial business by asking, "How's discovery coming along?"

Mike leans back in his seat and crosses an ankle over a knee. "The prosecution gets a month to start producing documents. They're starting to trickle in."

"It's been seven weeks!" I fume.

"Just over six since Francesco was arraigned."

I'm impatient to get started. The plan is to have me pore over the discovery documents: police reports, ballistics, witness statements, autopsy, toxicology reports—every scrap of paper they'll use to build their case. Mike will do his own review of the State's evidence, then we'll compare notes, hoping to find a mistake or something we can use to build our defense case.

"I'm anxious to see what they've got," I say.

"I think we can anticipate most of it."

Maybe *he* can. I have only the barest grasp of what to expect.

"You've got a big job ahead of you once that stuff arrives," he continues. "Hours and hours reading piss-poor photocopies, many of which will say the same thing over and over."

"You make it sound so glamorous. Why doesn't everyone do it?"

"Only a select few of us are dumb enough to be public defenders. Be patient, my friend. This is how it goes in the early stages... a whole lotta nothing for days at a time." After a pause, he asks, "Anything new on the job front?"

"As a matter of fact, I accepted an offer."

He smiles. "Whereabouts?"

"Fleiss Lansky LLP."

"Big firm. What'll you be doing?"

"Managing legal for the Fafnir America account."

"The hell's a Fafnir?"

"It's a Scandinavian multinational. Norwegian or Swedish —I can't remember which."

"You might want to brush up on that a bit," he suggests with a grin.

I return his smile. "I know a little! Fafnir bought up a bunch of American consumer goods labels and didn't re-brand them. That's probably why you haven't heard of them."

"When do you start?"

"Next Monday."

"Ain't that something to be thankful for, huh?"

"Definitely," I agree.

"What's happening with the house?" Mike asks next. "Francesco tells me you beat the eviction notice."

I nod. "The foreclosure's on hold, too."

"Outstanding!"

"I forgot to tell you that the contractor called," I tell Papa. "They'll be out to fix the garage next week. I paid the tax arrears."

He nods without comment.

Mike's eyes light up and he turns to Papa while hooking a

thumb at me. "This guy tell you about our little basketball competition?"

Papa shakes his head no.

"Whupped his ass, dressed him out, and wiped the hardwood with him when I was done," Mike says with a hearty laugh.

My mind drifts back to an image of Mike towering over me on legs resembling the Pillars of Hercules. He reached down to hoist me off the hardwood as if I weighed twenty pounds. I'd just been manhandled through three games of one-on-one that whistled by in a painful, confused blur. Team building exercise, my ass. With my hands braced on my knees and my head hanging almost as low, I was struggling to suck in precious thimblefuls of air while dreaming of smacking the smug smile off his face.

Mike's smirk from the gym returns when he looks back at me. "Let's hope you're a damned sight better in a courtroom than you are on a basketball court."

Doing what I can to stifle a chuckle, I hold his gaze with mine. "Don't get too cocky, Williams. There'll be a rematch."

He gets to his feet and claps me on the shoulder. "You turning into a man to be reckoned with, my friend?"

CHAPTER FOURTEEN

"What the hell's wrong with you?" Pat O'Toole snaps at me as soon as the bathroom door closes behind Brittany. My daughter's flight to Brussels leaves this afternoon at five-thirty. At Brittany's insistence, Pat is here for a farewell lunch.

"What are you talk"

Pat cuts me off. "This is gonna be a great memory of her last day here. You're surly, morose... an absolute bundle of joy."

"I can't help how I feel," I reply like a petulant little boy in a sulk—which isn't far off the mark.

"Save it for the morning. You want her to stay in Brussels?"

I shake my head miserably and begin collecting the Chinese carryout containers from lunch. Leftovers go in the fridge and the empties disappear into the garbage under the sink. Deano stands by, his eagle eyes scouring the floor for even a single grain of fallen rice. Pat has followed me and we're face-to-face when I turn around.

"Hold it together for the rest of this afternoon, for Brittany's sake," she says while tossing an empty rice container into the trash. "Give her a reason to come back."

"I'm angry she's going. Worse, I'm afraid of losing her for good."

Pat's eyes soften. "You need to set that aside for now. Let's talk about something besides how much you're gonna miss her."

Tough to argue with someone who's right, although I've tried it many a time. I sit down and manage a grin when Brittany walks back into the kitchen. "Gonna miss eating Chinese?"

"Like they won't have Chinese! I bet the Europeans like it, too," she says confidently. Then she steals a glance at Pat for confirmation. Tales of Pat's European travels have featured liberally in past conversations.

"Sorry, kid," Pat replies as she settles back into her chair. "Chinese *can* be found but not on every corner. Don't worry, though, they've got plenty of good food."

"Like what?"

"You've gotta try the wiener schnitzel in Austria."

Brittany's eyes go wide in surprise. "Wieners? You mean hot dogs?"

"Heavens no," Pat replies with a laugh while she leans back and crosses her legs. "Not friggin' hot dogs! They've probably never even heard of Oscar Mayer. Veal schnitzel is my favorite. Great stuff!"

Brittany wrinkles her nose. "Mom's against veal."

But pouring gallons of Coca-Cola into kids is okay.

"The Germans use pork, if that meets with your mother's approval," Pat says. "I happen to think the Austrians do it up right."

"I'll try some," Brittany says with a decided lack of enthusiasm. She's still standing, leaning her butt against the sink.

"You *will* insist on seeing more than Brussels, right?" Pat asks.

"What's wrong with Brussels?" Brittany counters with a hint of combativeness.

"Nothing," Pat replies easily. "It's just that there's much more to see and it's all easy to get to. Hell, a girl can spit clear across Europe. You can be in London or Paris or the Alps in a matter of hours—all without flying."

"Really?"

Pat nods. "Sure."

Brittany is catching Pat's enthusiasm. She sits down and leans her elbows on the table. "Sounds pretty cool."

"It is!"

Thanks, O'Toole, I say to myself. *Try to remember that I hope Brittany comes back.*

Pat winks at Brittany and then makes a point of looking at her watch before she stands up. "I'll let you two visit. I've gotta be somewhere soon."

I'm not about to argue. I'm glad she came and hope to patch things up, but I want a couple of hours alone with my soon-to-be departed daughter.

"You can't stay?" Brittany asks while following Pat to the front door. I seem to be the only one hoping for a final hour or two of family time.

Pat shakes her head. "Naw, I'm picking up my niece and nephew and we're going to The Field."

"The museum?" Brittany asks.

"Yup!"

I've tagged along to the front hall. "How old are the kids?"

"Six and eight."

"Taking six- and eight-year-olds to a museum? That's *gotta* be child abuse," Brittany deadpans.

Pat's eyes travel from Brittany to me and back. "I don't suppose you two have been?"

We shake our heads, me with some degree of guilt and Brittany with unabashed satisfaction.

"They've got some artifacts from the Hermitage and Catherine's Palace in St. Petersburg," Pat says. "Fabergé pieces, paintings, even a couple of items from the Amber Room."

"The what?" Brittany asks.

"The Hermitage is one of the greatest museums on earth," Pat replies. "Perhaps the greatest. I plan to go next summer. This'll be a great preview."

My daughter looks embarrassed. "We're not talking about Florida, are we?"

Pat chuckles. "Like I'd be this excited about going to rub shoulders with a bunch of fat old Americans in Florida. I'm talking about Russia! Home of Tsars, Catherine the Great, onion domes."

"Whatever," Brittany says with a distinct lack of enthusiasm. "It's still a museum."

"I can't argue with that," Pat replies with a laugh. Then she turns to me. "A chip off the old blockhead, isn't she? At some point, somebody's gonna have to civilize this kid."

"You volunteering?" I ask hopefully.

She shrugs. "Maybe we should start by civilizing you and hope for osmosis of some sort."

"Take *him* to the museum," Brittany suggests. "Give the kids a break."

Pat laughs again. "They're gonna love it."

"Uh-huh," Brittany mutters. Then, with tears welling in her eyes, she wraps Pat in a ferocious hug.

"You've got my email address, right?" Pat asks.

Brittany backs out of the hug, digs a scrap of paper out of the back pocket of her designer jeans, and holds it up. "Right here."

"I expect to hear all about your exploits traipsing around the Continent."

Brittany manages a weak smile. "Okay."

"I'll keep you up to date on Chubby's adventures here,"

Pat says before surprising me with a brief hug. "Hang in there," she whispers in my ear. Then she steps away and gives me a sad smile. When the door closes behind her, I wonder when I'll next see Pat... or *if* I'll see her without my daughter here to facilitate a visit.

Two hours later, Brittany is again in her room, completing "final packing" for the fifth time since Pat's departure. I'm in the kitchen flipping through brochures we collected from a couple of private schools we toured. Michelle and I exchanged a few emails about finding a school in Chicago with an International Baccalaureate program. Michelle is in favor of an IB program but was non-committal about my daughter returning to Cedar Heights anytime soon. Pursuing the IB angle wasn't much more than me clutching at straws, pretending my daughter will return to Cedar Heights in the foreseeable future.

When Brittany finally arrives back in the kitchen and sits down, I slide the brochures across the table. "Got a favorite?"

"Anything without St. Aloysius over the door," she replies grimly with barely a glance at the brochures. "You gonna buy a house pretty soon?"

"I thought we'd do that together when you get back. I'll stay here until then."

"I don't wanna live in this shitty old house."

My hackles rise at her callous dismissal of the Valenti family home. Things remain a little strained until it's time to go. Brittany plugs into her iPhone and bops away listening to who-knows-what all the way to the airport. I stew on that for a few minutes before realizing that she's simply being the daughter we raised her to be. As great a kid as she is, in some respects we haven't done well with her. That's hardly her fault. If she's inclined to indulge herself without much regard for those around her, the inclination surely came from watching her parents. As for her recent moodiness and uncharacteristically volatile behavior, is it really so different from my own? Through no fault of her own, her life has been upended and turned into a living hell. No wonder she's anxious to escape.

Because Brittany is a minor, I was allowed to accompany her to the gate. I've been studiously avoiding any mention of Brittany's possible return since Pat chewed me out for being all morose and shitty, but anxiety gets the better of me when the gate agent announces that boarding will begin shortly. I reach over and gently tug the ear buds away from her head. "Any idea how long you'll be gone?"

"I dunno. Long enough so I don't hafta go to St. Aloysius or live in Papa's house. I'm not liking all this court stuff, either. Maybe when that's over."

This is the first time she's mentioned the trial as a factor in her return. "It could be months before the trial ends."

"No hurry," she says with a shrug. "Pat and Mom make Europe sound like an adventure—tons of stuff to see and do."

"Your mother will be working. You know the kind of hours she likes to put in at the office."

"Yeah, I was kinda worried about that, but Mom said she won't be working so much. We're gonna have lots of time together."

Now, there's a broken promise just waiting to happen. I keep the thought to myself.

Brittany leans close and puts her head on my shoulder when they announce general boarding. "Sorry, Dad."

"Why?"

"I just realized that I wasted most of our last couple of hours together."

"That's okay."

"And I'm sorry for being kinda bratty."

"Don't worry about it, Britts. I haven't been at my best, either."

She doesn't argue but she does tear up. "I'm gonna miss you, too, y'know."

I brush a strand of hair away from her eyes. "I know.

"It'll be easier for you with me gone," she says br "You can stay in Papa's house and save some money."

She's probably right. But. "None of that matters as as having you with me."

"I know," she mumbles through a sniffle.

With Brittany on her way to Brussels, my first di alone on Liberty Street is reheated Chinese from lu washed down by one of a six-pack of Stella Artois I picke on the way back from the airport. The Belgian brew is a ra pathetic attempt to cling to my departed daughter. A discovering that beer definitely isn't the beverage of ch with Chinese food, confirmed by a second bottle to vali the experiment, I load the dishwasher and toss the remnants of lunch into the garbage. Then I tie off the garb bag, lug it to the back door, and follow Deano outside.

Where I stop dead.

Amy's mural shimmers under a luminescent full moon if she has just now applied the final strokes and stepped av with a wet brush in hand. The vision takes my breath aw No matter where life has taken me and whatever shit it dealt out in the process, the backyard of our home on Libe Street has forever remained an enchanted icon of warm chi hood and family memories. Here, Amy, Frankie, and I on ran and played with the reckless abandon of youth. This the sanctuary that Francesco and Maria Valenti devoted the selves to creating over the years. Stands of Papa's priz tomato plants have for years untold been planted along t north fence, hugging it for support while they bathed in t nurturing rays of the summer sun. Mama's rose bush splashed annual bursts of red and yellow and pink over t carefully arrayed milieu of her rock garden. Desperate to ke any remnant of Mama alive, Papa lavished this year's crop roses with the love and care usually reserved for his tomatoe In the center of it all stands a two-foot tall stone *Hummel* bo

fully decked out in *lederhosen* and rucksack with a t tucked into his peaked cap. He pours a bubbling strea water into a half-barrel from spring until autumn. I've nev quite figured out what a German totem is doing in our little slice of Italy, but Mama must have had her reasons. I should have taken an interest and asked while I had the chance.

A cloud crossing in front of the moon wipes the color and vitality from the scene. With the water shut off for the winter, a lonely drop of dew glistens on the cap of the *Hummel* boy before it falls on his empty watering can. Papa had cleaned out the tomato plants after the first frost but couldn't bring himself to prune the flowers from Mama's rose bushes. The final petals appear heartbreakingly forlorn in their wilted frailty. When the freshening breeze gently rocks the ghosts of Mama and Papa back and forth in the swing beneath the Hawthorne tree, I'm hammered by the realization that I am now well and truly alone in this house.

I slam the bag into the garbage can and smash the lid back in place, fuming at my daughter, her mother, my father, Pat O'Toole, and the whole horseshit universe in general. I pick up the lid and give it a final satisfying crash into position. A wet nose on the back of my hand reminds me that I'm not completely alone. Deano's sad eyes echo the emptiness of my soul. I scratch the crown of his head and head back inside with the dog at my heels.

As always, the cabinet above the stove holds a bottle of *Nonino Grappa*. The *Nonino* is a greatly refined version of the barnyard grappa Papa had grown up with, which Mama derided as peasant rotgut when she finally banished it from our home. I fill a water glass with a healthy shot and meander into the living room with the glass in one hand and the bottle clutched in the other. While I gaze at the pictures and keepsakes of the past, I brood over how the unfathomable twists and turns of life have led me to the dead-end of tonight. Then I head off to wander through the house.

After arriving unsteadily in the living room sometime later, I slip an old Dean Martin LP of Mama's onto the turntable of an antique RCA console stereo. The stereo, an obsolescent atrocity in the eyes of serious audiophiles, has occupied the same corner of the living room for decades. As Deano's mellow baritone croons "Memories Are Made of This," I study a fading family photograph of my parents, me, and Amy. The picture was taken while Amy was visiting during her senior year at the University of Illinois; it was her last Thanksgiving at home. We're all younger and smiling, still filled with hope for the future. There's no hint here that our family would soon be dealt the bitter loss of Mama and Papa's second born and, if I'm honest, far and away the best of their children. Alongside this picture hangs a blissful depiction of the whole family on a Christmas morning many years earlier. Everyone seemed happy in this shot, taken while we were still in grade school. Such good years they were—so filled with love, joy and the certainty that, whatever the future held, we'd see it through together. A crushing, desolate loneliness settles over me while I sink deeper and deeper into the bottle of grappa.

My wanderings take me to the doorway of Amy and Brittany's empty bedroom. I picture my daughter as she was last night, snuggled under the covers a few minutes after I'd tucked her in—an indulgence she'd allowed me on her final night at home. Then, as now, the only light in the room spilled in from the hallway. As quietly as I had last night, I step inside and settle into a well-seasoned armchair wedged between the dresser and closet. Many an hour had been spent sitting beside Brittany's crib or bed back when life was simpler. My mind's eye conjures up images of her as a sleeping infant and as the rambunctious and precocious toddler she became, a child who fell still only when asleep… and sometimes not even then. I steal away when the nostalgia gives way to a gathering melancholy.

After dropping the now empty grappa bottle into the recycling bin, I stumble back to the living room and collapse onto the sofa. Brittany is on her way to a new life, my parents are lost to me, my career is shot, and my broken shell of a marriage has finally shattered. What have I got to look forward to? What the hell is the point of even trying to move forward? It's probably a good thing that Papa's gun isn't in the house tonight. How easy it would be to resolve my future if it were.

CHAPTER FIFTEEN

Winter launches its first serious assault on Chicago forty-one days after Brittany's departure—not that anyone's counting. The blizzard's fury and resulting Friday traffic crawl remind me of a couple of reasons I fled south. Pat O'Toole called unexpectedly yesterday to suggest going out tonight for a quick dinner. It will be our first visit since Brittany left. Pat's due to arrive at seven. I eventually snowplow into the driveway with fifteen minutes to spare after a workday every bit as vile as the weather.

I hustle toward the house with a wary eye on the roof. It's smothered beneath the first eighteen of twenty-four forecast inches of snow and looks capable of unleashing a catastrophic avalanche at any moment. I pause to look up and down the block after muscling through a mountainous snowdrift to reach the front door. The winking holiday lights and festive decorations look to be in season for the first time since they sprouted after Thanksgiving, but even this winter wonderland isn't enough to nudge me into a festive mood. Most years, I slip into Christmas mode by the end of Thanksgiving weekend. This year, I just want it over with. I turn my back on the scene, scoop a handful of envelopes and flyers out of the mailbox, and go inside. Deano struggles up from a floormat to greet me with a few desultory wags of his tail while I sweep snowdrifts off my shoulders. I sigh and drop the mail beside the door, grab his leash from the closet, and drag the old bugger out to do his business. At least he doesn't linger. We're back inside within a minute or two.

I dump the mail on the kitchen table and head for my bedroom to get changed. I'm back two minutes later in a sweater and slacks, tumbler of Maker's Mark bourbon in hand. I've returned to my university bourbon of choice after drinking stupid expensive brands during the high-flying days in Atlanta. Maybe I have a crappy palate or something, but I can't tell the difference. Only two of the envelopes on the table merit my attention. One is from Butterworth Cole and the other is from the Village of Cedar Heights. I suspect both contain invoices. I gratefully set them aside unopened when the doorbell rings.

Pat's smiling face greets me when I open the door. The ends of her hair hang below a red ski cap, curling up on the collar of a forest-green knee-length wool coat. A red knit scarf is wrapped loosely around her neck, its ends dangling almost to her waist. She claps a pair of matching red Santa mittens together and laughs with delight. "Isn't it great?"

I wave a hand toward the Rockwellesque streetscape beyond her. "This shit?"

She pauses long enough to catch a fluffy flake on her tongue. "Pretty as a post card, isn't it? I can almost hear the tinkle of muffled sleigh bells and picture reindeer prancing through the snow."

"It took me the better part of three hours to get home from work," I grumble.

"Don't bitch about the traffic, Mr. 'I Won't Ride the L,'" she says, referencing my stated distaste for the iconic Chicago rapid transit trains. Then she breaks into song and starts to spin like a top with her arms outstretched. "Sleigh bells ring, are you listening? In the lane, snow is glistening—a beautiful sight, we're happy tonight, walkin' in a winter wonderland."

Her antics prompt a grudging smile from me. "You're happier than a pig in poop, aren't you?"

She laughs. "Where to for dinner, Mr. Grumpypants?"

"Not too far in this weather."

"What's close that you like?"

The nearest thing I can think of is a pizza place a mile away. "Lou Malnati's?"

"Perfect! Nothing like a little pizza and eggnog to put a gal in a festive frame of mind."

"Your car or mine?"

"Who's got the snazzy car with the big fat tires?"

I work my feet into a new pair of winter boots, then grab my keys and a leather coat before wading onto the front porch. The Porsche is already wearing a fresh inch of snow. Not for the first time, I wish there was room in our backyard garage, but Papa's old Buick and woodworking tools take up all the space.

"I hate to sour your cheery mood," Pat says while she watches me sweeping snow off the car.

"But?"

"The village has put Liberty Street and Independence Park redevelopment on the agenda for the January seventh board meeting."

I suspected this was coming but it's still a sucker punch in the pit of my stomach. I doubt our little victory over the eviction notice will stand in the way of a full-fledged redevelopment plan for the whole neighborhood. Of course, I don't know shit about most aspects of law, so that's just another uneducated guess from Tony Valenti, *Esquire,* Ignoramus-at-Law.

"I'm sorry," I say while we sweep snow off the car. "I was way out of line about Amy. I should have been thanking you for your help and friendship."

"You've got a funny way of showing your appreciation."

"I do a lot of stupid things."

Pat doesn't argue the point and we fall into an uneasy silence. She's probably reflecting on what an ass I am. At least she's speaking to me.

She eventually sighs. "Sorry. I know this isn't easy for you."

"What am I going to do to save the house?" I ask after we get in the car.

Pat pulls off the ski cap and shakes the snow out of her hair. "What did your folks do?"

"Got help."

"So, get help."

"Mr. Rosetti will know what to do. Mind if we stop on the way?"

"Nope."

We pull into the shoveled Rosetti driveway a minute later. Mr. Rosetti answers the door and waves me in.

"Hi, Mr. Rosetti. How are you?"

"Fine, Anthony. And you?"

"Frozen and missing Atlanta more every minute."

He rewards my lame humor with a tight smile. "I should have stayed in Florida. Perhaps the time has come to move down there."

"Seriously?"

He nods. "How can I help you?"

"Have you heard about the redevelopment hearing?" His blank stare is answer enough. After I fill him in on the details I have from Pat, he asks me to wait and disappears deeper into the house. He returns within a minute and presses a business card into my hand. I glance down at it: *The Citadel Foundation. Teresa Keebler-Jones, Director*.

My eyes rise to his. "I should talk to her?"

"She helped us two years ago. It is your fight this time,

Anthony. Teresa will help you." Then he surprises me by reaching to open the door.

"Thank you," I stammer as I step outside.

"You're welcome, Anthony," he says while pulling the screen door closed. I walk back to the car pondering the unwelcome ramifications of his seeming indifference. Mama told me that Mr. Rosetti had been a tenacious battler against the village in the last effort to turn Liberty Street into a shopping mall. I wordlessly hand Pat the business card after I clamber back into the warmth of the Porsche.

She reads the card and passes it back. "She can help?"

"I hope so," I mutter while tucking the card into my shirt pocket. After backing into the street, I begin inching toward Malnati's by keeping my tires in the tracks forged through the snow by other vehicles. We haven't seen a snowplow yet. I doubt we will anytime soon.

"Tough day?" Pat asks.

"Typical bullshit day."

"Tell me about this job. What are you doing?"

"It's with a law firm, handling one of their corporate accounts. Blowing off complaints and lawsuits from customers, fighting with the lawyers of other firms so we can all pile on billable hours to justify our salaries. Typical corporate law."

"Try not to sound so excited."

"It's a job."

"You sound like an everyday working stiff, Valenti."

A billboard advertisement we pass for the St. Petersburg exhibit at the Field Museum reminds me of Pat's outing with her niece and nephew. "How did it go at the Field?"

"Great! The kids loved it."

"As much as you?"

She grins. "Maybe not *that* much."

We arrive at Malnati's after a ten-minute drive. I was right about a dearth of snowplows along the way. The parking lot behind the restaurant hasn't seen a shovel or plow, either. Aside from several imposing snowdrifts and two cars, it's deserted.

"Let's hope the cook was at work before the storm hit," Pat says while we trudge through a Himalayan-sized drift between the parking lot and the entrance.

A waiting hostess greets us and leads us past a sea of empty tables covered in white and red checked tablecloths before seating us at a red and black booth for two. "Your server tonight is Madison," the hostess tells us brightly. "She'll be with you in a minute."

"Do you spend a lot of time with the kids?" I ask Pat after the hostess leaves.

"My nieces and nephews?"

I nod in reply.

"As much as I can. It isn't enough but I do my best. The worst is my nephew up in Canada. I only see him once or twice a year."

"Whereabouts in Canada?"

"They're out west in Calgary. My sister married a Canadian she met in college."

The waitress announces her arrival with a hearty, "Hi! I'm Madison! I'll be your server this evening! Can I start you off with a little something from the bar to warm you up?"

I order my second bourbon of the evening. Pat, being the designated passenger, asks for a cup of hot chocolate. I bitch about work while we wait, then smile at the ribbon of foam that appears on her upper lip after her first sip.

"So, tell me about this attack of conscience you seem to be having," Pat prompts. "You're suggesting your work has no redeeming social value?"

"Something like that."

"Wow. I'm fascinated by the concept of a conscientious lawyer."

I wave a hand in dismissal. "I'm just questioning the worth of what I'm doing."

She settles back and studies me for a moment or two. "Not a road you've travelled before, is it?" After I shake my head, she adds, "Maybe your subconscious is trying to tell you something."

"Could be... and that's all of *that* intriguing little topic we're going to discuss, Dr. Freud."

We're still chuckling when Madison! arrives with our pizza and two squat glasses of ice water in wide-mouth mason jars—authentic Italian mason jars, I'm sure. "Can I get you guys anything else?"

Pat shakes her head in response to my questioning gaze. "No thanks," I reply as the waitress transfers a slice of deep dish onto each of our plates. The zesty aroma of sausage, pepperoni, spinach, and heaps of mozzarella cheese stirs my dormant appetite.

"Enjoy!" Madison! exclaims before she departs.

That's easy enough to do. I like Malnati's. We down a couple of enormous slices each while chatting about her day at the Field Museum and her plans to visit St. Petersburg. "Good pizza," I announce a little later while pushing my plate aside.

"Done already?"

"Can't put it away like I used to," I tell her while rubbing my tummy.

"You disappoint me, Chubby."

"I'm in training."

"For what?" she asks with open skepticism.

"Hoops." My tale of woe on the basketball court at the hands of Mike Williams and my plans for revenge leave her in stitches until we get the bill and pay. Madison! leaves us with a couple of leftover containers.

Pat sits forward with her arms on the table. "Before we leave, let's talk about the second reason I called today."

I settle back in my chair and wait.

"It's about Amy's story."

So, it comes back to this. My initial flash of irritation is immediately snuffed out by the trepidation in Pat's eyes. After all my stupidity suspecting her motives, *The Trib* hasn't printed a word about Amy's death. The least I can do is hear her out. Besides, this has to be dealt with sooner or later if we're ever going to move beyond it. "Go ahead."

"Were you just having a bad day the last time we talked about this or did you really think I was angling all along to get a story out of you?"

"A little of both," I reply sheepishly.

"You're a stupidhead," she says with a wondering shake of her head. "God only knows how much money you spent on law school, yet here I'm the only one of us thinking like a lawyer."

I haven't got a clue what she's getting at, so I say nothing.

"You're familiar with the idea of infecting a jury pool?" she asks.

"Sure."

"The prosecution has been taking a good run at it, Tony. We've been running headlines like: 'Cop-Killer a Neighborhood Nuisance' and 'Cop-Killer Has History of Battling City Hall.' A story that stirs a little sympathy for your father in a potential juror or two may help his cause."

"Aren't you supposed to be impartial? Couldn't you get in trouble for taking sides?"

She laughs. "You're kidding, right? Believe me, my editors won't fire me for handing them a story about the government covering up the deaths of American soldiers in an illegal covert operation. Ask Mike Williams what *he* thinks. I bet he'd be happy to see the jury pool infected a little on your father's behalf."

How obvious is that? I ask myself. "I should have seen that you were trying to help when you first mentioned it. I've been known to look gift horses in the mouth."

"You're under a lot of strain. I hear that's a leading cause of idiocy."

"I feel like an ass."

"Only because you are, Valenti. What *do* they teach you people at law school anyway?"

"Advanced studies in maximizing hours billed and similarly arcane legal minutiae."

She shakes her head and laughs. "Fifty grand a year in tuition for that?"

"So now what?" I ask after I throw my hands up in a "what can I say?" gesture.

"That's up to you. Amy's story could probably run between Christmas and New Year's."

"Are you printing what I told you?"

"Not unless you tell me I can use it. I gave my editor the bare bones without naming you or Amy and he was excited. He heard much of the story from someone else a few years ago but needs a second source before he'll run the story."

"I'm that source?"

"No," she replies. "You weren't there. My editors want to speak to the guy who was with Amy in Colombia."

"Joe McIntyre. He exchanges Christmas cards with Mama and Papa, so his address must be around. Maybe his phone number, too."

"Perfect."

"Then what happens?" I ask. "You go to Colombia?"

"I'll be staying right here, thank you very much."

"They'll do the whole story from Chicago?"

She laughs. "That'll be the day. Our international staff will be all over this."

"What about you?"

"I'm strictly local. I'll look after the Chicago angle."

"Am *I* the local angle?"

"Don't flatter yourself," she replies with a chuckle. "You might be mentioned once or twice. Don't get delusions about seeing your name in print on a daily basis."

Such a small role for Pat doesn't seem right. "Isn't this a chance to be something more than a local beat reporter?"

"I'm just a simple Chicago gal," she replies. "I think what I do is important in its own way."

"I didn't mean to suggest it isn't. Why not advance your career?"

"Maybe I'm already sitting in the right seat on the journalism bus. Don't worry about me, Tony. I'm happy enough with my little lot in life."

"I'm jealous."

"Don't be," she says with a smile. Then she reaches for her coat. "Let's blow this place."

It's still snowing two or three feet per minute.

"How's Brittany doing?" she asks while we slog our way to the car.

"Good. Settled into school and liking it so far."

"How do you feel about that?"

"Happy for her, sad for me."

Pat looks at me across the roof of the car as we sweep off snow. "The little twit hasn't written to me once. Is she coming back for Christmas?"

"Afraid not."

"What are your plans for Christmas Day?"

"I'll be working on discovery for Papa's trial and probably trying to get something done about this eminent domain crap. Mike sent me a packet of discovery materials yesterday. I had a peek last night and I'll dig into it again when I get home. It's going to take a long time to get through it all."

She tut-tuts. "No one should be alone at Christmas. I talked to Mom last night. You're welcome to come by their place for Christmas dinner."

"Multiple O'Tooles?" I ask in mock horror as we climb into the car.

She grins. "A proper infestation."

Part of me is tempted, the rest cringes at the thought of being face-to-face with everything I've lost. "We'll see."

"You spent Thanksgiving alone, didn't you?"

I start the car and nod.

"Fun stuff?" she asks sardonically.

"Not so much," I reply before I put the car into gear and ease out of the parking lot. As if the night Brittany left for Europe hadn't been bad enough, I'd sunk even further into despair and self-loathing by the time I passed out on the couch after my Thanksgiving feast of PB&J sandwiches. I washed those down with Papa's last bottle of grappa before polishing off a half-bottle of bourbon.

Pat studies me with concern. "Think about Christmas, Tony. Being with happy people who care about you is never a bad thing."

I can't imagine where she plans to find people who give a shit about me. "I'll let you know."

She gives me a long look, followed by a shrug. "Whatever you think. There'll be scads of food. We eat around four o'clock. The invite's open right up until dinnertime."

"Thanks. I appreciate the offer."

"I hope you'll come."

We ride in silence until I turn onto Liberty Street and she says, "Let me know what that Citadel person has to say after you call."

"Sure."

A handful of snowmen in varying stages of completion stand here and there among the homes of our neighbors. Nowhere near as many as we used to build, of course, but kids still seem to populate Liberty Street. Grandchildren visiting, I suppose. A sled has left a set of tracks alongside the road in the general vicinity of the buried sidewalk. My blood begins to boil at the absurdity of condemning this neighborhood. "We're supposed to have property rights in this country. How can Zaluski get away with this crap?"

"People like Zaluski and Mayor Brown have been getting away with this crap for years."

I hammer a fist on the top of the steering wheel. "How?"

"Cedar Heights has a sketchy mayor paired with an overly ambitious village manager. That's a particularly toxic combination. You're in the ring with a tough tag team that is eager to auction off Liberty Street."

"David and Goliath stuff, is it?" I ask wryly.

"Compared to David, you're a pipsqueak without a slingshot, but otherwise, not a bad analogy."

"You going to be okay driving in this?" I ask when I nose into our driveway.

"Am I a Chicago gal?"

"So you say."

We exit the Porsche and stand together in the driveway for a minute, allowing the snow to drift down on us.

"It's beautiful, isn't it?" she asks softly.

"Unless you're behind the wheel or a shovel, I suppose it is."

She laughs and shakes her head. "Killjoy!"

I follow Pat to her car and help dig it out.

She leans her forearms on the roof when we're done. "You're gonna be in a fight to the death with Zaluski and the mayor. They're probably still pissed about the last time the shopping center project didn't fly. They won't want to lose twice."

"*They're* pissed? You think either of those clowns has more pent-up hostility to vent than I do?"

Her brows knit together. "They can't afford to suffer too many chinks in their aura of invincibility. They'll be ruthless."

"That'll make three of us."

"Be careful, Tony," she warns before climbing into her car. "Who knows what lengths they might go to?"

Far from accepting Pat's admonishment to tread carefully, the thought of assholes like Brown and Zaluski trying to screw my parents out of their home pisses me off. This is personal now; I want revenge for what these bastards did. The image of my shrunken father swimming inside his prison garb pops into my head. It produces my first inkling of the degree of helpless rage that likely sent a spasm through Papa's trigger finger.

CHAPTER SIXTEEN

State's Attorney to Seek Death Penalty for Cedar Heights Cop-Killer: Sources.

I stare at the headline for the umpteenth time since I sat down to my first cup of coffee this morning. My eyes stray from the screen to the silent phone on my desk at Fleiss Lansky LLP. Mike Williams has been in court all morning and is supposed to call when he breaks for lunch. It's now pushing eleven-thirty. I can either read the headline again, keep staring at the phone, or do something constructive. I reach for the business card Mr. Rosetti gave me and dial the Washington, DC telephone number of Teresa Keebler-Jones at The Citadel Foundation.

"The number you have called is no longer in service...."

Shit! Looking on the bright side, Keebler-Jones isn't a particularly common name and The Citadel Foundation is headquartered in DC. I assign the task of tracking her down to my legal assistant and call Papa's insurance agent, Jill, to see how our claim for the garage is progressing.

"It's early days yet, so let's lay low," she says. "It's not a good idea to lean on the claims people."

Time to light a fire under Jill. She's young, having taken

over the agency from her father when he retired a couple of years ago. This is the crap companies instill in young agents: sell, sell, sell, but don't bother the busy people in claims when pesky customers want their claims paid. "It's a straightforward claim, Jill. If you don't plan to pay it, just say so."

"You know I'd write you a check today if it were up to me," she says in that phony insurance agent (and lawyerly) schtick that says, "we're in this together."

"We're not going to play that game. Your job extends beyond peddling product and cashing commission checks. It's time a little cash flowed back to my dad."

"I'll call claims this afternoon," she replies sullenly.

She'd better. I need the damned money. Half my pay is now going to Brussels in child support. Another half goes to credit card and Porsche payments. Another half pays the utilities and buys mac and cheese. Yeah, that's right—three halves total 150%. Even I can do enough basic arithmetic to understand this budgeting conundrum.

"I'll look forward to your call," I say before cutting the connection.

My assistant Pam places a sticky note on my blotter. "Here's the number for Miss Keebler-Jones."

I nod my thanks and dial. "Is this Teresa Keebler-Jones of The Citadel Foundation?" I ask when a lady picks up.

"Who's calling?"

"My name is Tony Valenti, from Cedar Heights, Illinois. You helped my parents and their neighbors with an eminent domain issue a couple of years ago."

"I'm Teresa's sister."

"Can I speak with her?"

A stifled sob is followed by a choked, "My sister was murdered last week."

"I'm sorry," I mutter, sensing the inadequacy of the words as they pass my lips.

"Thank you," she says gracefully.

"How do I reach The Citadel Foundation?"

"The Foundation closed four months ago," she says. "Funding issues. They ticked off some powerful interests who exerted enough pressure to strangle Citadel's funding. Teresa was working on something new, but…."

We say our goodbyes. What the hell do I do now? I was banking on the expertise of Keebler-Jones for guidance.

Mike calls while I'm wallowing in despair. One of his death penalty murder cases went to the jury this morning. "How did it go?" I ask.

"Not well."

"Sorry." I pause long enough for him to elaborate. When he doesn't, I carry on. "You saw the *Trib* this morning?"

"Bastards!"

His anger surprises me. "You thought they'd shoot for the death penalty."

"That's no surprise. I'm pissed about them leaking the decision. I should have been told before they talked to some damned reporter."

"They've been leaking all along."

"Yeah," he grumbles, "but this is a helluva way for your dad to find out. Speaking of which, you still meeting me at the jail?"

"What time?"

"Now."

"I'll be fifteen, twenty minutes."

"See you then."

I hang up and grab my coat. We settle onto a pair of hard plastic chairs in the attorney-client room thirty minutes later and wait for the guards to produce Papa.

"I've been wanting to talk to you about something that might help us," I say while we wait.

"What's that?"

I give him a quick recap of my sister's demise and Pat's plan to run the story in the *Trib*.

"Jesus, that's awful," he mutters. "Not much of a Christmas fable, is it?"

Today is December twenty-third. "No. You've been reading the crap in the papers about Papa?"

He nods.

"Pat figures we should have a go at trying to infect the jury pool a little on Papa's behalf. She made a disparaging remark or two about my legal instincts when she realized I hadn't thought of that."

Mike grins. "You telling me that a *reporter* has better legal instincts than my co-counsel?"

"Looks that way."

"Shee-it," he chuckles. "She may have a point, though. It might work to our advantage in jury selection."

I may know squat about criminal law per se, but seeking every possible edge to use in court is universally a good thing. "Hopefully."

"You been through the discovery material yet?" he asks after we cool our heels for another minute or two.

"Some. I'll dig deeper starting tonight. You gonna tell Papa what was in the paper or should I?"

"I guarantee you he knows. That sort of news spreads pretty quick in here."

"Did you hear what was in the *Tribune* this morning?" I ask Papa in the midst of a brief hug after he's finally ushered into the room.

"One of the guards, he tell me."

Undoubtedly with a high degree of sensitivity, I think bitterly while imagining one of the asshole guards gleefully delivering the news.

Mike slides some magazines across the table to Papa. A loaf-sized package wrapped in foil follows. "Brought you a couple of Christmas gifts."

Papa flips through the stack of periodicals. Mike brought a little of everything—sports, entertainment, local stuff, a couple of weekly news magazines—probably hoping Papa will be interested in at least one of them. It's doubtful, but a couple might fill a few empty hours. Papa peels back a corner of the foil. Inside is a fruitcake.

"Mom's specialty," Mike says proudly. "She's been making them ever since I was knee-high to a June bug."

"Your Mama, she make the *panettone* each year?" Papa asks.

Mike points at the fruitcake. "You call this *panettone?*"

Papa delivers a solemn nod. "Yes, in Italy we say *panettone.*"

"Mom bakes me a bunch every year so I can spread a little holiday cheer," Mike says.

Papa's eyes settle on me. "What you do for Christmas, Anthony?"

"I'll be reading discovery materials, with a side of how to save your house."

"What is this house business?"

I fill him them in on the village resurrecting the redevelopment plans.

"You stop them, Anthony! They no have our home!"

"I'll try, Papa. I'll try."

"You come here tomorrow?"

"I'll probably stop by in the morning," I reply.

"What are you doing the rest of the day?" Mike asks me.

I sense an invitation coming and immediately head it off. "Pat invited me to spend Christmas with her family." I don't mention that I'm not planning to go.

"We eat *panettone* now," Papa announces while peeling back the foil wrapping from Mrs. Williams's fruitcake.

"That's for you," Mike protests.

Papa fixes him with an "I will be obeyed" look. "We eat now."

Mike shoots a grin my way. "Yes, sir."

"Anthony's Mama, she make *panettone* every year," Papa

says while breaking chunks off the cake and distributing them. "*Buon Natale.*"

"Merry Christmas," I translate.

"Merry Christmas," Mike mumbles around a mouthful of cake.

The cake is delicious, though it has little in common with Mama's *panettone.* Mama's loaf is a much lighter holiday fruitcake than the weighted footballs Americans indulge in.

"Tell us about your folks," I suggest to Mike.

"Nothing much to tell. Both career civil servants, devout Baptists, tough-as-nails parents."

I cock an eyebrow. "Tough as nails, huh? An abused child, were you?"

He laughs. "Hell no, but Mom and Dad—especially Mom—was a holy terror whenever we got out of line."

"Did all of you go to college?"

"My folks didn't give us a choice, God bless 'em. So, we got us a doctor, an Air Force pilot, an HR drone with the city, a cell phone engineer at Motorola, a state social worker, some dumbass working at the Public Defender's office, and a baby sister following in the dumbass's footsteps at Northwestern Law."

I arch my eyebrows theatrically. "Two attorneys in one family?"

"Hey, if we can accommodate *Doctor* Williams's ego *and* his snooty physician wife, there's plenty of room around the dinner table for the likes of me and Sara."

Papa smiles at Mike. "You have Christmas with your Mama and Papa?"

"Every year."

"You are good boy, Michael." I almost expect Mike to get a pat on the head. The wry grin he turns on me while Papa breaks off another chunk of cake suggests the same thought has crossed his mind.

"You go to the church at Christmas?" Papa asks Mike.

"We do."

Papa nods his approval. "What religion?"

"We're Baptists."

"You have the *presepio* at the church?"

"What's that?"

"A life-size Nativity scene. *Presepio* is a big Italian tradition at Christmas," I explain, remembering how badly Papa always wanted to take us to experience Christmas in Italy. "It's the centerpiece of an Italian church over the holidays. Papa used to do the carpentry and then we'd go on a tour of Chicago churches that had *presepios*. You should see some of them, Mike. Spectacular."

Mike looks at Papa. "You do some woodworking?"

Papa nods.

"His family's trade back home was carpentry," I say. "He's good. Unfortunately, Papa couldn't get his foot in the door with the trade here." It was always a sore point with Mama, who felt Papa should swallow his pride and do the trade school courses the State of Illinois insisted on before they would consider him a bona fide carpentry tradesman. Papa refused to suffer what he regarded as a humiliation and instead spent thirty years doing laundry at Cook County Hospital. It's not something he's dwelled on.

"Best is living *presepio*," Papa proclaims.

"We've only got a little nativity scene," Mike says. "But let me tell you, we Baptists *love* to sing. There's lots and lots of singing in our church come Christmastime."

"*Messa cantata*," Papa notes with approval.

"Sung mass," I translate. "The traditional midnight service on Christmas Eve."

"You go to Orsomarso for Christmas and *epiphania*, Anthony," Papa says. It's nice to see life stirring in his eyes, even if it's a yearning to relive the traditions of a hometown he'll almost certainly never see again. Given his obvious love of Orsomarso, I can't figure out why he never went home to visit. His explanation that "I am in America now" has never quite rung true.

"Is Orsomarso where you're from?" Mike asks Papa.

"Yes. Is small village in hills of Calabria. Very old."

"Tell me about it," Mike says.

Papa studies him. "Yes?"

"Please."

I settle back and listen to Papa relate tales of his childhood, peppering the stories with asides to explain the traditions of his homeland, such as the meatless feast on Christmas Eve and dressing in their finest for midnight mass. Yarns of Father Christmas follow (*Babbo Natale* in Papa's telling) and the excitement of *La Befana* visiting with gifts for the *bambini* on *epiphania.*

Mike expresses horror at the notion of making kids wait until January sixth for presents.

Papa shakes his head in response. "Is good, Michael, not same as here. Christmas is for store in America, all toys and money. Is not like this in Italy. Better, I think."

"Maybe so," Mike says thoughtfully. "Maybe so."

My thoughts turn to the upcoming exposé of Amy's saga. "The *Tribune* will be running the story about Amy soon."

Papa's brow furrows. "I no understand why you do this now."

I explain again about trying to infect the jury pool in his favor.

"I no understand this infecting."

"The State has been leaking crap to the press claiming you have a history around Cedar Heights of being a general pain in the ass," I tell him. "The hope is that—"

Papa's eyes flash. "They say this in newspaper?"

I nod.

"Because we try to keep our home?"

"Pretty much," I reply.

He squares his shoulders while fury flares in his eyes. "Is

time to stop this, Anthony! You stop them!"

"I'll try, Papa. I know how much the house means to you."

His eyes burn into mine. "For your Mama, Anthony. You do this for my Maria!"

We chat for another few minutes before Mike announces that he has to get back to the office. After Papa and I share our customary hug, Papa turns and surprises us by embracing Mike as well. *"Buon Natale,"* he says to us before he's led away by a guard. Mike and I wordlessly make our way outside.

"Welcome to the family," I say when we step into the parking lot.

"He's quite a fiery guy if the right buttons get pushed, huh?"

"He's got a long fuse," I reply with a chuckle. "You don't want to light it."

I ponder the unwelcome implications of Papa's temperament on a witness stand before Mike asks, "You ever been to his hometown?"

I shake my head. Michelle and I went to Tuscany a couple of times, but we didn't get to Orsomarso. Maybe we should have. I push the thought aside. More regrets I don't need. I wink at Mike. "Thanks for letting him go on about Italy. It's been years since I've heard him reminisce like that."

"It was interesting," he says. He takes a step toward his car, then turns back to me. "Experiencing him like that puts a different spin on things."

"How so?"

"I really like the guy. Wouldn't it be great to get him out of this hellhole and send him to Orsomarso next Christmas?"

I shake my head with a grim chuckle. "And you accuse *me* of having wild-ass dreams about winning this case."

Mike claps me on the shoulder. "That was before I started catching glimpses of how formidable you Valenti men are when y'all get riled up."

CHAPTER SEVENTEEN

When I was six, I woke up at three forty-five on Christmas morning terrified that Santa wouldn't leave presents if he found me awake. I squeezed my eyes shut and snuggled deep under the covers where I hoped Santa couldn't see me awake. Right, like I was gonna fool the guy who gets to every house on the planet in a single night. When sleep wouldn't come, I crept to the top of the stairs to peek around the banister to see if Santa had already been and gone. He had! Two hours of delicious anticipation followed while my mind's eye filled with images of the treasures that waited beneath the Christmas tree. Presents would be followed by hours of playtime and meals and treats and storytelling—our home fairly bursting with love and affection. But that was then, and this is now. A vintage Valenti family Christmas will not weave its traditional magic through this house today. It's Christmas morning and the alarm clock display again reads three forty-five, but this year I don't need to creep to the top of the stairs to confirm that Santa hasn't been here. I already know he isn't coming.

What the hell am I doing awake anyway?

Deano is wheezing and pawing at the bed. The poor old

bugger can't clamber up anymore, so what's he up to? I thought I heard something when I woke up, but I can't hear anything now. Maybe Deano thought so, too, but his hearing is going. After listening for a minute longer, I burrow back under the covers in an effort to shut out the world. For the first time ever, I'm free to do anything I like on Christmas Day, including sleeping it away. Sleep eludes me, however, leaving my mind free to wander down avenues best not explored. To realize that one walks the earth alone is at once profoundly terrifying and profoundly liberating. If nobody else cares, I don't have to, either. There are no longer expectations to live up to, no appearances to keep up, no possibility of continuing to fail myself and others. It occurs to me that Kris Kristopherson had it right when he wrote the lyric to "Me and Bobby McGee"—freedom *is* just another word for nothing left to lose.

Screw it, I decide while tossing the covers aside. So long as I'm awake I may as well put the time to use. While the coffee maker begins to gurgle, I realize that I've been smelling smoke ever since I woke up. A quick check confirms that nothing is smoldering in the kitchen, but the acrid smell is growing steadily stronger. While I'm on my way to check the basement, I notice the glow of orange and yellow apparitions dancing across the living room window. I grab the phone and hurry over to discover whose house is ablaze. When I look outside, it isn't a neighbor's house I see going up in flames. It's our front porch!

I cram my feet into a pair of boots and rush out the front door, where I almost topple right into the flames. My first thought after I stumble back is, *get the hose!* I've scampered all the way to the kitchen before I remember that the hose is tucked away for the winter. Does Papa have a fire extinguisher? I don't recall seeing one, so I gallop down the basement stairs and grab a pail. On my way back upstairs I realize that I haven't called 9-1-1. After sliding the pail under the kitchen tap and twisting the faucet all the way open, I dial 9-1-1 and report the fire while pushing Deano out the back door, then hang up and sprint to the front door to dump the pail of water onto the flames nearest the door. I've only been running back and forth with buckets of water for a minute or two when I hear sirens and see the reflection of approaching emergency lights in the windows at the far end of Liberty Street. A fireman is hurrying up the walk when I step back outside with my next pail of water. Good thing they're here—I'm sure as hell not getting the upper hand on the flames with the pail, though I've kept them away from the door. I spill water on the flames again and head back inside for a refill.

"Sir!"

"In here!" I yell back as I jam the pail under the tap again.

A fireman hurries in behind me. "Get out of the house!"

"One more pail."

"Sir, you need to get out. Now!"

Once the pail fills, I hustle back outside and empty it on the flames. Two firefighters are standing ready with a fire hose nozzle while another pair finish connecting the hose to the hydrant in the Vaccaro's front yard. I decide to keep battling the flames until they finish setting up. When I turn to head back in, the door is closed and the fireman who followed me in earlier bars the way inside.

"One more!" I shout, expecting him to step aside.

"I can't let you back in the house."

We're eye-to-eye when the first deluge from the fire hose crashes into the wall and soaks me from head to toe. It's only then that I realize I'm outside in boxer shorts, a t-shirt, and a pair of winter boots—shivering and shaking like a drenched dog.

With the firefighting officially taken over by the pros, I stumble down the steps to the sidewalk and into the driveway. Mr. Vaccaro wraps a blanket around my shoulders. A firefighter immediately supplements it with a foil blanket.

"I called the fire department, Anthony," Mr. Vaccaro tells me, which explains the arrival of the first fire trucks within a minute or two after my call.

"Thanks," I mutter. How in hell does a porch covered in snow burst into flames in the middle of a winter night? Not spontaneously, I'd wager. Brittany safely in Europe seems like a damned fine idea.

The firefighter who kept me out of the house walks up to us. "Any idea how this started?"

I shake my head as the last flames flicker and fail under the torrent of water from the fire hose.

"I smell gasoline," the firefighter mutters, eyeing me carefully.

I sniff the air and nod. "You're right."

"Hopefully, you'll never find yourself in this situation again but if you do, get out of the house right away and wait for us," he says. "Be thankful for the snow. That fire would have burned a lot faster if the wood had been dry. You gave it every chance to follow you in through the open door."

I meet his eyes. "Firefighting is best left to professionals *and* I should listen when I'm told to get my ass out of the house?"

"That's right," he agrees with a chuckle. "I got a wife and teenagers at home. I don't need people ignoring my orders on the job, too."

Six hours later, the sun is up, the fire trucks and investigators are gone, and the latest excitement at the Valenti home is over. I'm at the kitchen table with a cup of coffee and my laptop, searching through the real estate transfer records for the sales of the Palumbo, Priolo, and DeLuca properties. Mr. Rosetti wasn't kidding when he said they were offered a healthy premium above the market value of their homes two years ago. I'm intrigued to discover that the purchaser of record for all three properties was a numbered company. The printer starts spitting out copies of the records. I'll study them later.

A late breakfast of canned pears and toast is followed by a shower and shave. Then it's back to business. I hunt through corporate record databases in hopes of unmasking the beneficial owners of the numbered company that purchased the rental houses on Liberty Street. None the wiser after two hours, I conclude that I'll need the resources of Fleiss Lansky LLP to successfully deconstruct that puzzle—if it can be unraveled at all.

It's early afternoon when I finally put my computer to sleep and try to call Brittany. The call goes straight to voice mail. I slap together a ham and cheese sandwich and wash it down with a Stella Artois while I wait for Brittany to call back. When she still hasn't called by late-afternoon, I climb into the Porsche as darkness falls. Time to visit the family patriarch in jail.

Papa is a million miles away during my visit, uncommonly reticent to share the family memories and anecdotes that are his Christmas stock-in-trade. Neither of us is much company for the other. Despite being in the same room, Papa and I are each very much alone today. We're both relieved when I decide to leave after an awkward hour.

Pat's Hyundai is parked out front when I arrive home. She trudges up the driveway to intercept me when I step out of the Porsche. With a nod at the charred front porch as we climb the steps, she asks, "What happened?"

"Somebody decided to have a little bonfire."

Her eyes smolder. "Who?"

"The cops and fire department are investigating but between the fire itself and the firefighting effort, whatever evidence there might have been was trampled or melted."

"You okay?"

"Sure," I reply as my eyes drift to the street after I unlock and push the door open. An image of a bicycle-mounted figure wearing a hoodie pops into my mind. Could that be our mysterious arsonist?

She stares at me a moment longer, shakes her head, and then marches angrily into the front hall. "You've spent Christmas Day hiding from the world, haven't you?"

"I've been working."

"On what?"

I recite the laundry list of distractions I've used to pass the day.

"You're such an idiot," she says before handing me a gift-wrapped package. "Merry Christmas, Valenti. If it wasn't Christmas Day, I'd kick your ass."

"Merry Christmas. I didn't get you anything."

"All I asked for was a little time with my friend. You couldn't give me that?"

If she's hoping to make me feel bad about not showing up at her parents' house or even calling to say I wasn't coming, she's succeeding. The upside is that she referred to me as a friend. After she wriggles out of her coat and stuffs her mittens, scarf, and cap into a sleeve, I trail Pat into the living room like a whipped puppy. She stops dead to stare at tropical fish swimming around on the television screen. "*The Aquarium Channel?* You stood me up for *this?*"

I used to watch this channel with Brittany when she was a baby. It's been on in the background a lot since she left for Europe.

"You really know how to make a gal feel special, Valenti. I've been stood up before—maybe not on Christmas Day, mind you—but *never* for fish pictures!"

Sensing a lack of genuine anger behind her words, I risk a grin. "Better than me standing you up to watch a bunch of big sweaty men playing with a pigskin?"

She responds with a sardonic smile. "Just getting back from the jail?"

"Yes, and I stopped to see Mr. Rosetti to get current

addresses for the Priolo, DeLuca, and Palumbo families."

"How was your father?"

"In jail for Christmas," I reply with a shrug.

Pat's eyes stray to the printed copies of the real estate sales transactions that are scattered on the coffee table. "Are these the rental houses?"

"Yup."

She whistles after reading the first record and then glances at the others. "I don't get it. My parents' house is pretty much like these places and it isn't worth anywhere near this much."

"Helps explain why they sold out, doesn't it?"

She nods thoughtfully. "I've been digging into the *Trib* archives. The surest way to beat eminent domain seems to be by screaming bloody murder and making enough noise to give the politicians cold feet. That game plan worked here two years ago. It might work again. Quite a few of your neighbors were mentioned in the stories."

"But we already know most of them are out of the game this time."

"So, you need a Plan B."

"I've got a few days off after Christmas to canvass the neighborhood. I'll look for a few gamers."

"There's gotta be a story somewhere in here," she says after flipping through the real estate papers again. "Can I get copies?"

When I return from making copies in my kitchen "office," Pat is wearing a half-smile while she watches the fish.

"Pretty cool," she says. "I've never been able to keep fish alive. Do you have any idea how many goldfish might have been saved if I had this channel?"

I shake my head and laugh, but a deep stab of guilt follows when I think about the day. "I would have come if it had just been you and me for dinner."

"You got something against my family, buster?"

"I can't deal with anyone's family today, Pat. It's all too

fresh."

Her eyes drop to the package I still haven't opened. "Open your present."

I heft it and turn it over a couple of times, then give the package a shake and sniff around the edges. "Maybe a book?"

She rolls her eyes. "Why don't you open it and see?"

Sure enough, it's a book. *The Razor's Edge* by W. Somerset Maugham. "Maugham? Isn't he one of those guys English professors torment their students with?"

She laughs. "It's called *literature,* bozo. I'm not going to say I always lapped this stuff up in school, but I was lucky enough to find my way back to it when I actually knew enough about life and the world to appreciate books like this."

I remember writing an essay on Maugham's tale of a First World War veteran who turned his back on Chicago society to search for the deeper meaning of life. I still remember the gist of it. A maverick in the most un-American sense of the word, Laurence Darrell was that rare creature able to shrug off the straitjacket of societal expectations and conventions. Larry, who pointedly eschewed the desperately excessive lifestyle of his wealthy peers, was a character I had dismissed as something of a flake, or possibly an intellectual dilettante. If I remember this much, it must have made more of an impression than I realized at the time. Something in this story obviously matters to Pat. I resolve to discover what it is. "Thank you."

"How was Christmas in Brussels?" she asks.

"Who knows? I left Britts a message and haven't heard back."

"The little fart still hasn't sent me an email," Pat complains. "Maybe she's having too much fun in Europe to bother with us Yankees?"

We pass a few minutes discussing the Christmas gift haul of Pat's nieces and nephews, plus some O'Toole family news.

"It's been another lovely O'Toole family Christmas, Tony. Every year when we're all sitting around the table for Christmas dinner, I realize how lucky I was to be born into my family."

I'm in the kitchen digging out hot chocolate fixings when the phone rings. "We're about to find out how Christmas went in Europe," I say when the caller ID announces that it's Brittany.

Pat edges toward the door.

I wave her back in. Brittany will be pleased to have a chance to talk to her. "Stay. We can both yell at her."

I'm surprised to find Michelle on the line. "Merry Christmas, Tony."

"Merry Christmas."

"Let me put you on speaker so we can all talk," she says.

"Merry Christmas, Dad!" Brittany exclaims.

"Merry Christmas, honey," I reply with a grin. I put our phone on speaker and announce, "Pat's here. Say hi."

"Hi!" Pat and Brittany shout in unison.

"Did you guys spend Christmas together?" Brittany asks.

"We've been visiting for a few minutes while Pat drops off my present," I reply while spooning heaping piles of cocoa into a pair of mugs.

"What did you give him?" Brittany asks Pat.

"A book."

"I thought you liked him?"

I chuckle while Pat rolls her eyes.

"Which book?" Michelle asks.

"The Razor's Edge," I reply.

"Maugham?" she says with disdain.

Pat stiffens but holds her tongue.

"Who's Maugham?" Brittany asks.

"We had to read him in school," Michelle replies, taking pains to make it sound like an onerous ordeal. It's certainly not a book her father, the inestimable Prescott Rice III, and his fellow Wall Street tycoons and cronies would approve of, and Michelle is very much her father's daughter.

Brittany laughs brightly, oblivious to her mother's oblique bitchiness. "Why didn't you just give him a lump of coal?"

"What did you do today?" I ask before Pat can respond to Michelle's barb.

"We're skiing in St. Moritz with Morgan," Brittany says. "We're going back to Brussels tomorrow night."

Brittany didn't mention travel plans. "Morgan?" I ask lightly. "Girlfriend or some Belgian beefcake you picked up?"

"Morgan Tomlinson," Michelle clarifies.

What's he doing there? I wonder. Tomlinson is a blue-blood marketing executive with Coca-Cola. He'd still been working in Atlanta when we left. None of my business, I guess. Still, I wonder when that started. "No cell service in St. Moritz?" I ask with a touch of sarcasm.

"Well, it's late here and I just wanted to make sure Brittany had a chance to call before bed," Michelle announces. "Maybe you can call back at a more opportune time for the two of you to chat."

"C'mon Mom!" Brittany argues. "I'm wide awake!"

"Good night, Tony," Michelle says while Brittany continues to protest in the background. The line goes dead before I can reply.

"Wow," Pat says. "Nice wife you had there, Valenti."

"I'm sorry," I grumble through clenched teeth.

"No need to apologize for her."

The kettle boiled while we were on the phone. I pour the water and toss a handful of frozen mini marshmallows into each cup before sliding one across to Pat.

"I'm making progress at Village Hall," she announces while she stirs the marshmallows.

"Progress on what?"

"I've been asking around about what happened to your father's building permit application."

That's news to me. "And?"

She smiles. "I think I've got the license guy dead to rights."

"He deliberately held things up?"

"Yup. Not that I think he did it on his own initiative."

The initiative would no doubt be Zaluski's, the rotten bastard. "So now what?"

"I'll set up a meeting with him after New Year's."

"Will he give up Zaluski?"

"Be patient, Tony. Even if this guy implicates Zaluski, showing that the village dragged its feet with the building permit is a baby step. Taking Zaluski and the mayor down won't be easy… or quick. It's going to take time to get to the bottom of whatever's going on."

My doubts must be obvious. She touches my arm and says, "I've got faith in you, Tony. You'll rally the troops and come out of this on top."

I do well not to laugh in the face of her misplaced faith. As for rallying the troops, it's no secret that people don't much like me; didn't someone just try to turn me into the Christmas roast turkey?

I break out the Maker's Mark as soon as Pat leaves and am spiraling down into a black hole of despair by the time I finish draining the first bottle. My eyes land on the dog in his bed, chin resting on his paws as he gazes back at me. Good old Deano. Loyal Deano. Dogs don't just up and discard you. I stagger over to Deano's bed and lay on the floor, getting nose-to-nose to him with my chin resting on the backs of my hands. His sad eyes stare back into mine.

I know he wants Mama or Papa, preferably both. "I'm here for you, pal, but I'm not who you really want, am I? You mind if we feel incomplete together?"

Deano's chocolate eyes gaze back without comment. We stare deep into one another's soul for a minute or two.

"You comfort me a lot more than I comfort you," I

mumble before pushing myself back up.

After splashing more bourbon into a glass, I take the bottle for a visit to the Valenti family picture wall. My eyes settle on Frankie's high school graduation picture. Definitely the better looking of the Valenti boys, he was two inches shorter than me at the time but twenty pounds heavier. The extra weight was all muscle that he put to use as a brawler and destroyer of little brothers. My earliest memory of Frankie's animosity was being abandoned in a sandbox several blocks from home when I was four or so. Frankie had taken me well beyond Independence Park while babysitting me. I didn't understand the words he taunted me with when he left me behind in tears, but I did learn to recognize the cruel smile and mean little eyes that were seared into my psyche through the long reign of Fearsome Frankie. I've since learned that Frankie told Mama and Papa that I had run away from Independence Park that day when he had "looked away for a second." That was only the beginning. I didn't recognize the bullying for what it was until we got a little older. When I dared to push back, things turned ugly… and stayed that way. It had been followed by years of beatings, destroyed homework, broken toys, and public humiliation—particularly at school. Things had slowed some when Frankie finished high school and moved out, but never stopped completely. It had culminated a few years later when Frankie arrived on Liberty Street after overindulging in happy hour at the end of a day's work on a road crew. He found me home alone on semester break from my freshman year of college. I made the mistake of challenging his taunting rant about me being a school pussy by telling him that *I* wasn't stupid enough to skip university for beer money. I'd then pointed out that I'd be making something out my life while he dug ditches.

"I couldn't afford university," he'd erupted. "But you get to go, you pampered, spoiled little prick!" The first sucker punch had landed while I argued that I couldn't afford to go, either, but had busted my ass to earn my volleyball scholarship. A flurry of punches quickly put me down. Then he'd grabbed my arm, dislocating my elbow and shoulder while he dragged me into the basement with my head bouncing off the steps until it finally thudded onto the concrete basement floor. He pounded me into a bloody pulp, leaving me with a shattered orbital bone, my nose mashed across my cheek, two broken ribs, and a punctured lung. I'd only been saved by Mama and Amy arriving home from grocery shopping. Frankie, disheveled, out of breath, splattered with blood, and sporting swollen knuckles, had fled after telling them I'd fallen down the stairs. Amy found me in a crumpled heap behind the furnace and screamed for Mama to call 9-1-1. The hospital had stitched up the cuts, reset the broken bones, and removed my spleen. Poor Amy had later apologized for never intervening over the years; she was too afraid of our older brother to risk his ire. Neither of us saw him again. Although he'd gone on to join the Marines so that he and Amy were both service members at the time of her death, he didn't bother to attend her funeral.

"Why do you hate me?" I ask as I stare at his familiar smirk. "Answer me, goddammit!"

No reply, of course, just that smirk. I've wondered all my life what it is about me that makes people turn away. My own brother, for God's sake. Even Papa slapped me around now and again after a little too much grappa. My wife ditched me. Twice. Hell, even my own daughter can't stand to be around me. I reach out and touch Frankie's picture. "Maybe you were right all along. Michelle, too. I really am a worthless sack of shit. A waste of space. A malignancy in the genetic pool."

They'd called me all of these things and more. I knock back another slug of bourbon and stare at my sorry-assed reflection in the wall mirror beside the picture collection. I'm the human equivalent of a used condom—worthless, unwanted, and easily discarded.

CHAPTER EIGHTEEN

"Well, if it isn't my secret weapon," Mike says with a grin when I walk into the vestibule at the Cook County Jail on the evening of January third.

"What are you talking about?" I ask.

"Didn't you read the *Trib* this morning?"

I did. Gearing up for the trial, the state's attorney's reporter (as Pat calls him) wrote a little piece about how Tony Valenti, "fresh from his role as the principal attorney of disgraced Sphinx Financial," was now on the defense team of his father, "cop-killer Francesco Valenti," "lending his considerable legal clout *pro bono* to buttress the defense team assembled by the Public Defender's office." The asshole even slipped in a little blurb about me stirring up trouble in Cedar Heights, all the better to polish my bad-guy credentials. Subtext to potential jurors: *Don't trust this man!*

"My boss saw that," I groan. Lawrence Goddard ordered me to keep a low profile in my father's trial and around Cedar Heights. Fleiss Lansky LLP apparently has zero tolerance for troublemakers in the community.

"Isn't that Alex Dempsey a piece of work?" Mike says as we approach the security checkpoint. "The dastardly Tony

Valenti slinking back to Cedar Heights to undermine The American Way and all that is good and wholesome in the world."

"Like I'm some sort of legendary defense attorney." Dempsey would have a good laugh if he understood the inadequacy that lies at the heart of me. It will be apparent soon enough.

"You *must* be," Mike says. "Poor Alex makes it sound like they're totally outgunned by the two of us."

"Right. We've got them outnumbered two to thirty or thereabouts, plus all the cops they have at their disposal."

Mike cracks his knuckles and meets my gaze. "How's the job?"

"Most days I feel the need for a shower on the way out." He cocks an eyebrow, so I continue. "A Wisconsin court subpoenaed the engineering and testing documents about a Fafnir furnace component that allegedly failed and caused a natural gas explosion that annihilated a La Crosse home and its three inhabitants. Fafnir has ordered me to quash the court order by any means necessary. They're determined to keep the truth buried."

"That's soul-killing shit, brother. Makes me feel good about what I do—shitty hours, shitty money, and all."

"How did court go?" I ask. Mike had requested a continuance this afternoon, arguing that the prosecution's tardiness in delivering their psychiatric evaluation has delayed us ordering our own.

"No continuance. Judge Mitton wasn't sympathetic. He says we should have gotten our own evaluation done by now, regardless of what the prosecution was doing."

"Bastard!"

Mike raises an amused eyebrow. "You're anti-Mitton?"

"Hell yes!"

"I'm okay with old Myron," Mike says before putting a finger to his lips when we reach security. He expands on his point once we're through and climbing the stairs to the interview rooms. "His time on the bench is winding down, making him less susceptible to pressure. Sure, he's a little crusty, but that cuts both ways. He's never been one to coddle prosecutors."

"He hasn't seemed too fair so far."

"Francesco killed a cop, Tony. No judge likes that. We could have done much worse than Mitton. How'd you like some character two years removed from the state's attorney's office—another law-and-order butcher with political aspirations?"

"Things didn't go too well with Mitton today, did they?" I argue stubbornly.

"He was right, Tony. A continuance wasn't warranted. I *should* have gotten our shrink in to see Francesco sooner. Don't blame the judge. Blame me. *I* screwed up." Mike gives me a long look and says, "The judge sets the rules in the courtroom, decides what evidence comes in and what doesn't. No matter how much pressure the State brings to bear, Mitton will play this straight. He knows we haven't caught a break yet. When he thinks we've earned it, he'll toss us a bone or two."

Mike pulls a thin sheaf of papers out of his briefcase after we enter the conference room. "Here's the psychiatric assessment from the prosecution," he says with a sneer before reading from the summary. "'Subject presents tendencies suggestive of antisocial personality disorder.' They're not saying he's a little withdrawn when they use that term, Tony. This says Francesco is an aberrant personality inherently prone to violent behavior."

"That's so much bullshit," I scoff.

"Yeah, well, you know it and I know it. In fact, lots of folks may know it, but the judge and jury don't know it." His eyes drop back to the report. "'Shooting Deputy O'Reilly was a manifestation of a possible impulse control disorder known as intermittent explosive disorder.'" Mike stops and meets my eyes. "In other words, he can blow again at any time."

"Jesus."

He sighs heavily. "The judge is right. We should have done our own assessment."

"Why didn't we?"

His shoulders sag. "Same old story… not enough time, not enough money. I have someone coming to talk to Francesco tomorrow. We have to discredit this horseshit," he says while tossing the report on the table. "Francesco needs to be seen as a highly distressed man who lost control for an instant."

After getting to his feet to pace and blow off a little steam about other bullshit stunts he's encountered at the hands of prosecutors, Mike slides back into his seat and gives me a tired smile. "I read the story about your sister in the *Trib*. Anyone who reads that story oughtta be feeling a little sorry for Francesco."

"Let's hope so. Pat has another story about a jerk in the Cedar Heights licensing office taking a bribe to hold up Papa's building permit to fix the garage."

"A bribe in Cedar Heights, you say?" he mutters sarcastically.

The door finally opens and a guard lets Papa into the conference room. After we exchange greetings, Mike gives Papa a quick recap of the prosecution's psychiatric assessment.

"I not some crazy nut like they say," Papa retorts. "Why they say this?"

"The psychiatrist who wrote this works for the state's attorney, so he'll make things sound as bad as he can," Mike replies.

Papa's brow furrows in confusion. "He is the one I talk to after shooting? He was not a bad man. Why he say these things?"

"He's not the one you talked to, but they used that man's

report," Mike replies. "You'll be talking to another psychiatrist tomorrow. This one is ours."

"Why do this again?" Papa asks.

Mike cocks an eyebrow. "Do we believe what the first guy said?"

"No," Papa and I reply in unison.

"We've hired someone else," Mike explains. "We'll need to show the court that the prosecution's psychiatrist wasn't right."

Papa's questioning eyes look from Mike to me. "These doctors, they no tell the truth, just what lawyers want them to say?"

Such is the world of expert witnesses, I think before replying, "Something like that."

"This is not right! Is court not for truth?"

"You just answer the doctor's questions tomorrow as truthfully as you can, Francesco," Mike says. "Let us worry about the rest. Now—"

Papa cuts him off. "You answer me, Anthony."

"Two people can see the same event differently, Papa. In court, a judge or jury hears both sides of a story and then tries to decide which version is correct."

"That is truth in the legal sense of the word, Francesco," Mike adds. "My job is to make sure I tell the court everything they need to know to arrive at a just decision. I can't do that without your help. We need to hear your side of what happened that night."

I hold my breath while Papa thinks this over. He has so far refused to talk about the shooting. God alone knows why, but he's an obstinate old cuss when he makes up his mind to be. "Stubborn as an old ass!" Mama said more than once.

"Peter Zaluski is going to be a witness against you," I tell Papa in hopes of jolting him out of his reluctance to speak of that night. Zaluski is only listed as a potential witness. If he appears, we assume it will be to testify about how Officer O'Reilly came to be on Papa's doorstep the night he was shot.

"Zaluski!" Papa exclaims angrily. "He will tell more lies!"

"That's why we need you to tell us everything," Mike says patiently.

I lean in. "Tell us about that night, Papa. You were sitting in the kitchen with the *Trib* and a beer when the cop showed up?"

He nods slowly, clearly taking himself back in time. "As soon as I see this policeman at door, I know he will be trouble."

"Why is that?" Mike asks.

"He is bad policeman. Angry, always angry. That night, he angry again."

"Again?" I ask. "This wasn't the first time you encountered O'Reilly?"

"He yells at my Maria. He makes her cry!"

"When was this?" Mike asks. "What happened?"

"She see a boy break into swimming pool at night. She call police. This boy, he is police officer's son."

"O'Reilly's boy?" I ask.

Papa nods. "The police officer yell at Maria one day on street, call her bad names. He swear at her!"

"You saw and heard this?" Mike asks.

Papa nods. "He say his son is in trouble. Is Maria's fault. He say she not get away with making trouble for his boy."

"Why didn't you tell us about this?" I ask.

Papa shrugs. "I no think it matter."

"Everything matters," Mike says firmly. "Tell us exactly what happened on September seventeenth, Francesco. The doorbell rang?"

Papa settles back again, his eyes half-closed as he remembers. "When I open door, policeman try to open screen door. Is locked, so he kick it. He yell at me. Is crazy person!"

"What about the eviction notice?" Mike asks. "Did O'Reilly tell you he had court documents to serve?"

Papa nods. "He say I have to take papers he brings."

"And did you open the door then?" Mike asks.

Papa sighs. "I tell him I no open door. He should leave papers in mailbox."

"Why didn't he?" I ask.

"He say he come to kick me out of house."

"Were you afraid of him?" Mike asks. I immediately recognize how pivotal a question this is. Papa, looking a little ashamed as he does so, nods. Mike's eyes meet mine for a heartbeat before he again locks eyes with Papa. "How long did this go on, Francesco?"

"One minute. Two minute. Maybe more. Door is breaking."

"Why didn't you just close the inside door?" Mike asks.

"Then I can no get papers. He say I must have them."

And there's the impulsive madman of the prosecution's imagination, I think dryly. Facing down danger to carry out the orders of law enforcement… at least until he decided to shoot the guy.

"When did you take out your gun?" Mike asks.

"When policeman break door. Gun is by door in closet. I hope gun will scare him away."

"Did it?" Mike asks softly.

Papa is growing more and more distraught as the story unfolds. "No. He throw paper inside. Hit me with stick."

Mike's eyebrows rocket up. "He hit you with his nightstick?"

Papa nods.

"You kept telling him to leave?"

Papa nods again.

"That's when you shot him?" I ask.

With shame written all over his face, my father whispers, "Yes. After he hit me again."

"Sounds like Papa was provoked," I say to Mike Williams after my father leaves.

"Makes the shooting a little more understandable," he agrees. "No witnesses, though."

"None that we've found so far."

"So far?" Mike mutters grimly. "We've been through the discovery materials a thousand times. There's nothing there."

"Papa was there. Put him on the stand," I suggest as we gather up our papers and briefcases.

"No way, Tony. Dempsey will eat him alive. We need to take a closer look at who Sheriff's Deputy Andrew O'Reilly really was."

"I'm just a corporate weenie, so tell me how we do that."

"You *are* a corporate weenie," Mike says with a nasty grin as he dons a well-worn deep green mohair overcoat and opens the door. "I'll have our investigator look into O'Reilly. We'll need a copy of his personnel records from the Cedar Heights PD and Cook County Sheriff. I seem to recall a couple of excessive force complaints against him. Let's peek under that rock."

"I'll request O'Reilly's personnel records," I say while I slip into my red Gore-Tex jacket and follow him out of the conference room.

"The poor sonofabitch," Mike mutters while we walk. "Francesco must've come here with his head full of Hollywood dreams about the good life in America—streets paved with gold, boundless opportunity for everyone. All that glossy bullshit about America that we sell abroad."

"I suppose he did," I murmur.

"Look what he got. He couldn't practice his carpentry trade and ended up working his ass off for years at a menial job he could've gotten in Italy. Now this."

"He had a nice home. A family."

Mike chuckles grimly. "Maybe I understand this better

than you do, Tony. When *my* ancestors 'immigrated' here, things didn't work out so well for them, either."

"And your point is?"

Mike lays a hand on my shoulder. "They lied to him about what to expect, then turned around and took away what he managed to scrape together. Now they want to kill him. The dude must be feeling pretty bitter."

"So let's make sure this isn't the final chapter."

"Amen to that, brother," Mike says as a slow smile crosses his face. "Amen."

CHAPTER NINETEEN

The January seventh meeting of the Cedar Heights Village Board hasn't even begun and we're already a step behind Peter Zaluski and company. In fact, I've prepared for the wrong battle. I'd expected the board to discuss a potential redevelopment plan for Liberty Street tonight, but that discussion is nowhere to be found on the agenda posted in the Village Hall lobby. The board will instead be voting to establish a Tax Increment Financing (TIF) district in support of the Independence Park/Liberty Street Redevelopment Plan. Having no idea what the hell any of this means, I've used the village's Wi-Fi and my laptop to discover that passing a municipal TIF ordinance establishes a *prima facie* case granting legal authority for condemnation. In other words, a redevelopment plan has already been approved and the village is maneuvering to implement it. In another hour or two, Independence Park and the houses along Liberty Street could be formally condemned. How in hell am *I* going to keep that from happening?

I cross Village Hall's sterile lobby and continue on through a set of double doors that lead into the Council Chamber. The room, which also serves as a community hall when the

Village Board isn't sitting, is nothing if not utilitarian. Banks of fluorescent lights alternate with white acoustic ceiling tiles, bathing everything in a blaze of harsh white light. The walls are vast expanses of institutional eggshell white, on which plaques and notices hang at equidistant intervals. Chunky black speakers hang high in each corner, flanking a stage at the front of the room. The stage reminds me of the one in my elementary school gymnasium. In fact, the whole space reminds me of school gyms, right down to the basketball nets cranked up out of reach at either end. Several tidy rows of straight-backed chrome and fabric chairs for the public are arranged in the center of the room. A portable lectern with a microphone stands at the head of the aisle in front of the stage.

My post-Christmas effort to recruit Liberty Street neighbors to do battle with City Hall was a bust. Big surprise that people didn't line up with me. The denizens of Liberty Street exhibited surprisingly little interest in attending tonight's meeting—even after I explained their homes might be bulldozed. To say I'd been discouraged after two hours of that would be a gross understatement, so I'm inordinately pleased to see some elderly neighbors in the public seats. Mrs. LaSusa and her husband are here. The Vaccaros are also present. Even Mr. Rosetti is putting in an appearance. Pat has staked out a corner, pen and pad in hand. I walk over to her and explain the significance of the board adopting a TIF ordinance as opposed to the redevelopment plan we expected. She had noticed but wasn't aware of the implications.

"What do we do?" she asks. "You're the expert on this stuff."

"Then we're truly up the creek. To put this in lawyerly terms, what we have here is a classic case of the blind leading the blind."

Pat gives me an indulgent smile that carries a gentle reprimand for the self-denigration.

"When did they slip the redevelopment plan through?" I wonder aloud.

"After the November fourth board meeting. I've got a copy of the minutes. I'll ask about it."

We pause to watch Zaluski's entrance. He smiles and joshes with a handful of people milling around the seats reserved for village staff. I resist the urge to walk over and smack the smug smile off his face.

Seven people troop onstage and settle into black executive chairs behind polished honey oak workstations. The desks form a semicircle on the stage, from which the Village Board peers down at the rest of us. My eyes roam around the room and meet those of Mike Williams, who said he might "drop by to watch the show." He nods. I nod back before I leave Pat and slip into a seat amongst my neighbors.

His Honor the Mayor introduces Zaluski, Tricia Dix from Three Streams Development, and Hernando Mendoza from the architectural consulting firm Cormier, Marr, and Mendoza. My eyes lift to study this unholy trinity, who represent our opposition for the evening. My reading has taught me that Hector Mendoza is a hired gun specializing in unearthing blight conditions in properties that developers want condemned. Mayor Brown gives the trio a quick wink in greeting.

Last year's Cedar Heights High School valedictorian, Jeremy Spencer, earnestly recites the Pledge of Allegiance. The kid looks like the winner of a Howdy Doody look-alike contest who is well on his way to selling vacuum cleaners door-to-door. After we suffer through more civic banality, Mayor Brown calls the meeting to order. A marginally overweight man of average height in his mid-fifties, the mayor radiates the vanilla charm of a small-time politician. I've learned from Pat that he's a petty potentate who considers the village his personal fiefdom and its taxpayers his serfs. Supposedly, little happens in Cedar Heights without his knowledge and consent, which means the scorched earth campaign waged against my parents went forward with His Honor's blessing. Zaluski isn't my only enemy at Village Hall.

While the board takes care of routine business, I read through more of the TIF articles I bookmarked earlier. I tune back in when a trustee gets into a tussle with the mayor over the awarding of a telecommunications contract. Brown seems offended at being challenged.

A pair of Lilliputian glasses threatens to ski off the nose of Trustee Alvin Smith, the sole African American member of the board, who is sharply turned out in a tasteful charcoal suit, powder-blue shirt, and a fire-engine red necktie. Only a full head of tightly cropped, graying hair betrays approaching middle age. Trustee Smith is staring at the mayor. "Did the fact that an officer of Digital Wizardry is related to the mayor influence the village manager's recommendation?"

His Honor turns to Peter Zaluski. "Mr. Zaluski?"

"That was not a factor in my recommendation," Zaluski reassures one and all.

When Smith leans into the microphone again, his steely eyes betray his dislike of the village manager. "Based on what *specifics*, Mr. Zaluski?"

"Digital Wizardry offered the best balance of cost-effectiveness and professional ability."

"They must be *very* good to warrant a premium of fifteen percent more than the other bids," Smith retorts. "What makes these folks fifteen percent better?"

"Bid details are confidential."

When Smith continues to demand details, Zaluski's eyes appeal to the mayor for help.

"This has gone on long enough," His Honor says. "The village employs Mr. Zaluski to carry on the business of Cedar Heights, not to be a punching bag for the political aspirations of board members."

"I'm merely asking for the information I need to cast an

informed vote on the matter before us," Smith retorts. The exchange reminds me that Smith is rumored to be considering a run for mayor in the next village election.

"Discussion of this matter is closed," Mayor Brown proclaims with a rap of his gavel. "Please call the vote, Madam Clerk."

Trustee Smith objects loudly as the motion is polled and passed by a vote of five-to-one. The mayor doesn't vote; he's only called upon to break a tie.

Brown makes a show of consulting the agenda. "We'll now hear a report and recommendations from the Planning Commission. This relates to the urban renewal study commissioned to assess the Independence Park/Liberty Street Redevelopment Plan."

It's show time. A buzz circulates through our corner of the public seats.

"Village Manager Peter Zaluski will present the report," the mayor continues. "Tricia Dix and Hernando Mendoza will assist. All three will be available to answer questions afterward." He pauses to smile at his demolition team and then turns a beatific countenance upon the citizens present. "I understand some of you folks wish to speak to this matter?"

A few heads bob up and down.

"Excellent!" he says. "As you're recognized, please proceed to the podium and state your name and address. Who would like to go first?"

I pop to my feet and claim the point position. Mayor Brown beams at me.

"Tony Valenti," I announce. "Forty-seven Liberty Street."

A flicker of distaste registers in His Honor's eyes. "Our time for discussion is finite, so we'll limit questions to one per person."

"As I understand the TIF laws you propose to use in this matter," I begin, "the village must adopt a redevelopment plan before commissioning the study we'll hear about tonight. Is that correct?"

The mayor nods warily. "That's correct. Do you have a question?"

"When was this redevelopment plan approved? I haven't seen a copy of it or any mention of its passage on the village website."

Brown hands off. "Mr. Zaluski?"

"The redevelopment plan was initially adopted two years ago," Zaluski tells us. "After an extensive review, we determined that it remains viable."

"When was that decision made?" I ask.

His Honor shakes his head and tells me, "You've already asked your question. Please be seated." After I sit, he somberly studies the voters. "The village spent considerable time and expense preparing the original redevelopment plan for the Independence Park/Liberty Street project. After establishing that we are still legally able to utilize that plan, we concluded that it would be fiscally irresponsible not to do so. Mr. Zaluski will highlight the findings of the Planning Commission's report."

Zaluski rises. "Our plan calls for an exciting makeover of the Independence Park environment. When complete, the village will gain a new shopping center and several midrise condominium buildings."

Zaluski nods at Tricia Dix of Three Streams Development, who flips the cover page off an easel to unveil an artist's rendering of a futuristic multi-level complex where Independence Park now stands. It's flanked by a quartet of handsome condominium structures that replace the houses on Liberty Street. It looks great, albeit with no artistic license spared to spruce up the setting. Unless they bulldoze a few more residential streets, the area surrounding the proposed development won't be the upscale neighborhood depicted in the drawing.

"Not only will this development significantly improve the aesthetics of this area," Zaluski continues, "redevelopment will bring the village sorely needed new tax dollars. It will also enhance adjacent property values."

From what I've gleaned in my eminent domain studies, most of the communities pushing these projects end up offering developers sweetheart deals to locate in their jurisdiction. All too often, those municipalities end up eating the financing guarantees they offer to bankroll the commercial portions of the projects. Generous tax exemptions are granted to corporations for up to ten years. The developers unfailingly bluster and threaten relocation if their tax exemptions aren't extended every time they're due to expire. The individual condo owners who buy into these projects generally receive no tax breaks. Big surprise, that.

"We're pleased to have Hernando Mendoza here," Zaluski says. "Hernando is a partner with Cormier, Marr, and Mendoza, the architectural consulting firm Three Streams Development engaged to prepare an updated urban renewal study."

Mendoza gets to his feet. He's not a tall man, but there's a presence about him. Nice suit. Meticulously groomed. A confident air bespeaking cockiness. Hernando Mendoza wouldn't have been out of place in the Sphinx boardroom. I distrust him on sight.

A video screen glides down from the stage ceiling and a graphic appears, entitled: *Independence Park/Liberty Street Urban Renewal Study*. This is followed by a slide containing dense columns of numbers. "As you can see," Mendoza says, "municipal expenses are rising steadily. Experience teaches us that they will continue to escalate as long as this neighborhood remains in its existing configuration. Experience also tells us that once a neighborhood is in decline, crime gains a foothold and then runs rampant. Law enforcement costs rise in step with the breakdown of order, and public works costs skyrocket as vandalism explodes."

Mendoza turns a smile upon the Village Board as a new slide appears. "Fortunately, we can see in Table Two that Cedar Heights has an opportunity to turn the situation around before this neighborhood reaches the point of no return."

Table Two illustrates revenue numbers skyrocketing while expenses slide down the scale, turning the Independence Park/Liberty Street neighborhood into a fiscal Shangri-La. Disney couldn't script a happier ending. I'm reminded of Mama's old saying: "Figures don't lie, but liars figure."

Pictures of Independence Park pop onto the screen. Dilapidated. Forlorn. An eyesore without question. Used condoms carelessly discarded inside what remains of the change rooms. Feces litter the interior floors as well as the crumbling pool and surrounding concrete terrace, whether human or animal isn't clear. Drug paraphernalia is also present—used needles, the stubby roaches of joints.

Mendoza scrolls through picture after picture of the trio of rental houses on Liberty Street, cleverly multiplying the effect with shots from various angles—front, back, side views, even a couple of aerial shots. If I didn't know better, I'd think the whole street had gone to the Rottweilers.

"Don't be fooled, those pictures show only three houses," Mr. Rosetti booms angrily.

I'm relieved to see some feistiness from him, but cringe when the next pictures show the crushed corner of our garage with shredded black plastic sheeting flapping in the wind. Mendoza fails to mention that the village bears none of the cost of repairing our home while it reaps one hundred percent of the negative PR value from the situation.

Mrs. LaSusa gets to her feet. "I wish to speak about this."

"In just a few more minutes, Mrs. LaSusa," His Honor says with an indulgent smile.

I chuckle softly. Mrs. L, our neighborhood busybody, is apparently known at Village Hall.

"At least three indications of blight must be present for an afflicted neighborhood to meet TIF standards," Mendoza continues. "The area identified in The Independence Park/Liberty Street Redevelopment Plan has no less than *six* of the blight factors we were asked to investigate for."

Peter Zaluski gets to his feet. "Thank you for an excellent presentation, Hernando."

Mendoza beams and sits down; yet another corporate whore heard from. Tricia Dix leans over to whisper in his ear and places a hand on his arm as she does so. His grin widens. I imagine the conversation: "That was great, Hernando! Exactly what we paid for."

Mayor Brown also thanks Mendoza, then invites the public back into the discussion. I've been scribbling questions in a notebook and have distributed a few to neighbors.

Mr. Rosetti is first in line at the lectern. "How many properties show evidence of blight?"

His Honor looks to Zaluski, who looks to Mendoza.

"I don't recall the exact number," the architect replies, "but almost every house on Liberty Street was identified as a blight risk."

"Are you suggesting my home is an eyesore?" Mr. Rosetti asks indignantly.

Mendoza shakes his head. "Blight isn't only about appearance. We do an in-depth analysis in which many factors come into play."

"If I may," Trustee Smith interjects, not waiting for a reply before carrying on, "perhaps Mr. Mendoza will be kind enough to list the factors his study used to identify blight."

Mendoza shoots Zaluski a concerned look. The village manager in turn looks to the mayor for guidance. When His Honor gives Mendoza an almost imperceptible nod, I inch forward to the edge of my seat. So do my neighbors.

"We've seen some of the factors," Mendoza says, "such as increased crime evidenced by rising calls for police and fire department services."

"Does that include 9-1-1 calls?" Trustee Smith asks.

Mendoza nods.

Smith raises his eyebrows. "It seems to me that somebody calling 9-1-1 to report a fire or medical emergency is a pretty weak indication of blight."

"It's part of a pattern—" Mendoza begins.

Smith cuts him off. "How many of these calls to the police and fire department concern criminal activity, as opposed to citizens seeking medical assistance or a little help keeping their properties from burning to the ground?"

Mendoza's eyes cut to the mayor.

"I'm sure Mr. Mendoza will be happy to make that information available to us in due course," Brown says.

Mr. Vaccaro replaces Mr. Rosetti at the podium. "Independence Park has been rotting for years. Who will stop the crime when the police never come? Are we to suffer because the police don't do the work we pay them for? How much of this crime you speak of takes place in Independence Park?"

Once again, Mendoza has no details. Smith asks that they be made available. Mendoza promises they will be. This broken record could get monotonous.

Mr. LaSusa steps to the microphone clutching one of my notebook pages. Mr. L. is a smallish man who seems to be growing smaller still as the years pass; a quiet man who worked in the Marshall Field's furniture warehouse for years, loading and delivering. I've always liked him. He always had an encouraging word or some simple kindness for the kids on the block. "The village stopped fixing anything around Independence Park and Liberty Street years ago, yet most of Cedar Heights' other streets and sidewalks are kept in good repair," he says.

"Do you have a question?" His Honor asks.

Mr. L. nods. "When and why did the village instruct public works to stop doing maintenance work on Liberty Street and Independence Park?"

The mayor looks to Zaluski for an answer.

"Unfortunately, budget constraints don't allow us to do all we'd like to," Zaluski says. "Increased revenue from this redevelopment will help alleviate that problem."

Uh-huh. That's what this is all about.

"*Has* the village instructed Public Works not to make repairs on Liberty Street?" Trustee Smith asks.

"Certainly not," Zaluski replies tartly.

I guess they just decided to stop on their own.

A man I know only as Joe shuffles to the microphone to ask another of my questions. "What tax incentives and/or financing guarantees are we offering these people?"

"Negotiations on financial matters are confidential," Zaluski replies.

I'm overcome with a case of the warm fuzzies at this display of open governance.

I find Trustee Smith's thoughtful eyes on me. He offers the faintest suggestion of a smile before looking away. "Mr. Mayor, I hope Mr. Zaluski or one of your other friends is taking note of all the questions we'll be needing answers to."

Brown studiously ignores Smith and calls on another neighborhood old-timer.

"Why don't you tell us why our houses ain't worth keeping?" the man asks Mendoza.

"A prime focus of urban renewal is addressing imbalances between revenues and expenses," the slick prick replies.

And here I used to think urban renewal was about making our inner cities livable.

Mendoza continues, "We compare the neighborhood with others in the municipality in terms of average revenue generated per parcel of land in the subject area. Smaller, older homes simply don't generate as much tax revenue as newer and larger homes do, let alone commercial projects."

"*That's* a blight factor?" Trustee Smith asks as a current of repressed anger surges through the public seating area.

"We look at houses falling beneath minimum square footage parameters, those with a limited number of bedrooms and bathrooms, those without attached garages, the age of the houses," Mendoza explains. "These are key components of the study."

I stand up. "I have another question."

"Haven't *all* of your questions already been answered?" Mayor Brown asks me with exquisite sarcasm. He's apparently aware that many of the evening's queries came out of my notebook. "You've already spoken, Mr. Valenti. Be seated." The mayor stares me down for a moment before turning his gaze to the next person in line. He breaks into an enormous, shit-eating politician's grin as he booms, "Hello again, Mrs. LaSusa!"

She replies with a cursory nod and turns her attention to Zaluski. To scattered snickers from her neighbors, Mrs. L. announces that she's "not nosey or anything, but I walk my dog every day and I notice things. The pictures of the Valenti garage?"

Zaluski nods uncertainly. "Yes?"

She waves her cell phone. "I just saw a story about that on WGN."

Her words freeze me in my seat. I notice a little smile on Pat's face, a rather smug smile.

"What story is that, Mrs. LaSusa?" Zaluski asks anxiously.

"I'll get to that. I saw that truck smash into the garage."

I didn't know. I doubt anyone did. Why the hell hasn't she mentioned it?

"I went and talked to the truck driver so Francesco and Maria would know who should pay for the repairs," she continues. "The men said they were from the village, so I thought it would be taken care of. Why didn't you fix it?"

What the hell? We thought it was a hit and run—probably some kids or a drunk, maybe drunk kids. The police report recorded it as a hit and run.

The question clearly discomfits Zaluski. "We weren't doing any work there at that time, Mrs. LaSusa. Perhaps you've confused a village work crew with someone else."

Mrs. L. crosses her arms and glowers at Zaluski. "I am *not* confused, young man. I know what I saw out there and I remember speaking with your people."

"What date was this?" Trustee Smith asks.

"In the spring," she replies with a shrug, then searches the audience and meets my gaze. "Anthony probably has the date."

I nod back at her. "Late April. I'll get the exact date."

"You mentioned the news a moment ago?" the mayor nervously asks Mrs. LaSusa.

"WGN says someone at the village took a bribe not to give Francesco the building permit so he could fix his garage. They said Anthony had to take the village to court and get a judge to order you people to issue a building permit. Why did he have to do that?"

While Zaluski and the mayor start to squirm, I see that Pat is still smiling. The *Tribune* was until recently the owner of local television station WGN. The ties between some of the former colleagues remain tight, especially with long-running stories that predate the sale. I suspect Pat knew this story was breaking tonight. When she catches my eye and winks, I smile back.

"It's wrong that you people kept Francesco from fixing his garage," Mrs. LaSusa lectures, getting increasingly worked up as she goes. "What business do you have doing that? Now you show all these pictures pretending people in our neighborhood don't take care of their homes. You are a disgrace!"

The mayor looks mortified.

Mrs. LaSusa turns back to glare at Zaluski. "I'd like to know what you people were doing out there! Some sort of funny business is going on, isn't it?"

"All I can do is check with our Public Works Department to see if they had a crew there," Zaluski replies.

Having spoken her piece, Mrs. L. shakes her head in disgust, then turns on her heel and stalks back to her seat.

Pat steps to the lectern and digs a sheaf of papers out of her back pocket. "Pat O'Toole of the *Chicago Tribune.* I have here a copy of the minutes from the November fourth in camera executive meeting that was held after the regular board meeting."

The eyes of both Zaluski and Mayor Brown widen as they absorb the news that Pat has a source within the village administration. His Honor's icy eyes shift to the pack of village staffers, as if he's wondering which thumbscrew wasn't sufficiently tightened down. I hope Pat's source covered their tracks very, very well.

Pat continues with her eyes locked on the mayor's. "I'm told that this was a rather exclusive meeting, so exclusive that only a select few trustees were invited—just enough to achieve a quorum. Is that true, Mr. Mayor?"

"I don't recall the details," His Honor replies.

Pat glances between the mayor and village manager. "You told us earlier that you decided to proceed with the original Liberty Street redevelopment plan. That decision was taken during the November fourth in camera meeting. Why isn't it in the minutes?"

"I haven't seen a copy," Brown says.

"Would you like to see my copy before you answer?"

"We're not in court, Miss O'Toole," Mayor Brown retorts. He's losing his patience and his temper is fraying. This evening's meeting isn't going as planned.

Pat presses the point. "Who was present at your secret session on November fourth, Mr. Mayor?"

Trustee Smith taps his microphone for attention. "I would also like to know that. I was at the regular board meeting that night. This is the first I've heard about an in camera session."

"Do you recall Miss Dix and Mr. Mendoza being there?" Pat asks the mayor.

"I've spoken to Miss Dix and Mr. Mendoza a number of times. I wouldn't venture a guess as to when and where each of those encounters took place."

"You see a lot of them, do you?" Trustee Smith suggests acerbically.

"I'm told that Miss Dix and Mr. Mendoza were present at the in camera session and that discussions were held about how to sell this project to the public," Pat adds.

"The names of the people in attendance at that meeting, plus everything that was said, is a matter of executive privilege," the mayor snaps.

"So, you're telling us this plan was hatched behind closed doors with the hope that the voters of Cedar Heights would be none the wiser?" Pat asks.

His Honor looks away from her. "I'd like to thank everyone who took the time to participate this evening. Question period is over." The mayor looks to Zaluski and makes a cutting motion. A sharp crackle echoes through the speakers when Zaluski gets up and pulls the plug on the public microphone.

"I think we can proceed to a vote on this matter," the mayor announces, catching everyone by surprise. A rumble of angry voices rolls through the crowd.

Trustee Smith is on his feet. "No motion for a vote is on the floor at this time, Mr. Mayor. I move that the trustees discuss this matter before a vote is called."

His colleagues stare down at the incensed voters glaring

back up at them. Three nod in agreement. Along with Smith, the trio constitutes a majority.

The math isn't lost on Mayor Brown. "One minute each," he snarls.

Smith instantly seizes the floor and cites a litany of what he considers deficiencies in Mendoza's report. "You're making a mockery of this board, Mr. Mayor. We shouldn't bring this matter to a vote until we have answers to *every* question the people of Cedar Heights have raised here tonight. Until then, we can't possibly make an informed, intelligent decision. I, for one, would welcome the return of a little democracy around here."

Heads nod in agreement, both along the row of trustees and in the public seats.

"Time's up, Trustee Smith!" the mayor snaps. Then he turns to a woman who has her arm in the air. "Go ahead, Trustee Myers. One minute."

The waif of a woman the mayor has spoken to nods but refuses to meet his gaze. "I yield my time to Trustee Smith."

"Why, thank you, Trustee Myers," Smith purrs while Brown glowers at her. Smith pauses long enough to attract the mayor's attention, then stares straight into His Honor's eyes. "I move that the board defer consideration of any and all measures pertaining to The Independence Park / Liberty Street Redevelopment Project until our February fourth meeting."

Trustee Myers, perhaps still smarting from the visual darts His Honor fired her way, seconds Smith's motion. The mayor's smoldering eyes signal that he intends to make her pay for her impertinence.

"Please call the roll, Madam Clerk," Smith commands, all folksiness gone as he usurps the mayor's prerogative to call matters to a vote.

Faced with a *fait accompli,* Mayor Brown nods grimly to his clerk, who polls the trustees. The motion carries by a vote of four to two.

Trustee Smith has bought us a few weeks. It's all I can do not to run up front and hug the guy. Instead, I stroll over to shake his hand and congratulate my newfound ally on his success. His political clout will be a welcome addition in the struggle to save Liberty Street.

CHAPTER TWENTY

I've just pressed the brew button on the coffee maker when the doorbell rings. Mike has invited himself over to deliver trial news and to do a little Monday night "underdog strategizing." When he walks into the front room, he stops to look around and nods with appreciation. It's his first time inside our home. "Place is looking mighty fine for a condemned dump."

"Thanks," I chuckle while he hands me his coat.

He walks over and stops in front of the stone fireplace. "Is this Francesco's work?"

I nod. The stones are varied shades of gray, with purple tones and veins of pale blue and beige. A handsome carved mahogany mantelpiece bears a hodge-podge of family photos, pottery, plus statuettes and other knick-knacks Mama and Papa collected over the years.

"And the woodwork?" Mike asks while we admire the crown molding that tops the walls. Papa spent hours routing the edges, perfecting every miter joint, staining the alder to the exact bronzed fruity shade Mama had wanted. Then he buffed it all to a museum-grade gloss.

I nod again.

Mike whistles softly. "He's quite a craftsman."

"He is," I reply while leading the way to the kitchen, anxious to hear the trial news Mike has come to share.

He pauses in the doorway to the kitchen, his fingers tracing the intricate trim surrounding the doorframe. The fit is flawless; every notch and groove meticulously crafted to seamlessly kiss up against its neighbor. "Francesco did this, too?"

"He did."

"Those old European guys do amazing work, don't they?"

Feeling a little like a bobblehead doll, I nod yet again.

Mike's eyes roam around the kitchen, absorbing it all: hand-crafted alder cabinets (almost always alder with Papa), sunny terra cotta plaster walls, countertops inlaid with colorful miniature tiles, sixteen-inch ceramic tile flooring, and a rustic open pendant light fixture hanging from the open beam ceiling over a stout maple table. No hint remains of the banal kitchen the builder left behind so many years ago. He looks at me with a grin. "I trust you had nothing to do with this fine workmanship?"

"Not a thing. You said you have trial news. What's up?"

Mike drops into a kitchen chair. "We start on January twenty-eighth."

"That's only nine days away! Are we ready?"

"Nope. Which is why I'm here."

I take a couple of deep breaths to settle my nerves, followed by a serious slurp of coffee. "Okay, so where do we start?"

"Luke Geffen did the public records search on O'Reilly."

"He's your investigator, right?"

Mike nods. "We're getting a better picture of Deputy O'Reilly and it ain't pretty. There was an assault and battery charge after a bar fight. Looks like the cops on the scene torpedoed that complaint with some shoddy follow-up. There was also a domestic battery complaint filed by O'Reilly's sister-in-law after he beat the shit out of his wife and kid last year. That complaint was eventually withdrawn. No real surprises and nothing we can use so far, but Luke is going to reach out to the wife and sister-in-law."

"Maybe we can call them as witnesses?"

"They'd be hostile witnesses, at best," he replies. "That's always a crap shoot."

I'm tempted to point out that hostile witnesses are more witnesses than we have at the moment, but don't. I am, after all, Mr. Rookie Defense Attorney. "Any luck with O'Reilly's police records?"

"Some," he replies. "The Cedar Heights PD file came back pretty quick. He left there years ago, so I suppose they weren't too concerned about his record. The Cook County Sheriff's office is another story. Getting *that* file is like trying to access the crown jewels."

"Was there anything of interest in the Cedar Heights PD file?"

"I suspect he left under a cloud. There were a couple of excessive force complaints, not terribly unusual for a cop's file."

"Given Papa's version of events, that's significant."

"We'll need a lot more than a couple of poorly documented complaints to make hay out of his police record," Mike counters. "I have a hearing with Judge Mitton in the morning to see if he can speed things along with the Sheriff's office."

"What time? I'd like to come."

He cocks an eyebrow. "Where are you gonna find time to save the house, Francesco, and put in a proper day's work?"

"I've got all the time in the world. An Executive VP of Fafnir expressed concern about my work on their file in the matter of the exploding furnace. Fleiss Lansky found my involvement at the Cedar Heights Village Board embarrassing. I was reminded of the firm's warning to resolve my differences with the Village of Cedar Heights and to keep a low profile where Papa's troubles are concerned. Guess I didn't."

A scowl creeps over Mike's face as he listens.

"Trying to protect our home and keep my father from being executed are apparently matters of little import in the grand scheme of things. And that was that."

"They fired you?"

I nod.

"The *hell* is wrong with those people?"

"It's a law firm," I reply. "Appearances. Reputation. Billings. *That's* what matters."

"That's a bitch, man."

We spend a minute or two disparaging Fleiss Lansky before moving on to ponder the possibility of using Deputy O'Reilly's past to build a defense strategy. After twenty minutes, we reluctantly conclude that we don't have much to work with.

"We need to get Francesco's story in the record," I say.

"Easier said than done."

"Yoo-hoo!" Pat calls from the front door. She has also invited herself over to deliver news. "Mr. Valenti, sir? Are you home?"

She's closing the door with her foot and shrugging out of a Chicago Bears jacket when I arrive in the front hall. She glances up at me as Deano the Watchdog lumbers up wagging his tail. "Door was open. Mind if I come in?"

"What if I do?"

She rolls her eyes. "Shut up and take my coat."

I do so, then lead the way to the kitchen. Mike and Pat exchange greetings while I fill a coffee mug for Pat. Then I serve an Entenmann's coffee cake I picked up on my morning grocery run.

"You've been baking?" Mike asks with a smirk.

Pat snorts. "Don't give him any ideas. We don't want him burning the place down."

"Quite a job you've done, getting our boy in the spotlight," Mike says to Pat. He's referring to the ongoing saga of the village board hearing and its aftermath, which continues to unfold in the *Tribune*. I'm an occasional human-interest prop.

"Thank God it's been a slow news week," she says. "Valenti's not that compelling."

"Thanks. It's not as if I enjoy the limelight," I grumble, thinking of the Fleiss Lansky guillotine falling on my neck only hours ago.

Mike, whose thoughts must have gone to the same place, frowns and looks uncomfortable.

I turn to Pat. "To what do we owe the honor of your visit?"

"You go first," she says with her eyes traveling between us. "Your intrepid reporter smells a scoop! Trial news?"

I fill her in about the trial date.

"Wow, that's pretty close. You're plotting strategy?"

"Something like that. What have you come to tell us?"

"Peter Zaluski deigned to speak with me. They've fired Mr. Building-Permits-Withheld-for-a-Small-Fee. I think precious Peter might be running a little scared."

"Of what?"

"Probably the mayor. Or maybe the law. We'll see."

"The law?" Mike asks.

"Titan didn't go away after Tony's folks and their friends sent them packing two years ago," she replies.

"They didn't?" I ask.

Pat shakes her head. "Nope. The current Independence Park/Liberty Street scheme is basically the same redevelopment plan they put forward two years ago."

"Same old, same old," Mike says.

"That's not news," I agree. "They told us that at the board meeting."

"Right," Pat says. "But they *didn't* mention that Three Streams Development is a wholly-owned subsidiary of Titan."

"Bastards," I mutter.

Pat nods and adds, "Guess who owned the numbered company that bought your neighbors' homes two years ago? Guess who owns the management company that's letting those properties be run into the ground?"

"Titan?" I guess.

"Bingo. Our editors plan to do an expose on eminent domain abuse using this neighborhood as its basis." Her eyes shift to Mike. "I assume you're looking into Deputy O'Reilly?"

"Why do you ask?" he asks warily.

"Maybe I can help. Search the *Trib*'s archives and look for complaints about him. I'll follow up on that if I find anything, check with our usual sources on all things cop-related, and see if anyone around the paper has anything to say about the guy."

"I like it," Mike says. "How long will it take to poke through your records?"

"A day. Maybe two."

"Amen," Mike says while getting to his feet. "I gotta run. Just wanted to give my esteemed co-counsel a heads up about the trial. The state's attorney has his foot on the gas and won't be letting up anytime soon. Francesco's doughty band of attorneys is gonna have to do likewise."

"Just tell me what you want me to do," I say while he shrugs into his jacket.

"Give some thought to a few topics you're comfortable taking the lead on. We'll talk again at court tomorrow."

"Time and location?"

"Nine o'clock sharp."

"On California?" I ask to clarify the courtroom.

"Yup," he says before the door closes behind him.

"You have the day off?" Pat asks as we settle on the couch.

"You could say that," I reply before filling her in on my firing while boosting Deano up to lounge between us.

"Those bastards! Sue them!"

I respond with a morbid chuckle. "I wouldn't have a prayer of winning."

"This stinks, Tony. It really stinks."

Deano is nonplussed by my work news. He's worked his snout under Pat's elbow and has assumed the tummy rub position.

I brandish the slender straw I've been clutching for the past few hours. "Looking on the bright side, I'm available for Papa's trial and am free to help run Zaluski and Brown to ground."

Pat studies me for a moment. "I think we're going to find Titan's fingerprints all over what's been going on at the village. Some cash was probably spread around and a few rules were likely broken."

"No doubt Zaluski has pocketed a few bucks."

"Don't bank on it. Zaluski is a self-righteous, grasping bureaucratic yes man who really believes untrammeled government power is a good thing."

"And your point is?"

"Let's not rule out the possibility that he was hoodwinked," she says while she indulges Deano. "Maybe he's beginning to realize there may be more here than meets the eye. Including his."

Disinclined to view Peter Zaluski in anything but the worst possible light, I change the topic. "What about the slime bucket who took the bribe?"

"Henry Poindexter. I'm working on him. With luck he'll tell us who paid him off, maybe lead us to Titan." Pat takes her hand off Deano to lay it on my arm. "I want you to be very careful, okay?"

"How so?"

Deano squirms closer to remind Pat that she's supposed to be rubbing his tummy. She gets the message and resumes his massage. "I was concerned about what the mayor and Zaluski might do if they feel cornered, but Titan's a threat of a whole other magnitude, Tony. They scare the hell out me."

"It's a corporation," I argue. "I know a thing or two about how corporations think."

"And?"

"Big corporations can't afford to get involved in that kind of crap. It's not like they're a bunch of thugs or something. Think of the PR nightmares. Legalities. Reputation risk. Don't lose sleep worrying about Titan coming after me."

She gives me a doubtful look but lets it go.

My phone rings. The caller ID says it's Brittany calling at one o'clock in the morning Brussels time. *What's wrong?* I wonder as I anxiously pluck the phone off the end table.

"We're coming in two weeks!" she exclaims.

"Really?"

"Yeah. Mom's got a meeting in Atlanta. She's gonna drop me off at O'Hare on her way."

"How long will you be here?"

"A week."

"What about school?"

"I'll take time off. Can't stay here by myself among all these foreigners, can I?"

Heaven forbid! I think, attributing the parochialism to my ex-wife. Suddenly very aware that Papa's trial starts in less than two weeks, I ask, "When do you arrive?"

"February second," Brittany tells me after a quick conference at her end.

Uh-oh. "Papa's trial will be on. You won't mind coming to court?"

"Naw, might be kinda interesting." She falls silent for a moment. "How's Pat? Will I get to see her?"

"Want it straight from the horse's mouth?"

"Huh?"

I hand the phone to Pat and settle back to listen.

"Hey, kiddo!" Pat says with a smile. While she and Brittany chat about things European and possible outings in Chicago, I take the opportunity to study her. I've already screwed things up with her once. It can't happen again. She catches me looking and gives me a questioning smile while she says good-bye to Brittany and hands the phone back.

"Mom says we'll make the rest of the arrangements by email."

"Sounds good. You have to go?"

"Yup. It's late here. Mom just got home and told me we're coming. I couldn't wait to tell you!"

"I'm glad you did," I reply, wondering if Michelle is making a habit of leaving our child alone until one in the morning on weeknights. "Have a good week. Can't wait to see you."

"It'll be fun."

"Darn right it will. Love you."

"Love you, too, Dad."

After setting the phone back on the table, I lounge back and find Pat's thoughtful eyes on me. "Gonna be a busy week to have her here," she says.

"Better than a busy week without her."

"True. I'll pitch in as needed."

"Thanks."

She changes gears. "Remember me mentioning that I'd talk with our crime beat guy about O'Reilly?"

I nod.

"His name is Theo Wilson. I'm having lunch with him tomorrow. He found a cop who was on the force in Cedar Heights with O'Reilly. Better still, this guy and O'Reilly were also members of the same gym for the last year or two. Sounds like they were both into body-building and that O'Reilly was into steroids in a big way."

"Why is he willing to talk?"

"Says guys like O'Reilly are the bane of good, honest cops."

"Sounds promising."

"Let's hope so," she says.

"More coffee cake?"

"Sure."

After we head back to the kitchen, fix our plates, and settle down at the table, conversation circles back to the topic of my employment, or lack thereof. This continues into cleaning up afterward, with Pat bitching about how Corporate America screws over its employees with impunity.

I have no counter argument. Perhaps I've backed the wrong horse all these years? "Maybe I'm getting what I deserve in a karmic sense. After Sphinx and all."

Pat snaps a dishtowel at my butt. "That was on Hank Fraser, not you!"

"I'm not so sure about that anymore."

She smiles and touches my arm. "Well, the Tony Valenti I know today is a good man."

I know better but don't argue the point.

She notices my hesitation and laces her fingers through mine. "I may have had a schoolgirl crush on you twenty years ago, Valenti, but it takes more than popular preppie boy crap to impress me now."

"Yeah?"

"Yeah," she replies before releasing my hand and holding out her coffee mug. "I'll take some more of that coffee."

I smile and turn away to pour another cup when a pane from the kitchen window shatters and falls into the sink. A burst of pops follows. More glass shatters before it registers that someone is shooting at us. Pat shrieks and spins away, topples across the table, and crashes to the floor. She's face-down when I dive down beside her. My heart all but seizes up when I see blood streaming off the end of her nose and puddling on the floor. Pat's not moving and doesn't answer my anguished pleas to tell me she's okay.

The shooting seems to have stopped. I douse the lights and snag the phone off the counter while I dash back. For an interminable minute, I fixate on her blood as it pools on the floor. Now in full panic mode, I dial 9-1-1 and explain that Pat has been shot and is lying comatose in a lake of blood on my kitchen floor.

The operator asks me to hang on while she dispatches emergency services. "Sir, help is on the way, but I need you to tell me as much as you can about what's happening," she says when she returns. "Do you know who was shooting at you? Is the shooter in the house?"

"No. It came from the backyard."

"Are the doors locked?"

I check the back entry and run to the front door to confirm it's also locked, then scurry through the upstairs rooms to make sure the windows are closed and locked. "All good. I'll check the basement."

"Sir?"

"What?" I ask from the top of the stairs.

"Wait for the police and let them check."

Doesn't sound like bad advice. But. "You won't send paramedics in until they're sure the house and yard are clear?"

"Correct."

Well, that decides it. Pat needs help now. I flick the switch and scamper down the basement stairs, too terrified about her to be tentative. The windows are all closed. Nobody lurks around the corner with a gun. I tell the emergency operator that the basement is clear. "I'll check the yard now."

"Stay inside, sir!" the operator snaps with a trace of exasperation. "Police are on the scene."

Pat is still down amid a growing pond of blood. At least she's breathing. Deano is quivering and whining in the corner. "What about an ambulance?" I ask.

"Minutes away, sir."

"She's still breathing," I announce before peeking out the back-door window. Seeing nothing, I flip the switch for the outside lights and take another look.

"Police," a taut voice says from the other side of the glass. "Turn the damned lights off and unlock the door!"

I douse the lights and have my fingers on the lock before I gather my wits. How do I know who's outside? "I need to see you first."

"Sir?" I hear from the telephone handset still in my raised hand. "What's going on?"

"You talking to 9-1-1?" a deep voice shouts from outside.

"Yeah," I reply.

A big hand holding a shield appears in the window. "Give them my shield number. My name is Cho. They can confirm that from my shield number."

The voice on the phone is beginning to lose its calm professionalism. "Sir? *Sir!* Is everything all right?"

I relay the cop's name and shield number. She assures me that Officer Cho is legit, so I swing the door open.

The big cop steps inside and spins me against the wall and starts to pat me down. "Keep your hands where I can see them."

"Hey! This is my house. I made the 9-1-1 call."

"Then we won't have any problems, will we?" he says before pulling the wallet out of my back pocket.

"Hurry up! Pat's hurt!"

More footsteps enter the kitchen before he releases me and hands my wallet back. A menacing female cop stands in the open doorway. Our watchdog touches a tentative nose to her hand. She absently scratches behind Deano's ear.

Officer Cho nods at me. "He lives here."

Okay, so getting the new Illinois driver's license paid off.

"I'll clear the rest of the house," the newcomer says before she marches down the hall with gun in hand. Deano bounds along at her heels. Scratch his ears and he'll follow you anywhere. Anytime, apparently.

I stifle a strangled laugh as I watch them go, then turn to Cho. "Get the paramedics in here."

"As soon as my partner gives the all-clear," he replies as he drops to his knees beside Pat.

"How is she?" I ask anxiously.

"Breathing. Decent pulse. Can't tell you any more than that."

I sink into an empty chair. Pat may be breathing and her heart may still be pumping, but even I know that the outcome of a bullet to the head comes in varying shades of bad. Cho continues to monitor Pat, clearly concerned and doing what he can to help. Sure, he was a little rough with me, but I suppose walking into a shooting scene is a touch nerve-wracking.

"Sorry if I was harsh with you," I say.

He shrugs. "Harsh? That was nothing, sir. You oughtta hear some of the shit we get called for trying to help. No worries."

"All clear!" the woman cop calls from the stairs.

"Front door unlocked?" Cho asks me after he tells the 9-1-1 operator to send the paramedics.

"No," I reply as the reflection of emergency lights splashes across the living room walls. I'm off like a puppy to kibble, anxiously holding the front door open as a couple of paramedics hustle into the house with a crash cart. Try as I might to squeeze back into the suddenly crowded kitchen, I can't see what's happening with Pat before she's wheeled away and I'm alone with Deano and Constable Cho.

I grab my car keys, run out to my car, and give chase to the ambulance.

After two hours pacing the emergency waiting room, all I know for sure is that Pat is in a trauma room. I've been informed that only her family will be apprised of her condition. Nonetheless, I'm still here an hour later when I encounter a distraught woman at the coffee vending machine. A quick look pegs her as Pat's mother.

"Mrs. O'Toole?" I ask. When she makes eye contact, I continue. "My name is Tony Valenti. I'm a friend of Pat's. I was hoping—"

Pat's mother levels a shaking finger at me. "You got her mixed up in your troubles. My daughter was worried for you and look where it's gotten her!"

"I had no idea—"

"You will not see my daughter again if I have anything to say about it!" she shouts. "Stay away from her. You broke her heart in high school."

I did?

"I won't have you hurt her anymore!" After a final malevolent glare, she turns her back to me and stomps away.

While I'm stunned by the attack, at least it suggests that Pat's still alive.

CHAPTER TWENTY-ONE

I'm headed back to the vending machines when I spy morning daylight peeking through a window blind and glance at my watch. It's nearing seven o'clock. The hearing for a continuance in Judge Mitton's courtroom will be underway in just over two hours. I have time to get home and make it to court on time if I leave right now, traffic willing. It's not as if I'm accomplishing anything at the hospital anyway. Decision made, I purchase the biggest flower arrangement in the gift shop and leave instructions to deliver it to Pat. Then I hurry out. Thankfully, my car hasn't been towed from the Emergency parking lot—an unexpected miracle.

I tune in to WGN Radio for the seven o'clock news, which provides more info about Pat's condition than I received at the hospital. The *Tribune* and local television and radio will shamelessly exploit her shooting, citing her as "one of our own" to justify the exploitation of her life-and-death struggle. After recounting the scant details of the shooting itself, the announcer continues, "At this hour, we can tell you that Pat has survived several hours of surgery but her condition remains guarded. Her family has asked for privacy during this difficult time in their lives."

"And in *ours*," a solemn newsroom colleague adds.

"Yes. Stay tuned to WGN for updates and the latest on this breaking news story."

A Cedar Heights PD cruiser is parked in the driveway when I arrive home. A drab brown Ford Taurus sedan festooned with antennas that screams "unmarked police car" is parked on the street. The front doorway is again strung with yellow crime-scene tape. In a departure from the last time our home was a crime scene, a policeman is standing guard. I greet and thank him before going inside. The kitchen sink and counter are a mess of broken glass and debris, but someone has swept the glass off the floor and mopped up Pat's blood. Looking through the empty kitchen window frame, I'm surprised to see Detective Plummer standing in the middle of the backyard with Deano at his side. What is he doing here? Our eyes meet and I let them in.

"How's your lady friend?" he asks with evident concern.

I recite what little I know, then add, "I didn't expect to find you here."

"I heard about this on the radio and decided to stop by. Never know what will end up being of interest to a case."

Meaning Papa's case, no doubt. I don't want to consider the possibility of Pat's shooting turning into a matter for a homicide detective.

"I have to get showered and dressed to make it to court at nine."

"You go ahead," he says. "I'll see what I can find out about Miss O'Toole's condition."

After thanking him, I head inside to speed shower, speed shave, and speed dress. Plummer is poking around a bullet hole near the kitchen window when I return.

"Any update on Pat?" I ask.

"She's out of surgery and out of immediate danger," he

replies as he follows me into the living room. "The entry wound was through the eye. I don't know how deep the bullet penetrated or how much damage it did. I'm afraid she lost the eye."

I step back and lean against the sofa for support. A vision of Pat's bright green eyes swims into my head. I wonder how much of the intelligence that burns behind those eyes might be lost, then slide off the armrest and sink onto the cushion where she sat only hours ago.

I feel a hand on my forearm and look up to find Plummer kneeling in front of me. "You okay?" he asks. I nod. "Sorry to hit you with that. I thought you'd want to know."

I *do* want to know, but this is devastating.

Plummer carries on. "The doctors aren't telling us much. We won't be allowed to question her for at least a few days, so she's either doped to the gills or they're not sure she's going to pull through. Head wounds are unpredictable as hell, Mr. Valenti. I wouldn't expect to hear anything definitive for a couple of days. If you're so inclined, pray."

I struggle to process the news. An enormous lump in my throat precludes answering.

"I'll touch base if I learn anything else."

"Thanks," I manage to croak. I'll take any updates I can get. They sure as hell won't be coming from Mrs. O'Toole.

Plummer backs away and stands up. "You wanna hear my thoughts about what happened here last night?"

"Yes."

"A couple of the uniforms were talking about you being vandalized. Tires slashed and a fire set on the porch?"

I nod.

"The tires? Could be a random act of vandalism. Arson on your front porch a month later? Maybe the two incidents amount to targeted vandalism. But someone shooting at you here a few weeks after that?"

"Not vandalism?" I ask weakly.

"You should have been a detective. Come with me." He leads me back through the kitchen and out the back door. Then he walks over by the kitchen window and points to several small holes in the wall. "The people you're up against in this eminent domain business have a lot of money and power."

That's not exactly a news flash, Detective.

"Agreed?" he prompts while I stare back at him.

"Agreed."

"Whoever did this managed to put two shots through a big window from short range. We found ten shell casings out here, so that's eight misses. Our suspect isn't a marksman. If a professional had been sent to take you out, you'd be on a slab at the coroner's office."

"That's a comforting thought."

"This looks pretty amateurish to me. You might want to consider staying somewhere else for a while."

Like I should crawl into a hole and leave Papa in the lurch while the cops do whatever it is they're going to do about this? Not to mention letting Cedar Heights take the house unopposed? Absolutely not.

Perhaps reading my thoughts, Plummer sighs. "Amateurs are unpredictable. An amateur might come at you anywhere and at any time. Probably best that you're not out in public any more than you need to be."

The bicyclist again comes to mind, but that didn't involve Pat. Besides, I'm pretty sure it was just a kid on a bicycle, not a shooter. "Any suspects come to mind?"

Plummer looks me in the eye. "You tell me."

Have I pissed off anyone enough to prompt them to shoot me? Has Pat? We probably both have somewhere along the way. If we're talking recently, though, the eminent domain issue seems the most likely trigger. I leave for court with the unsettling specter of some nut stalking me with a gun. Someone I won't see coming.

CHAPTER TWENTY-TWO

I'm hands-free in the Porsche on Cicero Avenue, uncharacteristically weaving in and out of traffic at twenty miles per hour above the posted speed limit. If I don't hit anything or get pulled over, I should make it to court by nine. What the hell, if you own a Porsche, you should drive it like you're on an open Bavarian road even when you're in Chicago traffic on a winter morning, right? I'm waiting to be put through to Pat's boss at the *Chicago Tribune,* city editor Brook Atherton.

"This is Atherton." He sounds like a guy from the heart of Brooklyn. Based on his name, I had him pegged for a New England preppie. So much for my powers of deduction.

"My name is Tony Valenti."

"Pat's friend," he says immediately. "Do you have more news about her condition than we do?"

"I listened to WGN at seven."

"Then you know as much as we do."

Damn. I was hoping for more, figuring he would be in touch with Pat's family.

"What can I do for you?" he asks.

"I'd appreciate it if you could keep me up to date on Pat's condition."

"What does her family think of that?"

Honesty is probably the best policy. "They won't be updating me."

"If the family take us into their confidence, I won't betray that confidence."

Suspecting that I won't be hearing from Mr. Atherton again any time soon, I bid him farewell and mash the gas pedal against the floorboard. Having successfully dodged both vehicular mayhem and the cops, I meet Mike outside our courtroom with five minutes to spare.

"How's Pat?" he asks.

I tell him what I know.

He shoots a look toward the courtroom doors. "You gonna be okay in there? You don't need to be here, man."

"Better than sitting at home thinking bad shit," I say before leading the way into court. Once we're seated, I tell Mike about Pat's colleague Theo Wilson, including the fact that he has a source with info about O'Reilly's alleged heavy steroid use.

"Keep me posted on that," he says as court is called to order.

Two minutes later, Judge Mitton is staring down at us. More precisely, he's staring down at Mike. I'm sitting quiet as a church mouse so as not to screw things up. Watching with interest from across the aisle is Alex Dempsey.

"I have your motion for a continuance, Counselor," the judge says to Mike. "I'm not sure who to be annoyed at, you for coming to court with this so close to trial or the sheriff's office for dragging their feet getting the file to you. Enlighten me."

After telling the judge that we first requested the file weeks ago, Mike gives the court a quick overview of what Luke Geffen has uncovered. "Your Honor, in light of these new developments, we need to explore Deputy O'Reilly's background in as much depth as we possibly can. We've been handicapped in our trial preparation and need more time to prepare."

Alex Dempsey opens his mouth, then clamps his lips shut when Mitton casts a smoldering glance his way.

"Exactly how does this impact your trial preparation?" the judge asks Mike.

"This new information may go to our client's state of mind at the time of the shooting, Your Honor. The information we've compiled suggests that Officer O'Reilly had a lengthy history of belligerent behavior that may be relevant to this case."

"Have you turned this information over to the prosecution?"

Mike replies, "Our information comes from public records and the Cedar Heights PD, Your Honor, information that's readily available to the prosecution. Mr. Dempsey will have any discoverable information as soon as we do."

"He'd better," Mitton warns.

"He will. We would appreciate the assistance of the prosecution to obtain Deputy O'Reilly's personnel records from the Cook County Sheriff."

The judge turns his attention to the prosecutor. "Mr. Dempsey?"

"First I've heard of it."

Mike snorts.

"*Have* you brought this to Mr. Dempsey's attention before this morning?" Mitton asks.

"No, Your Honor," Mike admits.

This draws a withering look from the judge before he turns back to the prosecutor. "Can you help speed this along, Counselor?"

Dempsey shrugs. "You know how these things are, Your Honor."

Mitton's nostrils flare. "Tell me how things are."

"It generally takes some time to pry personnel records out of the sheriff's office."

The judge's frosty gaze lingers on Dempsey for several seconds before he begins scribbling some notes. He talks while he writes. "Mr. Williams makes a valid point. Let's see if I can help smooth the way for you gentlemen."

Dempsey scowls at Mike while the judge finishes working.

"I'll have an order ready within the hour for the release of Deputy O'Reilly's personnel records to your office," Mitton tells Dempsey. "Perhaps they'll respond promptly to a request coming from you. Have my order delivered to the sheriff as soon as you get it. A copy of the personnel records *will* be in the hands of defense counsel by close of business today."

"I'll do my best, Your Honor, but the sheriff's office is an independent agency. It's not as if they drop everything when we ask for a favor."

Unless it helps the prosecution, I think.

"You're not asking a favor of them, Mr. Dempsey!" Judge Mitton thunders. "You're delivering an order of this court. If the sheriff has any difficulty distinguishing between the two, tell him to give me a call. I'll be here all day."

"I'll do my best, Your Honor."

"Your best better be good enough," the judge warns Dempsey. Then he turns his attention to us. "The defense motion for a continuance is denied."

Mike sags beside me.

The judge's eyes shift back to Dempsey. "This ruling assumes that Officer O'Reilly's *complete* personnel file is delivered to the Public Defender's office by five o'clock this afternoon. If that doesn't happen, I'll reconsider the motion for continuance *and* impose sanctions against the prosecution." After a rap of his gavel, Judge Mitton dismisses us and calls for his next case.

Well done, Judge.

Dempsey surprises me by drawing Mike aside as soon as we exit the courtroom. They talk for less than a minute before Mike walks back.

"What was that about?" I ask.

"I think Alex has an inkling of what we're going to find in O'Reilly's file."

"Why do you say that?"

"He wanted to know what our position would be if they took the death penalty off the table."

"A plea deal?"

Mike nods. "Francesco pleads guilty to first degree and the State asks the Court to agree to a life sentence."

I think of all we've learned about Andrew O'Reilly. My mind revisits the crime scene photos of our battered screen door. I recall what little Papa has told us about that night. Then I decide that, if we plea at all, we'll plea for a damned sight less than first degree murder and life in prison. "What did you say?"

"I told him we'd think about it," he replies.

The hell we will.

CHAPTER TWENTY-THREE

We're down to our last full week of trial preparation and still don't have a concrete plan. Mike has invited himself over on Saturday afternoon to discuss strategy, sweetening the offer with the news that he's bearing a gift from his sister Sara.

"What's the latest on Pat?" he asks as soon as he steps inside.

"I talked to Plummer this morning. The bullet was a twenty-two. It clipped the bridge of her nose before plowing through her eye. Probably hit glass or the window frame on the way. The brain penetration was fairly shallow. The neurologists say we can't be sure of anything at this point, but I guess there's room for a bit of cautious optimism."

"Beats the hell out of them being pessimistic, brother."

"I suppose," I mutter. As much as I want to believe everything will turn out fine, I've heard enough about head wounds over the past few days to temper my optimism. There's also the distinct possibility that even if she pulls through, the Pat I know isn't coming back. I don't want to dwell on that, so I suggest getting right to work.

Mike nods before giving me a quizzical look. "You're talking to Plummer?"

"Not about our case." I explain about finding the detective at our home the morning after Pat was shot and how helpful he's been since. "I guess he's not all bad," I conclude sheepishly.

Mike nods, then settles in at the kitchen table, legal pad and pen at the ready.

"The screen door still intrigues me," I say to kick things off. "Mr. Vaccaro next door doesn't recall ever seeing it damaged."

"We've been over this," Mike says. "Nobody can testify with certainty that the door wasn't damaged before O'Reilly arrived, or that he busted it up."

The idea of putting Brittany and/or me on the stand to testify about the door is a non-starter. We're too close to Papa to be found credible and there's too many ways Dempsey might use us to muddy the waters. Still. "I'm not ready to let it go yet," I argue.

"Get me proof that O'Reilly busted it up and I'll run with it," Mike says. When I don't respond, he changes gears. "Luke reached out to the ex-wife, but she won't talk. If we decide to put O'Reilly on trial, we'll pencil her in as a potential hostile witness. Her sister was a little more forthcoming. She's a possible witness for us."

My mind drifts. Plummer told me that Pat is up and about a bit and talking but doesn't remember the shooting and is having trouble holding a conversation.

Mike is staring at me when I tune back in. "You hearing me?"

"Sorry. My mind's wandering a bit."

"You're back now?"

"You were telling me about the ex-wife's sister?"

"She described O'Reilly as an angry, insecure man whose

bullying was fueled by steroids. Unfortunately, that describes more than a few cops."

"We've got the makings of a case against O'Reilly," I say with a welcome note of optimism. The odds of a jury buying into Papa's story about an out-of-control O'Reilly increase as the documents and potential witnesses pile up. O'Reilly's Cook County Sheriff personnel file revealed a pattern of violent behavior similar to his Cedar Heights days. It also included the revelation that O'Reilly was suspended last year for abusing a teenager while serving an arrest warrant. There's a history of this guy going apeshit on citizens.

Mike rolls his eyes. I keep pushing the O'Reilly steroids angle, he keeps throwing cold water on the notion that it matters.

"Got some good news for you," he says. "My little sis was so pissed after you got fired that she started a crowdfunding campaign to keep you solvent."

"A *what* campaign?"

"Crowdfunding, old man," Mike says loudly and slowly. "It's something people do nowadays to help folks when misfortune hits."

The doorbell pre-empts further explanation.

"Expecting company?" he asks.

"Just Penelope Brooks from Butterworth Cole."

"She's still doing work for you?" he asks in surprise. Mike knows how much Butterworth Cole charges. He also knows that I'm about broke.

"I'll explain," I call over my shoulder as I leave the kitchen.

The story behind Penelope's pending arrival is a welcome bit of serendipity. Trustee Smith called me to discuss court action to stop the village's condemnation proceedings. For obvious reasons, he can't task a village attorney with the job. Penelope drafts a far better petition than I do, so I called to ask what it would cost to have her prepare the filing, only to learn that Herbert Cumming has fired me as a client. Nice of him to let me know. Penelope apologized and offered her regrets over my demise at Fleiss Lansky.

"I didn't say I won't do it," she said with a chuckle when I started to say goodbye. "This just means I can't do it officially and can't bill you."

"I couldn't ask you to do that."

"You didn't ask. I'm offering."

"Really—"

"Don't argue," Penelope had ordered me curtly. She gave me her personal email address and told me to send her the pertinent details. That was on Wednesday. She called last night to ask if she could drop off a draft today. She hands me a legal-size envelope when I open the front door. "Here you are, sir. One petition for an injunction. No charge."

"Much appreciated. Thanks for coming by on a Saturday."

"No problem. I'm on my way out to the burbs to see my brother and his family. You're on the way." Her concerned eyes focus on mine. "How's Pat?"

She gets the same update I gave Mike.

"I'll keep her in my prayers," she murmurs when I finish. Then she looks up and down the street and says, "Nice neighborhood. Love the trees. I miss that, living in the city."

"It's worth saving," I quip.

"Absolutely!"

"Wanna come in for a beer or something?"

She shakes her head. "That might be fun, but they're waiting for me."

I pat the envelope and turn to Mike, who has followed me to the door. After introductions, I say, "Penelope has been kind enough to draft a petition asking for an injunction to stop the village from proceeding with the condemnation. Pro bono."

"That's downright decent of you," he tells her.

"You won't report me to the ABA?" she asks with a playful smile.

"Screw 'em," Mike says with an answering grin. "Sounds like you've done some good work for Tony and Francesco."

Penelope's eyes cut to me.

I smile. "She sure has."

Her cheeks redden as she says, "Thanks." Herbert Cumming probably doesn't dole out much praise.

"Mike's little sister has started some sort of funding crowd thing to keep my head above water," I announce.

"Crowd-*funding*," Mike says with an exaggerated shake of his head. "Twelve-thousand bucks raised, last I heard."

"Cool!" Penelope exclaims.

"Twelve thousand dollars?" I ask incredulously.

"And she's just getting started."

I turn to Penelope and pat the envelope again. "Sounds like I can afford to pay you for this."

She waves my offer aside. "Stop. This is the least I can do after you bailed me out in court."

"What are you talking about?" Mike asks.

"I was floundering in court when we were arguing for the foreclosure injunction," Penelope replies. She smiles and hooks a thumb at me. "Then this guy gets up and blows the village attorneys away."

"Our boy Tony is a courtroom brawler?" Mike muses.

"I don't know about a brawler, but he's really good in a courtroom," she replies. "Quick on his feet. Smooth as silk."

"Interesting," Mike says thoughtfully.

"I should be off to my brother's," Penelope says. "Have a look at the petition and let me know if you want anything changed."

"Will do," I reply. "Thanks again."

"Happy to help. I feel as if I'm fighting on behalf of the good guys for a change," she adds with a grin.

"The mayor and his pals are in deep shit against you and

Trustee Smith," Mike says with a chuckle when the door closes behind Penelope. Then he slaps a hand on my shoulder and meets my gaze. "I gotta tell you, Tony, I'm stretched really thin at work these days and here you are, a courtroom wizard and suddenly a man of independent means with time on your hands."

"Independent means, my ass," I counter with a chuckle. "Thank Sara for me. Give her a hug, a smooch, whatever she wants."

"You got it, brother. Now, as I was saying, you sound like every public defender's wet dream. How about you take on a little more of the trial lawyering?"

"Such as?"

"Let's expand on my previous request. Argue a few more motions. Handle a witness or two or three."

"I'm not sure I have the chops to get up in criminal court without screwing up and sending my father to jail, or worse."

"Penelope says you do and I remember you bragging on how you kicked ass in moot court at law school. Don't sell yourself short, man. Believe in yourself."

He means well, so I smile and nod. The fortune cookie platitudes bounce harmlessly off the towering walls of self-doubt that surround me. I can probably handle some minor witnesses to take some pressure off Mike, but I won't let him make the mistake of handing me anything critical to our hopes.

CHAPTER TWENTY-FOUR

I awaken Sunday morning to find a legal pad in my lap, right where it was when I fell asleep on the couch last night. The scribbling on the pad is a list of the pros and cons of putting Sheriff's Deputy O'Reilly on trial. There's no question that he was guilty of bullying my parents, a score I have no way to settle. Putting him on trial is the only retribution open to me, a realization that gives me pause. I can't allow a subconscious desire for revenge to color my assessment of the best way to defend Papa. I set the notes aside and pore over the discovery materials from the state's attorney yet again. Nothing new there.

My thoughts turn to Pat, who has never been far from my mind over the past week. I haven't heard from Brook Atherton since I asked him to talk to Pat's mother about adding me to her hospital visitor list. A call to the nurse's station confirms it hasn't been done, so I decide to take matters into my own hands and call Pat's cell phone. The woman who picks up isn't Pat. With a sinking feeling, I suspect I'm speaking to her mother.

"May I speak to Pat?"

"Who is this?" she asks.

"Tony Valenti."

Mrs. O'Toole's reply is a dial tone. The phone rings two minutes later while I'm adding milk to a cup of coffee.

"Tony?"

"Pat?"

"Did you just call?"

"Yes."

"Mom!" Pat snaps before covering the phone so I don't hear what comes next. A moment later, sounding weary and exasperated, she says, "I got your flowers. Why haven't you visited? Are you okay?"

"I'm okay," I reply while relief floods through me. She sounds pretty much like herself.

"So, why haven't you come?" When I hesitate, not wanting to precipitate a dust-up between her and her mother, Pat quickly intuits the reason. "Jesus Christ, Mom! I *told* you I wanted Tony to visit. You didn't put his name on the list, did you?"

I can't hear Mrs. O'Toole's reply.

"I'll tell the nurses to let you in," Pat tells me. "Get your ass down here, Valenti."

I can't help but grin. *Yup, that's our Pat.*

When I arrive on her ward forty minutes later, a nurse tells me that Pat's asleep, orders me not to wake her, and then directs me to wait in the hallway outside the closed door of her room. A diminutive, rail-thin Black man with a close-cropped head of snow-white hair sits on the floor. I notice a cleric's collar when he looks up at me.

"Here to see Pat?" he asks.

I nod.

He gets to his feet to shake my hand. "Reverend Alvin Jakes. If I'm not mistaken, you're Tony Valenti?"

I return his handshake a little uneasily. How does this guy know who I am?

"Pat has mentioned you."

She hasn't mentioned Jakes to me. "Are you from Pat's church?"

"Lord, no!" he chortles. "My congregation is in Lawndale, Mr. Valenti. Has she mentioned the work she does with us there?"

"She hasn't." Lawndale is one of Chicago's longest suffering Black neighborhoods.

"We're working to reclaim the community. Pat has chronicled the work and championed the effort every step of the way. I don't think we could have kept the funding going without her turning a spotlight on Lawndale whenever the effort has flagged." He pauses to chuckle. "She's also held a few political feet to the fire as needed. Our girl even takes a regular turn wielding a hammer and paintbrush on a regular basis."

Why am I not surprised?

"I heard your phone call," Jakes says. "Don't be too hard on Pat's mother. This has scared the heck out of her."

I'm unable to muster much empathy.

"The important thing now is that you're here," Jakes says. Then he tells me that he's been following the tale of our neighborhood. "I've also been following the news about your father ever since Pat told me she knew him," he adds soberly. "I say a prayer for y'all every day."

"Thank you."

"Uh-huh. I did some time as a younger man, so I know something of what your daddy's going through. Getting caught up in our justice system is no treat. If there's anything I can do for you folks, be sure to let me know."

The reverend's good heart moves me deeply. "Thanks again."

"Just doing the Lord's work as best I know how."

I nod at the door. "How is she?"

"Getting better by the day."

The nurse I'd spoken to marches past us and into Pat's

room. Two minutes later, she steps out and smiles at Jakes. "She's awake. You can go in now, Reverend."

"Thank you," Jakes replies graciously. When the nurse frowns at me for taking a step to follow, the reverend takes my elbow. "Tony's with me, Alva. Pat's real eager to see him."

His endorsement wipes the frown from her face.

"Thanks," I murmur as he draws me inside.

"I'll leave you two to visit," he whispers before he slips out with a parting wink. It's hard to feel anything but positive in the presence of his mischievous grin and twinkling eyes. I didn't even mind when he characterized my profession as "trafficking in American justice" and likened us to practitioners of the oldest profession. All said with a smile, of course.

"Is that you, Tony?"

"It's me," I reply while stepping into Pat's field of vision. A bundle of wires and tubes snakes away from the bed to a bank of monitors and equipment that tower above her. She studies me with her remaining eye. A thick bandage covers the left side of her face, held in place by strands of gauze wrapped around her head.

She looks me up and down. "You're really okay?"

"I'm fine."

"I'm sorry," she says with a frown. "Mom means well but she can be a little overbearing."

"Just looking out for you," I reply diplomatically.

This prompts a sad smile. "I've been worried about you."

"I'm good. Do you remember what happened?"

"I remember you making coffee and recall hearing the window break. Then I woke up in the hospital. Who was shooting at us?"

"I don't know. You need to stay away from me once you're out of here."

"The hell I will," she says. Then she seems to lose focus.

When her eye settles on mine a moment later, I can tell she's lost the thread of our conversation.

"I'm serious, Pat. You should avoid me until the cops figure out what's going on."

"This probably has something to do with the village. I'm not going to let those bastards run me off."

I smile. "I'll have to run you off myself?"

"You're not getting rid of me that easily, Valenti," she retorts with a weak return smile.

My thoughts stray to what might have been if the bullet had been a fraction more accurate and resolve to be part of whatever life fate has in store for Pat, playing whatever role she wants me to.

"It hurts," she says wearily as she settles back onto her pillow. "Did you know that shockwaves from bullets cause nasty concussions?"

I shake my head and settle into a chair beside the bed. "You've got a concussion?"

"Maybe two. I had a cut and an enormous goose egg on the back of my head when they brought me in."

It all comes back now—Pat toppling over the table and crashing onto the tile floor.

"When they think I'm asleep, Mom and Dad talk about what the doctors and nurses tell them. I forget half of it, but I remember enough to know I'm getting better."

"So Reverend Jakes tells me."

She smiles. "You met the Reverend?"

"I did."

"I love that man," she says quietly. When she falls silent, I'm not sure if she's lost the thread again or if she's simply thinking about Reverend Jakes.

Her eye is only half-open when Nurse Alva bustles back into the room five minutes later and gives me a look of disapproval when she sees how tired Pat is. "Time for meds and a nap."

"At least they don't poke me in the ass," Pat mutters while the nurse sticks a needle into her IV line. When Nurse Alva tries to shoo me out, Pat's hand inches out from under the covers to rest on mine. "Let him stay until I'm zonked out."

The nurse nods and departs.

"What's happening on Liberty Street?" Pat asks.

I tell her about Penelope's injunction and add, "Trustee Smith held a press conference today and asked folks to keep you in their prayers."

Her eye widens in surprise. "What was that about?"

"He said he wanted to discuss the *Trib*'s story about redevelopment at the next village meeting and claims the mayor shut him down. He's questioning what's really going on, what the mayor's hiding. Then he presented a slide show of what he called the other ninety-five percent of the houses on Liberty Street that Titan and its minions were hiding from the public."

Pat smiles. "Sounds like the election campaign is underway."

I smile back. "Smith claimed that his little dog-and-pony show was designed to shine a little light in the dark corners where Mayor Brown and his cronies are trying to 'ram this travesty through in an undemocratic manner,' or words to that effect. He threatened legal action if the paper can't get to the bottom of it, then urged the attorney general and feds to get involved."

Pat's brow furrows. "How did I play into this?"

"Smith wondered if the shooting might have been related."

"Wow. That's pretty strong stuff."

I nod with satisfaction. "Yes, it is. Now we wait to see what comes of the village board meeting on February fourth."

But first, the battle for Papa's life is about to commence.

CHAPTER TWENTY-FIVE

It's eerily still in the Cook County courtroom on Tuesday morning as we await the start of Papa's trial. The chessboard that is pre-trial strategy has been carefully set. Preliminary motions have been heard and argued; opening moves have been painstakingly plotted. We're about to enter into the fog of battle, where the best-laid plans seldom survive first contact with the enemy. For the first time in my courtroom experience, the terminology of warfare seems wholly appropriate to the stakes.

The combatants are assembled and in position. I'm at the defense table with Mike on my left. Papa is seated to my right. Only my father's restless fingers and haunted eyes betray the fear and apprehension that must be churning inside him. He's dressed in a wine-colored suit Mama coaxed him into buying years ago at Montgomery Ward. The $700 suit I picked up for him to wear during the trial has been returned to the store; deemed unsuitable by Mike. "He's an elderly blue-collar guy. The jury should see him as they'd expect to see a man of his station in life."

Across the aisle sits Alexander Dempsey, decked out in a conservative blue suit replete with a miniature American flag pinned to the lapel. Beside him is a severe woman we've seen on and off in the pre-trial hearings. Sylvia Perez is an up-and-comer in the state's attorney's office.

Behind the tables for the prosecutors and the defense team, several rows of chrome and fabric chairs extend to the back of the courtroom. Detective Jake Plummer sits directly behind Dempsey and Perez, looking much as he did the evening this nightmare began. As lead investigator, he's one of only two potential witnesses allowed in the courtroom throughout the proceedings. The other is Plummer's partner, who is seated beside him. The partner is a little taller, a little older, and a little balder. His department store suit struggles to contain his swelling paunch. A couple of junior assistant state's attorneys sit quietly alongside the detectives, ready to run errands as needed. They remain in the background to promote the fiction that the respective sides in the courtroom have more or less equal manpower to draw upon. Given that the day will begin with jury selection, the courtroom is otherwise largely deserted.

When Judge Mitton arrives just after eight, I wipe my sweaty palms on the pant legs of my suit while my gut starts to churn out the first wave of what promises to be buckets of stomach acid. We spend fifteen minutes arguing about jury selection. When we're done, the judge spends a minute scribbling notes while the tension builds.

The courtroom has been updated to accommodate modern electronic and security requirements. Windowless off-white walls rise up to white acoustic-ceiling tiles. The carpet is a light shade of gray. Harsh fluorescent lighting pours down on the straight-edged minimalism of the bar, bench, and witness stand, all equally devoid of character. My mind wanders to mental images of comfortable old courtrooms conjured up by reading southern novels—aging rooms with imperfect glass in high windows that bend shafts of sunlight pouring in from a blue sky. Stately ceiling fans whirring overhead stir sultry air pregnant with human sweat and anguish. The picture strikes me as more humane, less contrived, less coldly calculated to deliver assembly line justice... less frightening for a fallen son fighting for his father's life.

Judge Mitton brings my meandering mind to heel. "We won't be leaving here today until we've sworn in our jury and gotten the prosecution case underway, so you can either cancel your evening plans or make sure we don't fritter away the day with needless delays. Understood?"

We get to work. Twelve jurors and two alternates are selected before lunch recess. The prosecution works hard to block minority jurors, but we manage to seat four. As Mike explains it, "If this trial turns on Deputy O'Reilly's behavior, the State's worst nightmare is a jury of folks who have plenty of experience dealing with cops like him."

We want those jurors for that very reason. What a system.

"Looks like Judge Mitton is going to keep things moving along," Mike says happily as we leave the courthouse to eat. "I hate trials that drag on longer than they need to."

"Billable hours," I remind him. "The name of the game."

"Not around here. How's Pat?"

I tell him about my hospital visit and finish by mentioning Reverend Jakes, launching into a brief explanation of who he is.

Mike holds up a hand to stop me. "So, you've met *the* Reverend Alvin Jakes, have you?" he says with a slow smile.

I nod.

Mike chuckles. "He's quite a character, isn't he?"

"He is."

"Pat's well-known in the Black community. She's done good coverage over the years—sympathetic coverage. A lot of folks regard her as a sort of honorary sister."

"I didn't know," I say with an inner smile. Physically, they don't come any whiter than Pat. Spiritually, maybe not so much.

When we return to the courtroom after lunch, the contrast from the sleepy atmosphere of the morning is startling. The press is out in force, including a contingent from *Court TV*. The reporters are seated behind the rows of seats reserved for family members of the victim. Only a few of them are filled, save for a handful of police officers and the public mouthpiece of the Fraternal Order of Police—the police union commonly known by the acronym FOP. More spectators are eventually allowed in to fill the empty seats.

Behind us sit Mr. and Mrs. Vaccaro, Mr. Rosetti, the LaSusas, and a handful of other neighbors and parishioners Mama and Papa befriended over the years. I recognize several men and women who worked long years alongside Papa in the laundry room at Cook County Hospital. The rest of the courtroom is filled with God alone knows whom. Mike calls them the usual collection of kooks and curiosities that populate a courtroom. Oddly enough, to me anyway, many of them seem to know one another. They carry on spirited conversations while we await the judge.

"All rise," a bailiff orders when the door behind the bench finally swings open. "Cook County Criminal Court is now in session, the Honorable Judge Myron Mitton presiding." The judge marches in and drops into the high-backed chair behind his bench. After arranging some papers, he settles back to survey his domain. He's fully engaged today. His eyes move from the prosecution table to ours and beyond, darting to and from in a bird-like display of alertness, an unsettling mannerism I've noticed before. It's never seemed as exaggerated as it does this afternoon, or perhaps that's just my tightly wound nerves amplifying events.

"Good afternoon," Judge Mitton says to the assembled host.

A chorus of reciprocal greetings echoes through the courtroom before the judge quiets the crowd with a light tap of his gavel. "Let's bring in our jury."

Alex Dempsey plants himself before the jurors once they're settled and begins his opening statement. After the usual rhetoric about how the prosecution will explain what happened on the evening of September seventeenth, Dempsey launches into an attack on my father. With a look of contempt and a voice dripping with disdain, he aims an accusing finger across the courtroom at Papa. "The defendant has a long history of defying the authority and traditions of civil society, ladies and gentlemen. While the rest of us pay our property taxes—perhaps with a little grumbling," Dempsey adds with a knowing glance at his fellow taxpayers, "the defendant thinks *he*'s entitled to a free ride. The Village of Cedar Heights felt otherwise and took action to recover its delinquent taxes. This eventually led to a foreclosure action. Sheriff's Deputy Andrew O'Reilly visited the defendant's house on September seventeenth to deliver an eviction notice, a task that is routinely completed without incident. But when this... this, *individual* was served, he flew into a rage. While the unsuspecting deputy stood on the defendant's front step carrying out his duty on behalf of society, the defendant ruthlessly gunned him down in a merciless barrage of bullets."

When Dempsey pauses for a sip of water, Mike dips his head and whispers, "Only one of which found its target from a range of two feet or thereabouts. Now *there's* a stone-cold killer for you. Alex is overplaying his hand."

Dempsey rattles on for a few more minutes, promising to prove his accusations "*well* beyond a reasonable doubt." He closes by pleading with the jury to "do the right thing and send a message that Cook County will not tolerate wanton violence against our brave law enforcement professionals who put their lives on the line for us each and every day." If nothing else, the prosecution's opening statement seems to bear out Mike's contention that Papa's prosecution is at least in part a bone being tossed to the FOP.

Judge Mitton turns to us. "Does the defense wish to make an opening statement?"

"The defense reserves our opening statement, Your Honor," Mike replies. Our opening will be the first salvo in our attack on the prosecution's argument when we present the defense case. It seems prudent to keep our near total lack of strategy to ourselves.

A procession of witnesses who establish the facts of the case fills the rest of the afternoon: the 9-1-1 operator who fielded the initial call; the responding police officers and paramedics; the police department evidence technicians who processed the scene; the coroner who performed the autopsy on O'Reilly. The coroner posits that the downward trajectory of the bullet that struck the deputy is best explained by Papa shooting from the top of the porch while O'Reilly stood at the base of the steps. Mike sits quietly through it all, voicing only a handful of objections when witnesses stray from fact into conjecture about motive or the unknowable circumstances of the shooting. Judge Mitton sustains them all. The prosecution trots out its psychologist following a brief recess. After an interminable recitation of the man's credentials and curriculum vitae, Dempsey finally gets around to exploring the shrink's findings about Papa. They spend a ridiculous amount of time on this, expounding upon theories of behavior and hypotheticals while the jurors do their best to follow along—not to mention simply stay awake. The shrink eventually finishes up by asserting that Papa is some sort of homicidal sociopath. This finally gets the jurors' attention.

Mike assures me that dueling psychologist testimony is seldom the turning factor in a trial. He begins his cross-examination by strolling over to stand a few feet away from the psychologist. "Would it be fair to say that most anyone in Mr. Valenti's position would be a little out of sorts after the shooting?"

"Out of sorts?"

"Not quite himself. Maybe in a bit of shock about what's happened?"

The doctor ponders this for a moment. "Perhaps somewhat. But given the socio—"

"So," Mike says to cut off an extended reply, "we've established that Mr. Valenti may not have been his usual self the night of the shooting."

"I didn't—" the doctor manages to say before Mike cuts him off again.

"Please, Doctor," he says with an engaging smile, "in the courtroom, *I* get to ask the questions and *you* get to answer them. If I'm ever in your office, then you can tell me whatever else is on your mind. Fair enough?" Mike casts a quick look toward the jury while he says this, the unspoken subtext being "Doesn't this guy ever shut up?"

Mike carries on conversationally, "Given that Mr. Valenti might not have been quite himself in the wee hours of September eighteenth, how many more times did you visit with him and, if you don't mind telling us, how often did you go? Every couple of weeks? Every month? Every other month?"

"Objection!" Alex Dempsey finally says in an effort to break Mike's stride.

"Grounds?" Mitton asks.

"Mr. Williams isn't allowing the witness to answer the questions. He's asking multiple questions at once."

"One question at a time, Mr. Williams," Mitton orders.

Mike bows his head towards the judge. "I'm sorry, Your Honor." He eases a little closer to the witness box and asks again how many times the doctor examined Papa.

"As is standard in such cases, my assessment is based upon the initial psychological assessment that was undertaken in the hours after arrest," the psychologist says tartly.

Mike cocks his head to the side for a long moment before he asks his next question. "Surely, you're not telling us that your findings are based entirely upon the bail report prepared in the Cedar Heights lockup by a social worker on the night of the shooting, are you, Doctor?"

"That is standard practice, Counselor," the doctor replies, "as I'm sure you know."

"No follow-up interview or additional assessments were carried out during the months Mr. Valenti has been incarcerated?" Mike asks in wide-eyed disbelief.

"There never is, Counselor, as you also know," the doctor replies testily.

"Interesting." Mike cocks an eyebrow and shakes his head in wonder. While Alex Dempsey probably wants his witness to answer the initial questions and shut up, Mike is making no effort to curtail the doctor's snide asides. "Let's back up to your initial testimony, shall we Doctor?"

"If you want."

"That was quite an impressive list of credentials you and Mr. Dempsey told us about," Mike observes.

The doctor nods. He's clearly pleased to have his qualifications acknowledged again.

"You have a great deal of experience testifying in court, don't you?"

"I do."

"In how many trials have you testified?"

The shrink puffs up. "I don't keep track."

"Really?" Mike asks.

"Really."

"During a trial in this courthouse just last month, do you remember being asked and answering that same question?"

"Vaguely."

Mike walks toward the witness box until he's looking down his nose at the good doctor. "Do you recall replying that you have testified upwards of two hundred times, perhaps as many as three hundred?"

"That rings a bell. Yes."

"And counting today, Doctor, how many of those times have you given testimony at the request of the prosecution?"

"Many times."

"Have you ever, even once, been asked to or offered your services to defense counsel?"

"I don't believe I have."

"Is your answer 'zero times?'"

"It is."

"Approximately how many days a year do you spend testifying in court?"

"Again, that's not something one keeps track of."

"Humor me, Doctor. You must keep track for income tax purposes, if nothing else. Would it be fair to say that you testify in one hundred cases per year?"

"Probably not that many."

"Fifty?"

"I really can't say."

"I did a little checking," Mike says. "Just locally, you know… Cook County, Kane County, Lake County, DuPage County, Will, McHenry. The Chicago metro area. Did you know that court records show that you've testified in at least five hundred and twenty cases in the past five years?"

"If you say so."

"That's over one hundred cases every year!" Mike marvels. "If you're in court for even one or two days in each of those trials and spend a day or so assembling your assessments, being an expert witness for prosecutors is pretty much a full-time job for you."

"Is there a question somewhere in there?" Alex Dempsey mutters.

"Would it be fair to say that you're essentially a full-time employee of local prosecutors?" Mike asks.

"I am not an employee of any prosecutor's office," the doctor retorts haughtily. "I am a professional psychologist in private practice."

"Do you actually see patients?"

The psychologist glowers up at Mike. "No."

"Your only clients are prosecutors. Is that a fair assessment of your 'practice,' Doctor?"

After the doctor answers with a sullen "one might say that," Mike walks away from him without a second glance, leaving Judge Mitton to dismiss the witness.

"We'll adjourn here for the day," the judge announces.

We feel like we've done well. While Mike has hopefully blunted the testimony of the prosecution's psychologist by painting him as a shill for the prosecution, he cautions against getting overly excited about it. "The best thing about that is that it ended the prosecution's day on a down note and court is dark tomorrow."

"But?" I ask.

"Alex was just laying the groundwork today. He'll do his heavy lifting starting Friday."

After replaying the afternoon in my mind, Mike's little triumph over the psychologist seems a minor blip against the hours the prosecution spent laying brick after relentless brick to build a solid case against Papa.

CHAPTER TWENTY-SIX

Just after noon on Thursday, ten days after Pat was shot, Nurse Alva wheels her out of the hospital in a wheelchair and brings her to my waiting car. After running battery after battery of tests, the neurologists have concluded that Pat's brain damage falls on the mild side of the Traumatic Brain Injury spectrum. Her motor skills seem to be in decent shape, although she's experiencing occasional dizziness and balance issues. Her concussion symptoms have subsided to intermittent headaches and moderate light sensitivity. She's prone to nausea and a little vomiting, which may manifest themselves more once she's out of the hospital and exposed to more stimuli. The biggest concerns are some memory issues, a bit of slurred speech, and anxiety accompanied by mood swings. These will require therapy but will hopefully improve over time. Her eye wound is healing nicely. The hospital—perhaps prompted by the *Tribune*'s health insurance corporation—is cutting her loose. She's excited to be going home. I'm happy to be taking her.

Nurse Alva hands me a bag of medications after we settle Pat in the passenger seat. "Take care of that girl. She's a special one."

"I know," I reply with a smile.

Pat fiddles with the Porsche's entertainment system until she finds WGN. "News junkie," she says fake-apologetically before she twists halfway around in her seat to focus her right eye on me. "What's with you? Any new job prospects?"

"I'm devoting all my time to Papa's trial and getting ready for next month's Village Board meeting."

"On a diet of mac 'n cheese?" she asks with a little grin. Other than the eye patch, she's working her way back to being the same old Pat.

I shake my head. "I'm not one-hundred percent sure how it all works, but Mike's sister Sara set up a crowdfunding thing for me."

"Cool! Tell Mike or his sister to call me. I'd like to help."

"Don't worry about that. Concentrate on getting better."

"Don't make me play the wounded patient card, Valenti. Just do as you're told."

I have the good sense not to argue.

"What's your take on day one of your dad's trial?" she asks as we enter the freeway. Sunshine pours in the windshield.

"About what we expected so far," I reply before catching movement in my peripheral vision as Pat slaps a hand over her good eye and groans.

"What's wrong?"

"Sun!"

I pop the glove box open and fish around. "Brittany's sunglasses," I say as I put the case in her hand.

She puts them on. "That's better. Thanks."

"You sure? I can take you back to the hospital."

"Absolutely *not,* Valenti! Now, what did I ask you?"

"You were asking about the trial. We'll probably start the defense case on Monday or Tuesday. We're still not sure what that is."

"That's leaving things a little late. What's the problem?"

I tell her what we've got, what we're hoping for, and that we'll most likely have to go after O'Reilly. "Mike doesn't think we have enough to make it fly."

"Did you talk to Theo Wilson?"

"Just once. Atherton didn't want him talking to me."

"That bastard. I'll make sure Theo calls you."

"You're going to get lots of R and R, O'Toole. I'll call Wilson myself if I feel the need."

I doubt I will. Wilson's source is a former partner of O'Reilly's named Beau Smith, whom Luke Geffen has already spoken with. Smith claims the steroid use and long hours in the gym began in O'Reilly's early days on the Cedar Heights police force—pretty much as soon as he realized that the combination of badge, gun, and swollen biceps was nectar to law-enforcement groupies. According to Smith, O'Reilly spent many an evening at a local watering hole for cops and their hangers-on called the Cuff and Billy Club, drinking and whoring when he should have been home with his wife and kid. Interesting tidbits to be sure, but we already know O'Reilly was an asshole. There's no defense angle in that, especially given Smith's newfound reluctance to testify or to let the *Trib* identify him as a source. He's undoubtedly correct that he'd be a pariah with a lot of cops for doing so.

"The prosecution laid a solid foundation for their case," I continue. "They also did a fair job painting Papa as an unrepentant villain. I'm not sure how to go about putting a human face on a man who killed a cop."

"I've got an idea that might help."

"Good. We're starved for ideas."

"I'm coming to the trial."

"No way, Pat. You should be home resting." *And keeping out of public view until the cops catch the bastard who shot you.*

"Me sitting behind the defense table with this damned eye patch will make an impression, Tony."

"That's all we need. Evidence that Papa consorts with pirates."

Pat punches my shoulder. "Stop with the class clown crap. I'm being serious here."

"Sorry."

"All modesty aside, I've got a pretty positive public profile around Chicago. It won't hurt to have the jury see me lining up behind your father."

My initial reaction is to object to using Pat as a human prop. My second take is that it's a damned fine idea. Will Mike approve? I decide to ask him before committing to anything. "We'll see."

"The hell you will. I don't need your permission."

"Point taken." I work the Porsche into the right lane. "Detective Carter called this morning."

"Who's that?"

"He's the detective trying to find out who shot you. They have a ballistics match between the gun used to shoot you and a .22 caliber cartridge and slug used in a gang shooting three years ago. The gun itself hasn't been recovered."

"I don't get it. What's a gang shooting got to do with me?"

"Nothing," I say as we exit the freeway. "Carter told me that most gang guns are throwaways that can't be tied to a specific person unless they're recovered at the scene of a crime."

"Oh," she murmurs.

I'm starting to wonder about her neighborhood as we pass train yards and a succession of ramshackle warehouses and industrial concerns. Not exactly what I'd want to see when I look out the kitchen window with my morning coffee in hand.

We drive through the southern reaches of Humboldt Park and pass Norwegian American Hospital before Pat says, "Turn left into the alley."

We park behind a tall, narrow three-story house and Pat

leads me inside. The back door opens into a bright, wide open kitchen with a huge island. The kitchen spills into an expansive, sun-infused living room that stretches to the front of the house. The floors are a fruity hardwood, not unlike our floors on Liberty Street. It's an airy, welcoming space.

"You like?" Pat asks when she sees me gawking.

"I do! It's all yours?"

"I live in the main house and rent out a suite in the basement. Want the twenty-five-cent tour?"

"Sure."

She points at the stairs. "Let's go up."

The second floor consists of a big master bedroom at the front of the house, an updated bathroom that I suspect has been substantially enlarged, and two narrow bedrooms. One bedroom is now a home office and the other is a modest guestroom; both have a very nice view of the garage and alley. Pat pauses at the base of a set of narrow stairs leading to the third floor.

"Secret hideaway?" I ask. "Sex chamber? What lies at the top of the stairs?"

"I don't know if I'm ready for this," she murmurs anxiously. She has turned pale and is a little shaky.

"Are you okay?" She doesn't answer. When I notice a sheen of moisture glistening on her forehead, I wrap an arm around her shoulders. "Hey, no worries. I can see this later."

"I need to face it now." She takes a deep breath and climbs the stairs with me in tow. We emerge into attic space that has been converted into a spacious painting studio. Pat has clearly put a lot of time and effort into setting this up—and likely some serious coin, as well. A pair of dormer windows and a skylight cut into the steeply pitched ceiling flood the space with natural light; several light fixtures hang throughout the room. A handful of canvasses hang on the walls and a substantially complete landscape sits on an easel, awaiting only the top third of a mountain to be complete.

Beside the easel, the once-white surface of a melamine table is coated in bright splashes of paint. The vivid colors also drip down the sides of a plethora of paint containers clustered at one end of the table. The floor around the easel sports an even greater riot of color.

"You're still painting?" I ask.

"Duh." Color me stupid with a giant brush.

"You were good in school, but this stuff is brilliant. Do you sell your work?"

"Some friends and acquaintances have pieces hanging in their closets and basements," Pat deadpans, but I can tell that she's pleased with my reaction.

"Wow!" I whisper when my gaze falls upon a painting that depicts a solitary figure sitting on a beach watching the sunrise. I don't know *how* I know it's a sunrise over Lake Michigan, but I do. The painting speaks to me of welcoming the day. "You did this?"

When she nods, a tear leaks out the corner of her good eye.

"Hey," I say, wondering what I've said wrong.

She sniffles. "I've lost my depth perception. I can't paint with one eye."

My mind is racing to retrieve something I read. "Got it!" I say triumphantly.

Pat pulls back and looks up at me. "Got what? A new eye for me?"

"There was an article in one of those airline magazines about a painter who lost an eye. He didn't think he could still paint but he could. If he can, so can you."

"I don't know."

"You can. You will."

"If you say so, Pollyanna," she says with a reluctant smile. "For the record, they told me the same thing in the hospital."

"Me, doctors, art schools… all on the same page. Maybe you should start listening to me."

"Not happening!" She nods toward the painting I was admiring. "I can picture that over your fireplace."

I turn to her in surprise. "You'd sell it to me? How much?"

"It's a gift, dummy."

"You've gotta be kidding. You can sell this!"

"Don't be gauche, Valenti. Gentlemen don't argue with wounded ladies."

I guess I own a painting.

"I'm a little tired," Pat murmurs. "Let's go back downstairs."

I take her by the elbow to steer her out of the studio and down the stairs.

"You want some water?" I ask when we reach the main floor. Looking into the kitchen, I notice that Pat's house has been stocked for her return. A small mountain of gauze bandages sits on the granite kitchen counter beside an enormous Costco-sized bucket of Tylenol and what could well be a small grocery store's entire selection of fresh fruit.

"Mom," Pat says when she sees me looking. "She'll be here in a half-hour or so."

"I'd best be out of here by then."

She grimaces and walks into the living room. "I'll take that water now."

When I catch up to her, water bottle in hand, Pat has settled onto a ruby red leather sofa and pulled her feet up under her. She takes the water. "Thanks. If Mom had her way, I'd be living at home and sleeping in my old bedroom for the next month or two."

I settle onto the other end of the sofa. "That's not a bad idea. I don't like you being here by yourself."

"Ha! Like that's gonna be possible. Between Mom and Reverend Jakes and his flock, I'll be begging for solitude before long. I'll expect to see you here on a regular basis… if you don't mind coming."

"I'll be here."

"You can have a Get Out of Visiting Pat card when you're in court," she adds with a thin smile.

We chat for a few minutes during which she continues to fade as the initial excitement of coming home ebbs away.

"You don't have to wait for Mom to get here," she mumbles as her eye settles to half-mast. "I'm not being very good company."

"I'll wait right here," I reply softly as her eye closes. I find a throw blanket in the coffee table drawer, drape it over her, and sit quietly until Mrs. O'Toole arrives. I sneak out the back door as she comes in the front.

On the way home I ponder all I've learned of Pat in the past few months. I'm struck by how deeply she's rooted in her hometown and how her Chicago isn't necessarily my Chicago. My Windy City is Michigan Avenue and State Street; Wrigley Field and Grant Park; a cheesy old tune claiming that Chicago is "My Kind of Town" and other nuggets of civic boosterism. Pat is familiar with all that, but she also inhabits a city I know little to nothing about. Reverend Jakes welcomes her to Lawndale, her civic anthem is "Sweet Home Chicago," and she's rehabbed *and* lives in a house on the fringes of the city. She's doing her part to put her neighborhood back on its feet. Pat understands the vast cultural milieu of the people who live in this city, including—maybe especially—the underprivileged, who have never quite registered on my radar. I feel bad when I see them on the news and hear their sad stories; sometimes I'm even moved to indignation that people live in abject poverty in America, but my commitment to helping has never gone beyond a tax-deductible donation to the United Way. Pat, on the other hand, embraces these people and feels their suffering. She moves amongst them and champions them in print. She shines a light into the murky nooks and crannies society hopes to hide them within. She demands that we do better. She *does* better.

Were we really raised a mile apart and educated at the

same schools? There was a time when I took pride in how far and fast I had traveled from my origins. I put great stock in my career success and the social heights Michelle and I scaled to reach the upper echelon of Atlanta society. Then again, Icarus also soared higher than he dared. Turns out neither of us can fly for shit.

Though she's never strayed far from her roots, perhaps Pat's journey has yielded richer rewards and taken her further in ways that count. She's inspired me to try to do better. To be better. To make a positive difference. We'll soon know if I'm up to the challenge.

A car door slamming close behind me after I park at home and climb out of the Porsche startles me. I look up to find Phil and Sandy Russo getting out of a silver Ford Explorer in the Vaccaros' driveway.

Phil smiles and lifts a hand. "Hey, Tony!"

I pause, then plow through the snowbank separating the driveways, extending my hand as I go. "Hi, Phil. How's it going?"

He comes around the Explorer to meet me. "Doing okay."

My eyes capture his wife's. "Hi, Sandy."

Sandy doesn't say a word before she turns her back on me and hurries into the house.

"I'm developing a complex," I tell Phil as we stare after her.

"Hell, I'm sorry, Tony. I've never seen her like this with anyone. You sure you didn't steal a lollipop from her or bust up a favorite doll when you were kids?"

"Not that I remember."

I'm still tossing and turning in bed two hours later when it occurs to me that I've never seen a statement from Sandy in the discovery materials.

Why not?

CHAPTER TWENTY-SEVEN

I'm meeting Mike at a local diner near the courthouse in response to my text telling him we need to meet before court begins. He swears by the place, which seems to be something of a go-to destination for flies. The food must be good, because the greasy spoon sure can't be renowned for its décor and ambience. Maybe the extra fly protein in the food sets it apart. Maybe a touch of fly shit spices up every bite? I order coffee with a side of water.

"What's so urgent?" he asks after ordering a Big Breakfast! special.

"Do you recall seeing a statement from Sandy Russo in the discovery materials?"

He shakes his head no.

"Everything the cops have should be in that discovery, right? I've seen everything they gave you?"

"That's right," he replies with a quizzical expression. "Why?"

"My neighbor's son-in-law mentioned his wife giving a statement to the police. If she did, it's not in the discovery."

"What did she see?"

"Phil said Sandy didn't see the shooting but she overheard them arguing."

Mike's eyebrows arch. "Francesco and O'Reilly?"

"Right. Her maiden name is Vaccaro. Her folks still live next door. Maybe the cops used the wrong name."

Mike ponders the news for a moment and then pulls out his cell phone to call Luke Geffen. "Hey, Luke. Go through all of our Valenti discovery one last time and make sure that a woman named Sandy Russo or maybe Sandy Vaccaro isn't mentioned in any police reports. Hell, check all the Sandies, Sandras, and any variation of the name you can think of. Plan on lunch at my desk and clear your calendar for the afternoon." Mike pauses and looks at me. "Do you have her contact information?" After I shake my head, Mike resumes his conversation with Luke. "The husband's name is Phil Russo. Find out where they live and plan to pay her a visit after lunch."

"Let's get to court," he says after he ends the call.

Day two of Papa's trial begins with Detective Plummer on the witness stand. Dempsey uses him to lay out the version of events the prosecution wants the jury to convict upon. This takes up the entire morning. Again, Mike is content to let them build their case with only a few objections.

We meet Luke Geffen for lunch at Mike's desk in the Public Defender's office. He's a surprise. I'd expected some sort of television hard-boiled private eye type. He barely looks old enough to drink legally—a scruffy, skinny-assed kid in ripped jeans and a well-worn Chicago White Sox jersey who lost the battle with acne somewhere along the way. But he's engaging, funny, and quick as a whip. Luke confirms that the names Sandy Russo and Sandy Vaccaro are nowhere to be found in our discovery materials.

"Bastards!" I snarl.

Mike settles back in his seat and gazes up at the ceiling. "There's a reason we didn't get anything about her. Why is that?" Without waiting for a reply, he counts off one finger. "Maybe there isn't a statement."

"Phil said—" I begin.

Mike shoots an annoyed glance my way and starts over. "Maybe there isn't a statement. Maybe she had nothing new to say and a lazy beat cop didn't bother writing it up."

I hadn't thought of that.

Mike counts off a second finger. "Maybe they took a statement and didn't pass it along to the prosecution."

"But they have to," I protest.

"They're *supposed* to. Not the same thing, my friend."

"No shit," Luke chimes in.

"Why wouldn't the cops turn it in?" I ask.

"Maybe they didn't think it was important enough to type up," Mike replies. "Or maybe it said something they didn't like. Maybe it just didn't square with everything else they had."

"Something damaging to their case?" I ask.

A smile creases Mike's face. "*Now* you're thinking like a defense attorney! Taking this a step further, maybe the cops don't want something she said to see the light of day."

I look at Luke. "Did you get an address? Are you going this afternoon?"

Looking a little bemused, he answers, "Yes and yes."

"I want a verbal report before you write up the transcript," Mike says.

Luke nods, seeming to approve of the order.

"What do you mean?" I protest. "We need that transcript right away!"

Mike shakes his head. "No, we need to *hear* what she says today. We need to be very discrete, gentlemen. If the prosecution gets wind of this, they'll put her on their witness list and either depose her themselves or demand a copy of her statement to us under reciprocal discovery. Luke here is a very busy guy. It might be a day or two before this overburdened fellow gets a transcript typed up."

The light bulb finally flickers to life in my razor-sharp legal mind. "Ah."

Mike's eyes twinkle. "If they're trying to hide something, I want them to think they've succeeded."

Dempsey starts the afternoon by trying to get Plummer to agree that Papa is some sort of homicidal menace to society. When Plummer resists the invitation to play into this narrative, Mike whispers an aside that perhaps all the players in the prosecutor's camp aren't singing from the same hymnal.

Mike starts his cross-examination by walking around the defense table and addressing Plummer as if they're making conversation. "Mr. Dempsey asked you to affirm that Mr. Valenti fits the profile of sociopathic murderers you've encountered in your duties as a homicide detective. You disagreed with that assertion. Correct?"

While Plummer takes a moment to formulate his answer, Mike casts a quick look at the jury. This is the first time today he's left his seat to approach the witness stand. Several jurors have inched forward, possibly inferring from his approach that this exchange is particularly significant—perhaps more so than any prior testimony. Several hours into the proceedings, this is the first hint of the adversarial police/lawyer drama that television and movies have conditioned them to expect in a courtroom.

"I'm not a psychologist," Plummer finally mutters. "I'm not the right person to ask."

"I understand that," Mike replies graciously. He's taking care not to attack the detective, who comes across as a credible professional whom the jury seems to like. He moves a step closer. "Yet Mr. Dempsey asked you that question, Detective."

"Objection!" Dempsey says. "Does Mr. Williams have a *relevant* question for this witness, or can we move on?"

"Of course, I have questions for this witness, Your Honor," Mike says. "I'm probing a topic Mr. Dempsey opened up on direct."

"Objection overruled," Judge Mitton says with an impatient glance at Dempsey. "Proceed, Mr. Williams."

"As I was saying," Mike says to Plummer, "Mr. Dempsey clearly believes that your experience with sociopathic killers allows you to make a qualified determination of whether or not Francesco Valenti fits that mold. When you observed him on the night of September seventeenth and early hours of September eighteenth, did Mr. Valenti strike you as a prototypical sociopathic murderer?"

I hold my breath. This may be a critical moment in the trial. While Mike is confident that Plummer will not make that assertion, asking the question is still an extremely high-risk, high-reward proposition. The jury will expect Plummer to support the prosecution's claim. If he doesn't, not only does the learned doctor look like a paid shill for the prosecution, the credibility of Dempsey will take a hit. If Plummer falls in line, Mike will have to find a way to undo the damage. While I've come to think he's not such a bad guy, my money is on Plummer being in the tank for the prosecution.

"Not when I spoke with him," the detective says.

I'll be damned. Is Plummer actually on the side of justice?

"Have you had occasion to speak with Mr. Valenti since that night?" Mike asks.

"No, I haven't."

"Thank you, Detective. That's all I have for Mr. Plummer at this time, Your Honor. The defense reserves the right to recall this witness."

"Does the prosecution have anything further to ask Detective Plummer at this time?" Mitton asks Dempsey.

He doesn't, so the judge dismisses Plummer and adjourns for lunch. We should be hearing from Peter Zaluski this afternoon.

Over lunch, I make a final play to be allowed to cross-examine him. "I want a piece of that son of a bitch!"

Mike shakes his head. "Hell, no!"

"The prosecution calls Peter Zaluski to the stand," Sylvia Perez announces when court is called back into session.

I work very hard to keep my expression neutral as the village manager takes the stand. It won't do to have Papa's son looking like a deranged sociopath while Zaluski is testifying.

After establishing that he is the Cedar Heights Village Manager and has been for the past several years, Perez invites Zaluski to tell the jury about the events that put Deputy O'Reilly on our front step on the evening of September seventeenth. Zaluski surprises us by starting with Titan Development's first attempt to acquire Liberty Street and Independence Park via eminent domain.

"Is there something about that time period I don't know about?" Mike asks me anxiously. "Did Francesco have a run-in with anybody?"

"Not that I know of."

"There was no question that the village would have been well-served had that project proceeded," Zaluski says. "But Mr. Valenti and his friends had other ideas. They disrupted our plans at every turn. They even imported agitators to stir up trouble in the community."

"The hell?" Mike whispers.

"No idea," I reply. Maybe he means Teresa Keebler-Jones? "Ask for specifics on cross."

"In the end," Zaluski says sadly, "Mr. Valenti and his cohorts prevailed, although a few of them did cash in a few months later. The neighborhood has been in steep decline ever since."

"Was that the last conflict between Mr. Valenti and the Village of Cedar Heights?" Perez asks.

"Unfortunately, not," Zaluski replies. "It came to our

attention some time ago that Mr. Valenti made improvements to his home without obtaining the necessary building permits. This allowed him to hide the improvements from the village to keep his property taxes artificially low. When this came to light, we reassessed the property and sent Mr. Valenti a bill for unpaid property taxes and penalties. He refused to pay."

The sonofabitch is relishing the opportunity to deliver a little payback to my father. When Zaluski pauses for a sip of water, I realize that he's coming across as a dedicated public servant intent on doing what is best for the village. I'm not buying. Zaluski would have to be an unusually naïve character not to have seen what Titan was up to.

"Mr. Valenti's neighbors began complaining last summer that the side of his garage was damaged and had become an eyesore," he continues. "This is detrimental to the neighborhood. The last thing we want is honest Cedar Heights taxpayers footing the bill for their neighbor's house repairs and maintenance, so we sent demands for Mr. Valenti to complete the repairs. He couldn't be bothered to do so. We had no choice but to initiate foreclosure proceedings."

"Your next step was eviction?" Perez asks.

"It was. I'm afraid Deputy O'Reilly was serving an eviction notice when Mr. Valenti decided to murder him."

"Objection," Mike snaps. "Assumes facts not in evidence."

Perez rolls her eyes, a stunt that does not escape Judge Mitton. "We can do without your histrionics, Miss Perez." The judge then returns his attention to Mike. "What facts are those, Counselor?"

"It hasn't been established that Mr. Valenti murdered anyone, Your Honor. We've heard no evidence about what prompted events that evening. Mr. Zaluski certainly doesn't know—unless he was there?" Mike concludes with a sidelong glance at the village manager.

"I was attending my son's Little League playoff game,"

Zaluski replies indignantly.

Mike dismisses him without asking about his claim that Papa had been an agitator two years ago. We want him off the stand. The sonofabitch has turned out to be an effective witness for the prosecution.

"It's getting late, Counselor," Judge Mitton tells the prosecutor. "We can take a fifteen-minute recess and come back or we can adjourn for the weekend. I would prefer to hear from another witness or two if possible, assuming you can wrap up by five."

Dempsey nods. "I *would* like to call one more witness today, Your Honor."

Mitton nods back. "Court is recessed for fifteen minutes. Let's all be back in place at three forty-five."

"Five bucks says we're gonna finish with the grieving widow," Mike says. "Too bad we didn't end with Plummer. That would have been a good takeaway for the jury."

Luke Geffen arrived during Mike's cross-examination of Zaluski and is waiting patiently in a seat directly behind us. As soon as the judge sends the jury on its way, Mike spins his chair around to face Luke.

I do likewise and blurt, "Did you find her? What did she tell—"

Mike slaps an index finger across his lips and cuts his angry eyes towards the prosecution table. "Quiet."

His concern is underscored when I look up and find Dempsey leaning toward us. Mike gets to his feet. "Let's take this outside, gentlemen."

After gathering our coats and briefcases, we follow Mike out. He leads us thirty feet away from the courthouse doors before he stops and turns to Luke. "What have you got for us?"

"I found Mrs. Russo. She wasn't happy to see me but resigned herself to talking. She didn't realize I was working for the defense when she agreed to talk."

"Tell me you told her the truth," Mike says sharply.

Luke smiles. "Of course, I did. Eventually."

Mike's eyes twinkle. "What did Mrs. Russo tell you before you were able to rectify that unfortunate misunderstanding?"

"Not much," Luke replies, dealing a crushing blow to my desperate hope that Sandy would ride to Papa's rescue.

"Anything useful?" Mike asks.

"She told the police what she heard and reminded me that she hadn't been able to see the actual shooting through the hedge. When I asked her if she'd heard the shooting, she nodded and gave me a funny look, like I should have already known that."

"And then?" I ask hopefully.

"She asked who I was working for."

"So much for the happy ending," Mike grumbles.

Luke answers with a grim smile. "I managed to ask if she'd be willing to give us a statement before she slammed the door in my face."

"Shit!" I mutter.

"We've got an ear witness," Mike says. "If Sandy Russo heard everything Francesco told us was going on, this could be significant."

"And if she didn't, or doesn't admit she did?"

"Not many upstanding citizens are willing to perjure themselves in a murder trial, Tony."

That's probably true of the Sandy Vaccaro I grew up with, but the Sandy Russo I've experienced over the past few months certainly isn't the same girl, so who knows? "There's something going on with her. She's scared of something."

Mike shrugs. "Time will tell."

"What should we do about her?"

"Tough call. One option is to say nothing and add her to our witness list after the prosecution rests."

"But we don't know what she's going to say." Even *I* know that a good lawyer never asks a question in court unless he or she knows what the answer will be. Putting Sandy Russo on the stand would be the epitome of recklessness.

"Exactly," Mike agrees. "Another option is to barge into Judge Mitton's courtroom screaming bloody murder because the cops buried Sandy Russo's statement. The good judge will order them to produce whatever they've got and will slap sanctions on the prosecution if they're hiding something. If they *are* hiding something, whatever it is has to help us, right?"

"And if it doesn't?" I counter.

Mike shakes his head and chuckles. "If it doesn't, Suzy Sunshine, it probably won't hurt us. If it's not exculpatory, why hide it? You can bet your gloomy ass they'd be using it if it helped their case."

Can't counter that logic.

"Whatever way we decide to go, we're not going to do anything today. I need to ponder our options and the upside and downside of each. I want you guys to do the same."

Luke nods. I nod.

Mike turns to me. "You'll be cross-examining the ex-Mrs. O'Reilly if she turns out to be the final witness of the day."

I turn to him in surprise. "She's supposed to be your witness."

"You can handle it. We need to get you into the game."

I worry that the jury's takeaway for the weekend will be me screwing the pooch on cross.

Sure enough, Dempsey calls Molly O'Reilly to the stand after the recess. O'Reilly's ex can't be more than forty or so years old, yet with thinning hair the color and texture of frayed twine, a thick waistline spilling over the waist of a pair of knockoff designer jeans, and a face as weathered as tree bark, she looks like she's at least fifty—and a hard-living fifty at that. Even so, I suspect Molly O'Reilly had once been an attractive woman. When she throws back her shoulders and strides to the witness stand with her head held high, it's difficult to imagine her as anything other than someone in control of her own fate. After establishing that the O'Reillys were married for seventeen years and that the love of her life had left behind an adoring fifteen-year-old son that the good officer doted on, Dempsey asks the widow if she recalls the fateful night of September seventeenth.

The jury leans closer to hear Molly O'Reilly answer in a voice barely above a hoarse whisper. "I'll never forget," she says tragically. "Never. It's the nightmare police wives live in fear of."

"How did you learn of the death of your husband?" Dempsey asks with a false intimacy that would do a daytime talk show host proud.

"A couple of police officers," *sniffle, sniffle,* "came to my door the next morning and broke the news to me."

Dempsey dwells on the drama a moment longer, then takes his witness on a quick spin through the halcyon days of her marriage to Andy O'Reilly. "I'm so sorry for your loss," he says while handing her more tissues. "How are you and your son managing?"

This question prompts another outburst of sniffling. "I don't think we'll ever get over this."

Dempsey stands back while his witness dabs at her eyes with her Kleenex prop. He lets her perform for a full ten seconds while he monitors the jury's reaction, then thanks her "for allowing us to intrude on your grief. You've been very helpful. I'm sure I speak for everyone in this courtroom when I wish you and your son Godspeed in the difficult days ahead. You can go now, Mrs. O'Reilly," he adds before pausing to look at us. "Unless the defendant's attorney wishes to question you?"

Quite a performance. What does Molly O'Reilly stand to gain by trying to bullshit the court about her late ex-husband and their rocky relationship? Maybe she's worried about collecting on all of his death benefits. The bigger question is what Dempsey's game is. Surely he knows the truth about the O'Reillys.

Mike leans close. "Be careful with this."

I meet his gaze and nod. "Just enough to pop the balloon." Then I get to my feet and look across the courtroom at Molly O'Reilly. "Were you and Andy O'Reilly living together on the night he was shot?"

The widow fidgets for a moment and then looks at Dempsey. "No."

"Were you still married to Andy O'Reilly at the time of his death?"

"No." She ventures a nervous glance at the jurors, a couple of whom avert their gaze.

Just to make sure the jury doesn't leave for the weekend thinking Molly O'Reilly carried a torch for "the love of her life" right to the bitter end, I ask one more question. "Did you divorce Andy O'Reilly over a year ago on grounds of physical and verbal abuse?"

She answers, "Yes," in a near whisper that seems more evasive than tragic. The jurors are staring at her with far less empathy than they'd shown a few minutes ago. My work is done.

When Dempsey declines the opportunity to re-cross his witness, I worry that he's got an unseen card up his sleeve that he's going to play when we least expect it. Judge Mitton sends Molly O'Reilly on her way without noticeable warmth and excuses the jury for the weekend.

"How much time will you need Monday morning to finish your case-in-chief?" he asks the prosecutor in a not-so-subtle hint to move things along after the weekend.

"I'm confident we'll finish Monday, Your Honor."

I wonder what evidence the prosecution can possibly have left. That's not my biggest concern, though. We still aren't sure what case we intend to present as soon as Tuesday.

CHAPTER TWENTY-EIGHT

I meet Brittany at O'Hare International Airport at noon on Sunday when she flies in from Brussels with her mother.

Michelle hasn't changed outwardly, and I suspect she hasn't changed a bit inside, either. She's arrived in her usual impeccably arranged splendor. A chic white raincoat is draped over the sleeve of a form-fitting burgundy dress. On another woman, the silky fabric clinging to her might be considered slinky. Michelle somehow manages to give it a conservative, executive-appropriate twist. Tall and willowy with long, lustrous raven hair and an almost regal bearing, she's graced with curves any stripper or starlet would kill for —assets she's never shied away from employing in either the boardroom or the bedroom. Not that she'd sleep her way through the executive suite or even seriously entertain a workplace tryst to advance her career. Michelle is simply aware of the numbing effect testosterone has on the male brain. She's used that knowledge to her advantage for as long as I've known her. In what is surely a sign of progress, her many charms leave me cold today.

"You won't have her in that house, will you?" she asks after a perfunctory hello.

"*That house* is our home," I retort.

"I will not have my daughter staying in a house where someone has been shot in the last few weeks!"

"She's not *your* daughter. Britts is *our* daughter and she'll be staying with me. She'll be fine. Get used to the idea."

"What security arrangements have you made for her stay?"

"I *said* she'll be fine."

Michelle bites off whatever angry reply is on the tip of her tongue and storms away to catch her connecting flight to Atlanta.

We collect Brittany's bags and head home. Fortunately, the insurance company contractor has replaced the front porch without building permit issues, so I don't mention the fire or vandalism. I reassure her as best I can about Pat's condition, bring her up to speed on the trial, and I'm current on events in Europe by the time we arrive at Liberty Street. I make hot chocolate and am just getting into the Cedar Heights saga when my phone rings. It's Mike Williams.

"I was gonna stop by but I know you and Brittany are catching up," he says after we exchange greetings. "I've got a quick question or two."

"Shoot."

"I've been thinking about how to play Sandy Russo's alleged statement."

"And?"

"I want to throw a tantrum about the discovery violation."

I don't disagree but I'd like to hear his reasoning. "Why?"

"What she heard has to help us."

I decide to play devil's advocate. "Probably so. If you're so sure of that, why not just put her on the stand and find out?"

"I've considered it, believe me."

"No time for the prosecution to prepare or dull the impact by getting her story out first," I continue. "If Sandy confirms Papa's story, the prosecution can't unring that bell."

"But then we'd need to put Francesco on the stand to tell his side of the story. You know how I feel about that."

Indeed, I do. "But if Sandy's testimony supports Papa's version of events, getting his story in front of the jury should outweigh whatever damage Dempsey can do to him."

"You might be right."

I pause and stare out the window while I think. "So, the question is whether or not to blindside Dempsey and hope it's a knockout punch or go a little more cautiously to guard against landing a haymaker on our own chin."

Mike chuckles. "That about sums it up."

I'm sorely tempted to swing for the fence on this. Mike sees the potential of doing so, yet he's holding back. Is he being overly cautious or am I being reckless? What gives me the right to gamble with Papa's life? Mike waits me out until I finally say, "Swinging for the fences appeals to me, but there's no Plan B if it goes wrong."

"That's right."

Prudence, Tony, I tell myself. "File the motion."

"I'll file it this afternoon. *Your* job is to park your butt at home and enjoy your daughter."

After we say our goodbyes, I find Brittany in the living room admiring Pat's painting of the beach at sunrise. I hung it over the fireplace the night I brought it home.

"Pat's work," I say.

Brittany looks at me in astonishment. "This is awesome! You didn't tell me she paints like this."

"I didn't know." I tell her about discovering Pat's painting room the day I took her home from the hospital.

"Can we call her?"

"We're going to see her tomorrow."

"*Please,* Dad?"

I put them on the phone together and putter while they chat.

Brittany walks in a few minutes later and hands me the phone. "Your turn."

"Hey, Pat," I say. "How are you?"

"Good. Sitting down?"

"Why?"

"I've been doing a little work the past few days."

I stifle the urge to give her hell for not resting. "And?"

"Titan targeted your house this spring. They sent a demolition crew to run a truck into the garage and then bribed Henry Poindexter in the licensing office not to issue the building permit. The *Trib* is running the story tomorrow. The article will suggest that folks higher up the village food chain were pulling the strings to use the damaged garage to foreclose and get your father evicted. We'll draw a direct line to how that effort had tragic results for your father and Sheriff's Deputy O'Reilly."

"Bastards!"

"Indeed," Pat agrees. "Your father and his neighbors aren't the first folks Titan has pulled this stunt with. They hire a bunch of punks to trash target neighborhoods and homes they covet. They've been running the same scheme in Phoenix, Tulsa, Sarasota, and who knows where else—always operating through cleverly disguised subsidiaries."

"How did you find out?"

"A Titan demolition team was arrested in action several days ago. I've been building a network of reporters around the country who are working on eminent domain stories of their own. When Titan's thugs got themselves arrested in Sarasota, a reporter there called me."

"How did the reporter find out?" I ask. "I mean, guys get arrested for vandalism all the time. Must be thousands of them. How was the connection made to Titan?"

"It's not like these bozos are the most savory critters around, Tony. They ratted out their boss before the day was out and the cops found *him* as easy to roll as a mangy mutt that wants its tummy scratched. And so it went, right on up the line until someone fingered Titan."

I shake my head in wonder. "Not much in common with the blue wall of silence, huh?"

"Nope."

"I should be able to use this at the Village Board meeting on Tuesday. I just need to figure out how."

"You'll work it out," Pat says confidently before we end the call.

I order pizza from Malnati's and carry it into the kitchen when it arrives. With the sky darkening, I walk over and close the wooden plantation shutters that cover the new kitchen window. Pretty hard for a shooter to hit what he or she can't see. At least that's what I've been telling myself.

When the doorbell rings five minutes later, Brittany bounces to her feet. "I'll get it."

"No! I've got it. Stay right here."

Brittany's inquisitive eyes widen at my display of skittishness.

I open the door to find a pudgy security guard staring back at me. "Is there a Brittany Valenti staying here?"

I stare back at him, wondering who the hell he is and what he's doing on my front porch asking about my daughter. A quick glance at the flashlight and other paraphernalia hanging off his belt suggests he's unarmed. "Who are you?"

"Who are *you?*" he asks back.

"I live here, so I'll do the asking. Who the hell are you and why are you here?"

"We're here to protect Brittany Valenti. Is she here?"

"Who sent you?" I ask while he snaps his gum. I doubt this guy would even be a match for the mysterious hoodie bike rider.

"Dispatch."

"Maybe you should call dispatch and find out who told them to send you here."

After his dispatcher assures him that he's at the right address, Brittany's prospective bodyguard squares his shoulders and once again demands to know if she's in the house.

"Listen pal," I inform him, "I don't know anything about this. You're *not* coming in."

Mr. Bodyguard inches closer to the door. "Sir, we've been hired to protect Brittany Valenti. I need you to step aside so I can confirm that's she's okay."

"Or what?" I scoff. "You'll call the real police?"

He's not sure what to say to that. He takes a step back.

"Until you can tell me who hired you, please get off my step before I call the police to report you as a trespasser."

When he doesn't move, I close the door in his face and start back to the kitchen, then begin to suspect what's probably going on. I divert to the bedroom and call Michelle's cell. She picks up immediately.

"Did you hire some sort of security service to watch Britts?"

"I did. If you won't see to her protection, I will. I have a call into our attorney to see what other steps I can take."

Maybe she'll have Brittany taken into protective custody until Mommy can whisk her back to Europe? When I recall the vision of Michelle's hireling standing on the porch, I can't quite suppress a chuckle. Unfortunately, Michelle hears it.

"You think this is *funny*?" she explodes. "My daughter is in a house that a killer is stalking, and you laugh at my concern?"

"You should see the clowns they sent out here. You're wasting your money. Call them off. I'll take care of things."

"I won't call them off! Even if you won't let them in the house to protect Brittany, I insist that you allow them to set up a perimeter."

A perimeter? I repeat silently. What a joke.

"Do *not* try my patience on this," Michelle warns when I don't reply.

I've had enough. "You don't insist on anything in my home. Call off your rent-a-cops before I have them arrested for trespassing." With that, I cut the connection and silence the ringer so we won't be interrupted by Michelle's outraged return calls. I coerce Brittany into playing along by silencing her phone to forestall a family telephone brawl. She can tell her mother that she forgot to take her phone off airplane mode after they landed at O'Hare.

The doorbell rings again forty minutes later. Michelle's SWAT team? I'm tempted not to answer but eventually relent. Maybe the poor little bastard has to pee. I peer through the peephole and see Detective Plummer standing on my front step. When I open the door, he's staring at the retired Ford LTD Police Interceptor parked at the curb.

"Hello, Mr. Valenti. I hope you don't mind me dropping by."

After we shake hands, Plummer looks back at the Shield Security vehicle. "What are those guys doing here? Everything okay?"

I wave him inside. "My daughter's visiting. My ex-wife hired them to protect her."

Humor dances in the eyes of the detective but he doesn't say whatever's on his mind.

"Come on in. We're having hot chocolate in the kitchen. Unless you need to speak to me privately?"

He shakes his head before following me into the kitchen to exchange greetings and a little small talk. "Me being here while we're in the middle of a trial doesn't look so good. No trial talk, okay?"

"What brings you here, if not the trial?" I ask.

"You'll be happy to hear that we've got Miss O'Toole's shooter in custody."

"Terrific!" Brittany exclaims.

"That's great!" I add to her cry of relief. For all my

bravado earlier with Michelle, I've been having second thoughts about Brittany staying here.

"Remember when we were talking in the yard the morning after it happened?" Plummer asks.

I nod.

"Once I heard that we'd been able to get a ballistics match on the shell casings and bullets through IBIS and it turned out to be a gangbanger's gun—"

"What's IBIS?" Brittany asks.

"Integrated Ballistics Identification System."

"Wow, a government acronym," she says with a smirk.

Plummer returns her smile. "Yeah. Imagine that."

"And?" I prompt impatiently.

"I asked myself why a gun that was used in a gang shooting resurfaced a few years later in Cedar Heights in the hands of some bozo who doesn't know how to use it."

"This isn't your case," I say. "Why were you looking into it?"

"The gangbanger gun bothered me. How did it end up here? Most of them go into the lake or down a sewer after they get used, but sometimes they disappear into a cop's pocket. Anyway, I had a look at the call sheets from a couple of hours either side of the shooting here and a name caught my attention."

"Who?" Brittany and I ask in unison.

"Andy O'Reilly Junior was pulled over for driving a little erratically in Daddy's car a little before midnight. Nothing else was filed, so I tracked down the beat cops who pulled him over. They recognized him as O'Reilly's kid, figured he was blowing off a little steam, and cut him loose with orders to go straight home."

"I guess that makes sense," I say.

Plummer nods. "Yeah, it does. I remembered you telling me about Brittany being harassed by the O'Reilly boy at school. It's no secret that the kid's a handful, so I dug a little deeper. I wanted to have a look for the gun at the kid's house. My captain laughed me out of his office when I suggested they get a warrant and check."

"Why did he do that?" Brittany asks.

"Cap reminded me that O'Reilly was one of our own and suggested I had a lot of nerve wanting to mess with the poor guy's family."

"Not that surprising," I mutter.

Plummer's eyes narrow. "That's not how the job works, Mr. Valenti. I went to see O'Reilly's ex. We chatted about the trial for a bit. Mrs. O'Reilly told me she worries about some of the people her husband had been running with before he split. Said she was glad there was still a gun or two in the basement. When I asked her about the guns, she gave me the insider nudge-nudge, wink-wink routine about cops picking up an illegal piece and bringing it home. Told me her husband did it a few times, as if everyone does."

"Do cops actually do that?" Brittany asks.

Plummer's brow creases in distaste. "Dirty cops do it, and some who aren't so dirty. Some guys keep them as an extra personal piece. Dirty cops plant them as evidence and worse. Anyway, I decided a little bullshit was in order to smoke out the truth, so I told her the kid was good for the tire slashing and arson here. I topped that off by telling her that a gun O'Reilly pocketed had just been used in an attempted murder. When she went pale, I knew I was onto something. Things played out pretty quickly from there—warrant, ballistics, confession."

"Did he slash my tires and torch the porch?"

"He did."

I meet Brittany's surprised gaze. "I'll explain the vandalism later."

"Okay," she says uncertainly.

I turn back to Plummer and angrily ask, "Did the mother know?"

"Who knows? Guess it doesn't matter one way or the other. Anyway, I gotta run. Thought you should know." Then he fixes Brittany in his gaze. "Last thing. It's against the law to disclose the name of a juvenile offender."

She stares back blankly.

"That means we can't breathe a word of this to anyone," I tell her. "Detective Plummer has done us a favor to let us know. He's trusting us not to jeopardize his career by popping off about it."

Brittany's expression is grave as her eyes track back to Plummer. "Understood. I won't let you down."

He smiles. "I know. I wouldn't have told you if I wasn't sure of it."

"Wait," I say when he turns for the door. "Why did he come after us?"

Plummer sighs. "Anger. Rage. Revenge. He's one screwed up young man."

Brittany turns to me. "The kid on the bike? I bet that was him. He's always cruising around on a bike like that."

"Kid on a bike?" Plummer asks.

Brittany explains.

"Could be," he mutters when she finishes. "I'll ask him… put your minds at ease."

Brittany smiles. "Thanks."

I can't figure Plummer. He's messing with my cop preconceptions; the guy genuinely seems to be a seeker of truth. Hell, he's even being helpful.

"I guess it's kinda sad," Brittany murmurs.

I recall the horrific vision of Pat lying in a pool of blood on this very floor. *Sad, my ass.* I'm glad the kid is off the streets and hope he stays off.

"But he's still an asshole," Brittany adds.

She and I chat for a few more minutes after Plummer leaves, but she's fading fast. I tuck her in ten minutes later.

Her hand creeps out from under the covers and tightens

on mine while another yawn overtakes her. "You've got a lot going on. Don't let me get in the way."

I tuck her hand back under the covers and lean down to plant a kiss on her forehead. "Don't be silly. I'm thrilled you're here. Have a good sleep, honey. I'll see you in the morning."

Her eyes close and she snuggles deeper under the covers with a contented sigh.

A profound weariness settles over me after I softly close the door. She's right. A momentous week lies ahead. The fate of this house and my father will likely be decided by next weekend.

CHAPTER TWENTY-NINE

At seven-fifteen Monday morning, a visibly angry Judge Mitton sweeps down the courthouse hallway toward Mike and me. Mike made an emergency call to the court yesterday to notify the judge that we would be moving for a continuance "due to an egregious discovery violation." The judge is dressed in a purplish paisley open-collar shirt and rumpled gray slacks. A fashion plate he's not. We exchange morning greetings.

"Lovely morning," I observe, hoping to lighten the judge's mood with a little levity. Another six inches of snow fell last night. With the wind howling off the lake, morning temperatures are flirting with absolute zero.

Mitton glances at his watch and scowls. The prosecutors haven't arrived. He pushes his door open and grumbles, "Knock when Mr. Dempsey arrives."

"Don't try to cheer him up," Mike says after the door closes. "We want him good and ornery when he lights into Dempsey."

Alex Dempsey, Sylvia Perez, and Detective Plummer arrive a moment later and we're all shown into Judge

Mitton's chambers. Considering how long the judge has been on the bench, his office is surprisingly modest. A few family pictures dot the walls or sit on top of a cherrywood credenza. Mitton sits behind a matching desk cleared of paperwork, save for a couple of files. Even the customary display of law school diplomas is absent, suggesting his ego is tucked away somewhere with his fashion sense.

Mike reveals that Luke talked to Sandy Russo on Friday afternoon, emphasizing that she seems to have spoken with the police on September eighteenth.

Judge Mitton's eyes settle on Dempsey. "I assume Detective Plummer is here to tell us what happened?"

Dempsey nods. "I asked Jake to find out who spoke with Mrs. Russo and why that interview wasn't included in the police reports we received."

The judge glowers at Plummer. "Let's hear your story, Detective."

"Pretty simple, Judge. A couple of O'Reilly's asshole buddies took it upon themselves to cover his ass one last time."

Mitton makes an impatient "come on" motion. "Details."

"We found out on the night of the shooting that Sandy Russo had been at her parents' house. She left before we started going door to door, so I sent a couple of uniforms to her house the next day."

"Why send uniforms?" the judge asks. "This was a potential witness from next door in a homicide case where you had no eyewitnesses."

"The Vaccaros knew nothing about the shooting. I expected the same from their daughter. My plan was to send a detective if she told the uniforms anything of interest."

Mitton nods. "That was done?"

"No. The jokers decided to erect their own little Blue Wall of Silence."

"How?" Mitton asks sharply. "You sent them. Why didn't you follow up?"

The detective pulls a piece of paper out of his pocket and hands it to Mitton. "This is what they turned in. They claim they don't remember her saying anything else."

The judge scans the page, silently hands the paper to Mike, and asks, "Have you seen this?"

"No," Mike replies tersely after reading it. He thrusts the paper at me before he turns on the prosecutors. "This wasn't in discovery."

"It wasn't in our paperwork," Dempsey says.

"Why not?" Mike asks.

"That's a good question," Plummer replies. "It's in ours and it's logged on the record of evidence transferred to the state's attorney."

Dempsey turns his palms up and shrugs. "No way to know what happened at this point. It's just one of those things, I guess. Let's move on... no good will come from pointing fingers."

The Report of Witness Interview I'm looking at consists of the date and time Sandy Russo was interviewed, confirmation that she was at her parents' house at the time of the shooting, and notes that she didn't see the crime take place. There's no mention that she heard anything relevant.

Mitton's eyes settle on Dempsey. "Quite a happy coincidence that the sole person in a position to shed some light on events wasn't supposed to be heard from, Counselor."

"It's an unfortunate oversight, Your Honor."

Mitton's eyes are aflame when he leans forward to address the assistant state's attorney. "How many times have you stood in front of a jury in my courtroom and stated that coincidences seldom hold up under scrutiny? Isn't 'where there's smoke, you can bet there's fire' a favorite line of yours when defense counsel has an awkward circumstance to explain away?"

"With all due respect, Your Honor—"

Mitton cuts him off with a raised hand and returns his attention to Plummer. "What is your department doing with the officers who pulled this stunt?"

"They're on administrative leave while the department investigates."

"And after a suitable interlude they'll be back on the street," Mike grumbles.

Mike's comment draws a scowl from the judge, who is working himself into a lather. Plummer is the target of his ire. "Whenever I wonder why a good portion of the public trust cops about as much as they trust their politicians, lawyers, and crooked salesmen, I only have to recall crap like this. Is there *no* oversight of the police department in Cedar Heights?"

Plummer sighs. "Judge, sometimes even I wonder."

"That's a pathetic admission, Detective."

"Yeah, it is."

Dempsey's eyes widen at Plummer's comment. I hope it never reaches the ears of the powers that be in Cedar Heights.

Mitton taps his fingers on the desk. "Our first order of business this morning was going to be a prosecution motion contesting the admissibility of Deputy Sheriff O'Reilly's law enforcement personnel records. The prosecution's motion to suppress is denied."

"May I speak to this matter, Your Honor?" Dempsey asks.

"Keep it brief."

"We object to giving the defense a chance to put a dead man on trial."

"He deserves to be on trial!" I snap.

"Save it for the jury, gentlemen!" the judge admonishes us. A sigh escapes him as he settles back in his seat and his eyes settle on Mike. "Let me guess. This wasn't the first instance of abusive behavior by Officer O'Reilly?"

"Hardly, Your Honor. The guy was a thug in a uniform."

"Officer O'Reilly's record was in many ways exemplary," Dempsey retorts.

Mitton all but rolls his eyes at the prosecutor. "Given what I've heard this morning and all the smoke you're blowing, Counselor, I'm inclined to let the defense dig. You better hope they don't uncover any other attempts to suppress evidence showing Deputy O'Reilly wasn't the choir boy the FOP has painted him to be."

"Your Honor—"

Mitton slams a fist on his desk as he cuts Dempsey off. "You *still* don't understand how angry I am, do you?"

"If I were you," Dempsey says, "I'd be upset—"

"You're *not* me!" Mitton snaps before he turns to Mike. "I'm giving you two extra days to find out what, if anything, Mrs. Russo has to tell us. We're adjourned until nine o'clock on Wednesday morning."

Dempsey leans forward to wade back into the discussion. A pointed glare from the judge stays the prosecutor's tongue.

"Discovery violations merit a remedy, Mr. Dempsey. Be thankful I'm not penalizing you further. The matter is closed."

And with that, the judge breathes life into Papa's defense.

"When we reconvene Wednesday," he continues, "the prosecution will continue its case-in-chief, which *will* conclude by the end of the day." Mitton's eyes traverse between Dempsey and Mike. "That deadline includes whatever cross-examination you see fit to undertake, Mr. Williams. The opening statement for the defendant's case-in-chief will start proceedings on Thursday morning. I'd like to wrap this up before the weekend."

We walk out of the courthouse five minutes later and stop dead. Twenty feet away, in the midst of television cameras and scribbling scribes, stands the spokesman of the Fraternal Order of Police.

"Judge Mitton showed with his outrageous ruling this

morning that he's no friend of law enforcement or the principles of law and order," the FOP SOB thunders. "Our members will remember this insult come election time!"

I wonder how the FOP already knows about Mitton's decision to allow O'Reilly's record into evidence. Then I notice Sylvia Perez watching the show with satisfaction. *Ah.*

"Asshole," Mike mutters.

"Doesn't the idiot realize Mitton is retiring?"

He shakes his head in disgust. "Tough to say. This guy never misses a chance to throw his weight around, preferably in front of a camera."

Dempsey catches up to us. "We should talk."

Mike's phone chirps and he turns away to answer.

"What should we talk about?" I ask Dempsey.

"I was speaking to Mr. Williams."

Mike waves me over. "Luke Geffen's excited about something," he whispers when I reach him.

"Should I wait?" Dempsey grumbles.

Mike asks Luke to hang on and turns back to the prosecutor. "What's on your mind, Alex?"

"We should keep the lines of communication open."

"Any reason in particular?" I ask. Dempsey gives no indication that he heard me. Funny how these guys pop up to chat every time they suffer a setback. In my previous legal life, it usually meant my adversary was worried about something coming to light. Stalling generally worked in my favor. I wonder if that's also true in criminal law.

"Can you give us a minute or two?" Mike asks the prosecutor. "I have to take this call."

Dempsey shrugs and pulls out his own phone. "I've got a few minutes," he says before he turns and walks away. We head in the opposite direction.

"Luke, what's up?" Mike asks when we're out of hearing range. "Interesting... what did she say?" Mike knits his eyebrows together while Luke replies. "This afternoon sounds good… let me know what she has to say… get a read on her, Luke, tell me how she'd come across on the stand… good work… thanks… later."

"The ex-sister-in-law just called him," Mike tells me after he hangs up. "She knows the kid is in custody and WGN just announced that O'Reilly's personnel records are coming in. She wants to talk to Luke this afternoon. I wonder why?"

"And if it's good or bad news for us," I say while Dempsey walks back to meet us with a smile on his face.

Mike looks unsettled. "I always get nervous when a smiling prosecutor wants to talk to me."

Dempsey wants to exclude me from his conversation with Mike, who argues the point for a minute before I throw up my hands and walk away. What the hell, Mike will fill me in when they're done.

I think about how things are progressing and my role in Papa's defense. The hours upon hours of research and late-night reading I've devoted to boning up on criminal law have paid off insofar as Mike has a partner, albeit a painfully green one. We shared a good laugh recently when he delivered the decidedly backhanded compliment that my criminal law skills now surpass my prowess on a basketball court. None of it seems funny now that we're deep into the trial. What if I ball things up?

After an animated discussion with Dempsey, Mike walks back to me. "They're offering to recommend a twenty-five-year sentence if your father pleads guilty to first-degree murder. Francesco could be out in fifteen years."

I guess we're not the only people who think Mike and I have an uphill struggle ahead, even with Andy O'Reilly's track record and character to work with. We've kicked this around a bit and the endgame remains a bone of contention between us. I'm inclined to put the case in the hands of a jury whereas Mike wants to angle for the best possible plea deal. He doesn't want to let an opportunity slip by; I don't want to settle for the first or second offer that comes along. Sooner or later, our diverging views are going to come to a head.

CHAPTER THIRTY

At six-fifteen the next evening, Pat and I watch from my living room as *WGN Evening News* airs a segment previewing tonight's Cedar Heights Village Board showdown. They've begun with a recap of last month's meeting, complete with the photos of Liberty Street and Independence Park that had featured so prominently in the would-be developer's presentation. A video showing the rest of the neighborhood in all its well-kept glory comes next.

Mr. Rosetti follows, looking every inch the dignified senior citizen. "I have lived on Liberty Street for over forty years. Like many of our neighbors, we bought our house new from the builder. Our children grew up on Liberty Street and played in Independence Park. We all did our best over the years to see that our neighborhood flourished."

"Until Titan Development took an interest," the reporter interviewing him prompts.

"That's correct. A handful of houses in the neighborhood were purchased by the developer, trashed, and then trotted out last month to suggest that Liberty Street is a slum in need of condemnation. Two years ago, those houses were as pretty and well-kept as the homes you just showed."

WGN moves on to a segment summarizing the *Tribune*'s bombshell reporting about the underhanded tactics Titan has wielded nationwide to expropriate property it wished to develop. We drive over to Village Hall at a quarter-to-seven and find a couple of open seats amongst my neighbors. I seem to have done a better job rallying the folks of Liberty Street than I'd thought. The public seats are filling quickly and the media has descended upon Village Hall en masse, far too many of them to squeeze into the cubicle-sized square of floor space allotted for the press. Cedar Heights is generally lucky to see a reporter or two from the community paper at a board meeting. This evening offers a feast of exposure. Pat was right about her media brethren. She says it only takes a drop or two of political blood to be spilled within sight of two or more reporters to get them circling. Linking corruption to murder incites a feeding frenzy.

A side door opens at seven o'clock and in troops His Honor the Mayor, followed by the village clerk and all six village trustees. I notice the eyes of a couple of trustees widen as they take in the carnival crowd awaiting them. An explosion of flash bulbs abruptly diverts their gaze. Mayor Brown turns a sour countenance upon the swollen press gallery before calling the meeting to order. Roll call confirms that the entire Village Board is present. The clerk matter-of-factly recites the Pledge of Allegiance. There is no prayer. There's every indication that Brown intends tonight's meeting to be over quickly. His hopes run into trouble immediately, beginning with the usually routine step of approving the agenda.

Trustee Smith looks up from the paper in his hands. "I see that you've taken the Independence Park/Liberty Street Redevelopment Plan off the agenda, Mr. Mayor."

The mayor's response is lost in the angry clamor sparked by Smith's disclosure.

"I'm sorry, Mr. Mayor," Smith says when the turmoil dies down enough for him to be heard, "I didn't hear your reply."

His Honor angrily hammers his gavel until the crowd falls more or less silent. "I said that as there's no representative from Three Streams Development here this evening, there's no point having it on the agenda."

As he speaks, I realize Zaluski is also nowhere to be seen.

Smith furrows his brow. "I was under the impression that we village trustees are the deliberative body in Cedar Heights, Mr. Mayor. Am I wrong?"

Brown sighs a long, heavy rumble of resignation. "You're quite right, Trustee Smith. Is there some point to your little speech or are you just playing to the cameras?"

Smith smiles tightly. "I move to reinstate discussion of the Independence Park/Liberty Street Redevelopment Project to this evening's agenda."

"For what purpose, Trustee Smith?" the mayor asks. "We don't yet have answers to all the questions raised at our last meeting."

"Perhaps you don't want the matter on the agenda with all this press here, Mr. Mayor?" Smith suggests.

"Nonsense," His Honor replies, turning an indulgent smile upon the media throng, wordlessly commiserating with them over his need to suffer such a fool. "I, for one, want answers to these troubling questions."

"Such as the suggestion that the United States Attorney is investigating allegations of improper dealings between Titan Development and the highest levels of this village's administration?" Smith asks sharply.

Mayor Brown glares at the trustee but, perhaps tellingly, doesn't dispute the claim. It was first printed in the *Tribune* this morning.

"I second the motion," Trustee Myers says, reminding everyone that there's a motion on the floor. The skittishness that was evident the first time she bucked the will of His Honor four weeks ago is nowhere to be found.

The motion reinstating the main event to tonight's card

passes four to two. A wave of relief surges through the public and press seating.

The clerk asks for the minutes of the January seventh meeting to be approved. They are. More minor village business follows. The hiring of an accounting intern is approved and a new liquor license is authorized. The Parks Department gets funds to purchase a new lawn mower. As each measure is introduced, discussed, and quickly approved, the elephant in the room hovers impatiently.

During discussion of a request from the fire department for funds to send a pair of paramedics to a certification class in Springfield, Reverend Jakes pulls me aside. His eyes roam across the press contingent and extra seats hurriedly brought in to accommodate the public. "Quite a turnout," he says.

I nod approvingly. "Who would've thought?"

"Anyone watching you pull all this together. None of this would have happened if you hadn't taken the initiative. You were the rallying point—the neighborhood leader, as it were."

If that's the case, it's a wonder anyone showed up. "Plenty of people worked hard to get things to this point, Reverend. Pat O'Toole. My neighbors. Trustee Smith."

A deep chuckle escapes Jakes. "I've got a wee bit of experience fighting city hall, Tony. You've done a fine job here."

"You give me far too much credit."

"Balderdash!"

I love how he says that. I smile gratefully and grasp his arm. "Thanks, Reverend. That means a lot to me."

Mayor Brown announces that Liberty Street is the next item on the agenda and informs the buzzing crowd, "I'm afraid time doesn't allow for public comment tonight. We'll make time at a future meeting." He raps his gavel to still the resulting commotion, then turns to the row of trustees. "Each of you will have a maximum of two minutes to address this matter."

"Pressing meeting with the feds?" a mocking voice calls out from the press pack.

His Honor's eyes snap to the reporters. "The press are invited guests here this evening," he snaps in a menacing tone. "The invitation can be rescinded."

The press area falls silent.

Brown puts off the main event as long as possible by inviting every other trustee to speak ahead of Smith. Myers leads off and counsels delay. Two other trustees echo her comments. The remaining pair of unabashed toadies to the mayor argue against this sentiment, deploring such ill-conceived efforts to stand in the way of progress. His Honor appears appreciative of their efforts.

"Something is terribly wrong with what's happening on Liberty Street," Smith says when his turn arrives. "I think it behooves us to put the brakes on this project before the mayor and his minions sneak it in the back door."

"I resent that accu—" His Honor starts to retort.

Smith rolls right over the budding objection. "I move that all funding for the Independence Park/Liberty Street project be temporarily withdrawn, effective immediately."

Trustee Myers seconds the motion. The measure passes four to two, momentarily rendering the discombobulated mayor mute. With the door thus ajar, Smith launches a follow-up strike before His Honor can recover.

"I further move that additional action pursuant to approval of the Independence Park/Liberty Street Redevelopment Plan be deferred until a new mayor and board of trustees are sworn in after the next Cedar Heights civic election."

Trustee Myers immediately seconds the motion. To my delight, a well-orchestrated palace revolt seems to be underway.

"The roll, Madam Clerk?" Smith prompts.

"I haven't called for a vote yet!" the red-faced mayor thunders. The clerk gives him an expectant look. His Honor can either call for the vote or keep the discussion going. "Call the vote," he mutters.

"Trustee Myers?" the clerk asks.

"Yea."

Two more yeas and a pair of nays tally before the clerk calls for Smith's vote.

"Yea!" he booms. The ensuing vacuum swallows the echo of his words.

"The motion carries four to two," the village clerk announces with an air of disbelief. His Honor, along with the rest of us, is equally stunned at the speed and totality of his defeat.

The clerk's announcement seems to throw a switch releasing the pent-up tension in the room. Dozens of voices explode. Residents whoop while reporters shout questions. The mayor's gavel restores some semblance of order. The fury twisting his crimson face is warning enough to retake our seats and still our tongues.

"I have an announcement to make," Brown says in a hollow voice. "Immediately before this meeting began, I reluctantly accepted the resignation, effective today, of Village Manager Peter Zaluski."

A few hands shoot up in the press section while less reserved reporters shout questions.

"Was Zaluski working with Titan?"

"Was the resignation forced?"

"Will Mr. Zaluski be charged with any wrongdoing?"

His Honor is banging his gavel and demanding a motion to adjourn when Pat grabs my sleeve to drag me out of my chair. "Come on!"

I follow dumbly as she leads me deeper into Village Hall. We stop abruptly outside a closed office door in a dimly lit suite of offices. The lights are on and we can hear activity inside. Pat's hand rests on the doorknob for a split second while she thinks. Then, with a decision apparently reached, she raps on the door. The office falls silent.

My eyes settle on the brass placard affixed to the wall beside the door: *Peter R. Zaluski, Village Manager.*

Pat hammers again, waits five seconds, then twists the knob and punches the door open. Zaluski stands frozen in place behind an enormous wooden desk. A copy paper box rests in the middle of the blotter. Another box sits on the floor nearby. Both are filled with the accoutrements and paraphernalia of long occupancy: plaques, diplomas, framed photographs, a personalized crystal paperweight, an engraved letter opener. Other odds and ends poke out of the piles in the boxes.

Pat walks in, continues to the desk, and leans on it for support. I follow, stepping alongside her, concerned that she's pushing herself too hard. Her eye is locked on Zaluski, who stares back without comment.

"Sorry about your job," I blurt, surprising all three of us.

Zaluski's eyes search mine for a long moment before he judges my words sincere. "Thank you."

"Wanna hear my theory of what happened?" Pat asks.

Zaluski says nothing.

"You were duped, Mr. Zaluski," she continues. "Like everyone else who wants to get ahead in Cedar Heights, you toadied up to Mayor Brown and his pals. I think you believed, and probably still do, that the homes on Liberty Street really should be razed for a shopping mall."

Zaluski stares back but still says nothing.

"Isn't that right?" she presses.

He nods.

"So, when these rental properties popped up and you found out the Valentis and Rosettis had potential property tax issues to exploit, I'm guessing you thought that was a little bit okay, huh?"

Zaluski doesn't reply, nor does he interrupt.

"Then along came the business with the Valenti garage. That was like *manna* from Heaven, wasn't it?"

Zaluski is now watching us like a fox cornered by baying bloodhounds on the hunt, desperate to plot an escape route before the men with guns arrive.

"I don't think you were behind the worst of what went on," she continues, "but you're certainly guilty of helping orchestrate the persecution of the Valentis."

Zaluski's eyes flicker to mine, confirming Pat's charge. I can imagine gears whirring behind those eyes. Excuses. Rationalizations. Perhaps he was "just carrying out orders."

"You were used by the mayor and his pals, weren't you?" I ask.

Zaluski doesn't answer. Instead, his haunted eyes return to Pat. He finds no succor there.

"You were used as callously as Tony's family and Officer O'Reilly," she snaps. "You were so blinded by ambition that you didn't see it. Isn't that right?"

Something in his eyes—is it possible to nod with your eyes?—conveys silent confirmation. Unquotable confirmation.

"The mayor knew, didn't he?" Pat asks.

No denial. No confirmation. No response at all.

Pat keeps hammering away. "You were his henchman through all of this, weren't you? Admit it. You were duped. Willingly, no doubt, but still duped."

Zaluski replies with an almost imperceptible nod.

Pat pushes harder. "The mayor knew what was happening all long, didn't he? He was in on this with Titan. Isn't that right?"

Zaluski finally responds. "Didn't you say in one of your articles that Mayor Brown knows everything that goes on in Cedar Heights?"

Pat nods.

"Whoever told you that knows this village."

A mirthless smile curls Pat's lips. She has what she came for.

"Can I get back to my packing now?" Zaluski mutters. "I'd like to be out of here before the rest of your colleagues find me."

Pat tosses a business card onto the desk. "Fair enough. Call me if you want to unburden your soul."

"Good luck," Zaluski says.

I look up to find his eyes on me. "You, too," I murmur. Then I follow Pat into the hallway. As she marches away, I pause and turn back to gently close the door on the premature termination of Peter Zaluski's public service career. My anger at him is spent, scattered like dust with the realization that his professional demise echoes my own at Sphinx Financial.

Pawns. The two of us.

CHAPTER THIRTY-ONE

Two hours later, Pat and I are quietly savoring our triumph while we sip mugs of hot chocolate at my kitchen table. Several neighbors have come and gone, even Mike popped in for a few minutes with his congratulations. I was among the few who avoided the media-fueled street celebration of our victory at Village Hall. I'm emotionally drained —euphoric over the outcome of tonight's meeting yet dogged by anxiety about what awaits us in court tomorrow morning. I excuse myself to tuck Brittany in.

She's already under the covers. "How would you feel about me staying?" she asks.

It's a question I've asked myself a few times this week. Brussels seems the best place for her right now. My daughter has gained maturity in the past few months and Europe seems to be broadening her perspective. She's traveled, seen new cultures, and met people unlike any she's known before. All in all, I like the change in her. I can't see a return to St. Aloysius turning out well and I can't afford private school. "Much as I'd love to have you here, maybe you're better off staying in Brussels for a while yet."

"How long?"

"At least the rest of the school year. We'll see how things are here come summer."

The tentative smile she pastes on doesn't mask her anxiety. "Don't want me around?"

"What kind of a doofus kid of mine thinks I don't want her around?"

My quip produces a chagrined grin. "Tell me why you think I should stay there."

"Do you like it?"

"It's kinda neat but I miss some stuff here."

"You don't get many chances to live overseas."

"I miss you."

"I miss you, too," I say while taking her hand in mine. "It's not like this is going to last forever."

"I know."

"You want to live here?"

"*Here?* In this house?"

"Yup. Right here."

She hesitates. "I thought you were gonna get a place in the suburbs?"

"I don't think so. Money's tight and the house is growing on me. Papa and I have been talking and I think I'm going to stay. Living here opens up a lot of possibilities for me when it comes time to choose a new job."

"You're still gonna be a lawyer, right?"

"I'm not sure."

Her eyes widen. "What else would you do?"

"Good question."

"Wow," she says with a little smile. "Maybe you can do something respectable and I won't hafta tell people my old man is a lawyer."

I reply with a playful smack on her arm. "Get to sleep. Big day tomorrow."

She squeezes my hand and snuggles deeper before we say our good nights.

"Everything going okay with you two?" Pat asks when I walk back into the kitchen.

"She was asking about coming back."

Pat's face lights up. "Soon?"

"I think she's better off in Brussels for now. Besides, she's not big on the idea of living here. She mentioned the suburbs."

"Have you closed the door on that idea?"

"I think so. I'm not sure what I'll do if she makes it a condition of coming back."

A frown signals Pat's disapproval. Part of me agrees with her. On the other hand, let her have a kid of her own, then we'll see how firmly she stands on principle. By silent agreement, we let the subject drop.

"Any plans for the next hour?" I ask.

She gives me a quizzical look and shakes her head.

"Are you feeling up to hanging around while I run over to the jail?"

"I'll be okay," she says, then glances at her watch. "It's awfully late for that, isn't it?"

I nod. She's right, but I want to tell Papa what happened tonight and get his input on tomorrow. We're meeting the prosecutors at seven-thirty to discuss plea deals. He'll suffer the consequences if what passes for our strategy blows up on us.

"Going now?" she asks.

I glance down at the last of my hot chocolate. "Maybe I'll finish this first?"

We sit in companionable silence for a minute, savoring tonight's victory and worrying about tomorrow. At least I am.

Pat breaks the silence. "I thought Brittany was enjoying Europe?"

"Maybe she's feeling a little homesick."

"She told me she gets bored sometimes."

"How? There's so much to do and see."

"Like Euro Disney?" Pat asks with a wondering shake of her head. "If you never do more than scratch the surface of life, anything gets old in a hurry. Even Europe, it seems. It'll be a shame if the kid gets saddled with her mother's provincialism."

"I suppose."

"Sticking to safe and familiar all the time is a shitty way to live."

I nod in agreement while *The Razor's Edge* comes to mind. Has the story influenced the changes in me over the past month, or has my evolution deepened my appreciation of the novel? I suppose it doesn't really matter if the chicken or the egg came first; the Tony Valenti who read the last page of Maugham's masterpiece isn't the same man who first cracked open the cover. My worldview today has much more in common with Pat's than it does with the one I shared with Michelle.

"I finished the book."

"Enjoy it?" she asks with a knowing smile.

"Very much."

We exchange a quick hug before I leave for the jail.

Papa is escorted into the attorney client room thirty minutes later. After we embrace and settle into our molded plastic seats on either side of a battered wooden table, Papa fixes his alert eyes on mine. "Why you come so late, Anthony?"

His eyes sparkle while I relate the outcome of the Village Board meeting and the fate of Peter Zaluski. "The feds are also investigating Mayor Brown," I conclude.

Papa smiles. "Is good, Anthony. As should be." Perhaps he feels as if some of the injustices and losses he's suffered have been partially redressed. There have been a few more smiles of late. We've knocked down several walls and are as close as we've been since I left for college. Papa seems pleasantly surprised to have me playing a role in his defense. As

I've grown more confident that I'm contributing something of value, I've even kicked around a little legal strategy with Papa. I've come tonight to do a little more of that. "I think the prosecution is bringing us a new plea deal in the morning."

"What is this deal?"

He shakes his head in annoyance when I start to explain what a plea deal is. "I know what plea deal is," he snaps impatiently. "What they say?"

"They'll recommend twenty-five years if you plead guilty. It's a possibility we need to consider."

He scowls. "They still call me guilty and I go to jail?"

I nod.

He fixes a steely gaze on me and states, "I no go to jail, Anthony."

He killed a cop, for God's sake. Short of getting the needle, what else does he think is going to happen? I can't imagine how we're supposed to reconcile Papa's demand with reality, but I know that look and that tone of voice. This isn't up for discussion. I get an unsettling sense that if Mike and I don't deliver, Papa will find a way to take his future into his own hands.

CHAPTER THIRTY-TWO

Papa's trial will resume at eleven this morning after our two-day recess. We'll be starting a couple of hours late to accommodate Judge Mitton, who is presiding over an emergency hearing for another trial. Aside from Luke Geffen delivering the written transcript of his interview with O'Reilly's ex-sister-in-law, Fiona Novak, the trial landscape hasn't changed since Monday. We've still got a huge hole in the heart of our case and are running out of time to fill it.

I take the garbage and recycling out to the curb, still wracking my brain for any germ of an idea that might lead to a coherent defense strategy. Sandy Russo exits the Vaccaros' front door. By the time she notices me, I've crossed into their driveway and am standing beside the driver's side door of her Ford Explorer. She pauses, probably deciding whether to go back inside or deal with me.

"Good morning, Sandy."

"Hi," she mutters without meeting my gaze.

I remain silent until she finally looks up. "You wouldn't talk to our investigator."

"I said all I had to say to him. The nerve of you people—

pretending that I was talking to someone from the police. Now, if you don't mind, I'm in a hurry."

"You might have information that will help Papa. Why didn't you come forward?"

"I talked to the police."

"They didn't tell us that."

She shrugs. "That's between you and them."

"No, Sandy, it's not. They're legally bound to give witness statements to the defense. They didn't tell us about you."

She looks confused. "Why not?"

"My guess is that they don't want anyone to know what really happened that night."

"Your father killed a policeman, Tony. End of story."

"But only Papa knows why."

"So he can tell the jury all about it."

"Who's going to believe him if it's his word against the State of Illinois?"

A hardness comes into her eyes. "I can't get involved."

"You're already involved. We can call you to testify."

"I don't think so," she shoots back.

"You think wrong."

She frowns as if her worst fears have just been realized. Then anger tightens the muscles around her eyes and mouth —exactly the expression her mother got when I'd crash through their hedge in pursuit of a baseball or football. "My daughter has to go to school with O'Reilly's son. Did you know that?"

I shake my head.

"The boy isn't much different than his father was and now, after what your father did, the O'Reilly boy is meaner than ever. How do you think it's gonna be for our daughter if I get up in court and tell what that boy's father did and said the night he was shot?"

"I didn't know—"

"There's always been a lot you didn't know, Tony. It's

been years since you had time to bother with Cedar Heights or the people here… including your own parents. They were mystified and hurt by your neglect. The only people you had time for were the ones who could help you escape our little one-horse town."

"I'm sorry, Sandy. I guess I can't fault how you feel about me, but this is for Papa. Can you at least tell our investigator what you heard?"

Not a hint of sympathy or forgiveness softens her features when she takes a step forward to force me out of her way. *"No."*

I'm sorely tempted to tell her that O'Reilly's kid can't bother her daughter now that he's behind bars, but I don't dare cross that line—especially as I'm an officer of the court. Sandy and I stare each other down for several seconds before I turn and trudge back to our house.

I head to the bathroom to shave and stand before the mirror, glaring at the ragged face staring back at me. Sandy's comment about me neglecting Mama and Papa has left me shaken. I hadn't paid enough attention—I realize that now—but neglect? Was it that bad? Enough that even the neighbors noticed? How could I have been such an asshole? I shake my head and turn on the taps to splash cold water over my face; maybe hoping to wash away the shame I see there. After another minute of self-flagellation, I grab a hand towel and dry off. Then it's off to court.

Judge Mitton calls us to order an hour later. Pat sits front and center amongst our neighbors with her lost eye symbolized by the black patch. This is only her second public outing since being released from hospital. She winks at me with her good eye when she catches me looking, prompting my first smile of the day. I appreciate her being here; she's nowhere near as fully recovered as she's pretending to be.

Mitton brings in the jury and calls on Dempsey to continue the prosecution's case.

"The prosecution rests, Your Honor."

A stunned silence falls over the courtroom. "The hell?" Mike mutters.

I think back to Friday afternoon and Dempsey intimating that the prosecution had more witnesses and/or evidence to present. "Guess he was just screwing with us."

Mitton pounces on the opportunity to move things along. "Is the defense ready to deliver its opening statement?"

"May we have a moment, Your Honor?" Mike asks.

After prosecutors complete their case-in-chief, defense attorneys often move to dismiss the charges by claiming the prosecution hasn't provided sufficient evidence to prove guilt. Such motions are almost always dismissed. We've been considering a plan to pitch a twist on the strategy. Thankfully, Mike's office worked up the motion yesterday. In hopes of buying time, we decide to play that card now.

"May I approach?" Mike asks the judge, brandishing a sheaf of papers that includes a copy of the Fiona Novak statement.

"Give it to my clerk."

Mike hands the paperwork to the clerk and returns. She glances at it, makes a notation, and passes it along to the judge.

I hand a copy to Dempsey and say, "We got the statement last night."

The judge's eyes settle on Mike after he sees what the clerk has handed him. "Another motion, Counselor?"

"Yes, Your Honor."

"Don't see many of these," Mitton mutters when he finishes reading and beckons the lawyers to the bench. We rush forward as quickly as decorum allows, then jostle for position, not unlike children struggling to be first in line at the Good Humor truck. The judge lifts the corner of the motion and looks at Mike. "A motion to set aside a grand jury finding, Counselor?"

"I believe the motion is fully warranted in this matter, Your Honor," Mike replies.

"Why is that, Counselor?"

"If the State had been in possession of the new evidence that has come to light—specifically Deputy O'Reilly's personnel records and the new statement from his ex-sister-in-law, we argue that the State would have brought lesser charges."

"Pure speculation, Mr. Williams."

Mike counters, "Given the current state of the evidence, bringing a capital charge in this case is demonstrably inappropriate."

"Your Honor—" Dempsey starts to say.

Mitton raises a hand to forestall him. "I don't necessarily disapprove of prosecutors giving themselves a little wiggle room by overcharging a case. We've all seen it done a thousand times. Often enough, it works out for the best."

Mike leans in. "Your Honor—"

Mitton waves him off. "I want to study your brief, read this new statement, and have my clerks do a little research. Everyone gets an extended lunch and I'll rule when we come back. Court will be recessed until three o'clock, but I expect you people here at two-thirty."

The judge's eyes move between Mike and Dempsey. "If you folks haven't already been talking, I suggest you try to find common ground."

Fat chance.

When we return from lunch, Mitton's clerk greets us and ushers us into the judge's chambers.

"Did you folks have a chance to talk about a deal?" he asks.

"Not a word," Mike replies.

Mitton cocks an inquiring eyebrow at Dempsey. "Counselor?"

"I spoke with State's Attorney Walker. Unfortunately, he

has commitments he couldn't reschedule. We'll get together this evening."

"Mr. Williams?" Mitton asks.

"The State knows where to find me, Your Honor."

Mitton appears satisfied. "Perhaps we should adjourn for the day and allow you folks some time to work things out."

"I see no reason to waste half a court day," Dempsey says.

I sense that Mike is about to agree. "Can I have a moment with Mr. Williams?" I ask the judge.

Mitton glances at me in surprise. "By all means."

"Thank you, Your Honor," I say while tugging at Mike's sleeve. "We'll just step into the hall."

As soon as the door closes behind us and I make sure we're alone in the hallway, I turn to Mike. "Walker's the top dog in Dempsey's office, right?"

"That's right. Cook County State's Attorney Timothy Walker. A real piece of work."

"You want to negotiate?"

"That's what the judge wants."

"It's not what I want, dammit."

"We don't have enough to hang tough," Mike says softly. "I wish it wasn't so, but it is. Time's run out on us."

"The hell it has. We haven't even started our case. The judge didn't rule on your motion."

"He won't rule in our favor. Even if Mitton agrees that the case is overcharged, he'll deal with that by pushing Dempsey to cut a deal for a lesser charge."

"Why is everyone pushing for a deal?" I ask.

"Business as usual, Tony. There's always pressure to clear the docket."

"I don't like it. Let's wait them out. They've just seen what Fiona Novak has to say. They've gotta start worrying about what the jury will think of O'Reilly when we're done with him."

"That's possible, but if they come back with a reasonable sentence, I don't care what we plead to."

"That's not your call," I counter. "I talked to Papa last night. He doesn't want to go to jail."

Mike gives me an incredulous look. "The hell?"

"You need to talk to him before we open, Mike. Trust me on this. We can open our case in the morning."

Mike ponders a moment longer. "If you say so."

"Good man."

"You handle things in there," Mike says before he opens the door to lead me back into chambers.

I'm initially taken aback at being appointed spokesperson, but it isn't as if I've never addressed a court. "Mr. Dempsey doesn't have a deal to discuss with us at the moment, Your Honor," I say once we're seated. "We'd like to hear what they have to say before we deliver our opening statement. If the prosecution brings us a deal to discuss, we'll fill you in on that before court resumes."

The judge nods. "Fair enough. Will you be ready to make your opening statement first thing tomorrow?"

"Absolutely, Your Honor," Mike replies.

"Absolutely" might be a little optimistic.

Mike seems to agree thirty minutes later when we leave the attorney-client room after Papa gives us our marching orders. Our job is to keep him out of jail, turning Mike's preferred strategy on its head.

"How the hell are we supposed to do that?" he asks in exasperation as we step into the cold outside the courthouse. "You need to make him see reality, Tony. We open in the morning and we still don't have a case. We need to cut a deal."

"The hell we do. Not the shit deals on offer so far."

Mike looks at me in disbelief. "You, too? The acorn didn't fall far from the tree."

"I want to be sure Papa has a say in what we do," I say with an edge in my voice.

"We both want the best possible outcome for Francesco."

"Maybe so, but we're miles apart on what that looks like."

Mike's expression is troubled when he says, "I'm starting to think so."

"With what Fiona Novak just gave us, we've got enough to raise the specter that O'Reilly was in the grip of roid rage," I say after an uncomfortable pause. "The guy was chock full of steroids when they cut him open. Think about it, Mike. He fits the mold."

"Even if he does, we've got nothing concrete to prove it."

"Let me dig. Have Luke Geffen dig, too."

Mike looks skyward and sighs. "Fine. Run with it, but let's not piss away what little time we have chasing rainbows."

I'm not finished tossing hand grenades. The only way to keep Papa out of jail is to convince the jury that he was defending himself. The only evidence we have of that is what he told us. "We may have to put Papa on the stand."

Mike spins on me. "The *hell* you talking about, man? No friggin' way is that happening!"

"Why not? We'll put a little old guy on the stand, a law-abiding citizen who's bewildered by what's happening to him —a simple man who wonders why the government is so determined to put him out of his home of forty years. Cedar Heights made life miserable for him and his wife. That's been proven. To his mind, the stress of that had a lot to do with her death."

Mike groans. "Come on."

"That's how he feels, dammit! That's what he'll say under oath. Can anyone prove otherwise?"

"Judge Mitton is going to tell our jury that their job is to decide whether or not Francesco shot and killed O'Reilly," Mike counters. "*Why* he did it isn't relevant."

"Papa will be a sympathetic figure to the jury," I argue.

"They'll hear his version of what happened that night. They'll hear how much O'Reilly scared him. We can put on a bunch of neighbors as character witnesses."

"The hell you been smoking? I'll tell you what happens if we put Francesco on the stand. He'll tell his story and then Dempsey will tear him apart. He's an absolute beast on cross."

"The jury is also going to hear the story of a legalized thug named Andrew O'Reilly," I counter angrily. "They'll hear his record. They'll hear from people who know firsthand what Andrew O'Reilly was about. I don't know about you, but if *I* were sitting on the jury, I know where *my* sympathies would lie."

Mike's eyes bore into mine. "But you're *not* sitting on the jury, Tony. Think about that."

I'm not throwing in the towel. "Papa will be a sympathetic figure."

Mike shakes his head in exasperation. "He'll be especially sympathetic when they stick a needle in his arm, won't he?"

Picturing that pulls me up short. Who in hell do I think I am pretending to know what to do in a murder trial?

CHAPTER THIRTY-THREE

Mike is chatting with Dempsey and Perez when I walk into the courtroom at seven-twenty the next morning. I stifle a yawn while Mike separates himself from the prosecutors and walks over to me.

"We okay?" he asks.

Are we? Nothing will be gained by us squabbling. "Sure."

"Has anything come out of the show at Village Hall Tuesday night?"

"An investigator from Papa's insurance company called yesterday to compare notes. They're going to pay the claim and go after Titan for reimbursement."

Mike grins and thumps the table. "Hot damn! Score one for the little folks!"

"No kidding," I mutter while envisioning the outstanding balance on my latest ABA credit card statement. My eyes drift back to Dempsey and Perez. "Where's Walker?"

"Always the last to arrive. The Alpha Dog waits on no one." He eyes me for a moment. "You look like hell. Did you get *any* sleep?"

"A minute here, a minute there. I'm a little groggy like Mount Everest is a little tall. But I'm pumped full of coffee."

He chuckles, then turns serious. "I thought about things last night. We'll play things your way this morning."

"How so?" I ask in surprise.

"Let's dip a toe in the water in terms of putting O'Reilly on trial and see how that plays."

The door opens and Cook County State's Attorney Timothy Walker marches into the room. He's a study in immaculate grooming, reminding me of any number of faceless C-suite corporate executives of my acquaintance. An elegant blue suit hangs perfectly on his trim frame. A red and blue striped rep tie stands out in sharp relief against a blindingly white dress shirt. His head of thick blonde hair is styled to display its owner's youthful vigor to maximum effect. A pair of black oxfords gleam under the brilliant overhead lights with each lengthy stride he takes. My fingers inch to my own striped rep tie. I resolve to go shopping to buy something less establishment.

Walker shakes hands with Dempsey and Perez, then chats with them for a minute before he turns and advances on us. We meet him beside the defense table.

He takes Mike's hand first. "Williams. How are you?"

"Fine."

"Tough case," Walker says, as if he's been losing sleep over it. He turns to me and extends his hand. "Timothy Walker, Mr. Valenti. May I call you Tony?"

I take the proffered hand. Piercing blue eyes study me carefully. "If you want."

"How are you holding up?" he asks. Although the question is couched in feigned concern, I sense that it's exploratory—a fighter sizing me up. I've played this game before and won't be telegraphing any sign of weakness to Papa's ambitious would-be hangman.

"Just fine."

Walker stares into my eyes for a moment before he turns

back to Mike. "Last time we locked horns was the Camponelli matter, wasn't it?"

Mike's strained response is filtered through a tight smile. "Maybe so."

Mike told me about the Camponelli case yesterday to illustrate who we're up against. Walker had clinched the endorsement of the FOP for his second Cook County State's Attorney campaign by winning death penalty convictions against two teenage gang bangers accused of shooting a narcotics officer. Mike told me that his clients weren't choir-boys, but there was no evidence that either one of them pulled the trigger; the cops couldn't even prove they'd been in the immediate vicinity when the shooting took place. It had taken the highly questionable testimony of a jailhouse snitch to seal the case. Two kids awaiting possible execution for a crime they probably didn't commit doesn't bother Timothy Walker. Not one bit. The important thing is that suburban voters lap up his tough-on-crime shtick. An undercurrent of animosity flows between the two men as they lock eyes.

"You sleep well when you think about those kids on death row?" Mike asks.

"Like a baby," Walker replies with an edge of surliness.

"Let's get to it," I suggest.

Walker slides effortlessly back into character by flashing me a winning smile. "I couldn't agree more," he says affably. He gestures for Dempsey and Perez to join us. After they do, Walker turns to me. "Alex tells me you're being a little stubborn?"

The condescension rankles. Instead of taking the bait, I reply with the hint of a shrug.

Walker shifts his attention to Mike. "Alex offered you first-degree and twenty-five years. What more do you want?"

"A serious offer."

"That's the best offer you're going to get."

Mike takes a step back. "See you back here in an hour or so."

"What the hell do you want?" Walker snaps.

"Something resembling justice," I retort.

"We'll seek the death penalty if you don't bend," Walker threatens. "We'll get no less than life in prison."

"And if we bend?" Mike asks.

"We'll be satisfied with twenty years."

"What's the difference to a sixty-nine-year-old man?" I ask.

Walker turns his palms up. He and his colleagues have taken several steps toward the door when Judge Mitton throws the door open and walks into the courtroom. He's once again a study in clashing attire. This morning it's a plaid long-sleeve shirt over a pair of faded brown corduroy slacks. His shoes cry out for a visit to the shoeshine stand in the lobby. The contrast between him and the Cook County State's Attorney turning to greet him is stark. Knowing that the rumpled judge holds the upper hand in the power equation between them must grate on Walker no end. I suspect Mitton isn't shy about letting Walker know who rules his courtroom.

After a quick round of greetings, the judge steps back to study us. "Have you come up with something workable?"

"We've made an offer," Walker replies smoothly. "The defense isn't receptive."

"What's the offer?"

"First-degree."

"Sentence?"

Walker meets his gaze. "Twenty-five years."

He's already walked back the offer of twenty years?

Mitton gives him a long look. "You haven't moved beyond that?"

"We've given this our best good faith effort."

The judge's expression telegraphs his dissatisfaction.

"With all due respect, Your Honor, it's not your place to tell us how to manage a case."

Mitton takes a step towards Walker. "I agree. On the other hand, misconduct in my courtroom is most assuredly my business, wouldn't you say?"

Walker doesn't bat an eye. "Misconduct is overly harsh to describe a clerical oversight."

"Don't try my patience. I'm not one of your pals at City Hall or down in Springfield. A pair of cops disposing of evidence to cover up criminal behavior by another police officer is hardly a clerical oversight."

"Reasonable people can disagree about what happened, Judge. The bottom line is that we must protect our communities and the folks who keep us safe. Where does it leave us when people think they can question the decisions and actions of the authorities?"

"In a free country," I retort.

Judge Mitton's eyes twinkle when he looks at me. Walker's lips tighten into a straight line.

"Are you prepared to rule on our motion to set aside the grand jury indictment, Your Honor?" Mike asks.

Mitton nods. "I am, but we'll discuss the discovery violation first. Be in my chambers at eight-thirty."

Walker turns to me as soon as the door closes behind the judge. "Willing to gamble with your father's life, are you?"

"I'm not willing to sacrifice him to your career aspirations."

"That's not what this is about," Walker says indignantly before he spins on his heel and marches out with his minions in tow.

"The hell it isn't," Mike mutters as we watch them go. "I thought they might come around."

We grab a couple of coffees from a vending machine and spend the next half-hour reviewing our opening statement and witness list. Judge Mitton's clerk shows us into his chambers when we arrive at eight twenty-nine.

The judge's eyes immediately settle on Walker. "Mrs. Russo spoke to the police the day after the shooting," he says without preamble.

"I haven't had much time to look into this," Walker says. "Mrs. Russo isn't even on our witness list."

Mitton's eyes smolder. "You've had this since September."

"As Mr. Dempsey told you, this looks like a clerical oversight."

Mike snorts. Mitton doesn't bother to admonish him.

"Technically," Walker continues, "this wasn't an eyewitness statement. Mrs. Russo told the police what she *heard*, Your Honor. I suspect someone misunderstood our instructions to turn over all *eyewitness* statements."

He's got to be kidding. I've generally considered allegations of prosecutorial misconduct on this scale to be so much sour grapes from defense attorneys. Goes to show how much I know.

Judge Mitton's eyes narrow. "That's quite a story, Counselor. I'm not buying. The failure to turn over Mrs. Russo's statement is an egregious discovery violation. Mr. Valenti's ability to mount a defense has been jeopardized by your misconduct."

Walker shrugs. "Friday was the first time we heard of Sandy Russo."

"That's the result of poor supervision of your investigators and weak administrative oversight within your offices," the judge says. "The defense is entitled to a remedy."

"We're well into this case, Judge. Whatever Sandy Russo may or may not have heard isn't going to make much difference in the outcome. A remedy is inappropriate."

"I'm afraid you're again mistaken on a point of law, Mr. Walker," Mitton replies before turning to Mike. "Have you given some thought to an appropriate remedy, Counselor?"

"We've been blindsided, Your Honor. Mrs. Russo won't speak with our investigator."

Walker spreads his hands. "Because she has nothing to tell them, Your Honor. This is no more than a red herring thrown out by—"

"I'm speaking with Mr. Williams!" Mitton snaps at the state's attorney. "You may speak when I tell you to. Understood?"

Walker flushes with anger. The judge invites Mike to continue.

"The circumstances of this shooting are not what we believed them to be, Your Honor. Given all that's coming to light, we may need to re-evaluate our position and reconsider Mr. Valenti's defense."

"How long do you think you'll need?"

Dempsey jumps in. "There's no need to delay the trial, Your Honor. If the Court orders Mrs. Russo to cooperate, we can send someone out to take her statement today. If she has anything relevant to say, we will bring that forward in rebuttal."

Mitton turns to Mike. "Counselor?"

"Sounds to me like the State wants to skate over its discovery violation, Your Honor. However much Mr. Dempsey and his boss try to spin what's happened, the fact remains that they withheld information about a key witness—deliberately, if you ask me."

Walker indignantly comes halfway out of his seat. "I object to—"

"Don't bother, Counselor," Mitton says. "I'm not persuaded that withholding Mrs. Russo's statement was an innocent oversight."

The state's attorney continues to look aggrieved. When Cook County voters finally wake up and throw his ass out of office, he's got a future in Hollywood.

Dempsey tries to step in. "Your Honor, you know I don't—"

Mitton shuts him down with an angry glare. "It happened! If your office hadn't played games with discovery we wouldn't be in this position, would we?"

Walker crosses his arms and stares at the wall above the judge's head.

Mitton turns back to us. "Remedy?"

"Given the prosecution's track record with this witness, it hardly seems prudent to trust them to do things right this time," Mike replies. "Perhaps the Court should order Mrs. Russo to speak with our investigator and then we'll decide how to use the information."

Walker jumps in. "We would, of course, immediately be given a copy of her statement, as per the rules of discovery."

"Mr. Williams?" the judge asks.

"They had their shot at this, Your Honor. Perhaps a suitable remedy would be to withhold Mrs. Russo's statement from the prosecution. They'll have a chance to cross-examine her if we choose to call her as a witness."

Judge Mitton thinks for a moment. "That sounds reasonable. It even includes a touch of poetic justice. Our second order of business is the defense motion to dismiss the grand jury indictment. The motion is denied." His eyes settle on Walker as he continues, "In light of the potentially exculpatory evidence withheld from the prosecution and defense prior to the grand jury hearing, the Court is sympathetic to the defense pleading that this case has been overcharged. I might have ruled differently if the motion had come before the prosecution rested."

Walker smirks while Mike and I try to mask our disappointment.

The judge slaps his hands down on the desk and pushes his chair back. "Now, go prepare so we can bring in our jury at nine o'clock and move things along."

We spend the next ten minutes getting organized as press and spectators filter into the courtroom. Brittany has joined Pat in the seats immediately behind our table. She mouths "hi" when I turn back to wink at her. The prosecutors are conspicuously absent, something we comment on as the minute hand creeps closer and closer to the top of the hour. Mike wonders what they're up to; I suspect their boss is throwing a temper tantrum. Dempsey and Perez stride in at one minute to nine, seconds before a door opens and a pair of sheriff's deputies march Papa into the courtroom. He settles into the seat next to mine. I fill him in on our fruitless meeting with the prosecutors while Judge Mitton sweeps in and settles behind the bench.

Once the jury is seated, the judge turns to Mike. "Are you ready to proceed, Mr. Williams?"

Mike nods and gets up to deliver our opening statement. It's a study in brevity. He asks the jurors to keep an open mind and then spends several minutes highlighting what we perceive to be the contradictions and holes in the prosecution's case. I admire his confident delivery. You'd never guess we're flying by the seat of our pants.

Mike directs the jurors' attention to the only prop he will use in his statement, a picture of the mangled screen door hanging from the frame of our front entry. "Have a look at this, ladies and gentlemen. This picture shows the screen door at the Valenti home as it was when the police arrived on September seventeenth. Ask yourselves if you've ever seen a screen door this beaten up. Ask yourselves how much strength it would take for a person to do this to a piece of metal. Ask yourselves what kind of rage must be behind such an act. This picture tells a story, ladies and gentlemen. We intend to tell you that story."

As Mike winds down, he stands in front of the jury box. "Ladies and gentlemen, we will show you the tragic events of September seventeenth from an entirely new perspective. The differences between the truth and what you've been told by Mr. Dempsey are stark. I find them deeply troubling. I suspect you will, too."

Mike walks back to the defense table and pauses for a sip of water. Then he walks around to stand behind Papa and utters the only part of our opening statement we can currently substantiate. "Francesco Valenti is a good and decent man who has lived an honest, productive, and honorable life. He worked at Cook County Hospital for thirty years. He's been a good and loyal husband, a loving father, and a doting grandfather. Mr. Valenti is a law-abiding citizen with absolutely no history of violence, a man who has made valuable contributions to his neighborhood for many, many years. He's the father and grandfather we all wish for."

He walks back into the well and looks each and every juror square in the eye. "Ladies and gentlemen, thank you for hearing me out. We look forward to presenting the *true* facts of this case, facts that will demonstrate that Francesco Valenti is a far different man than Mr. Dempsey's jaundiced portrayal suggests."

When my partner sits down, I cast a sideways look at Dempsey. He looks smug. Nothing Mike said countered the fundamental fact that Papa shot Deputy O'Reilly.

Judge Mitton raps his gavel. "We'll take a thirty-minute recess. When we return, the defense will present its case."

"Tony! Mike!" Pat whispers urgently from behind us after the jury departs and Papa is taken away.

We turn back to find Pat and Brittany at the rail behind the defense table.

"What's up?" I ask as we scoot our chairs back to them.

Pat pushes Brittany's cell phone into my hand. "Look!"

I stare at the phone for a long moment and then hand it to Mike. I'm speechless. Mike isn't. "Not a word," he cautions us before he pockets the phone and leads us into the hallway. Once he finds an empty alcove, he ushers us into it and stares at the picture again. He cautions us to keep our voices down, then softly asks, "Where the hell did this come from?"

"Dad took it before we went to school the night Papa shot the cop," Brittany whispers back.

I take a closer look at the picture. Brittany wears a pained frown and has her hands on her hips while she stands on our front porch, right in front of the pristine screen door. I belatedly remember the moment. She'd been bragging about the quality of the camera on her new phone while we were killing time before we left for St. Aloysius, so I'd turned it on her to snap a shot. The photo is date-stamped September seventeenth. Better still, it's time-stamped 6:07 PM—three hours before a police photographer snapped the picture of the broken, twisted door Mike used in his opening statement.

"Why the hell didn't you show this to us before?" Mike asks Brittany.

"Because she's been in Brussels and hasn't seen the picture of what happened to the screen door until just now," Pat reminds him tartly. "You should be thrilled to have the damned thing. Leave the kid alone."

"Sorry," Mike says to Brittany. "I'm just thinking about how much it would have helped to have this sooner."

"We're plenty glad to have it now," I tell Brittany. "Good work!"

Mike leads us back into the courtroom after he clarifies the details. He catches the eye of Detective Plummer and waves him over.

"What are you doing?" I ask.

"We need to get this into evidence," Mike replies. "The story of how the picture got here this morning needs to be told and corroborated as fast as we can make it happen. Chain of custody is going to come into play. That's going to be dicey. You can bet your ass the State will try to keep this out. The sooner we legitimize it, the better."

My knee-jerk reaction is not to share this with the enemy, but Mike's logic is sound. Still. "Can't we do it ourselves?"

Mike shakes his head. "Best to have the cops involved. Plummer will play it straight."

I'll be damned if I don't agree.

"What's up?" the detective says after he greets everyone.

Mike hands him the phone with the picture open. Plummer looks down at it, glances up at us, then studies the image some more. "Where did this come from?"

Mike explains.

"I've never seen what happened to the door before this morning," Brittany adds. "When I did, I remembered that Dad took this picture."

Plummer nods thoughtfully. "You keep all the pictures you take with your phone?"

"Pretty much."

He thinks that over. "This is the new phone you had on September seventeenth?"

"Yup."

"I remember you mentioning it. You were pretty excited."

Brittany blushes a little when she nods.

Plummer smiles. "Hey, don't be embarrassed. This is way nicer than my phone. I'd be showing this thing off if it was mine."

She gives him a grateful smile. "Yeah, it's pretty cool."

"I'll say. Mind showing me where you hide the pictures?"

Brittany angles the phone towards Plummer and scrolls through a gazillion photos.

"All date and time-stamped, huh?" he says.

"Yeah. I like to know when and where, y'know?"

"Sure do," Plummer replies. Then he turns to me. "Still got the sales receipt for this?"

"I do."

The detective turns to Mike. "What do you wanna do?"

"The phone needs to be taken into evidence but I don't

want it solely in police custody. We're going to need expert analysis to authenticate the picture."

Plummer thinks on that, then nods. "How are we going to do that?"

"My brother Reg probably knows what needs to be done," Mike replies. "He's a cell phone guy at Motorola. Not that this is a Motorola, but I imagine they're all similar enough."

"No way is a Motorola anything like *my* phone," Brittany says indignantly. Mike has apparently uttered a cell phone sacrilege. Given what I paid for the damned thing, it's probably true.

"That's a question for you attorneys to tackle," Plummer replies.

"I'll buzz Reg," Mike says before he takes a few steps away to call his brother. He turns back to us when he finishes. "Reg has a couple of ideas about who can do the work. He'll get back with me after he makes a call or two."

"Let's hear what the judge and Mr. Dempsey have to say," Plummer suggests. He walks over to the Clerk of the Court to tell her what's going on.

"I can't have my phone back?" Brittany asks with a tremor in her voice.

"If not, we'll get you a new one," I assure her.

"But my life is on there, Dad. I can't live without it!"

"They can transfer the data, can't they?" I ask no one in particular.

"I'll see what can be done," Mike says.

Pat rests a hand on Brittany's. "I'll take you to a cell phone store."

Five minutes later, we're in Judge Mitton's chambers explaining how the photo came to light.

He takes a long look at the picture, shakes his head, and looks up at Mike. "As you were saying earlier, Mr. Williams, the door tells quite a story."

"Having that phone turn up here literally minutes after

Mr. Williams made that exact statement in his opening is a little too convenient for my liking," Dempsey says.

The judge looks at Mike. "The same thought crossed my mind, Counselor."

"I can see why it might, Your Honor, but we brought this to the Court's attention as soon as Brittany showed it to us."

"Detective?" the judge asks Plummer.

"I'm no expert on this stuff, Your Honor, but it looks like it may be legit to me. We'll need experts to verify that the phone hasn't been tampered with, but I remember the girl telling me about the phone the night of the shooting. She said it was new. Mr. Valenti says he has the receipt, so that and store records should confirm ownership and date of purchase. It looks like she's kept all the pictures she's taken with it. It's not like the old days when a splice on a film negative showed right up, but the techies can tell if a picture file has been imported or manipulated."

"This is our piece of evidence," Mike says. "We want someone of our choosing to look at it. The police are welcome to send a technician along."

"Who is your guy?" Judge Mitton asks.

Mike pulls out his phone. "Lane Brown at Brown Photo and Electronics. My brother gave his name to me." Mike then fills Mitton and Dempsey in on his brother's occupation.

The judge nods. "Sounds reasonable to me. Mr. Dempsey?"

"The phone should be in police custody. I don't trust any of this and will move to suppress this picture on the basis of chain of custody."

"You're going to do that anyway," I retort. "It's not like you're looking for the truth."

"Let's wait and see what the experts can tell us," Mitton says. "Log this into evidence and arrange to have the experts look at it right away, Mr. Williams. I don't want to hold things up."

"But this is significant," Mike argues. "We'll need some time."

"You have some time. It's not as if you and Mr. Dempsey are needed to oversee the work. I'll send one of my bailiffs along to do that. Let the experts sort things out while you present your case. Assuming we can establish the picture is authentic and that the date and time are accurate, the story it tells is pretty much self-evident. You won't need a lot of time to show it to the jury and explain its significance."

"I need time to think about this," Mike says. "This may impact our order of witnesses and how we present our evidence."

"I'm sorry, Counselor, but we don't even know if this evidence will come in. I may give you some leeway at the end of your case, but we're starting on time this morning."

Mike is about to say more when I put a hand on his arm and speak up. "Fair enough, Your Honor. Can you extend recess an extra thirty minutes so we can get things organized?"

Mitton nods. "We can do that."

By the end of the recess, Lane Brown has agreed to tackle the job of investigating Brittany's phone, validating the integrity of the photo, and getting a report to us by nine o'clock tomorrow morning, all for a mere $6,500—money well spent if the picture makes it into the courtroom. Plummer called in a favor from a Chicago PD evidence technician and she has agreed to work with Lane Brown. Unlike the prosecutors, the detective seems to be on the hunt for as much truth as he can find, regardless of its impact on the proceedings. I hope it doesn't rebound on him. One of the judge's bailiffs is going along, as well, so we're all set.

"Things are looking up," I say to Mike before we walk back into court.

"Never count your chickens before they hatch," he warns me. "I just overheard Dempsey on the phone to Walker.

They're already preparing an injunction to keep the picture out."

"Mitton will let it in."

Mike nods thoughtfully. "Probably so. If he does, putting Francesco on the stand might not be such a wild idea, after all."

CHAPTER THIRTY-FOUR

The first witness we call is our psychologist, Dr. Angela Backstrom. Our goal is to reframe the jury's understanding of Papa to debunk the prosecution's depiction of him as a homicidal time bomb waiting to explode. When Dr. Backstrom finally leaves the witness stand after a furious cross-examination by Alex Dempsey, I think we've made progress. Mr. Rosetti, Mrs. LaSusa, and Mr. Vaccaro follow, adding their voices in support of Doctor Backstrom's depiction of Papa as a benign and admirable everyman. There's still the inconvenient fact of him shooting a sheriff's deputy to confront, but we hope the jury is now puzzled as to why he did so.

Our next witness is the recently unemployed Peter Zaluski. Mike has decided that it's safe for me to handle Zaluski when we recall him to the witness stand. I don't quibble with the former village manager over the chronology and facts of his prior testimony, driving instead straight to the motivations of the village in its dealings with my parents. "Let's go back a couple of years, Mr. Zaluski. Let's revisit the months immediately after Titan Development failed in its first effort to condemn and seize the Liberty Street/Independence

Park neighborhood for development. Do you remember that period?"

"Reasonably well," Zaluski replies.

"Offers to purchase were made to a number of Liberty Street homeowners in the months following this, correct?"

"Correct."

"Is it true that offers were made only to homeowners who played significant roles in contesting the eminent domain effort?"

"Objection!" Dempsey shouts. "We have no basis to believe Mr. Zaluski was involved in those negotiations."

"Counselor?" the judge asks me.

"Mr. Zaluski just told us that a few of Titan's opponents sold out in that time frame. I would like to explore the village's involvement."

Mitton nods. "Proceed, Mr. Valenti, but only if the witness has direct knowledge of those events."

"Thank you, Your Honor." I return my attention to Zaluski. "Do you know who decided which homeowners would receive purchase offers?"

"Mayor Brown and I were consulted."

"Who consulted with you, Mr. Zaluski?"

"Titan Developments. We were asked to provide a list of the homeowners who had been instrumental in thwarting the eminent domain effort."

"Were you told why Titan Developments wanted this information?"

"Titan wished to remove those homeowners from the picture before their next effort to acquire the parcel for development."

"They had a target list, did they?" I ask.

"Objection!" Dempsey yells. "That's hearsay! Mr. Zaluski was not privy to—"

"They did," Zaluski says while Dempsey is objecting.

Dempsey furiously demands that Zaluski's answer be

stricken from the record. Judge Mitton merely asks Zaluski to refrain from answering until an objection is either sustained or overruled.

"Do you have direct knowledge of discussions within Titan Developments at this time, Mr. Zaluski?" I ask.

"I do not."

"Were you involved in any discussions about future efforts to revisit this development plan?"

"Yes."

"Let's skip ahead to the tax reassessment of the Valentis' home. You said it came to your attention that Mr. and Mrs. Valenti had made improvements to their home without obtaining the appropriate building permits. Do you remember that testimony?"

"I do." Zaluski seems quite happy to cooperate today, which stands in sharp contrast to his efforts to obfuscate and otherwise obstruct Mike's efforts to get at the truth just last week. Perhaps his target for payback has shifted from Francesco Valenti to Mayor Brown.

"Can you tell us how that information came to your attention?"

"Titan gave us a list of improvements and suggested that we have Henry Poindexter in our permits department check to see if building permits were issued."

"Why Poindexter?"

"I didn't know, I just went along with the request."

"And this was done?"

Zaluski nods. "Yes. Poindexter was sent to inspect the property that week and initiate a reassessment."

"Is it unusual to have all that occur in the space of a week?"

"Very much so."

"Why was it done in this instance?"

"The mayor told us to."

"Was the rest of the process leading up to the eviction

notice also expedited at the direction of you and Mayor Brown?"

"It was."

"Would it be fair to say that Francesco and Maria Valenti were targeted for punishment because they helped defeat Titan Development's efforts to redevelop Liberty Street and Independence Park?"

"Absolutely," Zaluski replies. "Our goal was to drive the Valentis and others like them out of the neighborhood. Titan planned to bring the redevelopment plan to us again after the main opposition was neutralized."

I let Zaluski's answer hang in the air while I take a sip of water. "Neutralized," I mutter with distaste. "That's rather militaristic terminology for the public servants of a village to be using, isn't it, Mr. Zaluski?"

He looks somewhat chagrined. "I suppose it is."

"Did the administrators of the Village of Cedar Heights believe they were locked in conflict with any citizens who disagreed with Titan Development's plans for the Liberty Street neighborhood?"

"Mayor Brown certainly did."

"Why do you think that was?"

"You'd have to ask him."

I'm not here to beat up Zaluski. Not anymore. "I have no further questions for the witness."

Dempsey declines to cross examine Zaluski. He seems happy to see the backside of him.

Mike calls the former coroner of the City of Detroit. Coroner Jones has built a second career questioning coroner's findings he finds particularly egregious. He's costing us several thousands of my crowd funding dollars to call into question key findings of the Cook County Coroner. It will be money well spent if it works. He's smooth and authoritative on the stand. The jurors listen carefully. Are they buying? Who knows?

Mike's next witness is a doctor with extensive knowledge of steroids and experience treating abusers of steroids. Luke Geffen had looked her up two nights ago and somehow or other managed an interview that convinced her to appear a day later. Mike brings in autopsy toxicology reports confirming that O'Reilly died with startling levels of human growth hormone and anabolic steroids in his system. According to the doctor, the concentrations and mix of substances is indicative of a heavy steroid user at the apex of a stacking episode. She explains that steroid users are especially likely to experience incidents of uncontrollable rage after stacking. Deputy O'Reilly died on a night when he was decidedly susceptible to erratic and violent behavior—behavior to which he was no stranger. Dempsey is unable to blunt the damage on cross.

I'm up next, this time to trot out O'Reilly's personnel files. The records and witnesses from the Cedar Heights PD and the Cook County Sheriff's office show that he had a penchant for abusing suspects and other members of the public. Dempsey does his best to temper the damage. By the time we break for lunch, the jurors must be thinking Papa is a pretty good guy compared to Andy O'Reilly. When I share this thought with Mike, he agrees but notes, "Unfortunately, it doesn't excuse Francesco shooting him."

I recall Molly O'Reilly to the stand when court reconvenes. Mike and I debated the merits of bringing Molly's sister, Fiona Novak, to the stand before I attempt to shred Molly, but decided that Fiona might be an effective counter if Dempsey manages to rehabilitate Molly or has withheld some key point he hopes to spring on us at the last minute. If her answers to my first couple of innocuous questions are any indication of what's to come, Molly O'Reilly intends to fight back this afternoon. Suits me fine.

"When we last spoke, you told us that you divorced Andy

O'Reilly on grounds of mental and physical abuse. Is that correct?"

"No, it's not," she snaps. "You misrepresent the facts."

I pick up a copy of the court records from their divorce proceedings and hand them to her. "Is this an official copy of the papers from your divorce?"

She refuses to touch the papers. "They're not true."

"What isn't true, Mrs. O'Reilly?"

"Andy wasn't abusive."

I take a step closer to the witness box. "You swore he was when you filed for divorce."

"Well, I needed to say that to get support, didn't I?"

"You're telling us that you'll lie when it suits your purposes or to get what you want?"

"Of course, I do. How else—"

"Objection, Your Honor!" Dempsey shouts to shut her up. "Counsel is asking leading questions."

"Given Mrs. O'Reilly's prior testimony, I'll allow Mr. Valenti some latitude to do so."

I turn back to the ex-Mrs. O'Reilly. "You were explaining when and why it's okay to lie in court."

"Everybody knows you gotta say stuff like that to get what you've got coming to you."

"Do you know what perjury is, Mrs. O'Reilly?"

She snorts. "Yeah, legal mumbo jumbo that doesn't mean anything. Everyone lies in court."

"What makes you say that?"

"Andy always said so. So does everyone else. Cops have to lie in court—that's the only way to get around lawyers like you."

I notice Dempsey deflating before I cock my head to the side. "Did you rehearse your prior testimony with the prosecutor's office, Mrs. O'Reilly?"

"Yeah."

"Once? Twice?"

"Until I was sick of it," she says in exasperation.

I arch my eyebrows and step back as if I'm utterly shocked and scandalized by her answer. With all the wide-eyed disbelief I can summon, I ask, "They *knew* you were going to lie on the witness stand?"

"Objection!" Dempsey snaps. "We assumed our witness was being truthful with us. I resent the implication that we would knowingly allow a witness to perjure herself on the stand!"

"Do you have a specific objection, Mr. Dempsey?" Judge Mitton asks.

"Defense counsel is insinuating that our team is guilty of gross misconduct. He has no grounds to do so."

The judge cocks a skeptical eyebrow at Dempsey for the briefest of seconds and then turns back to me. "Do you wish to file a formal accusation of misconduct against Mr. Dempsey?"

I make a show of pondering the judge's question for several seconds. "Not officially, no. I don't think it's necessary at this point, but we'll reserve the right to do so."

"As you wish, Counselor."

I take a sip of water to let my "unofficial" accusation sink in. In my experience, no witness has ever worked so hard to impeach herself. It's hard to believe Molly O'Reilly did so without the prosecutors knowing she would. If I were a juror, I'd be mighty pissed with the prosecution right about now. "So, now you want us to believe that Andy O'Reilly never hit you?" I ask after a suitable interval.

"What happens in my home stays in my home. It's none of your business."

"Your Honor?" I plead.

"Please answer the question, Mrs. O'Reilly."

She looks daggers at the judge and then me. "He might have slapped me a time or two."

"Once or twice, Mrs. O'Reilly?" I ask. "Just a simple slap? Is that your testimony?"

"Yeah."

I hand her a copy of the domestic abuse complaint Molly's sister made on her behalf. "Do you recognize this?"

"Garbage," she snarls. "Bullshit from my sister."

"Please refrain from using profanity in my courtroom," Mitton orders her.

"Was your sister mistaken, Mrs. O'Reilly?" I ask. "Did she not take you to the Emergency Department at Maywood Hospital for treatment after your husband beat you and your son?"

"We had a little fight, okay?"

"Did you suffer contusions?"

"What's that?"

"Cuts and bruises, Mrs. O'Reilly." I hand her a copy of the Emergency Department record of their visit and then pass a copy to the clerk for distribution to the jurors. How in hell Luke Geffen can be nine places at once is beyond me but I'm glad he gets around so efficiently. "This is the hospital's official record of your visit. I believe you required stitches."

"Maybe a couple."

"Eleven, and two broken teeth?"

"Maybe. I don't really remember."

"And one broken and two cracked ribs?"

"Said I don't remember, didn't I?" she snarls.

"Could your foggy memory be a result of the concussion the emergency room doctor diagnosed?"

"Okay, so he beat the crap out of us. You happy now?"

"This was the last straw for you, wasn't it, Mrs. O'Reilly? You filed for divorce within a week of this incident."

"Yeah."

As much as I hate to humiliate her any more to demonstrate how often Andy O'Reilly resorted to violent behavior, I'm not done yet. "We heard testimony earlier about your ex-husband's steroid use. Were you aware that he used steroids?"

"Pretty obvious to everyone, wasn't it?" she replies sarcastically. "He wasn't exactly a little guy when we got married, but he was twice as big by the time we got divorced."

"We also heard that he did things like pyramiding and stacking to get better results from his steroid use. Did you witness that?"

"Yeah, he made me inject him with the damned stuff sometimes."

"Did you notice a change in his behavior after the stacking incidents?"

"Jesus God, yeah. I was scared to be around him for a few days after he did that. We'd go to my mother's until he wound down."

"Was he especially abusive after stacking?"

Her eyes flash. "Didn't I just say that?"

"If I were to tell you that your ex-husband ripped a screen door to shreds, what would you say?"

"Objection," Dempsey says. "Do we have to listen to defense counsel's storytelling?"

"You do," Mitton retorts. "Proceed, Mr. Valenti."

I uncover the post-shooting photo of the screen door. "On the night Deputy O'Reilly was killed, a screen door at the scene of his shooting was almost ripped out of its frame. Is this something you can imagine him doing in a temper in the day or two immediately following one of his steroid stacking sessions?"

She pauses before answering; perhaps realizing that an honest answer will be a damning indictment of her ex-husband. She elects to tell the truth but does so with a snarky codicil. "Yeah, he could do that. It wouldn't surprise me at all —but he couldn't have done it after your father pumped him full of bullets, could he?"

"He could have done it before he was shot, couldn't he?"

She shrugs. "'Spose he could."

"Last question, Mrs. O'Reilly."

"About time," she grumbles.

"According to the custody provisions of your divorce agreement, your son is supposed to spend Tuesdays with his father. September seventeenth was a Tuesday. Is it true that you didn't allow Andrew Junior to visit his father that day because you knew Andy Senior had just stacked steroids?"

"Yeah."

I give silent thanks to Fiona Novak for that revelation and add, "You couldn't expose the son you loved to Andy O'Reilly that night, could you?"

Her shoulders sag when she mutters, "No."

"Because you were afraid of what he might do to Andy Junior. Right?"

"Right," she admits with a poisonous look at me.

"I have nothing else for this witness, Your Honor," I say. Except contempt. My feelings shame me. It's not as if I don't know what being beaten black and blue does to your soul. I should be feeling a little pity for Molly O'Reilly, not the opposite.

Dempsey makes a half-hearted and unsuccessful attempt to repair the damage. How do you rehabilitate a witness who just told the court that she lies under oath when it suits her?

Mike and I decide that we're happy to leave the jury with this picture of the victim in mind for the evening. The suggestion that the prosecution willingly allowed and may have coached a key witness to commit perjury is bonus material. We have an engineer from the manufacturer of the screen door who can testify to its strength and the force needed to mangle it. We'll put him on the stand in the morning with the damning pictures of the door's destruction to refresh the jurors' memories.

Judge Mitton agrees to recess for the day after we assure him that we'll finish tomorrow. I wonder if we will. The matter of the photo on Brittany's phone needs to be resolved and we expect to hear from Sandy Russo. There's also the possibility that Papa will testify. We're undecided about putting him on the stand, but it seems ever more likely as the trial unfolds.

"Now what?" Brittany asks me while Mike walks away to call his office.

"Mike still thinks we should consider a plea deal. Probably second-degree murder."

"I'm hearing a lot of 'Mike thinks' these days," Pat says. "What does *Tony* think?"

"Tony's a corporate lawyer," I quip.

Pat crosses her arms and levels an unamused gaze on me. "He's also co-counsel in his father's trial. What do you think?"

"The corporate lawyer thinks we should be able to do better than that. Maybe manslaughter—especially if we can get Sandy Russo to corroborate Papa's version of events and Judge Mitton admits the picture from Britt's cell phone."

"And has the corporate lawyer had that discussion with the public defender?" Pat asks.

"Not exactly."

"The reporter," Pat says with a hint of a smile, "thinks the corporate lawyer should make his views known to the public defender post-haste as the reporter thinks the corporate lawyer has a good case to make to the public defender."

I smile back at her. "The corporate lawyer will take the reporter's views under advisement."

"The corporate lawyer better listen, buster," she concludes with mock ferocity.

"The European chick agrees with the reporter," Brittany adds with a grin as Mike returns.

We're discussing where to go for a quick bite when Luke Geffen calls. I listen to Mike's side of the conversation. "You gave her the court order? Wow… tell me what she said… no shit... that's some stubborn woman... no, don't bother... I'll take this to the judge." Mike hangs up and tells me that Sandy Russo read Judge Mitton's order to provide a statement to a representative of Papa's defense team, threw it back in Luke's face, and screamed "Screw you!"

Mike shakes his head and turns back to the courthouse. "Let's go see the judge before he leaves for the day. He needs to have Sandy Russo brought in. I want her declared a hostile witness before she gets on the stand."

We send Pat and Brittany on their way. Judge Mitton grants Mike's request twenty minutes later.

"I've got to spend some time tonight on another case," Mike tells me as we leave the courthouse. "Can you get with Francesco and talk to him about testifying? Walk him through how things played out that night and see if his story changes from what he told us at Christmas. We need to know what he's going to say. I don't think he's coachable."

I can't argue with his reasoning and agree to go, stopping along the way for a bite at a sub shop while I prepare for the chat. I want to be sure Papa understands the risks of testifying. Once I feel ready, I head to the jail. Papa listens carefully while I explain the potential downsides. "Mike says Alex Dempsey will come at you hard if you testify," I warn him when I finish.

"He will try to trick me. I know this."

"He'll do his best to make you look bad in front of the jury. If he can, things could go very badly."

Papa shrugs. "It will be as it should be."

What the hell does that mean? "Sometimes I almost get the feeling that you don't care which way this goes, Papa."

He studies me for a long moment. "You listen now, Anthony. I no tell you this before, I tell only Maria."

Some sixth sense warns me that I'm about to hear something I was never meant to know and will probably wish I'd never heard.

"This is not first time I kill a man, Anthony."

I'm speechless as his intense eyes bore into mine.

"You wonder why I no worry about what will happen to me now. You listen. If I die, maybe is judgment of what I do two times now. I no get punish first time, maybe this time I be punish for both, *capisci?*"

"No, I don't *capisci*, Papa. When did you shoot someone? Who? Why? How the hell don't I know about this?"

He doesn't appreciate my interruption. "I say you listen to me, Anthony!"

I sit back and cross my arms.

He rests his forearms on the table. "In Orsomarso, my Papa have gun in house to hunt the rabbits, shoot wolves and badgers when they come."

"Is this why you didn't want guns in our house? Mama told me something happened in Italy that put you off guns."

Papa is visibly annoyed, probably because Mama told me more than she was supposed to, or maybe because I've interrupted him again. Whatever the reason, the anger lines quickly dissolve into melancholy before he gathers himself to continue. "After my Papa die, bad men from *cosche* come to our house. Papa, he no like them, he no pay them, he no work for them. They no like this but Papa mind own business and do the woodwork for village, so they no bother him."

"Who are these people, Papa?"

"What is called in America the mafia, in Calabria is *Ndranghet*. In our village is *cosche*, the local people who are *Ndranghet*. After Papa die, they come, they want money to not bother us. If Mama no pay, they will kidnap my sister Alessandra to make Mama pay."

I didn't even know he had a sister. "Jesus, Papa. I never knew any of this. What did your mother do?"

"Mama do like Papa, she no pay and tell them go away."

"What happened?"

Papa's eyes narrow. "They take my sister."

Jesus Christ! "I'm sorry, Papa."

Pain swims across Papa's face as the memories wash over him. When he continues, his voice is haunted. "I take gun to hunt *Cosche* and find Alessandra. I find her at farm, they rape her and lock in barn with animals. I try to take her home. A man try to stop us. I shoot him and we run away."

"Then what did you do?"

"Mama and Alessandra go to hide with cousin at *monastero* in Abruzzo—you say the monastery, I think. I go with them, but I no stay."

"Why not?"

"I no spend life hiding from *Cosche* filth! Mama and Alessandra more safe if not with me. The *Cosche*, they try to find me. If they do, I die."

"So you came to America?"

"Yes."

"And your sister and mother? What happened to them?"

"Alessandra still in Abruzzo. Has husband and four children. My Mama, she die many years ago."

"Have you seen your sister, Papa? Do you write?"

He shakes his head sadly. "Is not safe for her. I hear sometime from cousins, have picture of her and family."

I've never seen the picture. "Surely it's safe to see her now?"

"If I no go to jail, maybe I go. Maybe *Cosche* no look for me no more."

We sit in silence for a minute or more before Papa looks up to meet my gaze. "So, Anthony, maybe God punish me now."

Neither of us believes in the traditional Catholic God, but maybe Papa is thinking of Karma or fate or something along those lines. I finally understand why he seems resigned to whatever fate awaits him in Judge Mitton's courtroom, yet I can't believe the cosmos intends to exact its pound of flesh for what Papa has done. His sister's kidnapper and rapist deserved his fate. From what Papa has told us about what happened on September seventeenth, Andy O'Reilly brought about his own demise. But that's just my opinion. What are the odds a jury will agree?

How the hell can we put him on the stand now? He's as honest as the day is long and will tell the truth if he's asked a question that even hints at past violence. We sure as hell aren't going to introduce the killing in Italy, but if the prosecution unearths it on cross, we're screwed.

CHAPTER THIRTY-FIVE

The picture on Brittany's phone is under discussion in Judge Mitton's chambers early Friday morning. The judge is reading the report produced by Lane Brown and police evidence technician Kyung-Soon Cho, who have determined that the photo and time stamp of Brittany in front of our screen door is authentic. Lane has attached the original phone invoice and activation record to confirm that the phone in evidence was sold to Brittany on September thirteenth, was activated the same day, and that she has been using it every day since. Records from her cell phone service provider and backups from her phone to the cloud helped with authentication. All in all, very impressive work by Lane and Cho in less than a day.

Alex Dempsey tosses his copy of the report aside. "Nothing here proves Brittany Valenti was in physical possession of that phone on September seventeenth or any other day. For all we know, the phone was spirited away to be tampered with—possibly without her knowledge." Dempsey pauses and stares us down. "No way does that phone belong in our courtroom. We'll be filing an injunction within the hour to suppress any and all images purported to have originated from that phone."

Mitton glances up at Dempsey. "You're not forgetting who's going to rule on that injunction are you, Counselor?"

"With all due respect, Your Honor, our office is prepared to appeal to the appellate court if you rule against us."

The judge taps the report. "These folks seem to know their stuff. You're kidding yourself if you think you're keeping this evidence out, no matter who you appeal to."

"We're not even sure who these two so-called experts are," Dempsey retorts.

"One of them is a veteran Chicago PD evidence technician," Mike scoffs. "Don't try to tell me you haven't worked with her."

Dempsey wordlessly fixes his gaze on the judge.

Mitton turns to Mike. "Will you be putting these folks on the stand?"

"Of course," Mike replies before his eyes swing to Dempsey. "I'll enjoy watching you rip into the competence of an experienced police technician, Alex. Just think of all the defense attorneys who will use the attack to undermine the competence and credibility of all police evidence techs. Your boss and FOP friends should love it, too."

Dempsey's expression morphs from anger to angst in a heartbeat.

"Do you honestly think you're going to impeach the testimony of these folks and discredit the picture?" Mitton asks him.

"We're going to try."

"You're not going to waste time in my courtroom doing so. I want both sides to stipulate to the authenticity of this photo. We're not going to drag this trial out while you try to suppress evidence, Mr. Dempsey."

"My office won't agree to that."

"The evidence will take us where it will, whether you and

your boss like it or not," Mitton retorts. "The jury will assess the credibility of the evidence and what weight to afford it. That's how our system works."

"State's Attorney Walker feels very strongly about this, Your Honor. He'll file for an emergency stay if you allow this evidence in. Perhaps we'd all be well-served by a short delay so we don't jeopardize the case."

The judge shrugs. "Do what you will, Mr. Dempsey. I'll review your petition before court this morning *if* you get it here within the next fifteen minutes. Otherwise I'll look at it during recess, but I'm telling you here and now that I will let this in. If another court reverses that decision, so be it. In the meantime, I want this photo stipulated to so we can move things along *and* to save you the embarrassment of trying to discredit a police technician in open court."

Dempsey hesitates.

"I assume you have Mr. Walker on speed dial?" Mitton asks. "Call him and hand me the phone."

"Mr. Walker," the judge says several seconds later. "Yes, he has… no, I'm not going to hold things up… you'll be free to appeal… we're going to stipulate to that, Counselor." Mitton scowls while he listens and then growls, "I didn't ask for your opinion, Mr. Walker. *We're going to stipulate…* have at it… good day."

"Let's get to work," the judge says after he hangs up.

I spend fifteen minutes with an engineer from the storm door manufacturer to establish that the steel frame is, in fact, highly resistant to bending. "It'd take a damned strong guy some time to do that!" he marvels as I linger beside the picture of the door and detail the damage done to it. Sylvia Perez asks a couple of perfunctory questions and quickly abandons her effort at cross examination. What's she going to do? Argue that for some reason or other our particular screen door was uniquely pliable?

Mike calls Fiona Novak as our next witness. She confirms

the story of taking her sister to emergency after Andy O'Reilly beat her up and of filing the police report, then goes on to paint an unflattering picture of her ex-brother-in-law.

Sylvia Perez gets to her feet and marches toward the witness stand to begin her cross-examination. "Why now? What's motivating you to dance on your brother-in-law's grave today?"

Fiona draws back in her seat. "Pardon me?"

Perez fixes a contemptuous glare on the witness. "You hated Andrew O'Reilly, didn't you?"

"Objection," Mike calls out. "Fiona Novak's relationship with or feelings toward Mr. O'Reilly were not explored during our direct examination."

"Objection sustained," Judge Mitton says. "Restrict your questioning to the topics opened during direct testimony, Counselor."

"Her motivations for attacking the victim are certainly pertinent," Perez retorts. "She's had nothing to say about any of this until today. We'd like to know why she's changed her tune."

After pondering Perez's statement for a moment, Mitton has a question of his own. "Does Mrs. Novak's testimony today contradict an earlier statement given in the course of your investigation?"

"That's exactly what I'm saying, Your Honor," Perez replies.

Mike glances at me and whispers, "Do you know where she's going with this?"

"Hopefully to hell in a hand basket."

Mitton relents. "I'll permit you to probe that topic very briefly, Miss Perez. The prosecution had the chance to call Mrs. Novak as a witness and did not, so you've limited yourselves to what you can explore. I won't allow you to circumvent that decision now."

"Understood."

"One last thing, Miss Perez," the judge says sternly. "You will not treat witnesses boorishly in my courtroom. Is that understood?"

Perez nods and rephrases her question. "In an earlier statement to police, you chose not to volunteer any of these stories you've come up with this morning. Why did you withhold this information when you were questioned?"

"The topic never came up."

"What did come up?"

"Not much of anything. I was asked when I had last seen or spoken with Andy. That was pretty much it."

"How did you answer that question?"

"The last time I saw or spoke with Andy O'Reilly was the day my sister was granted her divorce. I tagged along to help in case he decided to attack her again after court."

"Your Honor," Perez exclaims in exasperation, "I didn't ask Mrs. Novak why she went to court with her sister. Please have her last sentence stricken from the record, beginning with 'I tagged along.'"

"Is that comment in her original statement?" Mitton asks.

"No."

"I can corroborate that, Your Honor," Mike adds.

"Thank you, Counselor," Mitton says with a grateful glance at Mike. "Please strike the last sentence as requested by Miss Perez," he tells the court reporter before turning back to the witness. "Mrs. Novak, please answer only the questions asked."

"Sorry," Fiona Novak says. She doesn't look overly apologetic.

Perez takes a step toward the witness box, shoots a knowing glance at the jury, and says, "You didn't volunteer information to the police but now you suddenly tell all to the defense. Why is that?"

"The police officers I spoke with knew Andy O'Reilly. I assume they didn't ask because they didn't want that information on the record. Now that—"

Perez cuts her off. "Why did you decide to come forward at this late date with derogatory information about the victim of this crime?"

"As I was about to say," Fiona replies tartly, "my nephew was understandably upset over the death of his father. I saw no need to pile on by exposing him to the ugly truth about Andy. I was trying to protect him."

"Very noble," Perez sneers, "but here you are today slinging mud about his father."

"You asked 'why now?'"

"I did," Perez replies sarcastically. "Please *do* tell us."

Fiona glares back at her. "My initial inclination was to protect Andy Junior from the truth about his father. When I saw on the news that Andy's police records would come out in court, I realized that the truth couldn't be hidden. I already knew Andy Junior had been arrested for shooting Pat O'Toole at the Valenti house a few weeks ago—"

"Objection!" Dempsey roars from the prosecution's table. "Assumes facts not in evidence. Even if true, the identity of a minor charged with a crime cannot be disclosed."

Pat beckons me and I slide back to listen. "The *Trib* and WGN broke the story and reported the kid's name an hour ago. He's being tried in adult court."

I scoot back to the defense table while Mike and Dempsey argue about the objection. While Dempsey is taking a turn, I tell Mike what I've just learned while the clerk hands an envelope to the judge. Mitton glances at it and sets it aside.

When Dempsey finishes, Mike pipes up. "I have new information that bears on this discussion, Your Honor."

Mitton, who seems fed up with the bickering, waves Mike on. "Pray tell, Counselor."

"News outlets have reported that Andy O'Reilly Junior

has been arrested for the attempted murder of Pat O'Toole. He will be tried in adult court."

All eyes in the courtroom settle on Pat.

"I assume the state's attorney's office is aware of this?" Mitton asks Dempsey.

"I didn't know."

"The objection is overruled. You may finish your answer, Mrs. Novak."

"Thank you, Judge," she replies. "Now that Andy Junior's been arrested for trying to kill Mr. Valenti's son and Miss O'Toole, there's no reason to protect him from the truth." She looks at Papa. "When I look at what the village has done to this poor man and his family, how could I sit by and not speak up?"

I'm surprised when Dempsey and Perez don't challenge the statement, which allows Fiona Novak to twist the knife a little deeper.

"Francesco Valenti's probably lucky to be here today," she adds. "I imagine Andy was at his barbaric worst when he went out there that night."

"Nothing more for this witness," Perez snaps.

Mike declines to re-cross the witness. What more could she possibly say to help us?

"How many more witnesses do you have?" Mitton asks after Fiona leaves the courtroom.

"We need to consult on that, Your Honor," Mike replies.

Mitton glances at his watch. "We'll adjourn for thirty minutes and resume at ten-thirty."

"I'll see the attorneys at sidebar," he announces after the jury files out and the courtroom begins to empty. Once we gather, he looks Dempsey in the eye. "Your plea for an emergency stay has arrived. I had a glance at it while Mrs. Novak was on the stand. I'll see all of you in my chambers in twenty minutes to announce my decision."

"So, what have we accomplished?" I ask Mike when we're alone outside the courthouse.

"Everyone now knows Andrew O'Reilly was an asshole. His death was no great loss. Maybe the jury will believe he messed up the screen door. That doesn't absolve Francesco for murdering the lousy sonofabitch."

"Point taken, but the jury might buy into the idea that O'Reilly was on a steroid bender that night."

"We're not there yet," Mike sighs.

Twenty minutes later, Judge Mitton rules against the prosecution's request. Dempsey huffily retorts that his office will take the matter to appellate court.

Mitton shrugs. "That's your prerogative, Counselor. Now let's get back to work." He spends the next five minutes brow-beating Dempsey into stipulating to the authenticity of the photo, arguing that it might play to their advantage if the appellate courts rule against him.

When court reconvenes, Mike calls Brittany to the stand. A pair of easels face the witness and the jury. One holds a blow-up of my picture of Brittany in front of the screen door, the post-shooting photo of it sits on the other. Each is covered with a sheet of manilla paper.

After the preliminaries are complete, Mike uncovers the post-shooting photo. "Have you seen this picture before, Brittany?"

"Yes."

"Here in court?"

"Yes."

"Had you ever seen this picture before I showed it during my opening statement yesterday morning?"

"No."

"Have you ever seen the door in this condition?"

"Not until yesterday."

Mike uncovers the picture from her phone. "Was this picture taken with your cell phone?"

"Yes. Dad took it just before we left the house the night of the shooting," Brittany replies, prompting gasps throughout the courtroom.

"So, approximately an hour before the shooting took place." He then has her explain how she first realized the significance of her photo when she saw the door 'after' picture yesterday during his opening statement. Judge Mitton informs the jury that the defense and prosecution have stipulated to the authenticity of the photo. If any jurors still doubted that an altercation took place at our front door on September seventeenth, they should be convinced of it now.

Given the stipulation about the picture, Dempsey doesn't have much to cross-examine Brittany about. He's reduced to hammering away at the slender crack afforded to him when she can't swear to a certainty that her cell phone has been in her possession every minute of every day since she first activated it. If it wasn't in her hand at all times, maybe Dempsey can sow some semblance of doubt in the minds of the jury.

Then he goes a step too far. "If I were to ask if you had your phone with you on any given day, how often would you have to admit that you simply don't know, Miss Valenti?"

"Days I don't remember having it?"

"Correct."

"Oh, I've had it every day, Mr. Dempsey. There was, like, this one morning when I thought I'd lost it for a few minutes, but I left it in my jeans pocket when I threw them in the laundry. I live on that thing. It's my lifeline to everyone I know."

Dempsey is stumped. Seeing that, Brittany forges ahead to help out. "You can look, Mr. Dempsey. I send messages to my Dad and friends every day. Instagram, too."

Dempsey throws in the towel. "Nothing more for this witness, Your Honor."

After Brittany departs the witness stand, Mitton calls the lunch recess.

Mike and I make a beeline for his Public Defender office

and gobble down a couple of Italian grinder sandwiches while discussing how we should wind up Papa's defense. We feel we've shown that Andy O'Reilly was a thug and that he, not Papa, was the person most likely to have been the ticking time bomb that exploded on the evening of September seventeenth.

"Is that enough to push the jury to consider manslaughter or, better still, self-defense?" I ask.

"Self-defense?" Mike exclaims with an expression of utter disbelief.

"Why not? We haven't heard from Sandy Russo yet."

Mike throws his hands up in exasperation. "We have no idea what she'll say!"

"I think we have a shot at this, Mike."

"Putting on a self-defense case would be malpractice. We *may* have cracked the door open for a manslaughter plea deal."

"Papa won't go to jail, Mike."

"The hell does that mean? It's not his call."

"You need to talk to him."

He stares back at me, shakes his head, and plucks his briefcase off the desk. "I don't know what the hell has gotten into you two, but let's go."

Papa is shown into the attorney-client room ten minutes later. Mike makes his case. "You see the danger here, Francesco?"

Papa withdraws into himself for a moment. We fall silent while he works through whatever is on his mind.

Then Mike's cell buzzes. "Luke Geffen," he announces after looking at the caller ID. He takes the call and spends most of it grunting and nodding. He disconnects and takes a deep breath. "At the risk of further encouraging you two, Luke just talked to Beau Smith, the *Tribune*'s source for the steroid and weightlifting story. He's decided to testify, after all. His stories about O'Reilly abusing his family and being chased out of Cedar Heights PD will be inflammatory as hell."

Papa looks vindicated. I haven't mentioned his bombshell admission about killing his sister's kidnapper, which I'm sure was intended for my ears only. It's a wild card that scares the hell out me. I look from him to Mike and then level my eyes on my father. "If we can convince the jury that O'Reilly provoked you into fearing for your safety before you shot him, we may be able to argue self-defense."

"Then I no go to jail?" Papa asks.

"*If* we can convince the jury." I explain the possibilities of Sandy Russo's testimony, how it may have the potential to help or hurt our case. "We may have to put you on the stand to make that case, Papa."

Mike is appalled at what he's hearing. He turns a searing look on me before telling Papa, "That's extremely high risk, Francesco. We don't need to decide just yet."

"Is best," Papa says after a moment. "I think Anthony is right. O'Reilly scare me so I shoot. This is truth."

Mike looks to me for support.

"It's dicey, Papa," I say softly, horrified that my earlier enthusiasm for him testifying may end up walking Papa into a disaster of epic proportions. I should have known I'd mess things up. "We can't put you up there unless we have evidence to support your story *and* the jury is convinced that you're not prone to violence," I add pointedly, hoping he understands my oblique warning about the danger of disclosing what happened in Italy all those years ago.

Mike repeats his malpractice outburst.

Papa breaks the ensuing silence by reaching out to lay his hand alongside Mike's cheek. "Michael," he says soothingly, "I no want to live in this place. Better to die than live like animal." His beseeching eyes linger on Mike's for a long moment. "*Capisci?*"

"I hope you're not about to get your father killed by filling his head with pie in the sky bullshit," Mike snaps at me as we depart.

I envision a fitting epitaph for my gravestone: *One spectacular fuck up after another.*

CHAPTER THIRTY-SIX

There is a one-hour delay after lunch. Luke Geffen is bringing Beau Smith to court while Dempsey fulminates in Judge Mitton's chambers about "yet another defense ploy to sidestep discovery rules." Mitton listens to how Smith came to land on our witness list at the last minute. He accepts Mike's explanation and says we can put Smith on the stand.

When Dempsey continues to argue, Mitton stops him. "*You* chose to designate this a priority case, Mr. Dempsey. I'm mindful of the pressure that puts on the defense team and that you made this a priority case for exactly that reason. I intend to make sure Mr. Valenti is afforded due process, even if it gets a little messy due to time constraints. Understood?"

Dempsey's lips tighten into a straight line. He replies with a curt nod.

It does my heart good to see Mitton giving the sonofabitch a good dressing down. Damned if old Myron isn't growing on me.

The judge turns to Mike. "Hurry things along, Mr. Williams."

Mike calls Beau Smith and prompts him to share his recollections of the time he spent with O'Reilly on the Cedar

Heights PD, complete with the unsavory details of their carousing. They explore O'Reilly's stint as a fellow gym member of Smith's and dig into the details of O'Reilly's rampant steroid use. Smith is able to go into detail about O'Reilly's penchant for pyramiding—stacking and cycling different steroids to maximize the effects. He even relates an episode of O'Reilly experiencing roid rage. Perez subjects Smith to a brutal cross-examination that would discourage anyone from inviting him out for a beer but fails to impeach his testimony. Smith is on and off the stand in thirty minutes. The jury listened intently. I think it went well.

Time to roll the dice one more time. After wiping my palms on my pants, I get to my feet and announce, "The defense calls Sandra Vaccaro Russo."

At our request, Judge Mitton had Sandy taken into custody and delivered to the court this morning. With Brittany's picture of the screen door in play and yet another account of O'Reilly's volatility fresh in the minds of the jurors, evidence of an altercation between O'Reilly and Papa would be invaluable. We're gambling that Sandy will provide it. Given her refusal to cooperate with the court or anyone else, Mitton has granted us permission to treat her as a hostile witness. As I watch Sandy escorted to the witness stand and sworn in, I feel queasy in the pit of my stomach. Yes, this is a girl I grew up with, but I'm not her favorite person. I hope Mike is making the right call in having me question her.

Even though the hostile witness designation gives me plenty of latitude to work Sandy over in search of the truth, I decide to ease my way into the questioning. Maybe she'll be cooperative, maybe not, but the optics will be better if the jurors witness her making a deliberate decision to be uncooperative.

After establishing that Sandy grew up next door and was having dinner with her parents on the night of the shooting, I lob my first softball. "Did you make a statement to the police about the shooting that took place outside Forty-seven Liberty Street on the evening of September seventeenth?"

"I did."

"Can you tell us when the police questioned you?"

"The next morning."

I arch an eyebrow to signify surprise. "Not at your parents' on the night of the shooting?" Subtext: *What were the police doing that night if not talking to the people next door? What kind of shoddy investigation took place?*

"I guess I'd gone home by the time they rang the bell," Sandy replies. She's perched alertly on the edge of her seat with her hands resting primly in her lap.

"I see. Where did you make the statement?"

"At my house."

"Did the police tell you they were taking a formal statement?"

"Yes, they did."

Ah, but they didn't. I'll circle back to that later. "Did you witness the shooting, Mrs. Russo?"

"I did not."

I hold eye contact with her in hopes of establishing a little rapport. She's been surprisingly agreeable so far. "Would you mind telling us what you told the police the morning after the shooting?"

She's clearly surprised by the question. "They *still* haven't given you my statement?"

I notice a couple of jurors frown. I stifle a fist pump and lament, "I'm afraid not, Mrs. Russo. Perhaps you would be kind enough to tell us what you told the police?"

She fidgets in her seat and looks down into her lap when she answers. It's her first sign of discomfort. "I remember clearly."

Tread carefully, Valenti. "Do you need a moment? Perhaps a drink of water?"

Sandy's eyes rise to mine in appreciation. "Please," she

murmurs. The bailiff directs her to a bottle of water tucked away in a corner shelf of the witness box.

I let Sandy take a sip and resettle herself. "When you're ready to continue, please tell us what happened."

"Just like I told the police?"

"Yes, please. As best you can remember. I understand that you didn't see what was happening next door?"

"That's right. It started raining hard right after dinner. I couldn't remember if I'd closed my car windows, so I ran outside to check. That's when I heard what was happening next door."

I ease a step closer to the witness box and ask a simple question that totally unnerves me because I have no idea how she'll answer. "Will you please tell us about that?"

"Well, I could hear Andy yelling."

"By Andy, do you mean Deputy O'Reilly?"

"Right." She's addressing me directly, as if I'm the only other person in the room with her. Maybe it helps steady her nerves.

I smile encouragingly. "You were acquainted with O'Reilly?"

"In school. We were in some of the same classes. His son is in some of my daughter's classes at school this year. At least he was until they arrested him."

"Were you friends with Deputy O'Reilly?"

"No. I saw him around the school sometimes."

"So you knew who he was."

"Right." A look of distaste crosses Sandy's face. At the memory of O'Reilly? I resist the impulse to probe further; there's already more than enough uncertainty about what she might say.

"You know Francesco Valenti."

"He's been my parents' neighbor as long as I can remember."

"You would recognize his voice?"

"Sure. I heard him that night."

"You're certain the people you heard were Francesco Valenti and Andrew O'Reilly?"

"I am."

"How would you classify your relationship with Mr. Valenti?"

"We've been neighbors forever. He's always been nice to my family. My parents are friends with him."

"Francesco Valenti is a good neighbor?"

She nods firmly. "Yes. And a good man."

"Did you see him on the night of the shooting?"

"He waved at me from the porch when I arrived at my parents'. I didn't see him again after that."

"Did you see Deputy O'Reilly?"

"I did. I saw Andy pull up in front of your—the Valenti's house. You can't see their front door from our front step. There's a hedge."

"Deputy O'Reilly arrived in a police cruiser?"

"Yes."

"Did you see him get out of his car?"

"I did."

"Did you speak with him?"

"No, I was still in the house when he arrived. Andy walked up the driveway toward the Valenti's front door. I remember wondering what the police were doing next door and hoped everything was okay."

"What happened next?"

"I went to get my coat and keys and went outside. Andy was yelling and banging on the front door. Really pounding it."

"And then?"

"Mr. Valenti answered the door and said, 'What's this?' or something like that."

"You were close enough to hear clearly?"

She nods. "Yes. Our driveways are side by side. I was

fifteen or twenty feet away."

"Go on."

"Andy and Mr. Valenti argued."

I take a deep breath and plunge deeper into the unknown. "Tell us about the argument, as accurately as you can."

"Bad language and all?"

"Please."

"Andy did most of the talking… shouting, actually. He was very loud and aggressive."

"Was this normal behavior for O'Reilly, so far as you knew him?"

Sandy nods. "I guess. He was a bully all through high school. Grade school, too. Guess he never changed much."

I pause a beat to let the jury absorb Sandy's assessment before asking, "Officer O'Reilly was being abusive to Mr. Valenti?"

"Oh yes, I'd say so. *Very*. Andy shouted, 'Looks like you messed with the village one too many times, old man.'" Sandy blushes and looks into her lap when she swears. "'Only a dumbass wop right off the boat is stupid enough to keep pissing them off. You're gonna pay now,'" she adds. "Something like that."

"What did Mr. Valenti do then?"

"Well, I don't know what he did. I told you I couldn't see."

Feeling foolish, I ask, "How did Mr. Valenti respond?"

"He didn't say much. Andy called Mr. Valenti a dago and told him to go back to Italianoland, then started yelling at him to open the door. 'Open the fucking door!' he shouted."

"Did Deputy O'Reilly say why Mr. Valenti needed to open the door?"

"Yes. Something about having to give him papers so they could throw his wop ass out of the house. Then he screamed at Mr. Valenti to quit jerking him around or he'd rip the door off its hinges and come in after him. The banging started again, but louder and sharper, like maybe Andy was kicking the door or hitting it with something hard. He said it was about time the village ran Mr. Valenti's wop ass outta town."

"He seemed to like that expression," I observe, ruing the fact that I'd never get the chance to stuff O'Reilly's words back down his throat.

"That was Andy O'Reilly. Loud and rude and obnoxious. From the day he was born until the day he died."

"Objection!" Dempsey shouts. "Do we need to keep abusing the memory of this poor man, Your Honor?"

"I think you've made your personal feelings about Officer O'Reilly abundantly clear, Mrs. Russo," Mitton tells her quietly. "There's no need to do so again."

Sandy blushes slightly and nods.

"You *can* continue to tell us what you heard O'Reilly say and do," I tell her. "Did Mr. Valenti start yelling, too?

"Not really. Mr. Valenti's a pretty easygoing guy. He likes to play the stern patriarch role but he's pretty soft under all that. He's a marshmallow with the kids."

I smile. The jury should like that. I decide to keep quiet and see where Sandy leads us.

Her voice takes on an angry edge. "Andy said some real nasty things about Mrs. Valenti. Called her an old bitch who shoulda learned to mind her own business. Mr. Valenti got a little angry then. He told Andy not to speak ill of his dead wife—Mr. Valenti's wife, that is. She passed away last summer."

She looks up at me with a sad smile. "Real nice lady… but you know that." Then she seems to remember where we are and blushes.

I noticed a few jurors wince at O'Reilly's comments about my mother. "Did O'Reilly say anything else about Mrs. Valenti?" I ask in hopes of stoking their anger.

Sandy's brow furrows in fury. "Andy said he was happy when he heard she died. He joked that maybe the real estate developer poisoned her to help clean up the neighborhood."

I'm glad Papa shot the bastard. Too bad someone didn't do it years sooner.

I let the ugliness of O'Reilly's comments hang in the air for a moment. "How long were you outside listening to this, Mrs. Russo?"

"I can't say for sure. I almost missed dessert by the time I went back in. Maybe as long as five minutes."

"What happened next?"

"I remember Andy shouting that he was gonna turn the door into scrap metal."

"Did Mr. Valenti sound afraid while this was going on?"

"He did," Sandy replies. "Who wouldn't? Andy just went on and on shouting obscene, ugly words. He kept yelling at Mr. Valenti to open the door and calling him awful names and that he'd teach him not to mess with the cops. He said he was coming in and that Mr. Valenti would be one sorry wop when he did. God, it went on so long!" She pauses with a distraught expression and sounds stricken when she adds, "Then I heard what sounded like metal screeching and glass breaking."

"What happened next?"

"Andy shouted 'I've got you now, you little prick!' That just chilled me, you know? It sounded like he was going to do something awful to Mr. Valenti. I was thinking I should do something—call 9-1-1 or something. Mr. Valenti shouted for Andy to leave, to leave him alone. Then, almost right after that, Andy shouted, 'What the hell is this? That's it you little fuck, you're dead!'"

I wait quietly for the conclusion I'm sure is coming.

"That's when I heard the shots," Sandy says with haunted eyes. "I didn't hear anything after that, so I went back inside and called 9-1-1."

The courtroom has been deathly silent throughout Sandy's testimony, but a subdued buzz now surges through the courtroom. I let it settle before continuing. "You told the police all of this the morning after the shooting?"

"Pretty much," Sandy replies. "Maybe in a little less detail. They didn't seem interested, to be honest. They didn't seem surprised or much concerned about Andy's behavior."

"You never heard from the police again?"

"Not until they gave me a ride here this morning."

I lock eyes with Mike Williams across the room. He nods.

I smile at Sandy. "Thank you for coming forward, Mrs. Russo. Nothing further, Your Honor."

Dempsey's cross-examination fails to damage Sandy or diminish the power of her testimony. The judge calls for a recess.

I catch up to Sandy in the hallway after we leave the courtroom. Her husband and parents are with her, but she slides a few feet away from them when she sees me coming. We exchange greetings, albeit stiffly, and then I ask why she decided to quit fighting us.

"Aside from being hauled down here by the police?" she asks. She does so without rancor.

"Besides that."

"Phil wanted me to. So did Mom and Dad."

"I'm glad they did."

"That's not all," she says. "There were my memories of Amy and your mother. I imagined my father in your father's shoes. Seeing you take down those jerks from Titan made an impression, too. Maybe you do care about Liberty Street."

"I really appreciate it, Sandy."

"This will sound selfish," she says with downcast eyes, "but part of it was O'Reilly's kid getting arrested. I realized I could get up and tell my story without that little monster taking it out on my daughter. I'm sorry I almost let that get in the way of doing the right thing. I apologize for that."

"All's well that ends well."

"*Is* this going to end well?"

It's a good question.

CHAPTER THIRTY-SEVEN

Mike and I head for his office to map strategy.

"I guess you were right, after all," he says after we sit down. "The stage is set for Francesco to tell his story."

My mind's eye conjures up a vision of Dempsey asking my father if he's ever attacked or hurt anyone and Papa relating the story of killing his sister's kidnapper. How do I walk back my argument that he should testify without telling Mike about Papa's secret?

"Hey," Mike says when I don't respond. "You okay?"

"I don't want to put him on the stand."

Mike studies me for a long moment. "Why the change of heart? Cold feet?"

"I think we've made our case. Quit while we're ahead?"

Mike ponders that for a long moment. "Having the jury see and hear Francesco tell the story he told us might seal the deal, Tony. Like I say, the stage is set for that."

"What if Dempsey trips him up? What if Papa stumbles when he gets up there?"

"Did he have trouble telling you the story again last night?"

No. He told me a different story that I can't share. I shrug, not wanting to lie. "There were differences. He was a little shaky. I think the risk of things going wrong on the stand outweighs the upside. We've made the case for self-defense, Mike."

He takes a deep breath, steeples his fingers, and stares up at the ceiling for a good two minutes before his eyes drop back to mine. "Maybe you're right."

Maybe I'm not, I think while a crushing weight of responsibility settles over me.

"You sure about this?"

I swallow and nod.

He slaps a hand on the desk. "Okay then, my friend."

We turn our attention to our closing argument, which we've been assembling in bits and pieces for the past day. With the screen door photo and Sandy Russo's testimony in hand, we're no longer playing for favorable sentencing on a reduced charge.

"I like it," Mike announces after we work for a half-hour. "Hits the high points, casts a shitload of doubt on the prosecution's case, and sets us up to win this thing."

"I think we've got it right, so long as Dempsey hasn't saved any surprises for rebuttal."

"I want you to deliver our closing argument," Mike says after a sober pause. "You're better up there than I am."

What the hell has gotten into him? I shake my head emphatically. "I don't think so."

"Seriously, Tony. You're damned good in front of a jury. The way you dismantled Molly O'Reilly was a friggin work of art and your handling of Sandy Russo was dazzling."

"Dazzling?" I laugh. "Who the hell says that nowadays?"

Mike's eyes twinkle. "As in 'I was positively dazzled by the brilliant oratorical skills of my skinny-assed understudy,' my friend."

"You opened, Mike. You close. That's tradition. This is no time to mess with the natural order of things."

"Tradition don't mean shit to me, Tony. Let me make a

final point and then we can arm wrestle or something to settle this."

"What's that?"

"A son standing up there arguing for the life of his father would be some powerful shit."

"That's straight up emotional manipulation," I retort. "A lot of folks hate that. Me, for example. It may play well with some jurors, but it could backfire spectacularly with others."

"Good thing you're not on the jury then, huh?" he replies with a grin. "I like the idea of you standing up there."

"You're selling yourself short," I reply. *And way overselling me.* "Your opening was terrific and you've bonded with the jury. You're just the man to seal the deal."

Mike excuses himself for a bathroom break, leaving me alone at his desk with a six-inch mountain of case files. I wonder if I could do what he and his colleagues do. The system is stacked against most of their "clients" from the day they're born. Too many are guilty of nothing more than being born with the wrong skin color and living in the wrong neighborhood. All too often, pretty good kids unlucky enough to be in the wrong place at the wrong time become easy pickings for lazy policing and a justice system fixated on meeting arrest quotas and clearing cases. A lot of Mike's clients *are* guilty of everything they're accused of; after all, there's a percentage of bad apples in any demographic. My time in the business world and corporate law taught me nothing if not that. But it's also enabled me to recognize the disconcerting differences in how criminality plays out between different social milieus. Whereas a bad seed born to parents on Chicago's Gold Coast or the tonier suburbs goes to the best schools and learns how to perpetrate white-collar crime as a Wall Street bankster, the same kid born into poverty on the South Side becomes a two-bit gangsta in the hood. The white-collar crook hides behind the best legal defense money can buy; the kid from the wrong side of the tracks gets an overburdened and underfinanced public attorney. As a rule, the public defender is woefully outgunned by a richly funded justice system that devours the poor and then trumpets its supposed successes and commitment to achieving law and order. The more I learn, the more it disgusts me. I realize with a start that Papa's case is a variation on that theme.

Mike startles me when he drops back into his chair. "Where have you been?" he asks with a smirk. "Imagining yourself wowing our jury with your closing statement?"

Actually, my little reverie had pounded home the point that he has a wealth of experience arguing for people's lives. I, on the other hand, have exactly none. "Nope. I've been imagining you up there having your very own Perry Mason moment. You're closing, Mike."

He starts to roll up his shirtsleeve and clears some papers out of the way before he settles his elbow in the clearing with his hand up in the classic arm-wrestling pose.

I chuckle. "Not happening. No more discussion—you're delivering our closing argument."

"Aw shit, man, you ain't no fun," he grumbles, giving up easier and more gracefully than I expect him to.

We get into a discussion about Brittany's long-term plans on our way back to court; should she stay in Europe or should she come home? As for the short-term, Michelle is flying through O'Hare this evening and Brittany has a ticket to join her on the trip back to Brussels.

In a speak-of-the-devil moment, Brittany and Pat exit a cab in front of the courthouse when Mike and I are a half-block away. We catch up while Pat pays.

"Hey!" my daughter exclaims when I wrap my arms around her from behind.

"Good lunch?" I ask.

"Burgers and fries at Portillos," Pat replies. "What's not to like for a kid on her way back to the depravities of Europe?"

We all file back into court. The judge arrives and summons the jury.

"Mr. Williams?" he asks.

Mike stands. "The defense rests, Your Honor."

Mitton glances at Papa in mild surprise, as if he'd expected him to take the stand. The judge recovers quickly and turns to the prosecutor. "Please deliver your rebuttal, Mr. Dempsey."

The prosecutor looks as surprised as we had been when he rested. He turns a hungry gaze on Papa, then asks for another recess.

"We just came back in," Mitton says. "I'll give you five minutes to get organized." Then he turns to the jury. "Keep your seats, folks. Sorry for the delay."

Mike dips his head and mutters out the side of his mouth, "I wonder how much time Alex spent preparing to rip into Francesco?"

A lot, I'm thinking after seeing the predatory look Dempsey gave Papa. Maybe I was right about keeping Papa off the stand. Imagine that.

"We may have dodged a bullet there," Mike whispers.

I slide my chair back when Brittany summons me. "What happens now?" she asks.

I explain that the prosecution will offer any rebuttal witnesses they can muster to challenge the evidence we introduced in our case. "After that, Mike and Dempsey will deliver their closing arguments. Then the judge will give the case to the jury."

"What's that mean?"

"Judge Mitton will instruct them—explain how they should go about making a decision, point out what their options are, offer some suggestions to help them work through the evidence. Then he'll send them off to reach a verdict."

"Does that take long?"

"It shouldn't," Pat says airily. "Our guys kicked their asses."

"I hope you're right," Brittany says. "It's gonna suck big time if I have to fly to Belgium without knowing what happened."

"What time's your flight?" Mike asks.

Brittany looks to Pat for the answer. How would she have gotten through this week without Pat?

"You'll need to leave for the airport no later than five or so," Pat replies. "Things might be tight. Looking on the bright side, you've got that fancy new cell phone to keep in touch until your flight leaves."

That would be the fancy new $750 cell phone Pat and Brittany charged to my ABA credit card last night.

The prosecution's rebuttal, such as it is, lasts all of sixty-three minutes. I'm not surprised that Dempsey doesn't want to dwell on the gaping holes we drilled in their case. Judge Mitton, who is anxious to finish the trial this afternoon, makes Dempsey come right back to deliver the prosecution's closing argument after a twenty-minute recess.

The gist of Dempsey's forty-minute closing argument is that Papa broke a cardinal rule of civilized society by attacking a law enforcement officer carrying out his duty. He recaps the State's evidence in an effort to rebuild their case and bolster the narrative the prosecution wants the jury to carry into their deliberations. In Dempsey's telling, Papa's actions were the tragic culmination of a pathological killer's years-long battle to cheat the Village of Cedar Heights out of a few thousand dollars. He darkly hints that the very underpinnings of peaceful society will be undermined if Francesco Valenti is allowed to escape "the ultimate punishment for his assault on the law and order we all cherish. Do not allow Sheriff's Deputy Andrew O'Reilly to have been taken from us in vain!" he thunders righteously. "We ask that you, the jury, serve justice by convicting this murderer and sentencing him to death—as he sentenced Sheriff's Deputy Andy O'Reilly to death."

What a steaming, hypocritical load of shit, I think after Dempsey sits down.

Mike lays a hand on my shoulder when Judge Mitton calls on us to deliver our closing statement. "Mr. Valenti will do our closing," he announces while sliding our closing argument notes over to me.

My eyes shoot to his. What the hell do I do now? Argue with him in front of the judge and jury? I lean in close and angrily mutter, "What the hell are you doing?"

"Just remember that you're not on a basketball court," he says with a trace of humor in his eyes.

Sure. Big joke. How dare he put Papa's fate in the hands of a mediocrity like me? "What if this stunt costs Papa his life?" I seethe quietly.

"This *stunt* is designed to keep that from happening, my friend."

"Mr. Valenti?" Mitton prompts impatiently.

I gather my thoughts and take a few deep breaths to settle my nerves while I get to my feet, slip into my learned lawyer character, turn my attention to the jury, and begin, "I'll bet every one of you has seen movies, read books, or seen television shows about crime and courts and the police. Am I right?"

My question is met with nods and a few sheepish smiles.

"Sometimes I watch, too," I tell them with as much of a smile as I can muster. "Starting with the first cops and robbers shows I saw, I've heard the same mantra over and over again, as if it's the key to solving all crimes. Means. Motive. Opportunity. Have we all heard that?"

Once again, heads nod in the jury box.

"Let's apply that mantra here," I say as I wander over to stand beside the pictures of the screen door. "What has the prosecutor told us so far? He talked about law and order. He insinuated that Francesco Valenti is a stone-cold killer who threatens the fabric of civilized society. He told us that Sheriff's Deputy Andrew O'Reilly was a conscientious cop who was just performing his duty when Francesco Valenti suddenly attacked him without provocation or warning." I shoot a pointed look at the pictures and let the absurdity of that claim hang in the air while I return to the defense table and glance at our notes.

"Did Francesco have the means to shoot Deputy O'Reilly?" I ask when I turn back to the jury. "Yes he did. He kept a gun in the house to protect himself and his wife from the criminal elements that had recently moved into their neighborhood. Did Francesco have the opportunity to shoot Deputy O'Reilly? Yes, he did—he had that opportunity for several minutes before he felt compelled to protect himself with deadly force. Finally, did Francesco Valenti have a motive to attack Deputy O'Reilly? Mr. Dempsey would have you believe Francesco acted out of rage over a tax bill. The truth, of course, is that when Deputy O'Reilly rang the doorbell at the Valenti home, Francesco had absolutely no motive to harm his visitor. So, what happened, ladies and gentlemen? *Why* did Francesco end up having to shoot Deputy O'Reilly some five minutes or more after he answered his door? Did our prosecutor answer that question for you?"

He sure as hell didn't! I want to shout.

"We've told you a more nuanced story that fills in a great many blanks that the prosecution's narrative conveniently skips over," I continue. "The drama that culminated in the death of Deputy O'Reilly played out over several years—even longer if we consider O'Reilly's police and steroid abuse history. The real story is a complex puzzle that conspired to create a tragic confluence of people and events. The prosecutor has glossed over those complexities in an effort to sell you a formulaic law and order script that should end with the death of the mythical bad guy at the hands of the good guys representing law and order."

I pause to shoot the prosecution table a wondering look, then turn back to the jury. "What happened in Cedar Heights wasn't some high noon shoot-out in a western, folks. We've tried to get at the objective truth of what happened, or at least as close to it as *all* of the available evidence can take us. The evidence shows that Deputy O'Reilly's personal demons sometimes turned him into a violent, steroid-fueled monster. The evidence is equally clear that *this* is who Francesco Valenti was confronted with that evening."

I break again to read our notes and take a needed drink of water. The jury has been listening attentively. That's good, but I'm still nervous and scared.

"You're doing great," Mike assures me quietly when I turn my questioning eyes on his. "Much better than the corporate weenie lawyer you were only short months ago."

His gambit to relax me works. I keep my head down to hide the ghost of a smile that comes to my face.

"It's important to understand what was really going on in the lead up to September seventeenth," I tell the jury as I walk back toward them. "The Valentis were victimized by a predatory corporation and the Valentis' very own civic government. You heard Village Manager Peter Zaluski admit in this courtroom that he and the mayor singled out the Valentis for some particularly vicious persecution. It's interesting to me that Francesco knew all along exactly who was behind the misery he and his late wife suffered through. It's interesting because it seems to me that if Francesco were really the homicidal loose cannon of the prosecutor's imagination, he would have acted on that knowledge long ago. He didn't, ladies and gentlemen. He didn't because he has been a peaceful, honest, and productive member of our community for many, many years. Violence is not the way of Francesco Valenti, nor has it ever been—which makes the mystery of what happened that night all the more unfathomable."

I pause to see if a bolt from heaven will strike me down after I make that statement. Then I take a minute to recap the underhanded effort to hand our neighborhood over to Titan, emphasizing the toll it took on Mama and Papa. "Given the emotional trauma Francesco experienced over those two years, who among us would have blamed him for striking back by going to the media or by taking to the courts to defend his home? It was Maria Valenti, Francesco's dearly departed wife, who took up the legal challenge until she passed away several months ago. Francesco placed his faith in the American legal system, assuming that the forces of law and order would eventually prevail and save his home. The reality, of course, is that those supposed forces of law and order had conspired against him to steal his home. They conspire now to take his very life."

I take another stroll back to our table for a drink of water and a peek at our notes. Then I begin another trek to stand before the jury. "The story of how Deputy O'Reilly destroyed his life and the lives of those closest to him is a tragedy in and of itself. The fact that law enforcement agencies enabled and tolerated his rampages and excesses should outrage us all. If his employers had refused to tolerate his abuse of citizens, none of us would be here today."

I begin a slow walk along the length of the jury box as I continue, meeting the eyes of every juror as I go. "I'm going to talk a little more about the tactics of the prosecution in this case, but first, let me assure you that my comments are in no way a personal attack on the prosecutors," I say reasonably, somehow escaping a thunderbolt from on high for spewing a second whopper. Of course I'm attacking the bastards!

"It's simply my duty to prevent the travesty of justice that the State seeks to perpetrate here today," I continue. "In a few minutes, the prosecutor will talk to you about law and order.

He's going to urge you to send a message with your verdict, a message to deter others who would shoot a police officer. That's not why we have trials, ladies and gentlemen. The state's attorney's office has a pretty big PR department. They can get their messages out without your help."

I hope *that* message resonates with the jury while I walk right up to the rail at the edge of the jury box. "Whenever I hear prosecutors talk about sending messages, I suspect those impassioned sound bites are targeted at voters. 'I'm tough on crime! I'll keep you safe from the bad people! Vote for me!' But maybe I'm just being a little cynical," I add with a shrug before carrying on. "Prosecutors like to suggest that defense attorneys bewitch juries into believing outrageous fairy tale versions of events. They are particularly fond of this tactic when they can't explain away evidence and facts that undermine their case."

I resist leaping up to click my heels together when two jurors nod thoughtfully.

"I expect Mr. Dempsey to work himself into a lather while suggesting that we've put the victim on trial. He'll talk of how morally reprehensible it is to attack the victim—especially a victim who cannot defend himself." I pause and lift my shoulders in a little shrug. "Heck, who wouldn't get a little outraged by such a claim? I would… were it true. But it isn't true in this case, ladies and gentlemen. It's not true at all."

I make a final pilgrimage back to our table for another drink and gather my thoughts. My stomach is digesting itself as I prepare to launch the finale of our closing argument, the last words that will be spoken in this courtroom on Papa's behalf.

"They're eating out of your hand," Mike whispers.

My eyes settle on Papa. The calm veneer he's worn throughout the trial is beginning to fray. I can sense the tension emanating off him like heat baking off a stretch of asphalt boiling under a blazing desert sun. After taking a deep breath, I force myself to relax on the exhale and turn back to face the jury, making a point to look each of them in the eye as I approach. Try as I might to get a sense of which way any of them are leaning, I don't have a clue. I'll never play poker with a single one of these people.

"*Have* we put Andrew O'Reilly on trial here?" I ask. "Yes, we have. We did so because that's where the evidence led us. We did it because the sad truth is that the actions of Deputy O'Reilly on that night deserve to be put on trial. We did it because our search for the truth about the evening of September seventeenth yielded a set of facts that left us no alternative. The prosecution had the same facts available to them and tried to hide them from this court. They tried to hide them from *you,* ladies and gentlemen. The state's attorney and law enforcement have an obligation to seek the truth in criminal matters, *no matter where the evidence leads*. It's incumbent upon prosecutors not to abuse the considerable tools and advantages the criminal justice system gives them when they try a case. Yet, all too often, their goal is to win at all costs—justice and fairness and the constitution itself be damned. I submit to you that the prosecution of Francesco Valenti for murder is such an instance. How else can we explain the State's efforts to keep the truth out of this courtroom?"

I let the jurors ponder that question for several seconds, then reposition myself in front of a new set of jurors before continuing, "Recall, if you will, the efforts of the prosecution to suppress key evidence in this trial. They attempted to keep Officer O'Reilly's unsavory history as a law enforcement officer out of court by suppressing his personnel records. They did not want you to see the photograph of the screen door at the Valenti residence before Deputy O'Reilly arrived. In fact, the state's attorney appealed Judge Mitton's decision to let you see that evidence. What possible motive could the prosecutors have for that action other than to deny you the truth? The police and prosecutors even attempted to hide Sandy Russo from you, ladies and gentlemen. They violated the rules of discovery in our criminal statutes by attempting to hide the fact that they had even spoken with Mrs. Russo. They certainly did *not* do their duty to provide you with *all* of the available evidence. Time and time again they have attempted to hamper your ability to come to a just decision in this case. For that, ladies and gentlemen, perhaps a message *should* be sent via the verdict of this case. I will not make that argument." A cynic might claim that I just did. Still, no thunderbolt from Heaven. I must be golden today.

I pause for effect and reposition myself again before launching into our final roll of the dice. "Judge Mitton will speak to you about the law before he sends you to deliberate on all you've seen and heard here. Before he does, I would like to discuss a point of law that will be pertinent to your deliberations. Article Seven of the Illinois Criminal Code is a self-defense statute that specifies when it is legally permissible to use force against another person. This law permits the use of force—even deadly force—if you reasonably believe it is necessary to protect yourself and/or others from imminent bodily harm or death. Put simply, the law says Francesco was within his rights when he used deadly force to prevent Deputy O'Reilly from breaking into his home. Note that there is *no* exception allowing a law enforcement officer to illegally force his or her way into a home. Don't allow anyone to tell you otherwise."

In case my point isn't clear enough, I go a step further. "This point of law is central to this case. The fact that O'Reilly was attempting to serve an eviction notice in no way permitted him to force his way into the Valenti home. He had absolutely no legal standing to do what he did that evening. Mr. Valenti was under no obligation to permit Deputy O'Reilly to break into his home and assault him. Without an arrest warrant or a warrant granting him entry to the Valenti residence, O'Reilly violated the law by breaking into Francesco's home. O'Reilly was guilty of several crimes in those five minutes: he was guilty of criminal trespass, attempted assault, and uttering death threats, to name a few. According to the laws of Illinois, Francesco had every right to defend himself and his home using lethal force if he believed himself to be in imminent danger."

Having given the jury the dry facts of the law, I'm on the fence as to whether or not they're fully engaged in my narrative. I decide on the spur of the moment to go off script in an effort to bring the law to life. "Allow me, if you will, to recreate the scene at the Valenti home on September seventeenth."

The jurors inch forward almost as one while I take a few steps back and plant myself directly in front of them. The enormity of the moment threatens to overwhelm me. I freeze for a moment that feels like an hour, then take a deep breath to steady my nerves.

"Imagine if you will," I continue, "Francesco sitting at his kitchen table after dinner while he reads about his beloved Cubbies in the evening paper. He's enjoying his nightly bottle of beer. The doorbell rings. He sets the paper down beside his beer, folded open to the sports section he's been absorbed in. When Francesco opens his front door a moment later, Deputy O'Reilly confronts him. The deputy is on the type of steroid induced rampage that caused even his family to flee. Just how out of his mind was O'Reilly? The before and after photos of the Valentis' screen door bear testament to the unfathomable rage that consumed O'Reilly in the final minutes of his life. But I'm getting ahead of myself."

I pause to study the jury. "Imagine yourself in the position Francesco finds himself in. Sandy Russo told us that Deputy O'Reilly literally terrorized Mr. Valenti for at least five minutes and maybe more—however long it took

O'Reilly to destroy the screen door. That door was all that shielded Mr. Valenti from an enraged man nearly twice his size and half his age. Sandy Russo told us that O'Reilly kept up a steady stream of invective while he battered down the screen door. O'Reilly insulted Mr. Valenti personally, hurled ethnic slurs and insults, even gloated about the village finally ridding itself of Francesco Valenti. O'Reilly threatened physical harm again and again. Mr. Valenti demonstrated remarkable restraint in the face of incredible provocation, ladies and gentlemen. He maintained an almost superhuman control over his fear for five minutes or more. It was only when Deputy O'Reilly began hurling vulgarities directed at the memory of Francesco's recently deceased wife of over forty years that Mr. Valenti reacted with a measure of annoyance."

God, how I wish I could tell the jury that O'Reilly clubbed Papa with his nightstick, I think while I let the jury ponder Papa's forbearance while the bastard broke into our home.

I continue, "Ladies and gentlemen, to understand how truly remarkable this exercise of restraint was, let's ponder how long five minutes is. In five minutes, we might prepare and cook an omelet, sew a button or two, wash the supper dishes, or take the dog for a walk around the block. Imagine yourself being under assault for that period of time, beseeching your attacker for calm... all the while watching your last line of defense being shredded before your eyes. Imagine the terror Francesco must have felt as the door finally gave way and nothing stood between him and his attacker."

I ease closer and pause to let the scenario play out in the jurors' imaginations. "Mrs. Russo related O'Reilly's chillingly triumphant cry when he finally battered his way inside: *'I've got you now, you little prick!'*" I thunder. It's the first time I've raised my voice. The jurors appear shaken; Papa looks like he's just seen a ghost. I want the jury to sense the menace of O'Reilly's triumphant shout when he ripped the screen door out of his way in a final mighty heave and stood face-to-face with Papa. I hope I didn't overdo it.

I back off a foot or two while the jurors recover, then push the narrative forward. "It was only then, in that terrifying moment when he justifiably feared for his well-being, that Francesco Valenti finally reached for his only means of self-defense—a gun that had been within arm's length ever since O'Reilly's assault began. Deputy O'Reilly's response to Mr. Valenti's final desperate warning to leave him alone was, and here again I quote Mrs. Russo: 'That's it you little fuck! *You're dead!*' In his panicked effort to save himself, Francesco fired his gun five times. Contrary to the prosecution's depiction of this as a cold-blooded execution, Mr. Valenti managed to hit his target only once from a range of no more than two or three feet as O'Reilly burst into his home. Unfortunately for Deputy O'Reilly, that bullet struck a carotid artery in his neck. The prosecutor's coroner suggested that the downward angle of the entry wound from O'Reilly's neck and then down to his shoulder was best explained by Mr. Valenti walking to the top of the steps and firing down. You'll recall that Dr. Jones didn't buy into that theory. Everything we've heard today also strongly argues against it. The shots that missed O'Reilly lodged in the door frame and the porch near the door. How could that happen if the door and porch were behind Mr. Valenti? Not a single one of the stray bullets struck the sidewalk or yard."

I allow the jury enough time to absorb the implications of what they've just heard, then step right up to the edge of the jury box and mimic a person leaning forward and reaching for something in front of him. I use my free hand to draw a line down from an imaginary gun to my neck and then to my shoulder. "It seems much more likely that the angle of the entry wound is explained by O'Reilly lunging toward Mr. Valenti as the shots were fired. Coroner Jones seems to be sure that this is how the shooting happened. It's absolutely clear from Sandy Russo's testimony that the shots were fired in the midst of an altercation. The notion that Mr. Valenti walked out of his house and executed an unsuspecting police officer has been thoroughly debunked."

I pause while the jurors assess my assertion, confident they can come to no conclusion other than the one I just presented. "By any reasonable standard and certainly in the eyes of the law as it is written in Article Seven of the Illinois Criminal Code, it's clear Francesco Valenti shot Deputy O'Reilly in an act of justifiable self-defense. Given the evidence you've seen and heard in this courtroom, there is simply no other reasonable conclusion to be reached. The prosecutor is going to get up in a moment and try to tell you otherwise, but he can't use the evidence to assemble a credible case proving Francesco Valenti set out to shoot Officer O'Reilly that night. He can't even demonstrate that Francesco seized the first opportunity he had to do so… or the second, or the third, or however many opportunities he had to do so in a period of five minutes or more. It just didn't happen that way. I know it. The prosecution knows it. Most importantly, I believe you now know it, as well."

"The burden of proof is on the prosecution in a criminal trial, and never more so than in a murder trial," I earnestly tell the jury. "The prosecutor promised you he would prove Francesco Valenti cut down an innocent police officer standing at the bottom of the front porch. He told you Mr. Valenti did so in cold blood. Without warning. Without provocation. Mr. Dempsey will claim he has proven this." I walk back to the screen door pictures and stare at them until I'm sure the jurors are also looking. Then I look back to them and gesture at the pictures. "The evidence says otherwise. The law says otherwise. I trust you will also say otherwise. Thank you for serving on our jury, ladies and gentlemen."

CHAPTER THIRTY-EIGHT

Within two hours, Dempsey has done what he can to mitigate the damage we've inflicted on his case and Judge Mitton has instructed the jurors on the finer points of law before sending them off to reach a verdict. It's hard to imagine the jury doing anything other than setting Papa free or finding him guilty of a lesser charge with limited jail time. Then again, predicting a jury's decision is a fool's errand. They are as capricious as the weather, and often even more contrary.

A scrum of reporters has cornered Pat for her reaction to the news that Andy O'Reilly Junior is in custody for shooting her. We pause to listen.

"It's all very sad," she says. "The kid seems to have had a tough life, what with a broken home and seeing his mother abused for years. Losing his father at that age has to be tough, even if his dad was abusive. I hope the poor kid gets the help he needs to put his life back together."

Pat rejoins us while Penelope Brooks is congratulating us for what she describes as "one heck of a defense case and an amazing closing argument! Even the old law and order fogeys at Butterworth Cole had a good word or two to say about you guys. Anyway, gotta run. Good luck!"

"How long will the jury take?" Brittany asks after Penelope walks away.

"It shouldn't take long," Pat says confidently. "Chubby was brilliant. Hell, the jury might indict Dempsey for having the nerve to prosecute Francesco."

Mike rolls his eyes. "That's laying it on a little thick, sister."

"It's pretty damned clear that Francesco acted in self-defense," she counters.

We'll see. I believe we made our case and the prosecution didn't come close to making theirs, yet my stomach is in knots. "There's no telling how long the jury will take," I inform Brittany. "Sometimes they come to agreement fairly quickly, but not often. They need time to discuss things or for a majority to cajole a holdout or two to reach consensus."

"They'll see things our way sooner or later," Pat says before looking at her watch. "We should be on our way."

"Can't we stay a little longer?" Brittany pleads. "Dad says it's stupid to get to the airport more than thirty minutes before a flight."

"You don't wanna be one of those self-important idiots who holds the plane up," Pat says while giving me a knowing grin. I've been pegged as a chronic departure gate offender.

My farewell with Brittany is heart wrenching. We've agreed that she'll be back for at least the summer after school lets out in Belgium. What happens after that is anybody's guess.

Mike excuses himself to return to his office. Other cases await. I find a coffee shop down the block and settle in to wait, and to reply to numerous text messages from Brittany over the following hour. Her flight is delayed, but she's still in a panic about boarding without knowing the verdict.

I'm on my fifth cup of coffee when Mike calls. "You still at the courthouse?"

"Nope. Whiling away the day at a coffee shop down the street."

"The jury is coming back in. I'll see you in a few minutes."

My gastric glands are disgorging fire hydrant worthy waves of acid into my stomach by the time I reach the courthouse just ahead of Mike. Pat arrives seconds later. She gives me a thumbs up—whether for encouragement or to signal that Brittany is safely on her way, I can't tell. She hustles off to score a good seat while Mike and I make our way to the defense table. Dempsey and Perez are already seated.

Before I can sit down, Mike rests his hand on my shoulder and squeezes. With his eyes fixed firmly on mine, he seizes and pumps my right hand. "However this goes, it was an honor working this case with you, Counselor. Best damned rookie I've ever played with," he adds with a wink.

"I had a halfway decent coach," I say past the lump in my throat.

"This case got me thinking," Mike muses after we sit down. "Maybe I'm a little too quick to cut a deal in some of my cases. You reminded me that sometimes it's best to go toe-to-toe with the prosecution—especially when the plea deal on offer isn't much better than the outcome we'd get losing at trial."

The bailiff delivers Papa to us just before Judge Mitton returns. The clerk announces that court is back in session and the jury files back in. I reach over and squeeze Papa's hand. He squeezes back.

"Have you reached a verdict?' Mitton asks the jury.

The middle-aged black woman who was appointed foreperson of the jury replies that they have.

Just tell us what it is already! I rail inside while the formalities are observed.

The bailiff takes the verdict from the jury foreperson and

hands it to the judge, who reads it, seemingly one letter at a time with a long pause between each syllable. He finally looks up and asks Papa to stand. Mike and I rise with him while the judge hands the form back to his clerk, who prepares to read the verdict aloud. I hope my trembling legs will keep me upright until she finishes.

"The jury finds that the actions of the defendant in the shooting death of Sheriff's Deputy Andrew Sean O'Reilly constitute justifiable self-defense according to Article Seven of the Illinois Criminal Code. The defendant, Francesco Pascal Valenti, is therefore found not guilty of a crime punishable by law in the State of Illinois in the matter of the death of Sheriff's Deputy Andrew Sean O'Reilly."

Papa grips my hand while Dempsey rises and asks the judge to poll the jurors to ensure that the verdict is indeed unanimous and was reached free of any coercion.

After the jurors affirm their verdict, Judge Mitton winds things up. "The defendant is to be released from custody forthwith. You're free to go, Mr. Valenti. Good luck. Ladies and gentlemen of the jury, thank you for you service. You are dismissed."

CHAPTER THIRTY-NINE

It's one of those surprising mid-March days when the temperature surges into the seventies and prompts the question, "Is Spring here to stay?" Pat is lounging beside me on Mama and Papa's swing in the backyard; we each have a beer in hand. Mike came by for lunch and left a few minutes ago, but not before pinning me down on a date for our latest hoops showdown. The first rematch, played the week after Papa's acquittal, ended pretty much like our first contest. I'm looking forward to hanging out with Mike, though not to the whipping he promises to lay on me in the gym. It's a small price to pay for his friendship.

Penelope Brooks was by earlier. She recently hung out her own shingle after deciding she didn't want to be a big city law firm attorney, after all. I've hired her to explore a lawsuit against Titan Industries. I freely admit to spite being a motivator. I want to punish the bastards for the hell they perpetrated on my parents and our neighborhood. Our case's prospects brightened considerably this week with the announcement that the United States Justice Department is investigating Titan's activities in Cedar Heights and elsewhere. Penelope is also in discussion with Fleiss Lansky to settle my pending wrongful dismissal suit. Given the firm's slavish devotion to its image, we suspect they'll pay up to avoid a public slugfest with the newly minted local folk hero I've become. The media creation of Tony Valenti as a modern-day David slaying Goliaths is a curiosity I'm still shaking my head about. That said, I'm perfectly willing to use my fifteen minutes of fame to bludgeon the likes of Fleiss Lansky and Titan.

And Papa? Papa is in Abruzzo visiting his sister Allesandra and her family. He's paid his first visit to his mother's grave and plans to sneak into and out of Orsomarso to visit the grave of his father. I gave him Brittany's old cell phone to keep in touch. He's driving me crazy with text messages and pictures arriving at all hours of the day and night with no regard for the seven-hour time difference between Abruzzo and Cedar Heights. He wants me to bring Brittany for a visit. Maybe once school is out.

Pat has borrowed a knit sweater of Mama's to ward off the gathering chill as the sun sinks. She pulls her hands up inside the sleeves. Two months after the shooting, she's steadily getting better. Some memory lapses, speech a little slurred now and again, though less and less as the weeks pass. Her balance is almost back to normal and the mood swings are fewer and less severe. If she's to be believed, the occasional bouts of depression are over with. I hope that's true. I still worry about her.

"Should we go inside?" I ask.

"Uh-uh. I've been waiting months to sit outside."

"What's it like in St. Petersburg this time of year?"

She shifts to look at me. "Cold. Why?"

"Just curious." The truth is, all her chatter about the place has me intrigued enough that I'd like to tag along this summer. I haven't yet worked up the courage to invite myself, but I might.

"Hmm," she murmurs before she tucks her feet under

herself. Something in her smile suggests that she knows exactly what I'm thinking.

I reach up and run a finger over one of the buds sprouting on the Hawthorne tree the swing nestles beneath. Here and there in the yard, flowers are poking up through the soil. With the danger of freezing hopefully past, I've turned on the water and Mama's Hummel boy is once again emptying his watering can into his barrel. A shaft of sunlight illuminates the idyllic scene in Amy's mural. I take a deep, satisfying breath of the earthy smell of the damp peat Mama and Papa worked into the soil. Life is going to be good here, helping Papa tend to the yard and making time for other simple diversions. We've decided that he'll tend to the tomatoes while I try not to kill off the roses.

"I see one of the rental houses sold," Pat says. The former Priolo, DeLuca, and Palumbo properties all went up for sale a week ago, hopefully signaling the end of the effort to bulldoze our neighborhood.

"Pray that a family moves in," I mutter.

"Amen," she says. One of Pat's stories in the *Tribune* last week hinted strongly that Mayor Brown is about to be indicted on several charges of corruption related to accepting money and gifts from Titan Development. Funny how the U.S. Attorney—until recently all but invisible around Cedar Heights—is finally mining the deep vein of crime and corruption running through our little village. Welcome as the feds' attention is, I can't help wondering where they've been over the past few years.

"I was just thinking about eminent domain," Pat says. "Isn't it always the way? They take something good and bastardize it for the profit motive."

"Or self-aggrandizement."

She nods.

"Good intentions. That's how they sell it."

"We know where *that* paving leads," she says with a grim chuckle.

"Straight to hell. Hopefully Mayor Brown is hitching a ride."

Trustee Smith has proposed funds to clean up and restore Independence Park, a measure the village trustees quickly lined up behind. He's also called for a stepped-up police presence. I plan to be active in the rebirth of our neighborhood and have kept in touch with him. He aims to win the next mayoral election and it looks like he just might make it. I'll support him.

I think of my life. My work. Of modern society. Of what's happened in the past few months. I've been thinking a lot of Big Thoughts lately—after forty-some years of coasting, it's about time. All the chatter about me being a good lawyer is almost convincing in the wake of Papa's trial. Maybe I have a place and purpose in the world, after all. Looking ahead is almost exciting, but I'm not about to let my guard down. The urge to look over my shoulder in search of storm clouds is an ongoing distraction. I *know* they're lurking.

"What about Brittany?" Pat asks.

"She's going to finish out the school year in Brussels." I think about Papa's request and come to a decision. "Then I'm going to fly over so we can join Papa in Abruzzo with his sister for a couple of weeks. We'll come back here for the rest of the summer."

"Think she'll stay?"

"She says she wants to. I told her I'm not moving."

"Private school?"

"If we can afford it."

"Is the house still an issue for her?"

I nod.

"She'll come around," Pat says confidently. "It's a great house and she'll get to live with her grandfather."

"If he ever comes back," I say with a chuckle.

"Really? He's enjoying it there?"

I tell her about the pictures and texts. "He's having a ball, but I think he'll be back to grow his tomatoes."

"So all three of you under one roof," she says with a smile. "Sounds great, Valenti. Family matters."

"I know." It's been a tough lesson to relearn.

We rock quietly for another moment or two.

"And you, Tony? What are your plans?"

"I'll be okay." While I've given her the same answer many a time, this is the first time I actually believe it might be true.

"Yeah?"

"Yeah. What about you? Have you given any more thought to the polka dot eye?"

"Enough with that!" she replies with a laugh. When Pat went to be fitted for her first artificial eye, she discovered that it will be a temporary one; a placeholder until her eye muscles are ready for a permanent version. I suggested that she have a little fun with it and we kicked around the idea of various color combinations and other off the wall goofiness. She's not quite as sanguine about the experience of losing her eye as she'd have the world believe, but a little humor seems to help get her over the bumpy stretches. Hence the polka dots.

"I've got something to show you when we go in," I say.

"Tease."

"Who? Me?"

"Yeah, you, Valenti. Do I at least get a hint?"

A partnership agreement sits in a kitchen drawer. I've already signed. What the hell. Why be coy? "I've decided to become a respectable attorney."

She manages a face of absolute shock and breathlessly asks, "Pray tell, how does one manage *that?*"

"Penelope Brooks offered me a job. I'm going to accept. We're forming a partnership. She has some family money and

I'll chip in some of the settlement money from Titan and Fleiss Lansky."

"Where will you find clients?"

"Penelope has some connections and I've heard from a few people who followed the village business and Papa's trial. Strike while the iron's hot."

"Still going to need crowdfunding?" she asks with a smirk. I haven't come to terms with crowdfunding, helpful though it was. Pat thought I was being ridiculous when I tried to send the remainder of the money back after Papa's trial.

"Depends how many ambulances I'm able to chase down," I retort. "Don't worry, O'Toole. I'll get by."

"So, you're gonna be some sort of respectable attorney," she says after a minute. "What differentiates you respectable guys from the other ninety-nine-point-nine-nine-nine percent of the lot?"

"We'll seek out work with a heart—representing the little people battling the big boys, people who are disadvantaged in some way, worthy causes that need a little legal help."

"Lost causes."

"Probably some of those, too," I reply with a grin.

"You should get Mike to join you. You two were awesome together."

"I've thought about it."

"Well, think hard," Pat suggests. Then she smiles and briefly rests her head on my shoulder.

As the last rays of the sun paint Amy's sky warm, welcoming shades of pink and gold, I feel the certainty of Spring's arrival.

Dear Reader,

Thank you for reading *A House on Liberty Street*, the first novel in the Tony Valenti Thriller series. I hope you enjoyed it.

If so, please take a moment to leave a review at your book retailer. Reviews are invaluable to authors, particularly those of us who publish independently. A brief line or two about why you enjoyed the book is sufficient. A final tip about reviews: Please be careful not to include spoilers that may detract from future readers' enjoyment. Thank you!

Do you wish to be among the first to hear about upcoming releases, giveaways, and contests? If so, please join my exclusive Reader's Club on my website at **neilturnerbooks.com**. Your email address will not be shared or used for any other purpose. I promise! While you're on the website, feel free to poke around a bit to learn a little more about the books

My sincerest thanks again!

Take care, be well,

Neil

THE END

BOOK TWO - PLANE IN THE LAKE

BUY IT HERE (click on cover)

When the well-heeled owners of a crashed tour plane seek to pin the blame on the two-man team that does their maintenance, Tony is called to defend the outgunned partners. He's up against one of Chicago's preeminent law firms, a win-at-all-costs behemoth with resources that dwarf those of Tony's mom and pop firm. Only the truth can save his clients, yet Tony's search for facts is thwarted at every turn by adversaries who will stop at nothing to win. Suddenly, Tony is not only fighting to win a lawsuit… he's in a race to save the most precious people in his life.

BOOK THREE - A CASE OF BETRAYAL

TONY VALENTI THRILLERS BOOK THREE

BUY IT HERE (click on cover)

A woman is brutally slain and suspicion immediately falls upon her ex-husband. But should it? The suspect turns to Tony Valenti for help. The case is a bewildering maze with a mountain of contradictory evidence that points both to *and* away from Tony's client. What *is* the truth? Even Tony isn't sure of his client's innocence in a case where nothing is as it seems. Then a lethal terror from Tony's past surfaces to shake his faith in himself... and to threaten those dearest to him. Is Tony being pulled in too many directions to save anyone?

BOOK FOUR - A TIME FOR RECKONING

TONY VALENTI THRILLERS BOOK FOUR

BUY IT HERE! (Click on Image)

Tony Valenti and Penelope Brooks are enlisted to come to the aid of a young woman when her marriage turns sour in a remote corner of Wyoming. They don't practice law in Wyoming, but representing vulnerable clients battling impossible odds is what they do. They are quickly embroiled in a fight that may literally be to the death, with danger coming at Tony from several directions. Ill-equipped to face the battles he's forced to wage, he must rely on his guile and the help of unexpected allies to survive long enough to rescue his client… and himself.

BOOK FIVE - SCARED SILENT

BUY IT HERE (click on cover)

His choices: prison or death. Which scares him more?

When fifteen-year-old Denzel Payton is charged with the murder of a disabled veteran at a homeless camp, he's trapped in a no-win situation: remain silent and risk almost certain conviction, or name the real killer and face the wrath of a monster who terrifies him.

After Denzel's attorney is murdered, lawyers Tony Valenti and Penelope Brooks step up to defend him, despite the risk of becoming the killer's next targets. As the evidence against their client mounts and potential defense witnesses vanish, Tony and Penelope race to unravel a dark secret that may hold the key to the case. They'll need smarts, guts, and a little luck to save Denzel.

FREE - LAST EXIT ON THE ROAD TO NOWHERE

FREE READER'S CLUB SERIES PREQUEL NOVELLA

CLICK COVER IMAGE TO CLAIM YOUR FREE COPY

Last Exit on the Road to Nowhere is a prequel novella about the high-stakes dramas at work and home that precipitated Tony Valenti's move to Cedar Heights. These are the events that propel Tony and Brittany into the opening chapter of *A House on Liberty Street,* and will continue to reverberate through Tony's world in the novels that follow. What will ultimately become of Tony's family? His career? His life? It all begins here. Become a Reader's Club member and find out!

ACKNOWLEDGMENTS

There are a great many people to thank for helping to make this book possible. As the gestation period of *A House on Liberty Street* sometimes feels like it's been several lifetimes long, some of you may have forgotten reading it at all! A huge thank you to everyone who has been kind enough to read and comment on the story at some point: Susan Turner, Kyle Turner, Howard and Sharon Cornick, Free Dorfman, Diane Jurcin, Steve Petillo, Kim Strickland, Bridget Sabbia, others who chose not to have their name set in print, and anyone I've inadvertently left off this list (I'm *so* sorry!). Each and every one of you helped make this a better book as I've lurched in fits and starts along the way to publication. You have my unending gratitude. I'd be remiss not to mention the many people who've also helped me along the way at conferences, by writing how-to books and blogs, delivering courses, and all of you who shared your talents in workshops, not to mention all the members of networking groups I've been lucky enough to belong to. As solitary an endeavor as writing can be, people like you ensure that it need not be a lonely journey.

A big shout out as well to the amazing professionals who helped to get *A House on Liberty Street* across the finish line. For editing, my thanks to Erin Scothorn and Lucia Ferrara for making things so much better. To my brilliant cover and interior designer, David Prendergast, many thanks for patiently nursing a novice through the design process and producing a cover many leagues beyond what I had imagined possible. I hope the book is as good as its cover!

ABOUT THE AUTHOR

Neil discovered the thrill of losing himself in the pages of a book as a five- or six-year-old when Beatrix Potter and Thornton Burgess immersed him in the worlds of Jerry Muskrat, Peter Rabbit, and their furry friends. His mother and father had the good grace to indulge his excitement about being able to read *them* stories, which he thought was pretty darned cool. He's been reading and writing one thing or another ever since, but it was many years before the audacious idea of *writing a book* wormed its way into his head. He's lived throughout Canada, spent three years in Europe, and lived in Chicago and Arizona, somehow managing to squeeze a career in banking and finance into his travels. After doing an apprenticeship reading, reading, reading, taking courses, attending seminars and conferences, and churning out some truly atrocious manuscripts, After doing an apprenticeship reading, reading, reading, taking courses, attending seminars and conferences, and churning out some truly atrocious manuscripts, he began writing and stockpiling the Tony Valenti series of thrillers. The series will total four published novels by the end of 2021, plus a free prequel novella for members of my exclusive Reader's Club. There will be more titles to come in 2022 and beyond, probably at the rate of two or three per year . Stay tuned!

Neil lives in Ottawa, Ontario, Canada.